Aroused

Books by Sean Wolfe

Close Contact

Aroused

Also stories in these anthologies:

Masters of Midnight

Man of My Dreams

Midnight Thirsts

Published by Kensington Publishing Corporation

Aroused

Tales of Erotica

SEAN WOLFE

KENSINGTON BOOKS.
http://www.kensingtonbooks.com

Some people believe you have one soul mate and one true love in your lifetime. I used to be one of those believers. But not anymore. Because I have been very blessed in my life.

The first true love of my life, and the guy who made me believe in the existence of soul mates, was Gustavo Paredes. He taught me the difference between love and sex, and taught me how to really love another person and allow myself to be loved. He taught me the value of growing up and of commitment and of being true to myself. He was my partner and my life for thirteen years. Gustavo Paredes-Wolfe passed away in 2003. Gustavito—Te extraño y te quiero mucho. Siempre vas estar en mi Corazón.

And just when you think life sucks the big one and you'll never really love again . . . that your life will be filled with cheap and meaningless and anonymous sexual encounters . . . wait, that doesn't sound all that bad. Seriously, though. After two and a half years of being alone, the Universe was kind enough to grant me love again. True love and another soul mate. Everything about Kyle Martinez and I meeting and falling in love should have failed miserably. But it didn't. Instead, we fell madly in love very quickly and have grown closer with each passing day. Kyle is now teaching me the value of enjoying life, of holding on to my youth without letting go of the hard lessons I've learned throughout my life, and of sharing my life completely with another man, and allowing him to share his with me. Kyle, thank you for supporting me so wholeheartedly, for being proud of me, and for pushing me when I needed to be pushed. I love you and look forward every day to spending the rest of my life with you.

This book is dedicated to the two men who have made me the man I am today, and whom I will always love with every ounce of my being:

Kyle Martinez

Gustavo Paredes-Wolfe

Acknowledgments

Thank you to Austin Foxxe, former editor in chief of *Men* and *Freshmen* magazines, for believing in me and publishing my first erotic stories.

Thank you to the guys in my writers group: Matt Kailey, Jerry Wheeler, Jack Bumgardner, and Peter Clark. Your insights and constructive criticism of my work are invaluable and have helped make me a better writer.

Thank you to my angel on earth, Jane Nichols, for believing in me and supporting my dream, even if she can't bring herself to read any of my erotica.

And special thanks to my editor, John Scognamiglio. You never give up on me, and are always willing to go the extra mile. Thank you for giving me my start in publishing, and for giving me the creative liberties you have. You totally **rock**!!

Contents

Introduction

Most of us in the United States, with the possible exception of those of us fortunate enough to be from California or Florida or South Texas (on which the verdict is still out), are familiar with the "changing of the seasons." We generally have three months of winter, three months of spring, three months of summer and three months of fall or autumn (give or take a week or two with any season due to Mother Nature's sense of humor.)

Being from San Francisco, I didn't quite grasp this concept of seasons. In San Francisco it was always cold and foggy in the mornings, sunny and comfortably warm in the afternoon, and cool and crisp at night. That was my idea of seasons. That's just the way it was, and I liked it. Then I moved to Denver, and was shocked . . . shocked I tell you, to find myself thrust into real seasons that were as different as night and day, yet as predictable as Miss Texas being a top 5 finalist in the Miss America pageant. Fall came and leaves fell and everything turned gray and ugly. Winter came and it snowed and it was cold and wet and most inconvenient. That's just the way it was, and I didn't like it. But then spring came, the flowers bloomed, it warmed up, and I smiled again. When summer showed up and all the boys strolled around the park shirtless and in thirty different styles and colors of Daisy Dukes . . . well, all was right with the world again. And I liked it.

As I was pondering a theme for this book of erotic stories, I couldn't help but think about the seasons and how they apply to us as people, and especially as gay men. As we grow older, we go through a "changing of the seasons" of our lives and of our souls. What makes us happy in summer is not the same thing that makes us tingle with excitement in winter. It really happens in every aspect of our lives, but for the purposes of this book, I will be applying it to our sexuality as gay men, and how our perspectives of love and sex and sexuality and eroticism change as we experience our personal changing of the seasons.

We grow, we change, we see things differently as our library of life experiences expands and we grow as humans. For gay men this process is usually particularly difficult. As a community we are taught from a very early age (relative to our coming out as gay men) that youth and beauty and a carefree and fun attitude are all-important. That's great for us as we float through our gay youth. But as we grow older, it becomes more difficult to reconcile those deeply-seeded beliefs with what we feel as we mature. It's almost a whole new coming-out experience. The changing of the seasons.

The purpose of this book (other than the obvious, because this *is* an erotica collection, after all) is to celebrate all of the seasons of our lives. To learn the joys and understand the meanings of sex, sexuality, love, and eroticism within each of our seasons.

In this book, each season is represented by a specific age range and set of values within the gay male community. None of us are stupid enough to believe that *all* gay men place these values with their respective "seasons" (or age ranges). But we can't pretend to be naïve enough to believe that this system is not prevalent in our community, either. In this collection, there are four short stories for each season. As you read through the stories, try to recognize yourself. Are you currently in this season, or do you remember what it was like to have been there? If you're in spring or summer (not the temporal season), and you're reading a story in fall or winter . . . can you imagine yourself thinking what these characters are thinking, acting like the characters are acting, and feeling the things they are feeling? If you're in the later seasons of life, do you find yourself longing for your younger days of exploration and uncertainty, or are you comfortable with the experiences you've had and the wealth of knowledge you possess, and the level of sexuality and eroticism you are currently experiencing?

In the middle of the book, to break up the monotony, is a

novella, a longer story that follows two men through all four seasons of their lives. It deals with coming out, with lust and first love, with struggling with the meaning and demands of commitment, with infidelity and arguments, with finding common ground, and with realizing that true love is powerful enough to conquer all of the bad stuff life and society throw our way.

One thing to keep in mind as you're reading, is that the seasons of our lives—our sexual journey—by no means have to follow (and very seldom do) the temporal seasons of the calendar year. Your sexual awakening and coming out (represented by spring, in this book) might happen in the middle of January. Try to think outside the box and view these seasons as the significant times of our lives and our sexuality and our coming into ourselves . . . and not having anything to do with the months "typically" associated with them.

My hope is that you read all of the stories, and that you recognize yourself in a few of them. But more than that, I hope you will realize that we all have something very special to bring to the table of life, regardless of our age or background. By sharing and learning from and teaching one another, we grow as a community . . . and more importantly, as human beings.

We celebrate Gay Pride every summer with lavish parades and rallies and endless parties and orgies and other fun and exciting debauchery. Don't get me wrong . . . I love that. I came out at San Francisco's Gay Pride, and haven't missed a single one since then, regardless of the city I've been in at the time. But real gay pride can only be realized when we are proud of ourselves as good and decent human beings, and the endless possibilities of who we can become. When we embrace ourselves in every one of our incarnations and stages of life, then we are whole and complete and happy gay men.

Celebrate the "changing of our seasons."

SPRING

There are those of us who are analytical and studious and organized and like to color within the lines. And there are those of us who can't stay within the lines at all, love to think outside the box, and have an irrepressible need to fuck with the system. I'm a Gemini in every sense of the word, so I have a little of both in me. Okay, so I have a little bit of the analytical side and a whole lot of the "fuck with the system" side. It makes things interesting, and also means that every time I have sex with someone, it's really a hot three-way.

Dictionary.com defines spring as:

> 1. *The season of the year, occurring between winter and summer, during which the weather becomes warmer and plants revive, extending in the Northern Hemisphere from the vernal equinox to the summer solstice and popularly considered to comprise March, April, and May.*

> 2. *A time of growth and renewal.*

In our seasons of life as gay men, spring is a time of coming out. The stories in this section deal with young men, between the ages of eighteen and twenty-five who are struggling with their innermost feelings and desires. They address the urges we have and our inner battles of self-acceptance. They delve into our first sexual experiences with another man, and all of the excitement and intensity that comes with that. And this section speaks to the carefree nature that is so natural and paramount at this point in our lives and the feeling of immortality that dominates our belief systems.

In the spring of our lives as gay men, everything is new and exciting and life-altering. Each experience is a growing experience that makes the next one that much more exciting and alive. And as we open Pandora's Box, we wake up every morning believing wholeheartedly that our lives revolve around our sexual experiences and that our lives are great.

And they are.

Careful What You Wish For

"*Be careful what you wish for. It just might come true.*"

I remember my mother telling me this over and over when I was a little kid. It was one of those things your parents tell you that you think sounds stupid as shit when you're a snot nosed brat, but that comes back to haunt you when you move out and on your own. Had I known the truth in those words, I'd have taken my mother's advice and been a lot more careful about what I wished for over the years. But not this time.

My twenty-fifth birthday was amazing. A group of friends threw an awesome party for me, and made me feel really special. I got lots of great gifts, but I was a little surprised when my three best friends chipped in on one gift for me. I was even more surprised when they handed me a card and nothing else.

"What's this?" I asked, trying to hide my disappointment. "Where's my gift?"

"That *is* your gift," Brian said, and nudged Robert and Carlos on either side of him.

I stared blankly at them.

"Trust me," Carlos said as he leaned in and kissed me on the lips, "you're gonna love it."

I read the card. "Wish Upon A Star. Like every good Genie,

this card entitles you to three wishes, all guaranteed to come true. Happy Wishing!" It was a simple blue card with bright gold lettering. Cute, but not really what I was expecting from my three closest friends.

"Thanks, guys," I managed weakly as I hugged them, and then turned to replenish my martini glass. I heard them laughing, and when I turned to glare at them, they stopped giggling quickly and looked at the floor. But I could still see a smirk on their faces. The fuckers.

For the rest of the night I did my best to remain happy and cordial and to be the perfect guest of honor. But when it was time to say goodbye, I made short work of bidding adieu to my friends, making sure they knew I was *not* pleased with their cheap ass gift.

After brushing my teeth, I threw the blue Make A Wish Card on my nightstand, and climbed into bed. As the darkness overtook my room, my eyes began to get heavy. Despite being upset at Brian, Carlos, and Robert, I had to admit they really outdid themselves with my party. It must've cost them a full paycheck each. What kind of selfish bastard was I?

I wish Carlos and Brian and Robert were here right now so I could thank them, I thought as my eyelids finally gave in to the sleepy.

A couple of seconds later I felt the mattress on either side of me sink deeper into the bed. At first I thought I was imagining things, but then I felt a strong hand tweak my left nipple, and a pair of soft full lips clasp onto my own.

"What the . . ."

"Shhh," I heard Carlos say as he slipped his tongue into my mouth and kissed me hard.

It happened so quickly I didn't know what was going on. Carlos was kissing me tenderly on the mouth, Robert's hot mouth wrapped around my limp cock and sucked it deep into his throat and teased me into full hardness, and Brian licked and kissed my nipples until they stiffened in his mouth.

"Wow," Carlos said, as he broke our kiss and took a step back from the bed. "I had no idea this is what you'd wish for."

"But I didn't," I managed to croak as I took in a deep breath. Robert's tongue tickled my cock head for a moment and then he swallowed my cock in one slow move. "I just wished you'd be here so I could . . ."

"This wouldn't be happening if it wasn't really what you wished for," Brian said, lifting himself from my nipples and kissing me on the lips. "That's the way the card works. You get what you really wish for, deep inside. You might not even be conscious of it."

I moaned into his mouth as his soft tongue and Robert's hot mouth overtook every sensation in my body. I thrust my tongue into Brian's mouth and lifted my hips off the bed to slide my cock deeper into Robert's throat.

Carlos took advantage of my raised ass and turned me onto my side slightly, so that Robert could still suck my cock but so that he could also have access to my ass. A second later I gasped and moaned even louder as I felt his hot, wet tongue lick around my ass, and then slide slowly into my hole.

Brian kissed me gently one last time, and then stood above my head. With the moonlight streaming in from the window, I could see the silhouette of his cock. It was fully hard and throbbing about seven inches in front of him. He straddled my shoulders and then lowered himself closer to my face.

I reached out and licked the head, savoring the slick salty pre-cum that leaked from his piss slit. I wrapped my lips around his cock head and sucked on it for a minute or so, then slowly slid my lips down the full length of his shaft.

"Fuck, dude, that's hot," he moaned as the fat head slipped past my tonsils and deep into my throat.

I felt Robert's mouth slip off my cock, and was about to complain, when Carlos' hands settled on either side of my waist, flipping me onto all fours. The action caused me to let go of Brian's cock, and I suddenly felt completely empty. I was confused and started to say something, when I realized what was happening.

Carlos was standing at the side of the bed, and moving me, on my hands and knees, over to the edge of the bed in front of him. Robert was already lying on his back, sliding himself underneath me. Brian was still fully hard and still dripping precum as he placed one leg on either side of Robert's thin body and smiled at me as he slapped his cock against my cheeks.

"Fuck me," Robert said as he lifted his ass a couple of inches off the mattress.

My own cock throbbed in front of me. I leaned down and licked Robert's ass. He moaned and bucked his ass harder against my mouth, and I ravaged it as if it were my last supper.

"Fuck me," he said, louder and more persistent this time.

I grabbed my cock and guided it to his ass. I thought I'd go slow and take my time, allowing Robert some time to relax and be ready for me. But he was clearly ready, and had other ideas. When my cock head reached his hole, I stopped and let it rest at the entrance to his ass. But Robert took a deep breath and slid his ass all the way down my hard cock. He didn't stop until my balls rested against his ass cheeks.

"Fuck!" I moaned loudly.

"That's what *I'm* sayin'," Robert said with a grin as he gripped my cock with his ass muscles and then slowly slid up and down the length of my cock.

As I caught my breath and began sliding in and out of Robert's ass, Brian took a step closer and slipped his cock into my mouth. I sucked on his dick, savoring the soft silky skin against the hard muscle as it slid deep inside my throat and then almost out again. Then I felt Carlos' tongue licking my ass cheeks again, and slide slowly in and out of my ass. My head spun with overwhelming pleasure. I thought nothing could feel better than having Carlos' tongue sliding in and out of my hole as I fucked Robert's hot hole and swallowed Brian's hard cock deep into my throat.

But I was wrong. A moment later Carlos stopped licking my ass. I made an extra effort to stick my ass farther into the air as I withdrew from Robert's ass before sliding back inside. When he didn't return to eating my ass, I thought maybe he'd left to go to the restroom or something. But again, I was wrong.

A second later I felt the hot and hard skin of his cock head push against my ass. At first I tightened up and tried to take in a deep breath. But since my mouth was filled with Brian's cock, I only succeeded in choking a little. Then I relaxed, and as I did, Carlos pushed forward.

My eyes bulged as I stopped fucking Robert and just allowed Brian's hard cock to rest inside my throat. I'm certainly not a virgin to being fucked, and not even one to being fucked by big cocks. I hadn't seen Carlos' cock, but as it slid persistently inside my ass, I could feel that it was the biggest cock I'd ever had. He slid in slowly, allowing my muscles to get used to the thickness of his cock. With each inch, my muscles tore just a little, to allow him further access. It seemed to go on for an eternity, and when he finally stopped pushing forward, I knew I had at least ten inches of fat, hard cock deep inside me.

"You ready now?" Carlos whispered as he leaned down and kissed my ear.

My mouth was filled with Brian's cock, so my only possible response was to squeeze his cock with my ass muscles and slide my cock deep into Robert's ass, and then out again, causing my own ass to impale Carlos's huge cock.

That was all it took, really. The four of us began fucking like a well-oiled machine. Carlos shoved his cock deep into my ass just as I slid out of Robert's, then pulled out of my ass as I slid all the way into Robert again. Robert couldn't get enough, and moaned loudly as he bucked wildly up and down the length of my cock. Brian slid his cock in and out of my mouth, alternating between slow, deep thrusts and quick, frantic ones.

I'd never been so completely consumed with cock and ass, and never so completely satisfied. There wasn't an inch of my body that wasn't electric with pleasure. My ass and mouth were filled with cock and stretched to their limits. My cock felt like it was wrapped in liquid fire as I slid deep into Robert's ass. I literally saw fireworks in my head every time Carlos stabbed his cock all the way to the balls into my ass, and I wanted the feeling never to end.

"God, I wish I could feel your cock inside me forever," I said between loud moans as Brian removed his cock from my mouth to keep from coming too soon.

"Jason, don't say that. You gotta be careful . . ."

"Shut up and fuck me," I growled as I grabbed Brian's cock and sucked it into my mouth again.

We were out of control now. Carlos and Brian fucked my ass and mouth relentlessly, and I pounded into Robert like I was driving a stake through Dracula's heart. I was starting to get close, and I could tell everyone else was, too. Brian's cock was getting thicker in my mouth, and Carlos breathed heavily as he slammed into me. Robert was thrashing his head back and forth on the bed, and grabbing the sheets on either side of him.

"Not like this," I said as I pulled my mouth from Brian's cock. "Let me lie on the bed. I want you all to shoot all over me."

Robert pulled himself from my cock and slid from under me quickly, and moved around to the side of the bed. Carlos flipped me around onto my back, never allowing an inch of his cock to leave my ass, and laid me on my back on the bed. Robert was now at my left side, and Brian straddled my face with a knee on either side of me. His ass was right at my face, his cock pointing toward my feet. I couldn't see anything in front of me but his ass, so I reached out with my tongue and licked at it hungrily.

Everyone was moaning loudly now. My own orgasm quickly worked its way up my shaft, and I could tell by the way Brian's ass was flexing that he was about to shoot as well. I could still feel Carlos' cock deep inside me, fucking me harder and faster. Robert was to my left. I wanted their loads all over me, and didn't hesitate to let them know.

"Come on, guys. I want you to shoot all over my face. Brian, turn around. Carlos, pull out of my ass and come over to my right."

"What are you talking about, dude?" I heard Carlos say from directly next to me on the right. "I'm right here." He took a step to his left, and suddenly his long, fat uncut cock was an inch from my face.

But that can't be, I thought as Brian turned around and pointed his cock at my face as well. *I can still feel Carlos' huge cock sliding in and out of my ass.* It drove in an extra long and hard stab just to let me know I wasn't imagining things. And yet, I was staring at its angry red head an inch from my mouth.

"Fuck, man," Carlos yelled, "that's it. I'm gonna shoot!"

A second later my face was showered with hot cum. It sprayed all over me from every direction, and seemed to go on forever. My own load blasted from my cock, and from the sound of Brian's moans, it was landing all over his back. A minute later, my face was covered with jizz, and it dripped down my cheeks and neck as my three best friends tugged at their cocks to allow every last drop to splatter across my face.

I was still moaning and writhing my ass under Brian's body and against the bed.

"Dude, you already came, and we're all done, too," Brian said. "You can relax now."

"You're not gonna believe this," I said, as my eyes rolled in the back of my head, and I bit my lower lip lightly. My cock was still rock hard, and throbbed against my stomach.

"What?" Carlos said.

"You're still fucking me."

"What?" He looked at me as if I were crazy. "Dude, you're high."

"No, I'm not. I still feel your cock inside me, and you're still fucking me."

My buddies looked back and forth from one another, stunned.

"Oh, SHIT!" Robert yelled. "Remember earlier, Jason said he wished he could feel your cock inside him forever. That was his second birthday wish."

Carlos, Brian, and Robert started laughing as they watched me slide my ass back and forth against the invisible cock fucking my ass. I was vaguely aware of them around me as delirium took over my body, and I closed my eyes. A moment later my second load of the night flew from my cock and landed all across my chest and stomach.

And then I fell asleep.

The next morning I was awakened by the phone.

"Listen, Jason, I know you're not thrilled with our gift. I know it doesn't seem like much right now." It was Carlos. "But trust me, you're gonna love it. I promise."

I could still feel his fat cock deep inside my ass. It wasn't fucking me now, but just buried there, filling me up completely. The previous night came flooding back to me, and I remembered my first two wishes. I couldn't believe it was happening, but there was no denying the long, thick, hard cock I felt up my ass. I hadn't used my third wish, and for a moment, I thought about wishing I'd never asked to feel Carlos' cock inside me forever. I was soft, but just the sound of Carlos' voice was getting me plump, and as I got harder, the feel of his cock inside me began to move ever so slowly. I suddenly realized the little bit of control I had over the situation, and decided not to use my last wish just quite yet. I'd save it for another time.

"Jason, are you there?"

"Yes," I said softly, as my cock grew just a little harder, and I felt his thick cock slide in and out of my ass slowly. I closed my eyes and moaned slowly as I wriggled my ass against the pleasure it brought. "Hey, where did you guys go after the party last night?"

"We all went home. It was after three in the morning. Where else would we go? Are you okay?"

By now I was fully hard, and Carlos cock was sliding in and out at a quickening pace.

"Mmm hmm."

"Alright. Just one last thing, though, okay? Your gift is not a joke. You get three wishes, and they really will come true."

"Really?" I asked as I stroked my cock and felt him fuck me harder and faster. I was already close.

"Okay, I can tell you're mocking me. So I'm gonna go. Have fun with your gift. But Jason, promise me one thing."

"What's that?" I whispered as I bit my lip and the first spray of cum spewed from my cock and landed on my face.

"Be careful what you wish for."

He Made Me Quaker

Growing up in a small, northern Texas panhandle town of less than 500 is a burden and punishment I truly would not wish upon my worst enemy. I held my breath and tried my best to get through high school with as little attention and notoriety as possible. It was painfully obvious to me that I didn't fit in there. It was even more obvious to the other 499 residents who infringed upon my space and stole my air.

I came from a poor family, so I figured going to college was completely out of the question. Instead I focused my energies on researching other ways of getting out of the small, Bible-belt mentality, hopelessly redneck town and out into the real world. But my options were limited. My senior year in high school I felt like I was trapped and doomed to a life of riding tractors and plowing fields.

But miraculously, my belief and faith in the universe and its ability and desire to take care of us kicked in and proved my belief and faith were justified.

I attended a Quaker church. Though I didn't acknowledge it at the time, I initially went because there were a couple of really hot guys around my age who attended there, and I had the hots for them. It was a subconscious action, or reaction, and I certainly didn't realize it back then. But I know it now. Eventually, I actually found that my personal spiritual beliefs were very much in line with Quaker teachings, and I loved my church. And my involvement with the Booker Friends Church led me down a path that would forever change my life in many ways.

Most significantly, it announced in January of my senior year, that if I would be kind enough to accept the gift, they would be honored to pay my way through college. The one stipulation was that they wanted me to attend Friends University, a Quaker college in Wichita, Kansas. It was their sincere hope that I would get a degree in Bible and Theology, and eventually return to Booker and pastor my own church.

I was ecstatic, and agreed without hesitation. Wichita was a big city! I'd never been to a city of over 10,000, and so Wichita's population of 250,000 seemed like New York City to me at that moment. I was finally going to get out of Booker. It didn't matter that the church wanted me to return after my studies to set up permanent and binding residence and pastorship there. All I could see was an open door that presented a world of promises for me. I'd finally get a glimpse of reality. I'd finally see a real live Black person or a real live Asian person, rather than just seeing them on TV. I'd finally see tall buildings and subway systems and hear sirens racing through the streets at night.

But Wichita was a huge disappointment. It wasn't a real city at all. No tall buildings or subway systems. The only sirens I heard were usually the result of a cat that got caught in a tree or something similarly ridiculous. Wichita wasn't much different from Booker, except that it had approximately 249,500 more rednecks than did my hometown.

I did enjoy college, though, which was a relief, after having hated high school so much. It did present a few problems, however. I lived in the men's dorm, which had communal showers on each floor. We had about 200 young, virile, corn-fed Midwestern boys in our dorm, and though we were all attending a Christian college, and many of us were planning on going into the ministry, most of us seemed quite uninhibited, and were perfectly comfortable walking around the dorm in various states of undress, and in various states of . . . "happiness." I was not one of those uninhibited boys, but I took extreme pleasure in watching my dormmates lather themselves in the showers and walk around the hallways either completely naked and sporting hard-ons, or in just their tented boxers.

By my junior year at Friends University, I was still a virgin. My mind raced with thoughts and images and dreams of quite torrid sex with several of my fellow students. There were a couple of brothers, Mike and Loren Boettcher, who were particularly blessed, and about whom I could not stop thinking. Both of them had cocks that hung to their knees when soft, and both of them couldn't help but get half hard just by stepping under the shower. They often showered at the same time, and I often made every attempt to conveniently be in the shower at that same moment. There were also three or four other guys that I had the hots for as well, and I found myself spending more and more time strategizing on how to see them naked. And I spent more and more time daydreaming and fantasizing about all of them.

I'm no genius, but I'm not stupid either. It didn't take long for me to realize I had sexual identity issues. I was horny all the time, and I spent about every spare waking moment obsessing over Mike and Loren and Daniel and Cory and Kevin and . . .

The second half of my junior year, I finally decided to take action. There was a "dirty" bookstore and cinema about a mile from the school. One Friday evening I drove to the bookstore, and spent an hour and a half sitting in my car, trying to calm my heart down enough to go inside. I finally did.

The smell of sexual energy immediately assaulted my nostrils, and I got hard instantly. I looked around nervously, noticing the various magazines, the sealed video boxes, and the plastic encased dildoes of various sizes. The clerk barely looked up from the magazine he was reading to acknowledge my presence, but I slinked away to the nearest corner anyway, trying to will away the heated blush that had crept up my face.

At the back of the store was a door, with the words "Movie House – Pay Clerk to receive token." I swallowed my pride and purchased a token, dropped it into the slot, and jumped as the door buzzed and then opened in front of me. I stepped inside and was instantly overwhelmed with the odor of stale sex and even staler popcorn. It was completely dark inside the theater, and my shoes stuck to the floor and made a sucking sound as I walked forward. I heard loud moans and mumbled words from somewhere ahead of me. I walked into, and then pushed aside, a black curtain. On a large screen several feet from me was a naked woman lying on her back and a naked man lying on top of her, ramming his cock deep inside her as they both made exaggerated moans and grunting noises.

I stood there, motionless for a moment, taking in the sight before me. I'd never seen anyone fucking before, and I was mesmerized. Someone coughed, and I jumped and looked around. Seven or eight men were scattered throughout the theater. As the camera angle on the screen changed and filled the room with a little brighter light, I saw most of the men were middle-aged or older, and most of them were stroking their cocks.

I made a concerted effort not to look at any of them, and fumbled my way to a seat near the back. I sat down and watched the movie in front of me. It wasn't that I particularly tried to do so, but I automatically blocked the sight of the woman from my mind. All I could see was the naked man. His muscular ass flexed as he shoved his dick into the woman, and every once in a while the camera zoomed in and showed his cock as it pulled out and then slid back inside the woman.

I got hard instantly, and reached down to grope my cock through my jeans. It throbbed and begged to be released, so I pulled it out and stroked it slowly for a couple of minutes. In front of me on the screen, the woman began screaming, and the guy pulled out of her quickly. The camera focused in on his big dick, and I felt the stirrings of my orgasm building deep in my balls. A second later the actor moaned and huge streams of white cum flew from his cock. The first several shots landed on the woman's breasts, forcing me to acknowledge their presence for the first time. I almost lost my erection, but then the camera moved back to the actor's fat cock, and I was back on track. It took only a couple more strokes before my body tightened, a loud guttural moan escaped my throat, and I sprayed my load all over the back of the chair in front of me.

I lost my breath as jet after jet of cum flew from my cock. My legs quivered and my body shook with the force of my orgasm. When it was over I just sat there for a few minutes, letting the last few drops of cum slide down my still surprisingly hard dick. Then I stuffed my cock back inside my jeans and walked out of the theater.

"That didn't take long," the acne-faced clerk snickered.

I felt the flush come back to my face, and darted as quickly as possible to the restroom. Once inside I grabbed a handful of paper towels, wet them, and locked myself inside the stall. I quickly shoved my jeans down to my ankles, pulled my cock out, and began washing it with the wet paper towels.

Just being inside the bookstore filled me with conflicting emotions. I felt dirty and ashamed. If any of my schoolmates or friends knew I was there, they'd surely never speak with me again. I might even get kicked out of school. But at the same time, I felt alive for maybe the first time in my life. I was experiencing something I'd never given myself permission to feel before. And even after having shot a huge load in the theater a few minutes ago, I could not get my cock to soften. My heart was pounding hard in my chest again, and I knew I needed to cum again.

As I sat there half washing and half stroking my cock, I looked over and read a handwritten message on the wall. "I need to suck your cock. You need to suck mine. No troll here, you don't be one either. 316.555.4976."

I found it a little hard to breathe, and my chest hurt from the intense pounding of my heart. The number on the wall was only two digits different from my own, and I knew without thinking about it, that I was going to call it. I quickly stuffed my hard dick back into my jeans, pulled them up, and walked out of the restroom to the pay phone near the front door of the bookstore.

"Hello," the voice on the other end of the line said.

My heart stopped, and I almost hung up the phone. But then I mentally slapped myself. I hadn't come this far just to back out now. "Hi," I croaked out. "I'm at the Galaxy Palace and just read your note in the restroom."

There was an awkward moment of silence on the other end of the phone. "Yeah," the voice said hesitantly.

"Ummm . . ." I stuttered. "Do you want to meet?"

"How old are you?"

"Twenty."

"Cool," the voice said, and then waited for a couple of seconds before continuing. "We can't meet at my place. But I'm just a few blocks from the Blue Angel Motel. Can you meet me there?"

"Yes," I said, and felt my chest constrict with pain. I thought I was having a heart attack.

"How long will it take you to get there?" he asked, after giving me the address and room number.

"Twenty minutes."

"Right on," he said. "I'll leave the door unlocked. Just come on in. Don't turn on the lights."

Visions of being ambushed and beaten or even killed flashed through my mind as I pictured myself walking into a dark motel room. "Okay," I agreed way too soon, apparently not *overly* concerned about the dangers I might encounter.

The line went dead without a "goodbye" or "see you in a few" or any other such closing remark. I stared at the phone for a moment, and then rushed out of the bookstore.

* * *

The Blue Angel Motel was a local legend. Just a few blocks from Wichita State University, it attracted a score of college kids who wished to be discreet and rented the rooms by the hour. It was also frequented by prostitutes and drug dealers who needed a quick place to conduct their business off the streets and out of sight from cops. At Friends University we spoke of the motel in hushed whispers and sad, compassionate but self-righteous shakes of the head.

Room 115 was an end unit on the first floor. I found it easily enough and walked up to the door. It took me a couple of minutes to work up the nerve to go inside. Finally, I opened the door and took a step inside before I could turn around and run away. I closed the door quietly behind me and tried to get my bearings in the dark.

"I'm over here," the voice said. It came from in front of me and to the left, near the only window. "Strip and then come join me."

I tapped my hand against my right leg, a nervous habit I had when I was frightened and unsure of myself, and counted to ten. Then I stripped, letting my clothes fall to the floor next to the door, and walked slowly to the bed.

"Down here," the voice said.

I sat on the bed and reached out to feel for him. My eyes finally began to adjust to the dark, and I made out the shadow in the middle of the bed. I laid my hand on his chest and began rubbing the hard and smooth skin, tracing my fingers across his chest and stomach, and then lightly pinching his already hard nipples.

The guy moaned loudly, then reached up and put his hand behind my head and pulled me down to him. I could smell his scent, and my cock got even harder. He smelled clean but manly at the same time. A sweet cologne mixed with light sexually-charged sweat.

I was shocked when he pulled my face to his and I felt his tongue reach out to lick my lips. I drew in a deep breath, and then surrendered to his soft lips as they kissed mine. His tongue slipped inside my mouth, and I struggled to catch my breath as it slid deeper inside my mouth. It tasted like peppermint, and I sucked on it eagerly, as if it were a live candy cane.

I thought I'd pass out. This was a night of firsts for me. I'd never been inside an adult bookstore. I'd never seen a porn movie. I'd certainly never beat off in a public place. And now I was naked and hard and kissing another naked and hard man for the first time in my life. My head spun and a high-pitched ringing sound buzzed through my brain and behind my eyes.

My new friend released the back of my head, but I kept kissing him anyway. He reached over and took my hand in his, guiding it down to his cock. When I first touched it, I gasped in shock, and jerked my hand away. I closed my eyes tightly and concentrated on not biting his delicious tasting tongue. Then I slowly moved my hand back to his crotch. I opened my fingers tentatively and wrapped my fist around his cock. Or more accurately, I wrapped my fist around as much of his cock as I could. I moaned loudly as I sucked harder on his tongue, and squeezed my hand harder around his cock. It was so long and thick and hard that I couldn't wrap my fist all the way around it.

I kept my eyes closed and pumped my fist up and down the long length of his cock. It was hot and hard, and the veins were thick and pulsed against the palm of my hand as I stroked him. My new friend moaned loudly and thrust his hips up to help move his cock in and out of my fist.

"Suck my dick," he moaned loudly as he removed his tongue from my hungry mouth.

"I can't," I said. "It's way too big. I've never . . ."

"You don't have to take it all," he whispered and kissed my lips gently again. "Just lick it and suck on it a little. Whatever you can take."

"I don't think I can. I've never done any of this before. It's a little overwhelming."

"You're a virgin?" he asked, and propped himself up into a half reclining position.

I felt myself blush, and nodded my head.

"Holy fuck," he said, and just looked at me for a moment. "Are you sure you wanna do this?"

I returned his gaze briefly. The darkness was starting to recede, and slivers of light filtered through the small room. I could begin to make out the shape and general structure of his face. Something about him was beginning to feel oddly familiar. Was it his voice, or did the outline and shadows of his face remind me of someone?

"Yes," I said hoarsely.

"Then suck my dick, Sean," he whispered as he leaned in and kissed me on the lips again. "Please."

I returned his kiss and leaned down to start sucking his cock. Then I stopped midway, and froze in place.

"How do you know my name?" I asked, suddenly frightened. "I didn't tell you my name."

"Shhh," he whispered, and caressed my face in his hands.

"Don't shush me," I said, trying to control the panic that was quickly rising in my voice. "How do you know . . ."

"Promise you won't freak out?"

"I'm not promising anything," I said, sitting upright and beginning to stand up.

He leaned over and switched on the lamp next to the bed.

With the lamp on, he was even more beautiful than I had imagined in the dark. His long, lean body was lightly tanned and completely smooth. His chest was muscular and defined, and tapered down to a tightly muscled washboard abdomen. I'd never seen, or even imagined, such a huge and thick cock. It was a crimson red, and throbbed with thick veins that coursed through the shaft. Big, shaved balls hung between long but brawny legs. When I looked up into his angelic face, I nearly fainted.

"Loren?" I almost yelled. I couldn't believe one of the two Boettcher brothers was lying naked in bed, begging me to suck his cock.

"Please don't freak out, Sean," he said, and sat up in the bed. "I had no idea it would be you, or I never would have gone through with this. But by the time I knew it was you, it was too late to turn back. I really want you, Sean. And from the look of your cock, you want me, too."

I jerked my head down to look at my dick. It was jutting out in front of me, bigger and harder than I'd ever seen it before. I felt my face grow red again, and looked back up at Loren.

"No one has to know about this, dude. I certainly don't want word getting out about it, and I know you don't either. So let's just put the embarrassing part of this behind us and get down to doing what both of us are here for. I want you more than I've wanted anything in a really long time. Maybe ever. So, are you gonna suck my cock or what?"

I blinked stupidly at him, and took a couple of deep breaths.

Loren leaned in and kissed me on the lips again, caressing my chin and neck as he did. When I moaned, he broke the kiss and moved his face to my chest. He licked my nipples and chest and then snaked his tongue down my torso and around my bellybutton. I closed my eyes, thinking I'd never felt anything so right in my entire life.

And then I felt the most incredible wet warmth I've ever experienced. My eyes shot open, and I saw Loren's head slide up and down around my crotch while I felt his wet, warm tongue licking at my shaft as his lips wrapped around my cock and sucked more and more of me into his mouth. Bright lights exploded behind my eyes, and the room went fuzzy. The ringing in my ears grew louder, and my body grew light and dizzy. When Loren's mouth swallowed the last of my cock, and I felt my cock head slide past the back of his throat, my legs began to quiver and I moaned as the room spun around me.

"I'm gonna faint," I said softly.

Loren quickly slid his mouth off my cock, and leaned me backward so that I rested against the pillow. "You okay, dude?"

"Yeah," I answered, as consciousness filled the air around me again. "I'm sorry. I've just never done any of this before. It's all so much better than I thought it would be."

Loren smiled. "You ain't seen nothin' yet."

"Really?" I caught my breath and readjusted my body onto the middle of the bed.

"Mmmm hmmm," Loren said, and scooted up so that he straddled my chest.

His giant cock bobbed just an inch or so from my face. My mental ruler measured it at least ten or eleven inches, and I already knew that I couldn't wrap my fist around it. The head was bright red, and blue veins popped out along the shaft like a giant river. Loren was uncut, but the skin was pulled tightly back behind the head. A large drop of clear precum oozed out of his cock head and dangled from the end of his cock.

I reached out with my tongue and licked the precum from his cock head. It was slick and salty and delicious—all I needed to convince me that I wanted Loren's cock. I licked at the head for a moment, then wrapped my lips around it and sucked just the head into my mouth. Loren moaned loudly and tried to push another inch or so inside my mouth, but I pushed him back and just sucked on the head for a few minutes. And then something in me snapped, and I knew that I needed his dick inside me more than I'd ever needed anything. I took a deep breath and swallowed as much of his huge cock into my mouth as I could. I only got three or four inches in my mouth before it hit the back of my throat and I gagged.

"Careful there, stud," Loren said. "No need to hurry. Just take your time."

I took another deep breath and sucked softly on his cock again, slower this time. In no time at all, my throat muscles relaxed, and I lowered my head farther down on Loren's dick. My eyes bulged as more and more of his cock slid deeper into my throat. Before I knew it, his pubic hair was tickling my nose. His entire huge cock was buried deep inside my throat!

"Fuck me!" Loren almost screamed. He grabbed the sides of the bed with both hands as he slowly pumped his cock in and out of my mouth.

I couldn't believe how easily his giant dick fit inside my mouth and throat, or how good it felt filling me up like it did. I grunted and moaned like an animal in heat as I swallowed the entire thing and sucked on it hungrily. The fat uncut cock leaked a lot of precum, and my own cock throbbed harder each time a giant drop of the sweet liquid oozed from his cock and landed on my tongue and throat.

Loren breathed heavily and moaned as he bucked his hips up to force more of his cock into my throat. I stroked my own cock furiously as he fucked my face, and I could tell he was getting close. The feel of his hard cock pounding against my throat got me hotter than anything I'd ever experienced, and I felt the first stirrings of orgasm roll through my balls as Loren moaned louder.

"Oh, fuck, man," Loren groaned, and slipped his cock gently out of my mouth.

I'd never felt so empty so quickly, and my orgasm retreated back into my guts.

"What's wrong?" I asked as he twisted his face in a look of pain, and closed his eyes. "Why'd you stop? Does it hurt?"

"No," he panted. "I just don't want to cum."

"You don't?" I asked, a little stunned. "I thought that was the purpose."

Loren laughed. "I don't want to cum *yet*."

"Why not?"

"I want to fuck you."

I felt my eyes bulge as I stared at him. "You've got to be kidding me? There's no way I can take that monster up my ass. It'd rip me to shreds. You'd kill me."

Loren smiled, and leaned up to kiss me tenderly. "I won't rip you to shreds and I won't kill you, either. I promise."

"No. I can't take that," I said as I held his cock in my hands and looked at it lovingly. I couldn't help but lick my lips.

"I'll go really slow."

"It will hurt like hell."

"I'm not gonna lie to you, it will hurt for a little bit. But it wouldn't hurt any less if it were smaller. Your first time hurts for a couple minutes regardless of the size of the dick. But I'll go slow, and after a minute or two it won't hurt. You'll really like it, I swear."

"Loren . . ."

"Please, Sean. I want to fuck you. I want to feel my cock buried deep inside that beautiful tight little ass of yours."

"You think I have a nice ass?" I said shyly.

"You have the most gorgeous ass I've ever laid eyes upon."

I blushed, and knew at once that I would not leave that motel room a virgin. I leaned in and kissed Loren passionately on the lips, savoring the sweet taste of his tongue and the soft fullness of his lips.

Loren rolled me onto my stomach and pushed my legs apart. I'd never had my ass that spread open, and the cool air from the ceiling fan made goose bumps pop up all over my ass and legs. I clenched my ass hole instinctively. Loren leaned down and licked the crack of my ass, and I moaned as his tongue tickled my cheeks and snaked its way across my hole. He licked it several times, then slowly slid his tongue into my puckered hole.

"Oh my God," I cried out. "It hurts. Take it out."

Loren laughed, blowing air across my ass cheeks and my twitching hole. "Shut up, dude. That wasn't even my cock. It was just my tongue."

"Oh," I sighed. "Go ahead, then."

He laughed again, and then spread my cheeks even farther apart, attacking my ass with his mouth and tongue like it was his last supper.

* * *

There is more to the story, of course. But suffice it to say that I did indeed not leave the motel room a virgin. I can't kiss and tell every little detail . . . I have a need for some mystery in my life. But Loren was gentle and passionate with me the entire time. When the pain was too much the first time, he pulled out and let me catch my breath and relax. And then he went back in. The second and third time we fucked that night, I needed him *not* to be gentle and passionate, and he was more than willing and able to oblige then as well.

We fucked around a couple times a week for the rest of our time at school, and no one was the wiser. Loren eventually married, and he now has three kids and lives two blocks down the street from me. We are . . . cordial to one another, and wave as neighbors do when his wife is present. Aside from that . . .

Well, like I said . . . I have a need for a little discretion and mystery in my life.

Up With People

"You *are* kidding me, right?" I asked through a mouthful of Captain Crunch cereal.

"No, honey, I'm not," mom said as she set a glass of orange juice next to my bowl. "The church is really in a bind, and, well, I just couldn't say no when they asked me. They committed to hosting six people from the group, and only a couple of congregation members stepped forward. They still need to find homes for two more singers besides the young man I agreed to take in."

"Well, I don't care," I sulked. "We don't have room here. What were you thinking? I know you're not planning on having him sleep on the sofa for a month."

"No, I'm not. But you've got a big queen sized bed all to yourself and . . ."

"Absolutely not. I'm not sharing my bed with a complete stranger. That's not fair, mom. You should have asked me first."

"Well, you weren't here, and Pastor Bob had me cornered. I couldn't say no."

"Yes, you could have," I said. "You just didn't."

"Come on, Jeremy. Think of it as an adventure. José is from Mexico. You can learn about a whole new culture. It'll be a good experience, if you just let it."

"Oh, sure. I can see it now. Having some Third World visitor stay with us for a month. He probably doesn't even shower every day. Gross. And how are we supposed to talk with him?"

"Jeremy!" mom raised her voice as she sat next to me and poured herself a bowl of Grape Nuts. "Don't be rude. Of course he takes a shower every day. For crying out loud! And Pastor Bob has assured me that he speaks very good English. They all do."

"But, Mom," I whined. "It's my bed. I can't sleep with someone else in bed with me. It's just gross."

"Well, then," she said in that stern tone that I instantly recognized as meaning the conversation was now over and that she sincerely meant the next words that were to come from her mouth, "I guess if it's so gross to be a hospitable Christian and share your bed with a visitor, then *you* can sleep on the sofa for the next month. José can have the bed all to himself. I'm sure he wouldn't mind."

I chewed my Captain Crunch as quietly as possible, and swallowed carefully. "I guess it'll be okay," I mumbled, barely audibly.

Mom smiled. "Good. I knew you'd see it my way." She wiped her lips and stood up to leave.

"Like I had a choice," I muttered under my breath.

"Exactly," mom said as she kissed me on the cheek. She had the ears of a Rotweiller. And the bite of one too. "He'll be here when you get home from work this afternoon, so be on your best behavior."

"Whatever." I stood up and grabbed my backpack and walked out the door, careful not to slam it.

Work totally sucked. But that was nothing new. It always did. I worked at a local burger joint owned by a sweet old man and his wife. I could've worked at the only McDonald's in town, but it was over three miles away and I didn't have a car. The Burger Barn was only half a mile from my house, and there was just the three of us working there. It never got busy enough to hire anyone else. Officially I was the cook. Mr. Barker was supposed to be the cashier and Mrs. Barker was supposed to be the hostess/waitress. But I inevitably became host, waiter, cashier, cook, and dishwasher. It never failed that the Barkers ended up sitting at the booths with the patrons, who all happened to be old friends of theirs, and I ended up doing everything. But it didn't bother me. They were really very nice to me, and it was fun watching them gossip with their gaggle of old geezers who came in every day. For my eighteenth birthday a couple of months earlier, the Barkers made me the "Manager" of the joint. I got a fifteen cent per-hour raise and a new badge proclaiming my fancy new title. Woo hoo!

I couldn't stop thinking about José the entire time I was at work. Why the fuck did mom have to go and volunteer us to host some stranger for a whole month? A stranger from another country, no less. It had been hard enough living with mom since she and dad had divorced the previous year. She'd been very clingy lately, and it was almost impossible to find any time alone. And now she'd insist on me hanging around José as much as possible and showing him around.

Not like there were a million things to do in Perryton. It wouldn't take all that long to show him the "sites" around town. But I really valued my alone time. For the last couple of years I'd been struggling about some strong feelings for a few guys at school, and I spent hours alone in my room beating off to fantasies about them. I'd never been with another guy, and in fact avoided the showers after gym class as much as possible. I'd only seen a couple of naked cocks, and only at a quick glance. So my beating off fantasies were all I had. Now all of that was gonna change. I'd be sharing my room with a complete stranger from a stupid foreign country who probably barely spoke English. I'd spend most of my time flipping through the damned English – Spanish dictionary trying to explain what Hamburger Helper was and why José should eat it and not make a necklace out of it. And I'd have absolutely no privacy. Fuckin' great.

I took my time cleaning up after my shift, making sure every dish was washed, every floor swept and mopped, every counter and booth wiped down. The Barkers had left half an hour earlier, so I had the place to myself. I was just about to shut the blinds and beat off on one of the red vinyl booth seats, when the phone rang.

It was mom, wondering where I was. Dinner was waiting. Which really meant that José was waiting. I pinched the head of my dick to make my hard-on go away, grumbled, and headed home.

"Hi, honey," mom said in that sweet falsetto voice that dripped of June Cleaver. "You're late getting home this evening." She was speaking much more slowly and enunciating more clearly than usual, and was almost screaming, even though I was less than ten feet from her. "You must have been really busy at the diner tonight."

"Not really," I said with no enthusiasm. She knew we never had more than three or four customers at a time, and even with that mad rush, the old geezers only ever ordered coffee and a cinnamon roll. Every once in awhile a kid from school or a stranger passing through town would stop in and order a burger and fries. But that was the rare adventure at Burger Barn.

"Honey, I want you to meet José," she said as she grabbed the arm of the guy shutting the fridge door.

I set my backpack on the table and looked up. All day I'd been brooding about having to share my room with this guy, so I'd definitely built up an image in my mind about what he looked like. I was sure he'd be short and probably a little fat. He'd have bucked up teeth and acne all over his face. His hair would be buzz cut and greasy. And he'd struggle to get out a simple "hello."

I couldn't have been more wrong.

"Hey," José said, and stuck his hand out to shake mine as he popped a grape into his mouth. "How are you?"

His grip was strong and firm, yet his skin was softer than it had a right to be. I looked into his face and struggled to catch my breath. José was quite possibly the most beautiful guy I'd ever seen. He had shoulder-length, wavy black hair. His skin was smooth and perfectly copper colored. His eyes were hazel and almond-shaped, framed with thick, long, and curly eyelashes. When he smiled, dimples appeared from nowhere on either side of his lips, and his milk-white teeth sparkled.

He was a couple of inches taller than me, about six feet. Even fully clothed I could tell he was solidly built. His chest stretched the cotton fabric of his t-shirt and I could count the lines of his six-pack. His biceps popped out of the short sleeves and showed off thick, prominent veins. His legs filled out his jeans, and even though I only "accidentally" glanced at it, the bulge at his crotch couldn't be ignored.

I tried to speak as he tightened his grip on my hand, but found myself mute.

"This is my son, Jeremy," mom said loudly and slowly as she stared at me. "He has quite a wide vocabulary, really, and usually isn't this rude."

"I'm sorry," I stuttered. I released my grip on José's hand, and wiped my own sweat onto my dirty jeans. "I'm Jeremy," I said stupidly.

"It's great to meet you, Jeremy," José said with only the slightest trace of the sexiest accent I'd ever heard. "Thanks for letting me stay with you. I hope it won't be too much of an inconvenience."

"Not at all," I gushed out just a tad too quickly. "I mean, don't worry about it. I'm glad to help out."

Mom smiled and patted me on the back as she kissed my cheek. "Well, dinner is about ready. Wash up and sit down."

I did my best not to act completely stupid during dinner, but failed miserably. Hey, I admit it, I was all but catatonic. I couldn't stop staring at José. And the hard-on I got the moment José touched my hand didn't go away all throughout dinner.

"José, your English is superb," mom said as she kicked me under the table and gave me her patented evil eye, which this time I cannily interpreted as saying, *where the hell are your manners, and you'd better start chatting mighty damned quickly.*

"Yeah, it's really good," I said through a mouthful of soggy Spanish rice. Mom was trying to impress José with her Mexican cooking. I was praying we wouldn't be rushing him to the emergency room before we reached dessert. "Where'd you learn to speak English so well?"

"Oh, it's nothing. My mom is American, but has lived in Mexico since she met and married my dad twenty years ago. We speak both languages in my house. My dad actually does a lot of business here in the States, so we make a habit of speaking English quite a bit."

"Wow," mom said as she spooned another scoop of mushy chicken enchilada casserole onto José's plate. "That's very interesting, isn't it, Jeremy?"

"Yeah," I said as I struggled not to imagine José's naked body sitting across from me. "I wish I could speak two languages."

"It comes in handy. Especially when I'm planning on spending the next six months traveling through the States."

The rest of the dinner went fairly smoothly. José was a sport and ate every bite of the nasty food mom kept heaping onto his plate. When we were finished, mom insisted on doing the dishes (something she is usually adamant about *me* doing) and ushered José and me upstairs where I could help him unpack and get settled in.

After clearing a couple of drawers in my dresser and making room for Jose's clothes in the closet, I excused myself to take a shower while he unpacked. There was no door to the bathroom that connected to my bedroom, and the shower had a glass sliding door, so I was perfectly visible to José as I showered, and very much aware of the fact. As much as I wanted to, I didn't dare beat off in the shower. Instead, I turned and faced the wall, with my back to the glass door and showered as quickly as possible and with the coldest water I could stand. I just couldn't go back out there with a hard-on. When I finished, I wrapped myself snugly into my bathrobe and walked into the bedroom.

"Thanks again for sharing your room with me," José said with the sexiest smile I'd ever seen. I felt my cock stir just from looking at it. "Do you mind if I shower before I go to bed?"

"Not at all," I blurted out even before he'd finished the question. "There are extra towels in the cabinet above the toilet."

"Thanks," he said, and began to undress.

I turned away and quickly slid my briefs on under my robe, then dropped the robe to the floor and slipped under the covers and pulled them tightly around my chin. I heard José walk away, and a moment later the shower started. When I heard the sliding shower door shut, I rolled onto my back and stared into the bathroom. The glass was opaque, so I couldn't make out every detail, but I could see enough to spring a boner in just a couple of seconds. I watched as José lathered his entire body. When he raised his hands to wash his hair, I made out the dark of his underarm hair, and his muscles flexed in a way that made me moan. Then he reached down and soaped his cock, pulling up his balls and carefully washing under them. I swear I could see his dick grow a couple inches as he lathered it for several seconds. I felt my cock throb, and a small drop of precum leaked out of the head. "Shit," I mumbled, and turned around quickly as I heard the shower stop.

I forced myself to breathe slowly and deeply, pretending to be asleep as José pulled down the covers and clicked off the lamp. He climbed into bed carefully and rolled onto his side so that his back faced me. Even though I was under the top sheet, a blanket, and a comforter, I found myself shivering. And even though I was shivering, I swore I could feel the heat from José's body, despite the fact that he was at least a couple of feet and several layers of blankets from me.

I bit down hard enough on my tongue to bring tears to my eyes. It was the only way I could think of to make my hard-on go away. Even with that, it only went halfway soft.

A couple of minutes into that agony, I heard José snoring softly. I rolled onto my side and stared at the beautiful Mexican boy next to me. I could only see the back of his head and neck, and about half of his naked back. But it was enough. I popped a full boner instantly. I reached out tentatively then quickly pulled my hand away before I touched his back.

What the fuck was I thinking? I'd never been with another dude before. Shit, I'd done everything in my power to skip gym classes and lockers just so I wouldn't have to look at another guy naked. The fucking dreams and incessant daydreams I'd had over the past year were bad enough. I was beginning to think mom might have slipped a hallucinogenic agent in the enchilada casserole. Touching another guy. A naked guy. What the fuck was I thinking?

But the more I thought about how wrong it was and the horrible consequences it would bring, the more I found myself obsessed with the idea. I had to touch José's naked skin. I had to feel it against my own.

I scooted closer to him as slowly and carefully as I could. When I was only a couple of inches away from him, I stopped and struggled to catch my breath. I smelled the soap on his skin and it took my breath away. This close, I really could feel the heat of his skin, and it made me want to touch him more than ever. I felt light-headed and a little drunk, even though I hadn't had anything stronger than a soda with dinner.

José was still snoring soundly, so I leaned up on one elbow to get a better look at him. Bright moonlight shone through the window. I could make out every defined muscle on his neck and back and on the one arm that rested outside the blankets. I had to touch him. I had to smell him and feel the heat of his skin.

I reached over slowly and touched his shoulder. My god, I swear I felt a jolt of static rush through my hand and then my arm and then the rest of my body. I know it sounds impossible, but his skin was both hot and cool at the same time, and as smooth as silk. My cock throbbed just from the feel of his skin on my hand. My heart thumped a million beats per hour, but I couldn't stop myself. I leaned down and gently kissed his shoulder. As I did, I breathed in and was enveloped with his smell. The mix of my Dial soap and his natural scent drove me crazy. I felt the beginning stirs of orgasm building up deep in my balls, and I hadn't even touched my cock! So I pulled myself from José's body and lay right next to him, breathing deeply and slowly and trying desperately not to shoot my load all over my stomach.

As I lay next to José and squeezed the base of my cock to stop the quickly increasing inevitability of my orgasm, José rolled onto his back. As he did, he pulled the blankets down to his knees in one seemingly innocent and effortless move. I tried not to look at his body, but I was helpless against the temptation.

He was a study in perfection. Long and muscular, with not an ounce of fat, his body was magnificent. His body was hairless except for the patches of underarm hair I'd glimpsed earlier, and a thick line of short black hair that started at the bottom of his navel and disappeared into the waistband of his bleached white briefs. I swallowed hard as I saw the pouch of his underwear start to bulge.

I took a deep breath and casually moved my arm over closer to his side of the bed until my hand rested against his hip. My heart beat erratically, and I took another deep breath. Then I moved my hand up and rested it lightly right on top of his crotch. It felt big and strong and heavy, and I wanted it more than I'd wanted anything in a very long time.

And then it started to move. The bulge grew bigger and fatter. I stopped breathing altogether as José yawned and stretched his body across the bed, kicking the rest of the blankets to the foot of the bed and exposing his entire body. I took it all in and felt like crying. Never had I seen anything so beautiful or that I'd wanted so badly. His chest was very muscular, and as smooth as the rest of his body, with the tiniest nipples I'd ever seen. My eyes followed his chest down to his stomach, where very distinct lines appeared just below his ribcage on either side. And there was that damned sexy thick patch of hair again.

Now the bulge in his briefs was growing even more. A long thick line began snaking up the right side of his shorts, coming right toward me. I was mesmerized, and couldn't take my eyes off it. A few seconds later the elastic waistband lifted all on its own, and the head of José's cock poked out.

I tried to be good . . . to do the right thing, honest I did. But my head began to spin and bright spots of light floated in front of my eyes, and before I knew it, I was sliding down the bed right toward his crotch. When I was face-to-face with the bulge in his shorts, I didn't hesitate. I stuck out my tongue and licked the head of his cock, then slowly and carefully sucked it into my mouth.

WHAT WAS I DOING? I'd never sucked a dick before. Hell, I'd done everything in my power not to even think about them for the past couple of years. But now that I had José's cock head in my mouth, nothing had ever felt so natural. I just licked it for a few seconds, then kept it inside my mouth for a moment, relishing how it felt as it throbbed against my cheeks and tongue, savoring the salty sweet taste of his precum.

José was no longer snoring. I looked up into his face as I sucked gently on his cock head. His eyes were still closed and he was still breathing deeply and regularly. I was sure he was still asleep, so I very slowly pulled his briefs down just far enough so his entire cock and balls were freed. I gasped as I saw it fully for the first time. I knew that just the head had seemed quite a bit bigger than mine, but I hadn't given it a lot of thought. I didn't have much experience to compare it against, but even with my limited knowledge, I knew this was one huge cock. Freed from the confines of his underwear, José's cock lay across his lower stomach, a couple of inches past his navel, and I could barely wrap my fist around it.

I'd never seen an uncut dick before, so I was fascinated with the extra skin that covered the bottom half of his cock head. I played with it for a moment, completely enthralled with the way the soft skin covered his entire shaft and slid over the head as I slid my hand up and down the length of his giant cock.

Drunk with desire, I licked and sucked on it as best I could. I got about a third of it in my mouth, but choked a little when the head pressed against the back of my throat, so I stopped and just sucked on what I could get in.

José moaned and stretched out across the bed, causing his cock to slide a little deeper into me and this time I didn't gag as it slid another inch into my throat. I wrapped my lips tighter around it and sucked it in and out of my mouth. I'd never tasted or felt anything so good!

Soon José's hips were thrusting in and out of my mouth. I noticed he was breathing harder and moaning, but when I looked up into his face, I saw his eyes were still closed. He looked like he was still asleep, so I kept sucking.

I'm not sure exactly what I was expecting. I mean, I wasn't completely stupid or naive. Even though I'd never had sex or even gotten blown, I'd certainly beaten off enough in my life to know that eventually, with pressure and pleasure like I was giving, José's cock would release its load. But I wasn't prepared at all for the spray of warm cum that shot out of his cock and slid down my throat. He didn't grab my head or say anything or moan any louder than he had been since I'd started. Just all of a sudden his cock got thicker and harder and a split second later several forceful shots of cum splashed across the back of my throat and kept coming until my mouth was filled. It all happened so fast, I didn't have time to think about what to do, so I swallowed it before I choked.

I almost gagged at the first swallow, but it didn't take long before I realized I loved the taste of his cum. I swallowed it eagerly, and kept sucking on his cock for several minutes after he'd stopped spewing into my mouth. Eventually his cock got soft, and I reluctantly let it go.

I looked up at José and saw he was still asleep, so I pulled his briefs back up and crawled back up to my side of the bed. My own cock was as hard as it had ever been. So hard it hurt. I wrapped my fist around it and began beating off very slowly and very quietly.

"Want some help with that?"

I stopped mid-stroke and prayed my heart wouldn't pound its way out of my chest.

"What?" I croaked.

"Fair is fair." José leaned over and kissed me on the lips as his fist wrapped around my cock and slowly stroked up and down. At first he just touched his lips to mine and applied a little pressure. But then he licked my lips and slid his tongue inside my mouth.

I panicked. "José," I whispered, "what are you doing?"

"I'm kissing you," he said in that sexy accent, and then slid his tongue back inside and kissed me again.

I'd never imagined anything feeling or tasting so good. His tongue was soft and warm and minty, and it slid inside my mouth and licked my lips. Then he sucked my tongue into his mouth, and . . .

. . . I shot my load all over his hand. More than that, it flew past his hand and across my stomach and chest. My orgasm went on for what seemed like minutes, and when I was finished, my entire torso, and part of José's arm was covered in warm, sticky cum.

"I'm *so* sorry," I stuttered and panted at the same time. "I didn't mean to . . ."

"It's okay," José said, and leaned down to kiss me again. When he finished kissing my lips, he continued kissing down my chin and neck. Then he reached my chest and licked and kissed his way down my chest and stomach, licking up as much of my cum as he could.

My dick was starting to get soft after cumming so much. But when José slid back up to my face and kissed me again, I hardened instantly. His tongue was covered with my cum, and I sucked on it greedily. The combination of my still-warm cum and his tongue made me harder than I'd ever been.

"Are you ready for more?" he asked.

"More?" I said in a dazed whisper.

"Turn over."

I rolled onto my stomach without questioning him. He maneuvered his way between my legs and spread them apart with his own.

Never before had I been this exposed to anyone, let alone another guy, and I felt a little nervous and uncertain. A second later José's tongue found my ass crack and licked around it, and I tightened up like a San Quentin lockdown.

"José . . ."

"Shhh," he whispered. "I know. But don't worry. I won't hurt you. I promise. Just relax."

I bit my pillow and took a couple of deep breaths, and in a few seconds I indeed was relaxing. A moment later, when José's warm, wet tongue slid into my hole, I moaned much louder than intended.

"Shhhhh," José laughed, and then went right back in. His tongue licked around the hole for a moment, then slid slowly back inside my ass.

My cock throbbed painfully beneath me and threatened to shoot all over my sheets each time José's tongue snaked its way deep inside me. Those lights I saw earlier returned, and this time they were accompanied by a loud ringing noise in my head. Each time he pulled his tongue out, I arched my back and butt into the air, begging him to stick it back in.

José laughed and slid up next to me, then turned me around so that I was lying on my back next to him. He wrapped his arms around me and pulled me close. "There's so much more, if you want it," he whispered into my ear as he nibbled on it.

"I want it," I moaned.

"Are you sure?"

"Yes," I said, and leaned in to kiss him on the lips again.

"All right," he said, and rolled over until he straddled my chest. His fat, semi-hard uncut cock was only inches from my face, and he slapped it playfully against my lips and chin. When I reached out with my tongue to lick it, he pulled it away. "Nope. You've had that already."

"But I want it again," I pleaded.

"No. This time you get more."

"More?"

"Mmm hmm."

José spat into his hand a couple of times, then reached behind him and slid his fist up and down the length of my cock. I moaned and bucked my hips as he repeated the action a couple of times.

My eyes were closed and I grabbed the sides of the mattress as the sensations of his fist pumping my cock brought shocks of pleasure to every inch of my body. I felt his body lift from mine, and a second later my cock head was pressing against his ass hole.

"José, what are you . . ."

He slid down my cock just enough for the head to pop inside, then stopped and took a deep breath.

Fireworks exploded inside my head, and the room began to spin around me. José's ass muscles gripped my cock head and twitched all around it. His ass was hot and wet and tight and strong all at once. I couldn't breathe, and when I saw him lean down toward me, I thought he was going to give me mouth-to-mouth. Instead, he licked my lips and slid his tongue slowly inside to kiss me. As his tongue slipped into my mouth, he lowered himself onto my cock. When his ass finally reached the base of my cock, and squeezed my shaft teasingly, I thought I would pass out.

"You okay with all this?" he asked as he kissed my lips again.

"Oh yes," I kinda moaned, kinda whimpered.

"Then fuck me."

At first I panicked, because I'd never had sex before, and wasn't sure I knew how to do it. But I seriously doubted anyone had taken lessons before their first time, and that it probably came naturally. It did.

I slid my cock slowly out of José's ass until just the head remained inside, then slid it just as slowly back in. It seemed to do the trick, because he moaned loudly and planted his hands on my chest as he rode my dick. I looked up at him as we began moving together as a machine. My god, he was gorgeous. His chest was powerfully muscled, without being grotesque, and his tiny nipples grew hard as drops of sweat dripped down his chest and across them. Six deeply indented rows of hard muscle tightened across his abdomen as he slid up and down my cock, and I thought stupidly that I could get grill marks on a steak if I slapped it across his abs. His eyes were closed most of the time, but when he opened them, they sparkled as he looked into mine and smiled.

I was such an amateur at this, so it didn't take long at all before I lost all control and felt my balls tighten. I slammed my cock deep and hard into José's ass and made a noise that frighteningly resembled a frustrated horse trying to be corralled.

"Are you cumming, baby?" José asked as he leaned down to kiss me.

Just hearing him call me "baby" with that fucking sexy accent of his was enough to drive me way over the edge. "Yes," I whinnied.

He slid off my cock in one quick move, and maneuvered down my body so that his head rested on my stomach.

"Move, José," I said as I grabbed my cock and pumped. "I'm gonna cum."

"Like hell," he said.

The first shot flew right past his face and landed on my own lips. I instinctively licked it off and swallowed it as the next seven or eight spews of cum splashed across José's face. He moaned loudly as each spray hit him, and then hugged me tightly when he was sure there was no more.

"Are you ready for more?" he asked as he licked his lips.

"More?" I managed to squeak out.

"I'm so fucking close, I gotta shoot again," he said, and crawled back on top of my chest.

"Give it to me," I begged.

He stroked his cock a few times, and then cum was flying everywhere. It hit the headboard, the pillows on either side of me, and covered my face. I lapped up as much of it as I could, and José licked off the rest. Then he kissed me again, rewarding me with even more of his cum from his tongue.

We kissed for several minutes, then lay wrapped in one another's arms as we caught our breath. The last thing I remember that night was hearing snoring and not knowing whether it was me or José.

That month that I'd dreaded so much turned out to be the best month of my life, and passed way too quickly. José and I had sex every single night of that month. Mother was never the wiser. She was thrilled that José and I got along so wonderfully and that we spent every free moment together. She thought he was teaching me to speak Spanish, and although I did pick up enough to insult someone's mother and get my ass kicked, I hardly learned to speak the language.

Revenge of the Newbie

Patterson Hall. The name couldn't have been more plain or boring. The double-story red brick square building was nondescript and didn't have a single feature distinguishing it from any of the other dozens of buildings that dotted the hundred-acre campus of Bouvieux College.

I took a deep breath and lugged my four suitcases across the sidewalk and up the couple of steps that led to the main entrance. Inside was warm and a little overly furnished in Colonial décor. A small bell clanged as the door opened and shut, and a moment later I heard a voice coming from upstairs.

"Just a sec," the male voice said loudly. "I'll be right down."

I looked around and took another deep breath. Was this really a place I could spend the next four years? I felt like I'd stepped through a magical door onto the set of *Gone With the Wind*. Maybe I could transfer to another dorm after the first trimester.

"What's up, dude? How can I help you?"

I looked up and watched as the body accompanying the **voice** bounded down the stairs two at a time. He was shirtless and wore nothing but a pair of ratted and torn long gray gym shorts. A shiny layer of sweat covered every inch of visible skin, and I watched as a couple of drops dripped across his nipples and down his perfectly smooth torso. They got trapped inside the rippled muscles of his washboard abs, then gathered enough momentum to continue down his thin, but dark treasure trail.

"Hello?" he said as he came to a stop at the bottom of the stairs. He was now only a couple of feet away from me.

"Sorry," I mumbled, and forced myself to look from his naked torso to his face. His blond hair dripped with sweat and fell lazily across his forehead. His eyes were bright blue and sparkled when I looked into them. A light pink blush covered his cheeks and matched the color of his full and sensuous lips. He smiled, and twin dimples framed his mouth. I thought I would faint right there. "I'm supposed to check in with Tarik."

"That's me," he said, and held out his hand. It was strong and firm, yet surprisingly soft and welcoming to the touch. "You must be the newbie."

"I guess," I said awkwardly. "I'm Kent."

"Excellent," Tarik said, and looked me up and down. "Excellent. I'm the RA. You're gonna be in Room 214. Top of the stairs and all the way down the hall on the left. The rooms are small here, but we don't have to share them. At our age, that's a good thing, don't you think? I mean, boys need to be boys, right?"

I couldn't take my eyes off of his full, soft lips, but pulled myself together enough to laugh along with him.

"I'm in 212, right next door to you. Go on up and relax. Take a look around if you wanna. I was just working out, and smell like an overworked whore. I'm gonna grab a quick shower and then I'll stop by and show you around a little more formally. You can hang with me tonight and I'll introduce you to all the essentials."

"Thanks," I barely whispered.

Tarik turned and ascended the stairs two at a time, and disappeared down the hall.

"Shit," I said as I exhaled and concentrated on catching my breath.

I'd just graduated from high school a couple months earlier.

Layton, Texas, with a population of just under 2,000 is not exactly the picture of metropolitan life. For the last two years of high school I'd struggled with the dark secret of my obsession with and attraction to guys. There wasn't a single cute guy in Layton, or in any of the surrounding small towns, so keeping my secret hadn't been too hard. My only crushes were on TV or movie stars, and I could just slip into my room and beat off to the teenaged Clark Kent on the small tube or, on rare occasion, pop a video of a half-naked Brad Pitt or Orlando Bloom into the VCR and beat off until I was purple in the face.

My freshman year in college was really my first adventure into the real world, and as I stood paralyzed with my lust and desire for Tarik, I realized how totally unprepared I was. I'd never seen anyone as beautiful as him. The guys I'd grown up with in Layton didn't even come close. Even Brad and Orlando might have trouble holding their own were they in the same room with him.

I sighed, and lugged my suitcases up the stairs. Halfway down the hall, behind a closed door, I heard the shower running and Tarik's voice as it sang loudly to the latest Maroon 5 song. A few steps farther and I was looking into his room. A single-sized bed occupied one wall of the room, and a Soloflex workout station dominated the opposite wall. A small desk abutted the foot of the bed, and was overflowing with books, clothes and an open bag of Doritos. Strewn across the unmade bed were the gray shorts Tarik had been wearing, and a black jockstrap. His sneakers lay on their sides on the floor beside the bed. The raw and exciting smell of sweat and young man wafted out of the room, and I inhaled deeply to drink it all in. My cock hardened and I fought off the urge to grab the jockstrap and run off to my own room where I could be alone and naked with Tarik's sweat and scent.

Instead, I rolled my suitcases into my room next door and shut the door behind me. The room, empty of personal belongings, seemed small and cold and sterile. The only furnishings were a single bed identical to Tarik's, a desk attached to the foot of the bed, and a wooden chair in front of the desk. Already I missed home, and I lay on the bed without unpacking my suitcases. I'd never lived alone, or even been away from home for any period of time. I didn't know a single person here, and Layton and all my friends were a four-hour plane ride away. Maybe I'd made a big mistake.

Then Tarik's face appeared in my mind, with his perfect white teeth, seducing bedroom eyes, and soft pink lips, and I thought maybe I hadn't made a mistake after all. As I pictured his face, I imagined his kissable lips drawing my cock into his warm mouth and sucking on it until I couldn't breathe. I'd never had those kinds of thoughts about someone I actually knew, and thinking about Brad and Orlando with my cock in their mouths didn't really seem to count, so I was astonished at how strongly I pictured this act and how hard it made my cock.

I reached down and pulled my dick out of my jeans. It was already fully hard and throbbed in my hands as I stroked it. The big veins popped out on it and pulsed the blood through the shaft, and I moaned as my fist slid up and down its length. I shoved my jeans to my ankles and spread my legs as wide as I could without sliding my jeans all the way off. As my fist reached the base of my cock, I scooped my balls into my other hand and massaged them.

I moaned loudly and was just about to shove my finger into my ass when I heard a loud banging sound on the wall next to me.

"You in there, Kent?" I heard from the other side of the wall.

"Yes," I croaked out quietly and then repeated more loudly as I stopped pumping my cock in mid-stroke.

"Come on over. We can talk while I get ready."

I looked down at my cock, already red and starting to drip a little precum. I wanted more than anything to shoot my load and then curl up and fall asleep for a couple hours. "Ummm, now isn't a great time," I yelled into the wall.

"Get over here. You can unpack later."

"Okay," I said to the wall before I could stop myself. "Shit!"

I stood up and took a deep breath. My cock bobbed in front of me, defiant in its unwillingness to soften. "You bitch!" I hissed at it, and pulled my jeans up to cover its obvious insubordination.

I walked next door and stood for a moment, watching as Tarik stood naked in his room and dried himself off. His back was to me, and as he slid the towel up and down and across his body, I couldn't peel my eyes from his ass. It was perfectly round and hard and smooth, and white in contrast to the golden tan that covered the rest of his body. My cock jumped in my jeans, and I closed my eyes and counted to ten to help myself from creaming my jeans.

When I opened my eyes, Tarik was turned around and staring at me. The towel was draped around his neck, and he was holding it at both ends on either side of his torso. He stood with his legs about shoulder length apart. I tried to keep my eyes on his face, but it didn't work. They wandered down his chest, taking in the beautiful sight of his nipples standing erect and proud against his tanned chest, and even farther down past his six-pack abs and to the treasure trail I'd drooled over earlier.

And then it was there. Even soft, his cock was long and thick, and swung slightly between his legs as he swayed his hips. It was a shade or two lighter than the tanned skin on his legs and torso, and covered with a sheath of foreskin riddled with thick veins. As I stared, it bobbed up and down a couple of times, taunting me.

"Come in and shut the door," Tarik said as he tossed the towel onto the Soloflex machine.

I took a couple of steps inside and closed the door behind me. I just stood there for a moment, bewitched as I watched his cock thicken and harden in front of me.

"Come here," Tarik whispered.

I looked up at him and prayed that I didn't look desperate as I forced myself to swallow.

"Jeez, you look like you're gonna cry," Tarik said as he smiled. "Are you okay?"

"Yes," I mumbled.

"Then come here."

I put one foot in front of the other and closed the distance between us. When I was just a few inches from him, Tarik pulled me to him and hugged me. His hands traveled across my chest and back, and after a couple of awkward moments of trying to unbutton my shirt, ripped it from my chest. I gasped as he leaned down and licked at my nipples. They hardened instantly, and when Tarik sucked them into his mouth and swirled his tongue around them, my legs shook.

Tarik laughed softly and abandoned my nipples. He brought his face level with my own, and stared into my eyes.

His eyes were bright blue, and sparkled when they looked at me. His long eyelashes curled up at the end and matched the color of his unkempt hair. I couldn't stop gazing into them, and was surprised when Tarik matched my stare for several minutes. Then he winked at me and leaned in to kiss me.

When he touched his lips to mine, I fought to remain conscious. I just stood there for a moment or two, not sure what to do next. His tongue licked my lips slowly, tickling the nerves that coursed throughout my entire body. I'd stopped breathing, but wasn't sure how to start again without ruining the sensation that flooded my body and mind.

Tarik licked my upper lip slowly, and then slid his tongue into my mouth. Instinctively, I wrapped my lips around it and slowly sucked it into my mouth. It was soft and warm and sweet, tasting faintly like spearmint gum. Tarik let me suck on it for a little bit, then slipped it in and out of my mouth slowly. Then he slid his tongue under mine and lifted up, tickling the underside of my tongue. After a couple of licks, I realized he wanted my tongue inside his mouth. I tentatively slid it just inside his mouth. Instantly his lips wrapped around my tongue and sucked on it until it was deep inside his warm mouth. He sucked on it gently, then more forcefully, sliding his mouth up and down its length.

And then the unthinkable happened! Before I realized what was happening, or was able to stop it at all, I moaned loudly as my load shot through my balls and through my shaft. Spray after spray spewed from my cock and oozed down my shaft and covered my balls. My knees buckled and I began to fall.

Tarik caught me and held me against him. "Are you okay?"

"Mmm hmm." I said weakly.

"What happened?"

I looked at him as blood rushed to my head. I blush easily, and knew that I was as red as a beet.

"No way!" Tarik said excitedly, as he held me at arm's length.

I nodded, and looked away, embarrassed.

Tarik held my chin and pulled my head back to look at him. "Are you serious? You came?"

"I didn't want to. I couldn't help it."

"It's okay. I'm just shocked. We didn't even do anything."

"We didn't?" I asked.

He looked at me, and smiled. And then a look of enlightenment hit him. "Is this your first time?"

I blushed deeper and looked away again.

"Serious?"

"Yes," I admitted, then cringed.

"Fuck, man, that's hot. I would never in a million years think you were a virgin. You're hotter than hell, dude. I figured you'd have been with a million guys by now."

"No."

"Girls?" he asked.

I shook my head.

"Never? Nothing?"

I held up my left hand and showed him my palm.

"Fuck, yeah," he said as he grinned. "Is this okay with you? I mean, you wanna do this?"

I nodded and licked my lips.

"Cool. Then lean back." He laid me gently across the mattress so that my head and neck rested against the wall and my legs hung over the side of the bed. Then he slid my jeans down my legs and threw them across the room.

He scooted my legs apart and knelt between my legs. My cock was still rock hard, and the last couple of drops of cum were still leaking from the head and dripping down my shaft. Tarik licked at the cum and slid his tongue up and down the length of my cock on all sides until it was clean and slick with his spit. Then he wrapped his lips around the cock head and sucked it into his mouth. I couldn't believe how hot his mouth was, and how soft and hard at the same time his tongue felt as it tickled and slid across my crown. He kept just the head inside his mouth for a couple of minutes, and then, when I was able to breath halfway normally, he took more and more of my dick in his mouth.

I'd died and gone to heaven, of that I was certain. Never had I ever felt anything so deliriously good. Every nerve in my body tingled, and a soft, high-pitched ringing sound in the back of my head were the only things that kept me from drifting out of my body and into a weightless, bodiless, spirit state.

"Dude," I panted, "I'm gonna shoot again."

"Oh no, you aren't," he said as he quickly pulled his hot mouth off my cock. He stood up and waved his cock at me. "It's my turn."

I'm sure my eyes bulged as I looked at his cock. I'd only seen a couple of other cocks in my life. The limited access I had to classmates in the locker room at high school hadn't prepared me for the monster that bobbed in front of me. Easily eight or nine inches long, it looked almost as thick around as my wrist. The foreskin had peeled back to reveal about half of the red head of Tarik's cock. Fat blue veins popped all across the shaft, making his dick throb up and down in beat with his heart. His balls were huge, and shaved, and hung low beneath his giant cock.

"I can't take that," I protested as Tarik moved another inch closer.

"You don't have to take it all," he whispered, and clasped his hands behind my neck and gently pulled it forward. "Just lick it for a minute, then take it slowly into your mouth, like I did with yours."

I faintly remember my parents teaching me not to be a pushover and never to appear too eager for anything. But I'm comfortably certain they were not referring to sucking cock in particular, and I couldn't deny the fact that I wanted to suck Tarik's cock just about more than I'd ever wanted anything. For the past three years I'd imagined and fantasized about what sucking a cock would feel like and taste like. I wasn't about to forsake the opportunity now.

I reached out with my tongue and licked Tarik's dick. The hard and hot skin felt better against my tongue than I'd ever imagined, and though I began rather meekly, it didn't take long before I was devouring his cock. It was an out-of-body experience, and as much as I'd like to remember every detail of my first cocksucking experience, I can't. One minute I was shyly licking his cock head and the next his cock was buried deep down my throat. He was fucking my face so hard and fast that his face was red and sweating, and he struggled to catch his breath. A moment later I felt Tarik's body tense, and he moaned. Then my throat grew warm, and I instinctively swallowed blast after blast of hot cum. His cock was buried in my throat as he shot his load, so I didn't even taste it. I just felt wave after wave of the warm thick fluid slide down my throat.

I was covered in sweat, and when I gazed into Tarik's eyes and saw him looking into mine, a couple of drops of his sweat fell onto me and mixed with my own. I kept his fat cock in my mouth long after he'd finished coming, and until he began to soften. Then he pulled his dick from my mouth and collapsed onto the bed next to me.

"Fuuuuuck," he moaned a few moments later, as we lay tangled in one another's arms.

"That was the best thing I've ever felt in my life," I panted.

"So far," he corrected.

"What do you mean?"

"That's just the beginning."

I looked over at Tarik, and raised my eyebrows.

He smiled and scooted down the bed until his head was at my crotch. He didn't bother to lick my dick this time, but sucked my half-hard cock into his mouth. It only took a couple of seconds before his mouth got my cock fully hard again. I lifted my hips off the bed to thrust my cock deeper into his mouth.

"You're a natural," Tarik said as he let my cock slip from his mouth.

I laughed.

"You ready?"

"For what?" I asked. I couldn't imagine anything in the world feeling better than what I'd just experienced.

"I want you to fuck me."

"What?" I said a little too loudly.

"I want you to shove your cock up my ass and fuck me until I pass out."

"But . . ."

"Don't worry," he said and kissed me on the lips. "I'll do all the work. Just lie there and enjoy it."

"Okay," I said stupidly.

Tarik leaned over and reached into the drawer in his desk. He pulled out a bottle of lube and smeared some all over my cock, then slid some more into his ass crack. He raised himself onto his knees and straddled my body as he guided my cock to his ass.

"Ready?" he asked as he winked at me.

"Mmm hmm."

He lowered himself just enough for my cock head to enter his ass. Instantly, my cock was enveloped with a heat I could never have imagined. Tarik took a couple of deep breaths, then lowered himself further onto my cock.

Every inch of my cock slid slowly into his ass. His sphincter squeezed my cock and sucked it deeper and deeper inside him. I lost my breath and thought I was having a heart attack as wave after wave of pleasure shot up my shaft, through my gut and up my torso.

When my balls butted against Tarik's ass cheeks, he stopped and just rested with my cock buried inside him. He was breathing heavily and his eyes were closed. It looked like he was in pain, and for a moment I thought I should pull out. But then he moaned and his ass muscles began to squeeze my cock. At first they were slow and gentle squeezes, and then they grew quicker and more intense.

"Oh, fuck, dude," I moaned as Tarik teased my cock with his ass.

"You like?"

"Yes," I panted.

"Good," he said, and lifted his body off mine until my cock almost slid out. Just the head remained inside.

"Don't . . ." I begged.

Tarik laughed and slid all the way back down my dick until I was as deep inside him as I could go. Then he slid back up and then back down again. Each time he rode my cock, I felt as if I'd explode. He started slowly at first, and then rode me hard and fast. He leaned down and slid his tongue into my mouth and kissed me passionately as he fucked my cock. When I reached up to cup his chin in my hands, he pinned my hands above my head and kissed me harder. He licked my lips, then bit the bottom lip lightly as he sat up straight and looked down at me.

I watched in amazement as his steel-hard and smooth body slid up and down my cock. Every muscle was perfectly sculpted and he looked like a marble statue. I'd never in my wildest dreams imagined someone like Tarik would let another guy fuck him. Though I wasn't experienced in gay sex at all, I'd always thought hot and masculine guys like Tarik were always tops. But from the look on his face, he was definitely into my cock fucking his ass. I lifted my hips off the bed to drive my cock even deeper inside, and Tarik smiled and winked at me.

"You wanna take over now, stud?" he asked.

"Yes," I said, and rolled Tarik onto his back.

"Go for it, dude."

I lifted his legs and placed them on my shoulders. Then I pulled my cock all the way out of his ass.

"Fuck, man. Put it back in."

I slid my cock back into his ass, not stopping until my balls slapped against his ass cheeks. Then I pulled all the way out again and slammed back inside. Apparently that drove Tarik wild, because he began moaning and thrashing his head back and forth, and thrust his ass up to meet my assault. I lost control of my senses, and fucked him like I'd been doing it for a hundred years.

"Fuck, dude, your cock is so big. It's filling me up," Tarik said between breaths.

"Thank you," I said stupidly, and then blushed. Then I got upset at myself for sounding so childish, and I began fucking Tarik even harder and deeper.

"That's it, babe. I'm gonna shoot!"

I leaned down and kissed him on the mouth as I buried my cock as deep inside his ass as I could go, and left it there. A second later Tarik moaned loudly and sucked harder on my tongue as his ass twitched around my cock. The first three shots of his hot load splashed across my chin and chest as we continued kissing, and then the rest landed on his chest and stomach.

I began to lose my breath and knew I was close. I raised my body from Tarik's and pulled my cock out of his ass in one quick move.

"Bring it up here," he said.

I moved up his body and straddled his chest. A second later my load shot out and sprayed across Tarik's face. Though I usually have pretty large loads, this one surprised even me. No less than seven or eight large jets landed in his eyes, on his nose, and in his mouth. His head jerked with each forceful spray, and he started giggling after the ninth or tenth.

"Fuck, dude," he said as he spit cum from his mouth.

"Shut up," I said and let go with another couple of shots of jizz.

And then I laughed at how silly and unconvincing it sounded coming from my mouth.

My muscles gave way completely, and I fell on top of Tarik, struggling to catch my breath. Our sweat and cum mixed together and coated us both with a thick layer of sheen.

"What just happened?" I asked when I caught my breath and regained the ability to speak.

"You fucked my brains out, dude. That's what happened."

"No shit."

"So, what do you say we not let this be the last time we do this?"

"Sounds good to me."

"Don't let this go to your head, but usually I really fuck with the newbies. Give 'em shit and stuff."

"Yeah, well just consider this the revenge of the newbies."

Tarik laughed. "Right on. Here's to more revenge. Now, let's get up and let me show you around. Then maybe we can come back here and I can give you a little revenge of my own."

I looked at him curiously. He smiled and winked at me, and I knew then that in a few hours I would have his cock inside me, and that I'd love every minute of it. I remembered that just a little more than an hour ago I'd been questioning whether I'd made the right choice to attend college here. And now I was reveling in the most profound education I'd ever had. I couldn't wait to graduate!

SUMMER

Who doesn't love summer? I mean, really. I don't know a single person who doesn't love summer. They might not love the heat, but they love the long days and the energy of this time of the year. According to *Dictionary.com*, "Summer" is:

1. The usually warmest season of the year, occurring between spring and autumn and constituting June, July, and August in the Northern Hemisphere, or, as calculated astronomically, extending from the summer solstice to the autumnal equinox.

2. A period of fruition, fulfillment, happiness, or beauty.

God, I really love the second definition much more than the first. Okay, so all the "solstice" and "equinox" and "astronomical" science terms aside, summer is seriously the hottest season of the year, and I'm not talking strictly temperature here. Guys are outside wearing next to nothing and showing off the hot bodies that they've been working hard on at the gym for the past year. And something about summer just brings out the wild side of all of us.

The stories in this section of the book deal with the summer of our sexual lives. We've been through spring, where everything was new and maybe a little tentative and, for the most part, safe. We're a little older now; in these stories, all the main characters are between the ages of twenty-one and thirty. We tend to get bored easily and yearn for excitement. Just the missionary style or just doggie style simply doesn't cut it anymore. We need more. We experiment more with sex and are a little more open to the ideas of love and intimacy. Maybe not comfortable with them yet, but at least willing to look at them. But the key to this season of our lives is *danger* and *excitement* and *experimentation* . . . and allowing ourselves to be vulnerable just for the thrill of it.

In these stories, summer is all about letting go of control and leaving our safety nets behind and really stepping out there for that little something extra. That "something" that has the potential to hurt us or get us in trouble, but which ultimately brings us the greatest pleasure. Sex in public. Getting tied up for the first time. Being gang raped.

All of the things that we've all thought and dreamt about, but sometimes are hesitant to relinquish the control to try. These tales show some of the value of letting go and giving in to those desires.

The Voice in the Dark

<<Come on, dude. It'll be fun. You know you want to. You can't say no to me.>>

I leaned back in my chair and smiled as the metallic voice came through the speakers on my computer. Fucking cocky bastard, I thought, then reached down and groped my throbbing cock. It was harder than it'd been in a very long time. And it was all because of this guy and his bold proposal.

<<Yes I can.>> I typed.

<<NO. You can't.>>

I'd paid a lot of money for the voice system on my computer, and at times like this I was glad I had. I knew the guy on the other end of the line had capitalized the word NO—because my voice system emphasized it with a louder and more forceful tone. It didn't convey the real voice of the person, but at least it was pretty good at conveying a tone. Most of the time. My cock twitched harder in my jeans, and a drop of precum oozed out and slid down my shaft.

I was blinded five years ago in a freakish car accident. For the first year I'd thought my life was over. But eventually I adjusted and got back into the swing of life. I was able to go back to work. And I bought the voice system for my computer, which allowed me to stay in the mainstream of life. I was able to "read" e-mails, and most importantly, was able to participate in Internet chats and personals websites.

I'd been chatting with this guy for a couple of months. He was one of the few people who didn't freak out once they heard I was blind, and we hit it off very well. We talked about everything: our work, our family, our goals. Hell, he even shared with me his deepest and darkest sexual fantasy of being kidnapped and forced to have sex. And I shared with him my fantasy of having sex with a group of strangers. Lemme tell you, I beat off with him online more than I like to admit.

But now he wanted to meet in person, and that was a whole other ballgame. I wasn't sure I was ready for that. I mean, could I trust him? We'd chatted a lot, but that didn't mean shit. He could be a serial killer for all I knew. Online, people can tell you whatever they want. And without my sight, I was afraid I'd be completely out of control when meeting him. I'd not met anyone like this since the accident, and I wasn't at all sure I should do it. I was afraid.

<<What do you say, dude. Can I come over?>>

I took a deep breath and held it for several seconds as I pondered. What was at stake here? I could be killed. What did I know about this guy? He seemed nice, and up until now I'd trusted him. Why didn't I trust him now? Because I was a coward and afraid of my own fucking shadow. How could I overcome my fear and be the spontaneous and adventurous man I'd always been? I could let him come over.

<<All right.>>

<<Cool,>> the mechanical voice said flatly as I typed my address. <<Leave your door unlocked and be waiting for me naked in your bed. I'll have a surprise for you.>>

My heart skipped several beats. <<I don't like surprises.>>
<<Yes you do.>>

I was shocked at his indignant manner. And then I realized my heart was beating erratically because I was excited at the prospect of meeting him for the first time and at the thought of his surprise.

<<Okay.>>

I heard the door open slowly, and I thought I'd die with the pounding of my heart. I was naked and shivering, despite the fact that I'd turned the heater up to seventy-five before stripping and jumping excitedly into bed. My mouth and throat felt like sandpaper as I forced myself to swallow.

A moment later I felt him standing above me, right next to my side of the bed. I could smell his scent, a mix of soap and light sweat and the remnants of earthy cologne applied earlier that day.

His lips touched mine with the gentlest of pressure. I took a deep breath and opened my mouth just slightly. His tongue slipped inside and began exploring. At first I just allowed it to lick and kiss me. Then I wrapped my lips around it and sucked it deep into my mouth. It was soft and sweet.

We kissed for several minutes, and then I felt a hot, wet mouth envelop my cock and suck gently on my head. God, it felt so good, and I moaned around his tongue as I lifted my hips from the bed, to let another inch or two of my cock slide . . .

But wait. I was still kissing his mouth. How could it be sucking my cock? It took a long moment for me to realize the hot mouth sucking my dick was a different hot mouth than the one I was kissing. I panicked, and lost my breath as I pulled away and struggled to sit up in bed.

The hot mouth never let go of my hard cock, and strong hands gripped my shoulders and pushed me gently back down onto the bed. I felt the sweat begin at my face and work its way quickly down my body, and knew it wasn't from the heat in the room. My heart raced painfully fast, and I began to shiver again.

"Just relax," he whispered into my ear. His voice was deeper and stronger than I'd imagined, and despite my fear, I felt myself harden even more. "I'm not going to hurt you, I promise. No one here is going to hurt you."

No one here? What the fuck did he mean by that?

A second later I felt what seemed like a dozen hands caressing my body and keeping me pinned to the bed. All the while, the mouth on my cock never relented, and sucked my dick until I thought I'd explode.

I opened my mouth to protest, but before I could utter a word, it was filled with a semi-hard cock. I was speechless and struggled to breathe through my nose as my mouth wrapped around the cock. Despite my fear and the shock of it all, I was harder than ever and adrenaline rushed through my body like it was competing in the Indy 500.

I sucked tentatively on the head for a moment, then took another couple of inches into my mouth and lapped at it hungrily. It didn't seem to be very long, but it was really fat, and took no time at all to fill my mouth.

"That's it, baby," my friend whispered into my ear, and I realized it wasn't his cock I was sucking on. "Suck his cock, dude. It's so thick and sweet, isn't it? You should see his face. You're making his eyes roll into the back of his head!"

I took another inch of the cock into my mouth and sucked greedily on it. I was drunk with the taste of it, the feel of the warm wet mouth sucking my own cock, and the sound of my friend's voice urging the action on.

A couple of seconds later I felt another pair of hands on my ankles. They spread my legs far apart and then lightly caressed their way up my legs. When they reached my hips, they rolled my balls around for a moment and tugged on them gently. Then they let go of my balls and moved down to my ass. I took a deep breath as I felt the fingers tickle my ass hole and pry my cheeks apart slightly. I felt the inevitable orgasm begin to build in my nuts, and moaned loudly.

The other guys must have known I was close, because all of a sudden everything just stopped.

"Don't stop," I tried to yell around the still hard, fat cock in my mouth.

There was a flurry of motion all around me, and I felt disoriented. A moment later I felt a pair of hands on either side of me grab me under the arms, and another pair of hands on either side of me grab me under the knees. I was lifted effortlessly off the bed, and floated through the air, carried by strong hands all over my body. Then I felt myself being lowered.

"It's my turn now," my friend said from below me. "I want you."

"I want you, too," I growled, unable to rein in my desire. His voice was so strong and deep and sexy. It sounded completely in control and so different from the mechanical voice I'd heard on my computer. I wanted him to control every inch of my being.

His cock head was hot and hard as it just grazed my hole. I gasped as it touched my sphincter, then I relaxed and shuddered in anticipation. The hands carrying me lifted me a couple of inches, just out of reach of his dick, and I felt the air in the room kiss my hot hole. I wanted my friend's dick in me more than anything, and when I felt myself being lowered again, I moaned and squirmed in their grip. Again I felt his cock head, but this time the hands allowed me to remain in contact with it.

"Let me fall," I said desperately. "I want his cock inside me."

I heard a few laughs, but the hands lifted me again.

"No," I moaned, and struggled to get closer to his cock.

"Don't be mean, guys," my friend said, and I nearly shot my load just at the sound of his voice. "Let him have it."

I felt myself being lowered again, and drew in a deep breath.

This time when the head kissed my twitching hole, the hands didn't stop; they allowed the fat, hard head to slip inside my ass. I moaned with delight as my ass muscles danced around his hot cock head.

"Fuck, dude," my friend moaned. "That's awesome. Lemme have some more, guys."

And they did. The hands around me relaxed a little, and I felt myself lower another couple of inches on my friend's cock. It felt really long and thick, and I shuddered as my ass opened up and slid down it. After a couple of inches, my ass tightened up and I stopped. I felt like I was on fire. I felt like I'd never been fucked before, and I was eating it up.

"Ready for the rest of it?" my friend asked.

"Yes," I panted.

This time, instead of the hands just allowing my body to lower with its own weight, they pushed me gently down on the giant cock in one steady but strong move. My ass opened up easily and welcomed the big dick deep inside.

"Fuck me!" I almost yelled, and my friend did.

His big dick slid in and out of my ass for several minutes. He went deep into my gut and stopped only when his balls rested against my ass cheeks. Then he withdrew until only the head remained inside my ass. He slid back in and repeated his actions until I thought I'd die.

Soon I felt a hand open my mouth, and a second later I was sucking on a long hard cock. I could tell it wasn't the one I'd sucked earlier. This one was much longer, not as thick, and was covered with a thin layer of foreskin. I sucked on it hungrily as my friend fucked my ass. I loved the taste of the cock, and the feel of the thick vein that ran underneath the shaft as it slid across my tongue.

I don't know when it happened, exactly, but a little later I realized that as I was sucking the cock and being fucked by my friend, someone else was sucking *my* cock. The mouth was hot and very talented, and I knew it wouldn't take too much more of this before I shot all over the place.

Just then another pair of hands pushed on my shoulders gently from behind. I leaned forward a few inches, which probably made it a little awkward for the guy sucking my cock to continue, but he was persistent and kept sucking like a baby on its last bottle. The guy in front of me refused to let his cock slip from my mouth, and followed me lower onto the bed. I had a big dick in my mouth, another up my ass, and a hot mouth wrapped around my cock. I didn't think it could get any better than this. But I was wrong.

"Just relax," my friend whispered. "Take a deep breath and don't think about it."

Think about what? I wondered. And then I felt another cock head press against my hole. *There's no way*, I thought as I took a deep breath and pretended not to think about it. *The cock in my ass is already filling me up completely. There's no way!*

Apparently there *was* a way, because a second later the head slipped inside. I gasped in ecstasy that should have been pain. The cock rested inside my ass for just a second, then slid deep inside in one slow but steady move. When both cocks were buried deep inside me they just lay there for a moment, throbbing against one another.

Then both cocks slid in and out of my ass in synch with each other. As my friend slid deep inside my ass, the other guy slid almost all the way out, until only his head remained inside me. Then he slid slowly back inside as my friend withdrew his big dick. There wasn't an inch of my ass that wasn't being fucked with hot cock for even a fraction of a second.

There was no way in hell I was gonna last very long with all that action going on. The guy sucking my dick clamped down tightly and sucked with a vengeance. He obviously wanted to drink my cum. And now. I followed suit and flicked my tongue around the cock in my mouth as I sucked it deep into my throat. Both cocks slid in and out faster and deeper with each thrust.

The guy in my mouth shot first. His cock was buried deep in my throat when he let go with his load, and I swallowed all of it hungrily before allowing him to withdraw. That was all it took for me, and I moaned deeply as I tensed my body and shot my own load. The mouth wrapped around my dick wasn't as skilled at finishing me off as he was at getting me there. He only took a shot or two of my cum in his mouth, then pulled off and allowed the rest of it to shoot wherever.

Wherever was apparently all over my friend's face and chest, because he moaned loudly, and then I felt him wiping at his face. A second later he pushed me up and off both big cocks in a move that left me feeling empty and lonely. I lay on the bed next to him and allowed myself to be wrapped in his strong arms. At the same time I felt the foot of the bed shift, and knew the other guy who was fucking me had stood up and was now towering over me and my friend.

"FUUUUUUCK," the guy groaned.

My friend pulled my face up to his and kissed me tenderly on the lips just as I was showered with hot cum. I felt it coming from the guy above us, and also from my friend's cock at my side. It seemed to go on forever, flying across my arms, stomach, legs, and face.

When it finally stopped, everyone stood perfectly still and quiet. I eventually regained my ability to breath, and squirmed just a little bit beneath my friend's firm hold.

"Thanks, guys," he said in that voice that drove me fucking crazy. "I think we're good from here on out. I'll see you tomorrow."

Then they were gone. As quietly and undetected as they'd arrived. When we were alone, I caressed my friend's stomach and hairy chest with my fingers. I traced his strong, masculine face and leaned down to kiss him.

"So . . . I'm Mike," I said.

He laughed and hugged me tightly to him, then rolled me onto my side, and pressed his hard cock against my ass.

1 + 1 = 9

"Fuck You!" I screamed at the alarm as it screeched at 7:15 in the morning. I pulled my hands from beneath the blankets and slapped at the clock. When I couldn't locate the sleep button, I ripped the cord from the wall and flung the clock across the room. My roommate yelled something unintelligible at me, and then rolled over and pulled the blankets back over his head.

I am not a morning person. Never have been.

But today was a particularly bad morning, because in less than two hours I would be facing the defining moment of the rest of my life. Whether or not I remained in school, eventually graduated, and ultimately landed my dream job and became a very wealthy man.

My Statistics final exam. Math is not my best or favorite subject. Never has been. And Statistics is the mother of all math classes. In high school I had barely passed my Algebra and Calculus required courses. And now that I was in college I found I had to take another, and harder course. It was almost, but not quite, enough to make me switch majors. But I wanted more than anything to be a psychologist, so I agreed to the mandatory class, and moaned and groaned my way through it. I'd pissed away my freshman year with fluff classes and ones I knew I could sail through. But now, at the end of my sophomore year at Stanford, I was faced with the inevitable. I couldn't go any further without passing this one test.

"Fuck you," I said again at no one or nothing in particular. I swung my legs from under the covers and stumbled naked to the showers.

Our dorm was one of the oldest on campus, and didn't have private showers in each room, as some of the newer ones did. Instead, each floor, which consisted of fourteen rooms, shared a communal shower and restroom. Truth be known, it was the one deciding factor in my choosing that particular dorm over some of the more modern ones. That, and the fact that it cost about half the price.

I flung my towel over one of the pegs outside the shower entrance, and stepped inside. I was the first one in the shower this morning, as I almost always was. Setting my clock fifteen minutes earlier than everyone else gave me a few strategic moments to wake up, lather up, and get it up, just in time for the onslaught of my fellow dorm mates. I stood under the flow of steaming water, allowing it to warm my skin for a few minutes. Then I squirted some shower gel across my torso and began rubbing it in.

I lift weights for two hours every day, and also play on the basketball and track teams at school, so my body is in great shape. The wandering eyes of the other guys in the showers doesn't escape me, and I really get off on feeling and rubbing my own hands across my hard, muscled body. I spent a little time tweaking my nipples, and caressed my chest and stomach, closing my eyes and reveling in the hot water and soft touch of my own hands. Then I worked my way down past my tummy to my cock.

It was already rock hard. It doesn't take long to get me there. Never has. Fully hard it's just a bit over eight inches, and very thick. I'm a real blond, and the short clipped hair around the base of my cock seems almost white against the dark tanned skin around it. I was circumcised as a baby, which was probably a mistake. My cock gets so hard that it strains to stay in its skin and turns bright red with any exertion whatsoever. Sometimes I'm so hard it hurts.

I wrapped my fist around my cock and slid my soapy hand up and down its length. Instantly, a shock of pleasure rippled through my thighs and down my legs. A couple more strokes, and my cock turned red and stretched to the point of a little pain. I liked that, so I stroked it another three or four times.

Just then I heard a shuffling noise behind me, and turned to look. Jason and Tyler, roommates who occupied a room just a couple doors down from my own, stepped into the shower. Each of them walked over and stood under a spout at the extreme opposite ends on either side of me. The shower stall held eight heads, so the boys were several feet from me. I feigned surprise, and turned to hide my hard and soapy cock from them.

But I continued to stroke it, and even added more soap when the water had rinsed away most of it. I noticed out of the corner of my eyes that Jason and Tyler were both standing with their backs to me as well, but were straining to look at my cock. I teased them for a few minutes, then turned around so that my hard cock was pointing into the center of the shower.

"Fuck, guys," I moaned. "I'm sorry. I was trying to finish this before anyone else got here. I can't do a thing this morning before I take care of this. I hope you don't mind. It won't take long." I slid my hand up and down my thick shaft again, and looked at the two roommies.

"Nah," Jason said, turning around to reveal his own hard dick. It was nowhere near as big as mine, but not bad in its own right. Maybe seven inches, and fairly thick. "It's cool."

"Yeah," Tyler echoed, and shyly turned around to show his smaller but equally hard cock.

"It's kind of embarrassing," I said, as I grinned at them both. "I wake up every morning with a raging hard-on like this, and it refuses to go away until I shoot my load."

"I know what you mean, bro," Jason said, and stepped closer to me. He reached down and wrapped his fist around my cock, and fisted me like a pro. "I got the same problem. But Tyler here usually takes care of it for me before we hit the showers. He didn't feel up to it this morning, though."

Tyler blushed and covered his cock with his hands.

"Awww," I said, and looked at Tyler. "Is that true, Ty?" I asked, and winked at him.

"I had a headache."

"We can take care of that for you," I said, and turned to face Jason. "Can't we, buddy?"

"Mmm hmm," Jason said, and wrapped his fist tighter around my cock as he slid it up and down my shaft.

"Come here," I ordered Tyler.

He took a couple of steps but stopped about a foot away from me.

"Get on your knees."

Tyler knelt in front of me and moaned loudly. I could see in his eyes that he wanted my cock more than anything. But I had another idea. I wanted to tease him a little. When he leaned forward to suck my cock, I pulled back.

"No fucking way, dude," I said as I pulled my cock from his mouth. "I'm not a fag." It was a lie. I was the biggest fag in the school, and it was no secret at all. But I could tell Tyler was a little shy and confused, so I wanted to mess with him a little.

"What?" he asked, and shook the water from his face.

"I said I ain't no fucking fag." I watched the look on his face grow more puzzled, and struggled not to giggle.

"But . . ."

"But your buddy here is. Aren't you, Jason?" I looked over at the stud to my left and grinned.

"Hell, yeah," Jason said, and moved forward to slide his cock into Tyler's gaping mouth.

Tyler was more than happy to have Jason's cock in his mouth, and he sucked on it hungrily. Jason slid his cock in and out of his roommate's mouth and moaned louder and louder. Tyler stroked his own cock as he sucked Jason's big dick, and his body began to shake a little after a couple of minutes.

I could tell both boys were getting close, and I wasn't far off myself. I slammed my fist up and down my shaft several times, and then felt a ball of fire shoot up through my nuts and up my cock.

"Fuck, dude, take my load!" I yelled as I pulled Tyler from Jason's cock and pointed my own at his face.

Jason lost it first. The second Tyler's lips left his cock, he sprayed several shots of jizz across his friend's face. A couple of shots flew past Tyler's face and landed on my tummy, and that was all it took for me. I blew my load up and over Tyler's face and onto the floor behind him. The last few drops of cum drizzled out of my cock, and Tyler couldn't resist. He reached out with his tongue and licked them off of the head.

"I told you I ain't a fag," I said roughly, as I pulled my cock from his mouth and pushed him gently to the floor. I grabbed my towel and walked toward the door.

"Is he serious?" Tyler asked as I walked out.

"Shut up and let's go back to the room. I need to fuck your ass," I heard Jason say as I laughed and walked to my room.

It was a warm Northern California morning and predicted to get even warmer. I hastily threw on a pair of cutoffs and a tank top. As I walked to the Math building, I tried to remember some of the stuff I'd crammed for the night before.

Fuckin' Mr. Wynette. He'd hated me from day one, and I just knew he was going to throw in some surprise problems only to trip me up. At seventy-two years old, he was one of the school's oldest professors. He was cranky and old and wrinkled and pissy. Just looking at me seemed to irritate him beyond explanation, and he often spat insults at me as if he couldn't go another moment without getting them out of his system. He obviously resented my hot body and good looks. Not that he wished he'd had them back; I'm sure he never had them to begin with. I think he was born old and wrinkled and cranky and pissy. Which made him hate me even more. I'd have done almost anything not to have had to take this test today.

I walked into the classroom and took my regular seat at the back. I stretched my legs out beneath the desk and crossed my arms behind my neck. I yawned and closed my eyes for a moment, hoping the test wouldn't be too hard or too long, and that I'd be able to get to the gym fairly early.

When I opened my eyes, I thought I'd fallen asleep and was dreaming. As the bell rang, a young man, not much older than me, walked in and set his suit jacket and briefcase on the chair behind Mr. Wynette's desk. He was, without a doubt, one of the most beautiful young men I'd ever seen. He was tall and solidly built, with dark black hair, light blue eyes with long lashes, and a tiny mole just below his left nostril. His skin was naturally copper colored, and looked as smooth as silk. When he smiled, a big dimple creased his right cheek, and bright white teeth peeked through the most kissable pair of lips I'd ever seen.

"Hey, class," he said with a deep voice that melted me in my seat, "I'm Ricky . . . ummm . . . Richard. Mr. Wynette is sick today, so I'll be monitoring his classes today as you take your exams."

I caught my breath, and stood up and walked to the front of the class. There was an empty seat in the front row, and I was not about to let anyone else take it. I looked around the class and noticed a look of relief on everyone's face.

The sub explained that we had an hour and a half to complete the exam, and passed the test papers out. When he reached my desk, I thought I caught a glimpse of a smile on his face, and he held my gaze a little longer than he had to. I lost my breath again and felt my cock stir in my shorts.

Ten minutes passed and I hadn't written a single answer on the test. I couldn't pull my eyes away from Ricky. Instead of sitting at the chair he leaned against the desk, crossed his feet at the ankles, and read the newspaper. He was wearing expensive-looking brown slacks and a starched white shirt with a tie. I couldn't peel my eyes away from his crotch, which bulged impressively against the thin material of his slacks.

And then it happened. As I stared at his crotch, it jumped in his pants. At first I thought I was imagining it, but when I didn't look away, it happened again. I shifted my eyes from his crotch to his face. Ricky was looking at me from behind the newspaper, and smiling. I blinked a couple of times, and swallowed. Ricky winked at me.

Holy shit! My cock got hard instantly. I reached down and rubbed it, hoping it wasn't too obvious. But Ricky's eyes followed my hand, and he licked his lips as I rearranged my dick inside my shorts. When I stopped rubbing, he raised his eyebrows and looked back at my cock. He wanted more!!

I looked around the room. Everyone was deep in concentration. Besides, with the way the desks were arranged, and with the right positioning of my legs, no one would be able to see my cock if I pulled it out.

So I did.

I unbuttoned my shorts and hauled out my cock. I pulled my balls out and let them hang over the top of my shorts, holding my cock out in front of me so Ricky could see it in all its glory.

A noticeable blush covered his face as his eyes bulged. He was riveted to my hard cock. After a couple of seconds of staring, he looked up at me and licked his lips. The bulge in his own pants was noticeably longer and harder. He looked around the room to assure himself that no one was watching, and then flexed his own cock inside his pants. It grew bigger, and Ricky moved the newspaper down to cover his lap.

I stroked my cock a couple of times under the desk, and felt a big drop of precum ooze out the head and down my shaft. I reached for it with my fingers and slid it across my head and the first inch or so under the head. By now my cock was starting to hurt with the pressure of my erection. I knew it was turning red at this point. As I watched Ricky's reaction, I knew my cock was as big and hard as it had ever been.

"Class, I'm going to have to excuse myself for a few moments," Ricky said suddenly, and looked over at me. "Please keep your answers honest, and the chat to a minimum while I'm gone."

He pushed himself off the desk, rearranged his cock inside his pants, and walked out of the room. As he closed the door, he looked back at me and motioned with his head for me to follow him.

I stuffed my dick back inside my shorts before anyone could see it, and sat there dazed for a few minutes. Then I got up and left. The restroom was several doors down from our classroom. As I opened the door, I saw Ricky's shoes under the door of one of the stalls. I walked over to it, and without hesitating or knocking, I walked in and shut the door behind me.

Ricky had already removed his shirt and had his slacks down around his ankles. He was sitting on the toilet, and his cock jutted up between his legs. It was easily as long and as thick as mine. But it was the same copper color as the rest of his skin, and a thin layer of foreskin covered the shaft and about half of the head. It took my breath away; I stood there dazed and unable to move.

"Come here," Ricky said in that deep voice of his, and I did.

The stall was small to begin with, so it only took a step before my crotch was an inch or so from his face. He grabbed my shorts on either side and yanked them down in one move. My cock sprang out in front of him, and without flinching, he reached out with his tongue and licked at it. Then he grabbed my cock with his hand and held it steady as he wrapped his lips around the head and slowly slid his mouth around it. He swallowed my cock slowly, but didn't stop until my balls rested against his chin.

I thought I'd shoot my load right there. No one had ever been able to deepthroat my cock. A couple of guys had taken half of it, maybe a little more. But no one had ever swallowed the entire thing. Ricky did, though, and I watched stunned as my cock disappeared through his mouth and down his throat. He tightened his mouth and throat muscles around my cock, and I saw stars behind my eyes.

"Dude, I can't take much of that, or I'm gonna shoot," I panted.

Ricky slowly pulled his mouth from my cock. His eyes were watery and a little glazed over. "We don't have much time," he said hoarsely.

"Yeah, I know."

"So let's get down to business."

"Okay."

"Fuck me."

I blinked a couple of times, and swallowed hard. I just stood there, with my cock bobbing up and down in front of me.

Ricky stood up and turned around so that his back was to me. He bent forward and stuck his ass out toward me.

I fell to my knees and dove my face into his ass. It was the most perfect butt I'd ever seen. Mocha brown, smooth as marble, and muscular. I spread his cheeks and licked the tiny hole in the center of his crack. Ricky moaned, and I felt it on my tongue from deep within his ass muscles. It took all I had not to cream right there. His ass was soft and hard at the same time. It was so smooth I couldn't imagine a hair ever having touched it. It smelled lightly of baby oil, and tasted sweet and clean. I licked it for what seemed an eternity, sticking my tongue deep inside then pulling it out and licking the outside of his ass.

"I need you inside me right now," Ricky whispered.

I stood up and spat on my cock head. His ass was still slicked with my spit, and I didn't hesitate. I placed the head of my cock at the opening of his crack, and waited for Ricky's response. When he moaned and shoved his ass toward me, I slipped my cock head inside and waited.

Ricky's ass spread open and enveloped my cock. He moaned

loudly and gasped as his body tensed and he stopped moving. He was so hot inside I thought it would cook my dick. I kept just the head inside his ass for a moment, praying I woudn't shoot my load too soon. When Ricky's ass relaxed, and another couple inches of my cock slipped inside, he groaned loudly and I slid all eight inches of my fat cock deep inside.

He tightened his muscles around my cock as he shoved his ass onto my cock. As hungry as I was for his ass, he was just as hungry for my dick, and slid up and down the length of it several times. He rode my cock like he was competing in a bronco-riding contest, and his moans and begging for me to fuck his brains out echoed through the restroom.

As I slammed my fat cock in and out of Ricky's clutching ass, I leaned down to kiss him on the neck. His skin was soft and hot and glistened with sweet perspiration. I was drunk with his aura. I couldn't get enough of him.

Ricky tilted his head up and back to kiss me. I left his neck and kissed him on the mouth, savoring the softness and intoxicating taste of his supple lips. When his tongue slipped into my mouth, I groaned softly, feeling the first stirrings of my orgasm building in my balls.

There was no way I could stop it now. I reluctantly let my lips leave his, and stood up. I held Ricky's hips, and slammed my cock deeper and harder into his ass. I'd never felt such animal lust. I pounded his ass so forcefully that I struggled to breathe.

"Oh, fuck, dude," Ricky said as his ass muscles squeezed and spasmed around my thick cock. "I'm gonna explode."

He stood and gripped my cock one last time, holding it prisoner inside his ass. His tunnel convulsed around my dick, and as he moaned loudly I looked over his shoulder. The first three shots of his load splashed powerfully against the metal wall of the stall and slid down in a blaze of white heat. The next several spurts fell to the floor in front of him. With each shot of his spunk, his cock thickened and grew bigger, the river of veins popping out impressively.

That was all it took to send me over the edge. I pulled out of his ass quickly and pushed Ricky to his knees in front of me as he turned around to face me. I looked down at his face. Never had I seen a more beautiful man. His brown skin was as smooth and perfect as any supermodel's. His bright blue eyes were large and almond shaped, and spoke of untold mysteries wanting to be shared. The lashes were long and curly, and beckoned me to come inside. His lips were soft and pink and full and begged to be kissed and fucked. The dimples on either side of his perfect smile were the last touch of perfection that caused my heart to skip a beat. For a moment I thought I'd be so overcome with his beauty that I might not be able to cum.

I was wrong. My load shot from my cock with tremendous force. Seven or eight giant spurts splashed across his perfect face, covering it in white jizz that completely hid its beauty. Ricky gasped as each squirt plastered his mouth and nose and eyes, and he licked at the cum around his lips. When he closed his eyes, I wasn't sure if it was in appreciation for the taste of my cum, which he seemed to enjoy immensely, or to keep it from stinging his eyes.

I'd never had such an explosive orgasm, and when it finally drizzled off after at least ten huge shots, I leaned against the door to keep myself from falling. Ricky laughed, and wiped the remaining jizz from his face as he wrapped his arms around my legs to help steady me. Then he stood up and kissed me passionately again. I tasted my own cum on his lips and tongue, and despite having just spewed the load of my life, felt my cock begin to harden again.

"We gotta stop, dude, or I'm gonna pass out from it all." I laughed and steadied myself against the door again.

"Wimp," Ricky said, and hugged me tightly against his hard and muscular body.

"You think anybody missed us in class?"

"Oh, shit!" Ricky almost yelled, and reached down to quickly pull up his slacks. He dressed as hurriedly as he could while I watched and grinned.

"You know I'm not gonna pass that test, right?" I said coyly as I pulled him to me for one last hug.

"I don't think you have to worry about that," he said as he grinned and returned my hug.

"But I'm terrible in math." I reached behind him and squeezed his ass.

"Really?"

"Mmm-hmm."

"What's one plus one?" he asked as he touched his chest and then my own.

I reached down and squeezed his cock, feeling it twitch at my touch. I smiled and kissed him again. "Feels like about . . . nine, I'd say."

"Bingo. You get an A+. And you said you were no good at math!"

We both laughed and walked out of the restroom together. Ricky kissed me on the lips in the hall, and then entered the classroom. I didn't even bother. I whistled to myself as I walked down the hall and out into the warm day.

Maybe I'd change my major to Math.

Good Ol' Boys Club

"That was your last hand, Eric," Cameron said as a huge grin spread across his face. "You know what that means."

"Come on, guys," I pleaded. I set my cards down and looked around the table. Andy, Richard, and Victor all stared back at me with unforgiving smirks. Cameron had been the instigator, but they'd all jumped on board rather quickly. "We aren't really going to go through with this, are we?"

The five of us met at freshmen orientation three years ago, and quickly became inseparable. Ours was the friendship that paperback books and medium-budget chick flicks are made of. We ate together, studied together, played ball together, dated together and failed all the same classes together. We were THE boys club on campus. Every guy in school hated us and wanted desperately to be a part of our little clique. Every girl on campus publicly despised us and secretly wanted to wear our letter jackets.

Nothing could separate us. We all believed it and we all reminded one another about it every chance we got. Nothing could separate us.

Except having the four of them walk into my dorm room unexpectedly and finding Mitch Barton's cock buried deep inside my ass. They'd decided we were all going out to play some pool, and had come to inform me of the fact and to pick me up. I, unaware of the plan, had taken advantage of the rare moment without the gang, and had finally given in to Mitch's persistent requests to fuck my brains out.

"Eric, my man," Cameron yelled as they stumbled through the door. "Get your . . ." He halted mid-sentence, causing the others to bump into him. They all stared, jaws dropped, at my long legs wrapped around Mitch's naked, sweaty body as he buried himself inside me and gazed straight ahead at me, refusing to look at my friends behind him.

We must have stayed there like that for a full five minutes. Mitch with his cock still hard inside me, looking straight into my eyes. Cameron, Andy, Richard, and Victor alternated looking at Mitch's naked ass and into my eyes. I looked back and forth from Mitch's eyes, wanting more than anything for him to continue pounding my ass, and my friends' eyes, wanting second more than anything for them to turn around and leave so Mitch could finish pounding my ass.

"Guys, ummm . . ." I stuttered.

"Can you guys just leave?" Mitch finally said, flexing his cock inside my ass and grinding his pelvis against my ass. "Eric will be done here in a few minutes."

The guys mumbled and stumbled over one another, and fled the room almost as quickly as they'd crashed into it. Mitch finished fucking my ass, and left without saying a word. I lay there in bed afterward, covered in sweat and cum, and cried for about an hour.

Then there was a soft knock on my door. It was the guys, and they needed to talk. How could I be gay? How could I like "doin' it" with another dude? How could I have lied to them all this time? How could I have kept this big a secret from them? And on and on and on. We talked for a couple of hours, and when we finished they were all okay with me being gay. A little uneasy, but committed to maintaining our friendship at all costs. And so was I.

That was last week, and the last thing Cameron told me before they left my room was that "We gotta finish all this shit later." Tonight, when Cameron called and informed me that the whole gang was getting together to play cards, something in his tone told me we'd be doing more than just playing cards, and that I didn't have the option of arguing.

"We're not really going through with this, are we?" I asked again.

I sucked at poker, and everyone knew it. In three years I had never once won a game. I very seldom won even a hand. And they all knew it. So when they insisted we play poker, I became a little suspicious. When they explained the wager, I understood perfectly. The loser was at the complete mercy of the other players and had to do whatever was instructed. "Whatever," Victor reiterated with an evil smile on his face.

"Oh, yes, we really are," Richard said, and scooted his chair back from the table and spread his legs out in front of him. "Get over here."

I took a deep breath and walked over and stood directly in front of Richard. He'd always taken my breath away. He had the All-American looks every guy wanted. Light blond hair and deep blue eyes, strong and muscular corn-fed body tanned by the sun (not a booth), angular clef chin, and dimples as deep as the Grand Canyon.

He spread his legs even wider and glanced down at his crotch. "It ain't gonna suck itself." He was the cocky smartass of the bunch. I pretended that it got on my nerves, but secretly it turned me on more than anything.

I looked at the others. They were all smiling and arranging their chairs into more convenient positions. Then I dropped to my knees and unbuttoned Richard's jeans.

His cock was fully hard as soon as I released it from the confines of his jeans. It was long and thick. The pinkish-tan skin was riddled with blue veins that throbbed visibly across the shaft. I licked the large drop of precum from his cock head, then slid my mouth slowly down his cock until it was buried in my throat.

"Fuck," Richard moaned, and lifted his hips to get even more of the big dick deeper inside my gullet.

I looked up at his face while I sucked his cock. He was struggling a little. He'd never done this before, I knew, and his fiancé would probably have a very hard time understanding it. He was as straight as they come. But I'm a very good cocksucker, and it was obvious Richard was loving the feel of my mouth wrapped around his cock as it slid deep into my throat.

"My turn," Victor said, and got up to stand next to me. He whipped out his cock and slapped it against my face.

His cock was an inch or so shorter than Richard's, but it was so thick I couldn't wrap my fist around it. I pulled the fat head into my mouth and sucked on it like it was a cough drop. It leaked a large drip of precum, and I savored the sweet taste before swallowing it. Victor slid his thick cock in and out of my mouth slowly at first, and then faster and deeper.

"Yeah, dude, fuck his mouth," I heard Cameron say a foot or so to my right as I felt Richard slide my ass around so that it faced him.

As I did my best to swallow Victor's fat cock, I was vaguely aware of my pants being pulled off me from behind as I squatted in the doggy position. My head was spinning with the excitement and surprise of the evening, and with the dizzying ecstasy of feeling and tasting Victor's big cock. When my pants were all the way off, I felt cool air tickle my ass and my cock, and I wondered if I would be able to make it another five minutes before I shot my own load.

A second later I felt a warm mouth around my cock. I hadn't seen who had maneuvered behind and then underneath me. But I could imagine who it was. Andy was the most quiet and timid of the group. He had a beautiful smile, and a kind Southern manner, and his exceptional good looks made him a natural magnet for guys and girls alike. But he was a little soft spoken and never took the lead in anything. I'd often wondered if maybe he was gay. I was pretty sure it was his tentative tongue and soft warm mouth playing with my cock right now.

Victor was fucking my mouth like it was the last fuck of his life. I gagged several times as he forced more of his fat cock into my throat, and that just drove him even crazier. Behind me, I felt Richard's tongue lick between my ass crack and slowly work its way toward my hole. Andy's mouth was getting a little more confident, and now instead of just licking my cock head, I felt him take my entire head into his mouth, and then another inch or so deeper into his throat. I looked from the corner of my eye and saw Cameron take a couple of deep breaths and swipe his hand through his hair. He'd had a little more to drink tonight than the rest of us, and I wondered if all of this was a little too much for him.

I needn't have worried.

"I wanna fuck him," Cameron said as he moved behind me and around Richard.

"What?" Victor asked as he stopped pumping and just rest his cock inside my mouth.

"I wanna fuck him."

All the action just stopped. Victor stopped fucking my mouth and I stopped sucking his cock. Richard stopped licking my ass and raised himself up onto his knees. Andy stopped sucking my cock and let it rest in his warm mouth.

"Dude, I don't think that's a good idea," Richard said.

"Eric, is it okay with you if I fuck your ass?" Cameron asked.

I reluctantly let Victor's dick slip from my mouth. "Fuck me."

"A'ight," Cameron said with a smile as Richard gasped.

Cameron lay on his back on the floor. His cock was fully hard and sticking straight up from his body. It wasn't as long as Richard's or as thick as Victor's. But even throbbing hard, the skin looked as soft as silk. A thin layer of foreskin covered the shaft and about half of the head.

"Sit on my dick, Eric," Cameron said.

I looked into his face. His green eyes shone mischievously, and a sly smile pierced his full pink lips. I thought there might have been some meanness to his desire to fuck me, but in his face I saw nothing but passion and desire. I stood up, straddled his torso, and lowered myself toward his up-pointing cock.

His cock head was small, and my ass was well-lubed from the rimming Richard had given me, so my ass grabbed hold of Cameron's cock and gripped it tightly as I slid all the way down his shaft in one move.

"Fuck me!" Cameron moaned as the last of his cock slid inside my ass. He held me firmly by the hips, and closed his eyes tightly as I felt his cock thicken inside me.

"No, fuck *me*," I said, and pushed his hands away from my hips as I slid up and down the length of his cock.

The others just stood around and stared for a few minutes as I fucked Cameron's cock. They stroked their own dicks as they watched. Cameron's cock felt great inside my ass, but before long I needed more.

"Victor, lemme suck your cock again," I said as I bounced up and down Cameron's dick.

Victor lunged forward and slipped his cock back inside my mouth, and that snapped Richard and Andy out of their trance. Andy dropped to his knees and took my cock in his mouth. He was much less tentative now and sucked my dick eagerly. I reached up to wrap Richard's cock in my hand, but he had other ideas.

"I have to fuck you, Eric," he said as he walked around behind me.

"No way, dude," Cameron said, fucking me even harder.

"Come on, Cam," Richard said. "Lemme have a turn."

"I'm not about to let go of this ass. Next time, man."

"Like fuck, next time," Richard said, and maneuvered himself between Cameron's spread legs. He pushed me gently forward at the shoulders, so that my ass, even though it was still impaled by Cameron's cock, was also exposed to him. "I'm goin' inside there, too. Relax, okay, Eric."

I'd never had two cocks inside me at the same time, but I'd always wondered what it would feel like. And I was hotter at that moment than I'd ever been in my life.

"Dude," Cameron said, "that's not cool. There's no way he can . . ."

"Yeah, man," I moaned as I stopped squeezing Cameron's cock with my ass muscles. "Fuck me, Richard. Lemme have both of your cocks inside me."

Richard knelt and placed the head of his big dick at my hole. Cameron and I took a deep breath at the same time, and Richard leaned forward. His thick cock pierced my hole and slid halfway inside in one move.

"FUCK!" I moaned as the first five inches or so slid into me.

"I'm sorry," Richard said as he leaned down and kissed my ear. "Want me to pull out?"

"Don't you fucking dare," I said through clenched teeth. "Give it to me."

He slid all the way in, and rested his cock deep inside, allowing me to get used to both cocks. It took me a couple of minutes, and then something clicked in my head, and I needed both of them to fuck me.

"Fuck me," I almost yelled as I bounced up and down on both cocks.

"Jeez, Eric," Andy said as he lifted his head, "are you sure . . ."

"Shut up and suck my cock," I said as I pushed his head back down to my crotch. "Victor, get over here and fuck my mouth."

I saw the look of shock on his face. I'm sure this wasn't how any of them had pictured the evening going. They probably thought they'd "teach me a lesson" or some silly shit like that. But I was in control—and loving every minute of it.

"Now!" I commanded.

Victor smiled and slapped my cheeks with his heavy cock, then slid it deep into my throat in one swift move. I gagged on it a couple of times.

"Don't even try it, you cock whore," Victor laughed as he fucked my face deeper and faster.

"You guys!" Andy said as he came up for air on my cock. "Do you have to talk like that?"

I laughed around Victor's fat cock.

"Shut up and suck his dick," Victor said, pushing Andy's head back down to my cock.

I'd never been filled with so much cock. Victor's fat dick filled my mouth, and Richard and Cameron's cocks slid in and out of my ass in perfect synch. Andy had truly found his niche in cocksucking and was lapping my cock hungrily.

"Fuck, dude," Cameron said to Richard, "I feel your big dick sliding against mine. I'm gonna cum."

"Me too," Richard moaned as he breathed heavily and thrust his cock deeper and faster into my ass.

"Not inside me." I released Victor's dick from my mouth.

"Oh, fuck!" Victor yelled just as Cameron and Richard pulled out of my ass. "I'm gonna shoot."

And he did. I'd never seen so much cum in my life. It splashed all across my face and chest and stomach. A couple of shots even flew past my head and landed on Richard's face. That's all it took for him. With a loud groan he sprayed himself all over my back and ass. Cameron followed suit and shot his load across my ass and balls from beneath me.

With all of that hot cum on me, I couldn't hold back any longer. "That's it, Andy. I'm gonna cum. You better pull off now."

He didn't let go. In fact, his mouth tightened around my cock and sucked even harder.

"Andy?" I moaned.

He grabbed my leg and squeezed as he sucked harder on my cock.

"An . . ." My entire body shuddered as I sprayed my load deep into Andy's throat. I thought he'd gag and come up spitting, but he swallowed my entire load like a pro and licked my cock clean when I was finished.

Everyone collapsed onto the floor in a heap. Then I realized Andy was the only one who hadn't cum. When I mentioned it, he laughed.

"Fuck that," he said, and turned red. "I came the second Richard's cock slid inside your ass with Cameron's." He pointed to a huge puddle of clear fluid on the hardwood floor.

"I can't believe we just did this," I said.

"Yeah, well believe it," Cameron said. "And remember, we're the Good Ol' Boys Club. We share everything. No more secrets, okay?"

"Okay," I said.

"And get rid of that Mitch dude. He's got pimples on his ass. You don't need him anymore."

"I don't?"

"Fuck no," Victor said. "You've got us. What more do you need? You ain't got any more holes to fill."

We all laughed, and fell asleep in a huddle in the middle of the floor. From that night on, the Good Ol' Boys Club was closer than ever.

Unseen and Unspoken

It had been undeniably the longest summer ever. I hated my job, I was fighting with my parents, and my car had been stolen. I broke up with my boyfriend of a year and a half at the beginning of the summer, and spent the next ninety days desperately searching for my next ex. I found three of them, and they lasted four weeks, three, and one and a half, respectively. Apparently, I'm "difficult" and "impossible to live with." I finally decided I made a much better hot and sexy bachelor than I did a loving and committed boyfriend, so I settled comfortably into a life of meeting and fucking a new guy almost every night.

There was no shortage of takers, or places to meet them. The Internet was inundated with sex and hookup sites, and I had a profile on every single one of them. I was never able to keep up with all Instant Messages I received no more than a minute after I signed on. There were more than twenty gay bars in the city, and at least one of them was packed to the beams every night of the week. I don't wanna sound conceited or anything, but I've never gone home alone unless I've wanted to. The universe has been very good to me. At twenty-five, I stand just a little over six feet tall, with 185 very lean and naturally muscular pounds, wavy black hair and baby-blue eyes. I've always been the envy of every guy around me.

So I'm usually a very content person. But for the past two weeks, I'd been especially on edge. No guy was hot enough. I'd even sent a couple of online hookups right back home after opening the door and not being satisfied, even though they were not by any means unattractive. I found myself having to bite my tongue at work to keep from saying something I'd certainly regret to my boss. I'd even very harmlessly stolen some candy from the supermarket on more than one occasion despite the fact I had more than enough money to pay all my bills and still live what most called a lavish lifestyle.

What was the problem, then, I'd wondered several times daily for the past couple of weeks. I flipped through the channels on the TV without watching long enough to see what was playing. I dusted and vacuumed my entire apartment until I could eat off the floor, and then I dusted and vacuumed again.

I'd had Adrian, my best friend, over for dinner that night. He was still there, reading through the local gay rag, with his shoes kicked off at the door and his feet propped up on my coffee table.

"I'm fucking bored," I yelled loudly as I slumped back into the sofa.

"Jesus, Bradley," Adrian shrieked. "You scared the fuck out of me."

"Well, I am. I'm bored as hell."

"Yeah, I heard."

"Let's do something. If I don't get out of this apartment, I'm gonna frickin' blow my brains out."

"All right. We could head over to Butch's. Tonight is the wet briefs contest."

I rolled my eyes. "I've had every single one of those guys. And my cock is bigger and my ass is tighter than all of them. They bore me."

"OK. We could go to ManHole. It's half-price night. Always busy."

"Nah. I don't feel like drinking tonight. I'm bored with alcohol."

"What about a movie?"

"Oh, yes, please," I said sarcastically. "Let's go see *Bambi* again. I'm bored, I said. If I have to sit in a dark theater with you, I will scream and strangle you. I swear I will."

Adrian laughed and went back to his newspaper. I slapped the back of his head softly as I stood up and went in to clean the kitchen again, even though I'd just cleaned it less than half an hour earlier.

"Hey, here's an idea," Adrian said enthusiastically. He sat up straight and turned around to face me. "Fantasy night at Rendezvous."

"A *bathhouse*?" I asked incredulously.

"Have you ever been to one?"

"Of course not!"

"Well, then, you probably wouldn't be bored. And it actually sounds like fun. Listen to this: 'Ten dollar lockers for all first-time customers. Twelve different rooms to fulfill twelve forbidden fantasies. Free booze and snacks. Leave your clothes and your inhibitions in your room or locker. Open your mind and find the man of your fantasies.' I think it sounds hot."

"Adrian, it's a *bathhouse*," I said in my best indignant tone, careful not to look at him. I already felt my resolve melting away as my cock plumped up a little.

"Oh, grow up. You said you were bored. So do something you've never done before. It could be exciting."

"I don't know. What if I see someone I know?"

"So what? You think they're gonna judge you? They're at the same place."

I wiped the counter again, and chewed on my bottom lip. It was a habit I had when I was nervous. And it was a dead giveaway that I was actually going to do it. "Go with me?"

Adrian smiled, and we both grabbed our wallets and headed for the door.

I almost chickened out right before walking through the front door, but Adrian pushed me through before I could turn and run. I stumbled into the foyer and lost my breath almost immediately. The sex might all occur in various rooms and areas behind the door and window in front of me, but the smell of it was definitely all around me. I scrunched my nose and turned to look at Adrian.

"We'll take two lockers, please. It's our first time here. I guess we get a discount?"

"Yeah, tonight's a special night," the young guy behind the counter said and smiled at Adrian. "Ten bucks apiece, and I'll need your IDs. You'll have a great time."

"Promise?" Adrian asked and smiled back at the attendant as he slid our IDs and twenty bucks under the glass window.

I slinked against the wall in the corner closest to Adrian and the window.

"Oh, yes," the cute guy said, and winked at Adrian as he registered us.

About two minutes after we entered the building, we were buzzed into the main part of the building behind the mysterious door. My heart raced, and I struggled to keep my breathing normal as I hitched my finger into the belt loops on Adrian's jeans and followed him as closely as possible. He laughed and led me to the lockers, where we stripped and locked up our clothes. Clad in nothing but a skimpy once-white towel, I felt naked and vulnerable. The smell of bleach and sweat and sex assaulted my nostrils, and I tried to feel mortified. In reality, though, my cock throbbed painfully hard against the skimpy towel.

"Looks like someone's not so bored anymore," Adrian teased as he glanced at the long line that ran along the right side of my leg.

"Shut up," I said, and pushed him toward the hall that led out of the locker room and into the unknown.

The corridors were dark, the only light coming from a purple fluorescent bulb high above us. Tiny, closet-sized rooms dotted the halls. Most of the doors were closed, but a few were open. Inside, older, heavier set men lay on a single-sized mattress and beat off as they stared at TV screens bolted to the ceiling next to their doors.

"Eww," I whispered into Adrian's ear. "This is disgusting."

"I'm sure it gets better." He took my hand as he wound his way through the maze of rooms. We turned a corner and found ourselves in the middle of a large, overly-decorated locker room. We were apparently in the middle of the Princeton team's sacred room. Banners and uniforms were scattered about. There were four older guys partially dressed, but with their pants around their ankles. Six or seven younger guys knelt in front of them wearing nothing but jock straps and sucking the cocks of their coaches.

"Suck my dick, boy," one of the coaches yelled out at the kid on his knees in front of him. "If you want a place on this team, you're gonna have to do better than this." The kid on his knees moaned and gurgled and deepthroated the coach's big dick as he doubled his effort.

"You two!" another of the coach's yelled at Adrian and me. "Get your asses over here and suck my dick."

I tried not to giggle, and pushed Adrian toward a side exit from the room. "Sorry, that just made me laugh," I said.

"I thought it was kinda hot," Adrian said as he looked back behind him.

"Serious?"

"The coach leaning against the wall was hot. I'd have sucked him off."

I looked at Adrian closely to see if he was serious. He was. "Keep going, Bucky," I said as I laughed and pushed him forward.

We passed several other fantasy rooms. Father and son. Priest and altar boy. Teacher and student. Cop and robber. Each of the rooms was occupied with eager participants, but none of them did anything for me. I was beginning to regret coming.

Then we turned a corner and found ourselves in total darkness. My eyes struggled to adjust to the complete absence of light, but to no avail. I heard noise off to my right side, and my heart skipped a beat. Someone was breathing close to me, off to my right. Despite my disorientation, my cock started to harden. Adrian let out a quick yelp, and then his hand was ripped from mine and he was gone.

"A . . ." A hand clamped over my mouth at the same moment that two strong arms pulled mine behind me and another set held my feet together. I felt myself being lifted and moved deeper into the dark. I struggled to catch my breath and figure out in which direction Adrian had been dragged. My heart pounded painfully fast in my chest.

A moment later I was pushed to my knees and then up against cold metal. It took me a few seconds to realize it was a chain link fence. Invisible hands grabbed mine and flattened them against the fence, and a second later I felt warm leather straps wrap tightly around my wrists. The hands on my mouth were removed, and I took the opportunity to express my displeasure.

"Hey, I'm really not into . . ."

A piece of fabric replaced the hand and was tied behind my neck, rendering me silent.

"I don't remember asking you if you were 'into it' or not," a husky voice whispered into my ear.

The voice was rough, and so were the strong hands that tightened the leather straps around my wrist and then fastened them to the chain link fence in front of me. The restraints were attached to a short length of rope, so I had a little mobility, but not enough for my comfort. I panicked a little as the towel was ripped from my waist; when several pairs of hands pinched and squeezed my nipples and ass, I panicked for real.

Where was Adrian, I wondered as my ass was spread wide and thick fingers probed inside. He'd been yanked away so quickly, and

I had no idea if he was even still in the same room or not. I blinked a few times in vain to try and see better. The gag was ripped from my mouth and tied tightly across my eyes and behind my head.

"Don't say a fuckin' word or even think about screaming," the tough voice said. "I've got better plans for your mouth. Open up and suck my dick."

Despite my fear and the ache in my chest, I opened my mouth and stuck out my tongue. I was hungry for this tough guy's cock, and a moment later I was rewarded with it.

He rested just the head on my tongue. It was hot and heavy, and enough to let me know that the cock attached to it was massive. I licked it eagerly, then sucked it into my mouth. A large drop of pre-cum trickled onto my tongue, and that was all it took to set me off. I moaned loudly and sucked more of the long, thick cock into my mouth as several hands spread and caressed my ass. I deepthroated the big dick and wriggled my ass against the probing hands.

"Fuck, man," the guy in front of me said huskily, "this dude's gonna make me cum."

Although I wanted this moment to last, I wanted even more to make this tough guy shoot his load before he was ready, so I tightened my throat around his cock and licked around his shaft with my tongue.

"FUUUUUUUCCKKKK . . ." he yelled, and held my head tight against his crotch as he emptied his load into my throat. I couldn't taste or feel his cum, because his cock head was deep in my throat, but I felt his cock grow thicker with each spurt, and I knew he was shooting a huge load into my belly.

The guy left his cock deep inside me for a couple of minutes after he'd spent himself in my throat. When his cock was fully soft, he pulled it out and I heard him walk away.

"Okay, now the real fun begins," someone else said from my left. "You," he said, and his voice turned away from me, "get over here and get on your hands and knees."

Someone groaned from a few feet away, and it sounded like he was being pushed around. I was being manhandled so that I was sitting up on my knees. My wrists were still shackled to the fence, and they hurt. But when I tried to suggest that my captors loosen the grip just a little, someone reached under my legs and squeezed my balls tightly. I shut up.

"That's it," the new voice said. "Move him into position."

I heard rustling just inches in front of me, and then the warmest, wettest sensation I'd ever felt enveloped my cock. I moaned loudly and thrust my dick deeper inside the mouth until my balls slapped against a chin. God, this guy was good, whoever he was. Not many guys can take my entire dick. A couple of skilled cocksuckers could take it all the way, but they always choked. This guy had all ten inches deep down his throat, and hadn't even gagged a little. And his hot throat muscles squeezed my thick cock appreciatively. I struggled to keep my knees from buckling as I thrust my cock in and out of his hot mouth.

The guy sucked me for at least five minutes, and then I felt the load building in my balls. "I'm getting close," I warned him.

He quickly pulled his mouth from my cock. "Not yet. Not like this."

"What . . ." I groaned, and thrust my dick into empty air in front of me.

A second later I felt warm muscle rub up against my cock. "Fuck him," the familiar voice said. Cold fingers grabbed my cock and directed it to the hole of the ass in front of me, and someone spat on my cock head. Then from behind me, hands pushed me forward. I slowly slid inside the ass. The muscles tightened around my dick, and the moan I heard from what seemed like a block away told me my entry was not easy. I tried to slide in slowly and easily, but the hands on my back and ass were insistent, and I was pushed forward until my hip met with the meaty ass cheeks in front of me.

"Oh fuck, that feels go . . ." I started to say, but my mouth was suddenly filled with another thick cock. I sucked on it greedily and slid my own cock in and out of the hot unseen ass in front of me.

I felt movement and heard rustling all around me. I couldn't tell how many people were there. At least two pairs of hands massaged and played with my ass, and then another thick finger slid inside me, and I moaned again. I felt the guy whose cock I was sucking straddling the guy whose ass I was fucking. And from the sound of things, my hot partner had his mouth filled with cock as well.

My entire body tingled with the heat of all the sex around me. And then, without warning, the thick finger inside my ass pulled out. A second later I felt the hot skin of a hard cock head press against my ass, and I panicked. I'd only been fucked a few times by my last boyfriend. I was almost always a top, and with a ten-inch hard, thick cock, that had never really been an issue. I wasn't comfortable being fucked by an anonymous guy I couldn't even see. I choked on the cock in my mouth as every muscle in my body tensed up.

I tried to pull my mouth from the cock, but the guy pulled my head back onto his cock. "Don't even think about it, dude," he said, and slid his cock deep into my throat.

There was a lot of moaning around me on all sides. The guy behind me spat on his cock, and spread my ass cheeks apart. A second later a hot searing pain shot through my ass and all the way up my body. I moaned loudly, trying not to bite down on the cock in my mouth. My own cock began to soften inside the hot ass in front of me, and I closed my eyes even against the blindfold. I felt tears building up behind them.

The guy behind me let his cock head rest inside me for a moment, and then slowly slid in and out of my ass. The first few pumps hurt like hell, and I fought back the pain and tears. Then, before I knew it, my cock began to harden again inside my unseen partner's ass. The searing tingling inside my body was still there, now it was pure ecstasy. I moaned and felt my ass muscles relax.

My fucker felt it too, and took that as his cue to go to town. He slid his big dick almost all the way out, until only the head rested inside, then slammed it back in. At first he was a little rough and awkward, but then he slowed down and found his groove. Before long I was moaning and swallowing the cock in my mouth and slipping into the ass in front of me as I slid off of the dick behind me.

Everyone was moaning and groaning from every direction, and I was caught up in the excitement of it all. I'd never felt anything so hot in all my life. Every nerve in my body was on fire. And then, without warning, the guy behind me pulled his cock unceremoniously out of my ass. I could actually hear the "plop" as it exited my ass, and moaned my disapproval. But I needn't have worried. A couple of seconds later I was filled again with as little fanfare as I'd been vacated. It was a different cock, though; I could tell that right away. Nowhere near as long or as fat. But once the guy got going, it felt pretty good, and I fell right back into my mojo. I swallowed the big cock in my mouth as I slid off of the cock behind me and into the warm, wet ass in front of me.

Sweat dripped from every pore in my body as I worked like a machine with the guys around me. Our moans grew louder and more intense, and filled the room. I still didn't know how many guys were there, but I did know that at least five or six dudes shoved their cocks up my ass. Each time someone new entered me, I felt like a new person being born into sex for the first time. I couldn't get enough cock inside me, and I bucked back onto their cocks, begging for more. All the while my own cock was rock hard as it pounded the invisible ass in front of me.

"I'm getting fucking close," the guy in my mouth said, and I felt and heard the other guys close in around me. The guy behind me fucked me faster and harder, and I did the same to the guy I was fucking. "Here I cum, man!" my mouth fucker yelled, and a second later he did. He pulled his cock out of my mouth and sprayed his load all over my face.

That was enough to send everyone over the edge. The guy behind me pulled out quickly, and I suddenly felt a shower of warm musky cum from every direction. Loud moans filled the room, and cum landed on almost every inch of my naked body.

As the sticky liquid covered me, I pounded my cock into the ass a few more times, then pulled out. My hands were still tied to the fence, so I couldn't touch my cock. But I didn't need to. It took a couple of second after I left the hot hole, but when it finally came, my load exploded from my cock. I felt seven or eight huge spurts spew from my cock, and then several smaller ones. Everyone gasped, and someone was amazed that I'd shot a couple of shots "way over the dude's fuckin' head."

I struggled to catch my breath as I heard the guys around me gather their belongings and leave. A soft, warm mouth sucked on my lips and kissed me as tender hands untied my own.

"You guys were hotter than hell," a soft and surprisingly tender voice said as I let my arms fall to my sides. "You make a great couple."

"What?" I asked as I felt the blood rush back into my arms and heard the man leave. I knew they were all gone now, and I shook my hands for a moment before I removed the blindfold.

The room was still pitch black, and my eyes stung as they dilated and tried to adjust to whatever light they could find

"You all right?" I heard Adrian ask, out of breath.

"Adrian?" I asked with disbelief.

"Down here."

I felt around the floor in front of me and found him easily.

"My hands are still tied," he said. "Untie me."

I quickly untied him. "Are you okay?"

"Yeah," he whispered as I threw the leather strap that had bound his hands to the side.

I sat there in the dark, thankful that I couldn't see my best friend as I quickly realized what I'd done. "I'm so sorry, Adrian. I didn't know . . ."

"Neither did I," he said. "At first."

"What? You mean you knew it was me?"

"Yeah, after a few minutes."

"I would never have done that if I'd known . . ."

"Yeah, I know," he said, and sighed deeply as we both sat with our backs leaned against the cold chain link fence. "So, lucky for both of us you didn't know, right?"

"You're okay with this?"

"More than okay with it."

"You liked it."

"More than liked it."

We both laughed, and helped each other stand up. It was no easy feat. All of our limbs felt like wet noodles. I took one of his hands in one of mine and felt around the walls with my free hand.

"Come on, let's get outta here," I said. "This dark is getting to me."

"Not so fast," Adrian said, and pushed me against the wall as he kissed me.

I'd never kissed him before, and was more than a little surprised to find myself getting hard as he slid his tongue in and out of my mouth. Adrian reached down and stroked my cock to full hardness.

"What are you doing?" I asked and kissed him again.

"Remember the teacher/student room?"

"Yeah."

"Well, directly behind it was a sling room. No one was there when we passed through a while back. Maybe it's still empty."

"You've got to be kidding me!" I said with a laugh.

Adrian just squeezed my cock and kissed me again.

I grabbed his hand and led the way through the maze and toward the sling room.

A Life Much More Than Ordinary

A Novella

PART I

You Know You're Gay When . . .

Coming out wasn't so much a process for me as an accidental discovery that became the main form of entertainment for my entire family throughout my senior year of high school. We were in no way anything like the Cosbys or the Camdens or even the Carringtons, from what I remember of the syndicated reruns of *Dallas* that I was addicted to. We were more like the Connors . . . you know, the Roseanne Barr/Arnold Barr show where, instead of everyone in the family lifting one another up and supporting one another, they thrived on the misery and failure of each other. That's kinda what it was like for me growing up.

There are three children in my family; myself, my sister who is three years older than me, and my brother who is almost to the day a year older than me. Not only do we not "come from" money, but we barely had any. With my parents' income, it was a struggle to keep us all in clothes, put food on the table, and come up with the rent for a small three-bedroom apartment. My parents had one room, of course, and my sister, being the only girl, and a teenage one at that, had her own room. Which meant that JJ and I shared a small room.

I'd been struggling with my sexuality for the past couple of years. In my sophomore year, while sitting in the waiting room at my dentist's office, I was flipping through old magazines and ran across a full-page CK1 ad. The Ricky Martin look-alike was shirtless, and his tattered jeans were unzipped about halfway down, revealing not only his rock-hard six-pack abs, but a thick, black patch of pubic hair and a significant bulge just out of sight under his jeans. I'd popped an instant boner and sneaked off to the boy's room to beat off before seeing Dr. Mason. I stole that magazine from the dentist's office that day, and beat off to that ad almost every night for the next two years.

The inevitable happened one Saturday night halfway through my senior year. I avoided dating at all costs, under the pretext of throwing myself into my schoolwork and striving for a scholarship. My parents were so proud of their little boy. But JJ and Amber were both out on dates. Dad was at work, and mom was completely oblivious to the world. She worked during the day, and wasn't able to watch her soap, so she taped the entire week's shows and then watched them all at once, fast-forwarding through the commercials, on Saturday evenings. Armed with a quart of Chunky Monkey ice cream and five hours of *Days of Our Lives* she could be distracted by nothing.

So I didn't think twice about shutting myself off inside my room and beating off to my fantasy boyfriend with the ripped abs and jeans and that treasure trail from heaven. The rest of the magazine was tattered and torn almost to pieces, but that one page was in perfect condition. I didn't tear out that one page, and laminate it or frame it, but instead kept it inside the rest of the magazine for cover. If anyone had found just the page with my boyfriend on it, I'd be found out. But no one in my family read, not even the trash tabloids, so I knew they wouldn't pick it up and notice the perfect page with my perfect boyfriend and come to the perfect conclusion that I was a faggot.

What I didn't count on that night was JJ arriving home early and bursting through the bedroom door.

"Fuck!" he yelled as he slammed the door. "That bitch wouldn't put out again tonight. Said she's . . ."

He stopped mid-sentence as he looked up and saw my naked body lying on my bed, one fist wrapped around my hard and throbbing cock and the other clutching the open magazine to the page with CK, my boyfriend-in-waiting.

"What the . . ."

"JJ, please don't say anything," I pleaded as I threw the magazine to the floor and grabbed the blankets to cover myself.

He ran to the other side of the bed as I scampered to cover my naked body, and picked up the magazine. It was still opened to the page with CK.

"Oh, my God," he nearly yelled. "You're a fuckin' homo."

"Come on, JJ," I said, grabbing the magazine from him. "It's nothing, really. Just don't say . . ."

"Mom," he yelled as he pulled the door open and rushed out into the living room. "Kyle's a fucking homo!"

Finesse and tact are not qualities that run in my family.

I pulled the covers over my eyes and cried myself to sleep. The next morning I tried to sneak out the door to school without being seen. But there was no way to get out without walking through the kitchen, where everyone was having breakfast. Mom and Dad and JJ were having eggs and bacon and fried potatoes. Amber was having her usual half a grapefruit with artificial sweetener. Normally my plate would be filled with the same food as JJ and my parents. But this morning my plate had a frozen waffle on it. It was topped with pink whipped cream, and a single strawberry capped it off.

I sat down and buried my head in my hands, and everyone at the table laughed at me until they had tears in their eyes.

College was such a blessing. Not so much because I loved school or was even among the brightest. I wasn't a jock or a computer nerd or a standout in any other way whatsoever. That, in fact, was one of the blessings. I could just get lost among all the other kids and not be noticed, and not a whole lot was expected of me.

The other was that I was away from my family. I love my family. But damn, could they ever get on my nerves. Most of the time, every word out of their mouth made me want to cringe and scream and pull my hair out. I suppose I wasn't unlike every other teenager in that aspect. But once they knew I was gay, it got worse. They never stopped teasing me. It wasn't at all mean-spirited or anything like that. Just teasing and poking and prodding and asking when I was bringing my boyfriend over to meet the Fockers. To them it was funny and their way of showing me how open and accepting they were. I love them for that. But for me it was embarrassing and got old after a while and I just wanted to go into a coma or something for a few months until I could get out of the house and be on my own.

Leaving the small, redneck town of Rock Springs, Arkansas, and heading off to college . . . alone for the first time in my life . . . in the big city of Denver, Colorado, was the experience of my life. No one knew me in Denver, and that meant no one would know that I was gay. That was fine with me, because my only experience of people knowing I was gay was with my family, and I could certainly live without that.

I lived in the dorm on campus, and actually enjoyed it a lot more than I thought I would. I made a lot of friends there, and there was some kind of party going on almost every night of the week.

My roommate's name was Tony. Tony was Mr. All-America: five feet ten inches of solid, rock-hard muscle. He was a star on the wrestling and gymnastics teams. Dark blond hair, emerald green eyes, and a smile that put Tom Cruise to shame. To me, he was the perfect guy. He was shy and quiet and sweet, and a real nice guy. And yet he was popular and always the center of attention. He had a way of making everyone feel wanted and appreciated, and he was great at being a leader in everything he did. At the same time, when he was alone with me he confided that he really was shy at heart and was always a little uncomfortable with all the attention.

I had a huge crush on Tony. I wanted to crawl into bed with him and cuddle and kiss and make love. I wanted to lick the valleys that dipped between Tony's eight-pack abs.

During wrestling season, he would ask me to help him work through some moves. I am not a jock, and am, in fact, one of the clumsiest people I've ever known. And so the first few times he asked me to wrestle around with him, I vehemently refused. But one time, after we'd had a few beers and were getting a little restless as the night drew closer to midnight, when Tony asked me to wrestle with him, I agreed. I'm a very cheap drunk.

When he started to undress, I panicked. "What are you doing?" I squeaked as I tried very hard not to look at his smooth, tanned and perfectly muscled chest and legs.

"You can't maneuver in your clothes, dude," he said as he slid his jeans off and threw them aside. He stood in nothing but his boxers. "They get in the way and you can't grab hold."

I just stood there and looked at him with a mixed expression of stupidity and horror.

"Strip down, dude. To the underwear."

There was absolutely no excuse I could give that wouldn't make me sound completely retarded or completely gay. So I stripped down to my white Hanes briefs and just stood there.

Tony had had quite a bit to drink, so I could chalk up a lot of his actions and reactions to the ten or so Coronas he'd had. But as I stood there in only my briefs, shivering like it was twenty below zero inside the room, he looked me up and down and sized me up in a way that led me to believe it was more than just the beer. I'd seen other straight guys check out girls in that same way, and I'd snuck a few similar looks at hot guys around campus myself.

He showed me a few basic moves, then started attacking me for real. He came at me from the front, from the back, from the side. His smooth skin was so hard and warm and sweaty as it rubbed against mine. It didn't take long at all before I felt my cock harden, and I panicked. Tony must have noticed too, because he flipped me onto my back so my hard-on couldn't be hidden beneath me, straddled my chest and pinned my arms with his legs. We were both breathing heavily and his crotch was only a couple of inches from my face. His fly was spread wide open, and I could see his dark bush and the base of what looked like a very nice and very thick cock. It was definitely on its way to full hardness.

Tony looked into my eyes, and I somehow found enough courage not to look away. He leaned down toward me, and I braced myself for him to kiss me. At last, the dream of my life would become reality. Tony's lips would gently touch mine and linger there for a moment before he slipped his tongue into my mouth and kissed me passionately. He would break the kiss and hold my face in his hands and tell me he loved me and wanted us never to be apart.

But that didn't happen, of course. This was no Harlequin romance. Instead, Tony fell forward and planted both hands on either side of my head. He turned to one side and vomited all over the floor right next to me.

"I'm so sorry, dude," he said when he'd finished and collapsed on top of me. He looked like he was going to cry.

"Don't worry about it," I said, as I helped him up and half-carried him to his bed. As I laid him on top of the covers, the fly of his boxers opened again. I couldn't help it. I looked inside and saw his beautiful hard cock in all its magnificence. It was every bit as long and thick as it seemed in my preview a few moments earlier, and pink with big hairy balls that lay low between his legs. He was dead to the world at this point, so I could have taken advantage of him then and there, and he'd never have known. But I didn't. I went to bed, climbed under the blankets, and beat off to the picture of his cock that would forever be engrained in my brain.

I was in love with Tony. There was no denying that. But I couldn't ever tell him that, or let anyone else find out either. There were no rumors at school that I was a fag. There were certainly no rumors that I was some butch jock or lady-killer, either, but I didn't have to put up with any prods or pokes like from my family, and no pink whipped cream frozen waffles and no whispered words behind my back or uneasy stares as I walked about campus. And I wanted to keep it that way. So I could never let on that I barely ever looked at CK anymore, or even thought of him, for that matter, but that instead I beat off quietly under the blankets of my bed every night as I watched Tony sleep across the room from me.

My ruse was working pretty well, too, until one fateful Thursday night in early May. I'd been studying for my Psych final exam for the past three nights, and was almost to the point of committing myself. My Tony never studied . . . he didn't have to, and he had a habit of leaving me alone in the room when I needed to concentrate on my books. So I was alone when my cell phone rang. From the caller ID I saw it was Amber, and I almost didn't answer it. But her birthday was this weekend, and I was heading back to Rock Springs to celebrate with the family the next day, so I picked up.

"I've decided what you can get me for my birthday," she said excitedly, even before I had a chance to say hello.

"A brain?" I teased.

"No. I want a porno DVD."

"A *what*?"

"A porno DVD. You know there's no place here in Rock Springs to get something like that. There must be hundreds of stores in Denver where you can get them."

"I wouldn't even know where to begin to look for one of those places."

"Check the Internet or the Yellow Pages under 'porno stores' or 'sex shops', or something like that. You're smart, I'm sure you can figure it out."

"But Amber . . ."

"Make sure you get me a straight one. You know, with a man and a woman."

"Very funny," I said, and stuck my tongue out at the phone.

"And make sure the guys on the cover are cute. God, some of the pictures I've seen on advertisements for those things are horrible. The men look like they've just been found in the caves of Afghanistan."

"I am *not* going to go looking for a porno video for you," I said. But already I was Googling sex shops in the area.

"Please," she begged. "I'm twenty-three years old, and have still never seen one. That just can't be normal. I should be on Springer or something."

"I think you were, just last week. I saw you pulling some girl's hair out because she was claiming to be your boyfriend's baby mama."

"Fuck you. Are you gonna get me the damned tape or not?"

"Yes, I'll get you a hot porno tape. You nympho."

"Fucking faggot."

"Good night, Amber. I love you."

"I love you, too, sweetheart. See you tomorrow."

There were several shops within a mile or so of campus, but I didn't want to chance running into anyone I knew, so I drove all the way downtown to a sleazy stretch of Colfax Avenue, and found a store very inaptly named Romantix. There was nothing romantic about it. The second I walked in the door I almost vomited a little in my mouth. The stench was overwhelming, and the dozen or so TVs behind the counter were all showing porn videos with the volume turned up a titch too loud.

I kept my head down and walked as purposely as possible to find Amber's DVD. It didn't take long; there was a whole room filled with them. There were a few people browsing the DVDs, but no one I knew, so I loosened up and took a few minutes to find one I thought she might like. Okay, so I found one *I* liked. There were two guys on the cover, and both of them were gorgeous. Smooth and muscular and model-pretty. And they both had huge cocks that I couldn't take my eyes off. The black guy's cock was as thick as a beer can, and buried halfway up the blonde girl's snatch, and still I could see several inches. The white guy's cock wasn't quite as thick, but covered with thick veins, and from the look of the chick's puffed-out cheeks and expanded throat, he was pretty deep inside her from the other end, and again I could still see enough of his cock to get instantly hard. I thought Amber would like that one, so I picked it up and headed toward the counter.

It was then that I saw another whole room with a white neon sign hanging over it that heralded "Gay." I instinctively dropped my head, so as to keep anyone from seeing me, and walked inside. Hundreds of gay porno DVDs surrounded me. My already hard cock throbbed painfully, and I knew it wouldn't be long before I stained the front of my jeans. So I reached out and picked up the closest DVD and rushed to the counter, where I paid for both DVDs, and then bolted from the building as quickly as possible.

Back at the dorm room, Tony still hadn't returned. It was only nine o'clock, so he'd probably be out for at least another three hours. I shoved Amber's DVD into my suitcase, then popped the movie I'd bought for myself into the DVD player. I undressed and lay on the bed, completely naked, and was fully hard even before the opening credits finished. I spat into my hand and slid it up and down the length of my cock as I watched a couple of cute guys kissing and undressing one another.

I was so engrossed in the video that I didn't hear the door open. It took me a couple of seconds to realize Tony was standing just inside the door, which was wide open, watching me beat off. I instantly had déja vu of JJ walking in and catching me in this same compromising position and outing me.

"Can you shut the door, for fuck's sake?" I grabbed the blankets and tried to cover myself.

Tony closed the door, and it was then that I noticed he was wearing nothing but a pair of his infamous boxers. They clung to his muscular ass in a way that is illegal in thirteen states. When he turned around, the fly of his shorts tented out in front of him.

"What the hell have you been up to?" I asked, trying to divert the attention away from me.

"A few of us were playing Truth or Dare down in Karen Thomas's room, and things got a little out of hand." He was holding onto the door to brace himself, and I was afraid he was gonna fall.

"Well, it doesn't look like you were too put off by it all," I said, and glanced down at the very obvious bulge in his shorts.

"Oh, that," he said, and squeezed it harder. "I didn't actually get that until I walked in here and saw you beating off."

"Really?"

"Yeah," he said, and strutted toward my bed. My heart raced and my cock grew harder. When he reached my bed, he stood right in front of my face and pulled his cock out of the fly of his shorts. "So why don't you suck my dick?" he said in a deep and sexy voice that almost made me cream right there.

I reached out with my tongue and licked the salty head of his cock, savoring the sweet taste of his precum. I wasn't a pro at cocksucking at that time . . . in fact, I'd had no experience in it at all. But I did what felt good for me, and Tony seemed to enjoy it as well. I pulled his foreskin back and sucked on just the head for a few moments, and then took a couple more inches into my mouth. It was all I could handle without gagging, which I so did *not* want to do. I sucked on it for a few minutes, and then slid my lips up and down the length of his cock, or at least as much as I could take.

Sucking his cock was the best taste and feeling I'd ever experienced. He leaked a lot of precum, and I lapped it up like I a bear after honey. His cock was thick and long and veiny and hard, and intoxicated me with desire. I wanted all of him. I was in love, remember.

"I wanna fuck you," Tony said, and then turned me onto my

stomach, with my naked ass raised in the air. In a matter of seconds, he had my cheeks spread and was fingering around my hole.

"Tony, this isn't such a great idea," I said as I tried to find enough spit to swallow. Every ounce of energy in my body wanted him to fuck me. I'd dreamed about it from the moment I met him, and had beat off to that fantasy a hundred times. But I wasn't ready. As much as I wanted to be, I wasn't ready.

"Come on, dude. You can't fucking tease me now," he said, as he spat on my ass. "You got me fucking harder than a rock."

"I'm sorry. I didn't mean to," I said, and then cringed as I realized how stupid that sounded. "It's just that . . ."

"Just that what?" Tony asked as he slid one finger up my ass all the way to his knuckle.

I gasped as he wiggled his finger deep up my butt. I truly meant to cry out in pain and shock and horror, and to demand that he stop. Imagine my dismay when instead I moaned and wriggled my ass against his finger, wanting more.

"I've never done this before."

"Yeah, right," he said as he slid a second finger inside me. and I moaned louder and squeezed my ass muscles around his fingers.

"Seriously, Tony, I've never done anything like this," I said as I tried to pull my ass from his fingers and turn around onto my back.

But he was much stronger, and horny as hell, so he kept me pinned on my stomach and continued to finger fuck me.

"Well, that's cool," he said nonchalantly. "Then you're a natural, because your ass is begging for more than just my finger. And let me tell you, it feels fucking hot up inside there."

"Thank you," I said, and cringed again as I realized how utterly ridiculous I sounded.

Tony kicked off his boxers and lay on top of my back. His legs lay across my legs, and were smooth and hard. His cock was hard and hot and throbbing against my ass cheeks, slipping between them and rubbing against my hole. I expected him to lean down and kiss my neck and nibble on my ear . . . to whisper in my ear and tell me to relax and that it'd all be okay. But instead he massaged my back and shoulders. Then he leaned down and whispered into my ear, "Open up that sweet ass and take my cock, dude. You know you want it."

Not exactly the romanticism I'd expected or hoped for on my first time out, but I did as he told me. I took a deep breath and relaxed every muscle in my body. Tony lifted his hips and positioned his cock head at my hole. When he felt me exhale, he covered my mouth with one hand and slid his cock all the way inside me.

His cock was long and thick and hard, and it hurt like no pain I'd ever felt before. It felt as if muscle tissue was being ripped from my bones, and I imagined I could actually feel myself bleeding to death. I tried to scream, but it was muffled by his hand over my mouth. I tried to fight him off and squirm out from under him, but that only drove his big cock deeper inside me, and made him more excited.

"Yeah, you love that cock up your ass, don't you, bitch?" Tony said as he slid in and out of my ass.

Tears streamed down my face, but I couldn't say anything because his hand was still covering my mouth. The thought ran through my head that I was being raped, but I knew it wasn't true. I'd never told him "no" at any point, and in fact, had very willingly sucked his cock and gotten him all worked up. I'd flirted with him a little over the semester and knew that at least a few times he was watching me beat off in the dark while I looked over at his naked body lying on top of his blankets. This was not rape in any way. I wanted this, and I wanted it badly. I just needed to go about it differently. Go about it the right way.

I relaxed a little more, and licked Tony's palm that was covering my mouth. I felt him tense up a little when I did that, and when he started to move his hand from my mouth, I pulled one of his fingers into my mouth and sucked on it.

"Oh, fuck," Tony moaned and slid in and out of my ass a little faster.

In the blink of an eye, the pain in my ass became complete and absolute pleasure. I lifted my ass to meet Tony's thrusts, and tightened my ass muscles around his cock as it thrust in and out of me. I whimpered with pleasure each time his cock slid all the way inside me and tickled my prostate. My own cock throbbed painfully, and when I wiggled it against the sheets, my ass writhed around Tony's cock.

"See," Tony said as he slid his finger from my mouth and grabbed my waist from both sides. "I knew you wanted my fat cock inside you." He held my hips in place and slammed into me deeper and harder.

"Fuck me harder," I said a little too loudly, and spread my legs further apart so just a little more of him could get just a little deeper inside me. *Where the hell did that come from?* I wondered. But only for a second, because before I knew it, I felt my orgasm building deep inside my balls. "I'm gonna cum, man," I whispered hoarsely, as my cock slid against the sheets and bright colors floated in front of my eyes.

"Shoot your load, dude," Tony said as he leaned down and bit me hard on the neck.

I did. With his cock deep inside my ass and his mouth latched onto my neck, I shot a load I thought would never stop. With each squirt, it felt like every ounce of lifeforce in me was being drained. I shuddered and quivered as my ass tightened even more around Tony's cock and I shot my load into the sheets.

"Fuck me!" Tony yelled, and quickly pulled his cock out of my ass. He was barely out before the first shot of his hot load sprayed across my ass and back. I didn't count how many shots there were, but when he finished, I was covered in his warm, sticky cum.

I felt his knees give way, and a second later he was lying on top of me. He was breathing heavily.

"You okay?" I asked.

"Yeah, just a little tired," he said.

I expected him to roll off of me and head to his own bed. But a few seconds later, he was snoring, still lying on top of me. I started to push him off, and rolled over onto my back. But then something strange happened. Tony was snoring loudly and was definitely asleep, but his cock began to harden again as it still lay between the cracks of my ass. It took less than a minute for his cock to get fully hard and throbbing again, and as tired and spent as I was, . . . I found myself hard and horny again.

I twisted and wriggled just a little to one side, and Tony's cock was positioned right at my hole again. I pressed my ass against his cock, and this time it slid in with no resistance, and made me quiver as he slid all the way inside my ass. I thought that would wake him up, but he continued to snore and didn't move. So I began thrusting my ass up down the length of his cock. Even with him asleep and snoring on top of me, his cock was very much alive.

His breathing pattern didn't change at all, but mine did as I fucked his dick. I slid my hand beneath me and grabbed my cock. It only took a couple of thrusts. The feel of my hand around my cock as Tony's thick pole was up my ass . . . and knowing that I was in control this time around . . . sent me over the edge. I sprayed another load into my hand and shuddered with pleasure.

It wasn't long at all before I fell asleep too. Tony was still fully hard and buried inside my ass, as my last conscious thought went through my head.

It must have been a couple of hours later when Tony finally woke up.

"What the FUCK?" he said, as he pulled his cock out of my ass in one swift move that felt like I'd had a wisdom teeth pulled.

"OWWWW!" I cried out.

"What the fuck happened here?"

"You were at a party in Karen Thomas's room last night and had a little too much to drink."

A foggy look of confusion crossed his face. "Yeah?"

"I was asleep when you got back here. You were really shit-faced and crawled into bed with me."

Tony pulled the blankets up to cover his nakedness, and looked at me with those puppy dog eyes that were about to cry. I might not be the brightest crayon in the box, but I could tell that his biggest fear at that moment was he was a fag.

"You kept calling me Karen and rubbing me up. You told me that I had great tits and that you wanted to fuck me."

"I did?"

"Yeah."

"But . . ."

"You were drunk as shit, hard as a rock, and much stronger than me. So I just thought it'd be easier to let you fuck me and get it over with. I didn't want to fight with you."

"I fucked you?" He looked like he was gonna be sick.

"Yeah. But you thought I was Karen Thomas."

"So I'm not . . ."

"No, Tony," I said, and held his chin in one of hands. "You're not gay."

He just stared at me.

"Yes, Tony. I *am* gay. You fucked me thinking I was a girl. So you're not a fag. I liked it a lot. It felt great, so I let you do it. So I am a fag. But you must not have liked it very much, because you didn't even finish. You fell asleep pretty quickly after starting, and then I must've fallen asleep right after that."

"So that's why my dick was inside you just now? We fell asleep with my cock inside your ass?"

"Yes."

"And you're okay with that?"

"Yes. It's a very nice cock."

"Thanks. So I'm not . . ."

"No, Tony, you're not. But I am. You cool with that?"

"Yeah, sure," he said, but got out of the bed with the sheets still wrapped around him and walked into the bathroom to shower.

There were three weeks of school left, and Tony and I barely spoke to one another after that. I could tell he was nervous around me. He came to the room very late at night, long after I'd gone to bed, and slipped into bed fully clothed. When we did have occasion to speak, it was as brief as possible and mostly superficial.

To his credit, Tony never said a word about me to anyone at school. It might have been because he couldn't out me without divulging his part in my first experience. But it was more likely because he was a really good guy at heart and didn't want to hurt me.

That night . . . that experience . . . changed my life. I became a man that night. I became my *own* man that night. I no longer felt the need to hide who I was or make excuses or lie. I came out to my friends and my family. Some of them were cool with my newfound confidence and pride, and others were not. That was, and still is, okay. I became me that night, and knew I'd never turn back.

When school started again in the Fall, I joined the Gay/Straight Alliance and became active in their political and social activities. I learned Tony had joined a fraternity and was no longer living in the dorms. It was a good thing, really. We'd never have been able to be buddies again. It would always be awkward between us. And I wanted him to be happy and secure in himself. The fraternity would provide him with that. And if by chance he got a little too shit-faced again, I was sure the fraternity would be able to provide him with more of what he needed as well. And that, conveniently, no one would remember it the next morning.

As for me, I was stuck with a pimply-faced computer nerd from Mississippi. His name was Robert, and he was totally obsessed with me from day one. He followed me around like a lost puppy. Even offered to carry my books to class, if you can believe it. I caught him beating off under the covers several times at night when he thought I was asleep. Sometimes I'd sleep naked and on top of the blankets, stretching and flexing my muscles—a couple of times even fully hard—and watch him with one eye as he looked at me and sprayed his load all over himself.

Then I'd grin and fall asleep.

wsny u >> and hit "Send" before I could correct my spelling mistakes. "Shit!" I yelped, and slapped myself lightly across the face.

<< LOL. That's cute. I wsny u 2 >>

I giggled again, then butched up my laugh, even though I was alone. This guy was cute *and* funny. I had to continue chatting with him. So I did, but before I knew it I was pulled from my trance when the phone rang.

"Hey, hag." It was Josh, one of my best friends. "Listen, whatever you had planned for tonight, forget it. I need you."

"Why? What is it this time? Do you need your nails painted again? Or does your dress need hemming?"

"Well, you're on the right track. I just got a call. One of the girls canceled for the show at Charlies tonight, and they asked me to sub for her. I need your help getting ready. And I really need your support during the show. You know how nervous I get when I perform."

I glanced back at the screen and the chat window with Gemini_Angel. I couldn't believe we'd been chatting for over two hours. And I really wanted to hookup with him. But Josh was my friend, and I couldn't say no to him.

<< Can u meet me at Charlies tonite at 8?? >> I typed awkwardly as I balanced my cell phone to my ear with my shoulder.

"I'm not hearing an answer," Josh said.

"Just a minute," I said. Why was it taking Gemini so long to respond?

"What do you mean, 'just a minute'? Are you really thinking of not coming?"

<< OK. Yeah, I can meet you there at 8 >>

"No, of course I'm not thinking of not coming," I said as I breathed a sigh of relief. What time do you want me at your place to help tuck and tape?"

<< Good! I'll see you there >>

"NOW! The show is in two hours. I'll never have enough . . ."

"Calm down. I'm on my way," I said as I hung up.

PART II

Through the Eyes of Geminis

Kyle

I walked into the living room and threw my bag onto the floor. I closed my eyes for a second, and took a deep breath. It worked in the movies sometimes, so what the hell, it couldn't hurt right? I clicked on the light and opened my eyes. No movie magic here. Dirty clothes were strewn around the living room and the pizza box with one lingering two-day old slice of pepperoni and sausage still sat perched atop the kitchen counter. The sink was full of dirty dishes. So much for movie magic.

I sighed and waded my way through the clothes on the floor to my bedroom. It was just as bad there, but at least I could tell the pile of clean clothes on the floor from the pile of dirty clothes on the floor, and I discarded my work clothes into the dirty pile and plucked up a pair of wrinkled jeans and a T-shirt from the clean pile and put them on.

My roommate of the past six months went and got himself a boyfriend, and moved out a couple of months earlier. There was no way I could make the rent on a two-bedroom apartment in Denver's gay ghetto and ridiculously overpriced Capitol Hill area all by myself. Shit, I was only doing temp work. I was lucky to afford my staple of Kraft Macaroni and Cheese (the powder cheese variety, not the fancy squeeze cheese kind), Ramen Noodles and the occasional luxury of Domino's Pizza.

And so, since Markus moved out, I'd let myself and my place go a bit. Okay, more than just a bit. But hey, I was twenty-three years old and on my own for the first time in my life. I had a right to stress over my current situation. Both of the months I'd lived alone I received a three-day notice to "pay or quit the premises." Trust me, there was nothing I would have liked more than to "quit the premises," but I couldn't. There was no way I was moving back in with my parents. And even one-bedroom apartments in this area were outrageously overpriced. It was cheaper to stick it out and try to find a roommate to take the second bedroom than to find a place of my own.

But I hadn't had much luck in that search. And one simply cannot function normally under such duress. Certainly a clean apartment and washed and folded clothes was out of the question.

I boiled a couple of cups of water and dropped the beef Ramen noodles into it, and sat down at the computer. There was no doubt where I'd be going. There never was when I was feeling like this. I needed to get laid, and there was really only one place for that.

Manhunt.net.

I logged on and scrolled through the profiles of the guys in the Denver room as I slurped the noodles into my mouth. There were three or four friends that I'd chatted with before, and I said hi to them. But chat was not what I was looking for, so I continued searching the profiles.

One in particular caught my eye because of his screen name. *Gemini_Angel*. I am a Gemini myself, and my screen name was *Dark_Lil_Angel*. I couldn't ignore the similarities, so I pulled up his pics and profile.

Angel or Devil . . . You Decide!

Me: 35 y/o, 5' 7", 140 lbs, slim athletic body, br/br.

I'm a typical Gemini, and can be either an angel or
a devil . . . it's all up to you.
Mostly bottom, but will top for the right young,
smooth hottie.

You: 20–35, in shape, HOT, energetic and TOP.
Your eyes and lips will catch my attention first.
Dimples will get you anything U want.
Latinos and Blacks move to the front of the line!"

The profile sounded pretty hot, so I opened up his pic There were five posted. Two of them were really cute pics face, and the other three were downright HOT. One was a shot with his face covered in cum that got my dick rock ha soon as I looked at it. His tongue was sticking out and licking of the cum from his lips, and I almost shot a load looking at i other two photos were of his cock and ass, and they were so thought they had to have been doctored. But I didn't care. I h chat with Gemini_Angel.

<< Hey, wassup? I love your screen name >> I tried to p cool and coy.

I stroked my cock and looked closer at his pics while I waite his reply. It came about a minute later.

<< Not too much. Goofin off a lil. You are HOT! >>
I smiled and felt myself blush.

<< Thanx. So are you. I love your pics >>

<< Ditto here. I wouldn't think you'd need to be on this s find sex. From the looks of your pics you could have anyon want >>

My smile grew bigger, as did my cock, and I couldn't supp little giggle. *Damn it*, I thought, *butch it up. This guy's ho sounds interested. He wants a butch top, not a giggling little s girl. You can do this.*

I took a deep breath, then typed out quickly, << thanzz. I

<< OK. I'll be wearing a red sweater and black jeans >>

<< Can't wait to see you. I'll be wearing a blush on my face and a hardon >> I typed quickly and then logged off before I started giggling some more.

Charlies was . . . well, it was Charlies. I love the bar, don't get me wrong. It's my hangout, and I'm there at least a couple of times a week. But if it's not the way-too-busy half-priced drinks Thursday, or the slightly less crowded Saturday night, it can be a little depressing. Like Denver itself, the bar is very eclectic. It is first and foremost a cowboy bar, and has been for the past twenty years. But a couple of years ago they converted a struggling attached restaurant into the "Party Bar," which played contemporary high-energy dance music, and drew a much younger and diverse crowd. It's a lot of fun on Thursdays and Saturdays to watch the middle aged cowboys mingle with the spiked and painted twink goth punks.

But anytime other than those two busy nights the place can be a little dreary. And this was a Tuesday night. The Party Bar was hosting the fundraising drag show that Josh . . . excuse me . . . Sookie . . . was performing in. At 8:00 there were maybe a dozen people scattered to watch the show. I already was bored and didn't want to be there, and I started fidgeting. Where was Gemini_Angel?

"Go on, girl, just go ahead and call him," my other best friend John said as he made a production of turning around and passing out Tuaca shots to me and a group of three other friends. "You know you're dying to." He raised his glass and we all clinked ours to his. "Here's to going down . . ." he batted his eyes and smiled that Julia Roberts smile of his. ". . . smoothly and gently. Cheers."

We all tossed back our shots, and then I pulled out my phone. Even though it was only ten after eight, I was afraid I was being stood up and I was beginning to panic. This would not do, so I was gonna call and give this guy a piece of my mind. I'd been hurt more than I'd wanted in the past six months, and I wasn't about to let this stranger be the next in line. I listened to the voicemail message on the other end, and my heart melted. He had a very sexy voice and sounded so sweet.

"Hey, you hot little angel, you. This is Kyle," I said, and then remembered we'd exchanged phone numbers but never got around to giving our real names. "Ummm . . . I mean, the guy you chatted with online earlier. It's a little past eight, and I'm just calling to see if you're still planning on meeting me at Charlies. Gimme a call. You have my number."

I hung up and looked over at John.

"Aww, sweetie, don't look so sour," John said as he turned around to order another round of Tuaca shots. "Those puppy dog eyes look much better when they're sparkling and not crying."

"Oh, please! I'm not crying. Especially not over someone I just chatted with online," I said, hoping it sounded convincing.

Even though I hadn't even spoken with this guy, I felt there was something different about him. Our conversation wasn't the usual online bullshit. We didn't even talk about sex at all. Instead we talked about our work and Latino culture and our favorite movies. He made fun of the fact that I'm Mexican and don't even speak Spanish and rubbed it in that he was a gringo and spoke Spanish fluently. I teased him about his age and called him a cradle robber for flirting with a boy twelve years younger than him. There was nothing sexual about our chat; it was fun and innocent. And yet my heart fluttered and my cock hardened as we interacted.

"Fuck him, anyway," I said bravely, trying very hard not to slip into my patented pouting voice. "He's the one who's missing . . ."

Standing just outside the door, next to the ATM was a guy dressed in jeans and a red zip-down sweater. I was sure it was him. He had his phone to his ear, but didn't seem to be talking. Was he checking a message?

I grabbed John's arm just as he was going to toss back his shot. Instead it splashed all across his shirt.

"Hey!" he screeched. "Those aren't cheap, you know."

"I think that might be him." I gripped his arm tighter.

"Where?" John asked, forgetting about the shot.

I nodded toward the door.

"Oh," he said as he cupped one elbow in his other hand and rubbed his chin. "He's kinda cute. A little old . . ."

"I like a little old. I'm tired of all these twinks who don't know what they want out of life and don't know the difference between their ass and a hole in the ground."

". . . a little short . . ."

"I like a little short. Makes it easier for me to . . ."

"Well, don't justify it to me, girl," John said as he pushed me forward. "Go meet your man."

Preston

What the fuck was I thinking? I thought to myself. I looked at the picture of the guy on the screen. He really was beautiful, and exactly my type. Young, Latino, and with a cocky expression on his face. I'd never been able to resist guys like him. Not that I was complaining, mind you. Though falling for his kind had brought me more than my share of pain and anguish, it had also brought me some of the hottest and most precious moments of my life.

We'd chatted for a couple of hours and really clicked. I'd gotten so used to all the Internet bullshit that I'd almost forgotten what it was like to actually meet and chat with someone who knew how to be real. I popped a boner just from chatting with him . . . and we weren't even talking about sex.

But who was I kidding? He was just a kid, twenty years younger than me. My profile stated I was thirty-five years old, because most people guessed me to be between thirty and thirty-five . . . and more truthfully, because in the gay community anyone whose real age begins with anything higher than a three might as well have their age begin with a nine or even a ten. Even with my false age of thirty-five, I was twelve years this kid's senior. When I mentioned it to him, he said he liked older guys (which caused my heart to tighten painfully), and that thirty-five was the perfect age for him. That made me smile and feel really good . . . until I remembered that I was actually the non-perfect age of forty-three.

And now I'd gone and agreed to meet him. Had I gone mad, I wondered as I ransacked my closet for something to wear. I dug to the back of the closet, where I kept my *"happenin' clothes."* The jeans were all strategically ripped and faded, and the shirts were all clingy and made of material undoubtedly manufactured on another galaxy and accentuated my hours-at-the-gym sculpted body. My happenin' clothes had always been good to me and had gotten me more action than anyone my age had a right to get. And usually with guys whose age really did still begin with a two.

But in my epiphany stage, which had begun a couple months earlier, I'd come to an understanding of who I really was, and that I needed to stop behaving like—and dressing like—and pretending to be—a twenty-something. I needed to be comfortable with my real self. And not only did I need to stop trying to be a twink, but I also needed to stop being attracted to them. It was time I found someone my own age and settle down and grow old with him. But that had proven much, much more difficult than it sounded.

I began to hyperventilate and panic deep inside the closet, among the hanged shirts and folded pants and jeans. I dug myself out quickly, and crawled over to the bedroom door, then looked out into the living room and at the computer screen. His picture was still there, looking at me seductively and winking. Just as I was about to blow a kiss at it, the picture disappeared, and my animated fish screensaver popped up. Nemo looked directly into my eyes and then blew out a big bubble.

"Fuck you," I said out loud to the defenseless fish on my computer screen.

As much as I wanted to bring out my happenin' clothes and slip back into a pattern that was very comfortable, I knew I couldn't. I couldn't turn my back on all I'd learned about myself the past few months. I couldn't pretend I was half my age. And so, the hot twenty-three year-old Latin boy-god would just have to meet the real me and determine whether I was something he wanted or not. I felt fairly comfortable, after our two-hour chat session, that he would. But I was still hesitant and afraid as I pushed my happenin' clothes back to the rear of the closet and worked my way to the front of the row of hanged clothes.

I settled on what I'd told the guy I would be wearing anyway, even if it meant he'd be able to spot me immediately and run the other way if I wasn't what he'd imagined. Maybe that was better. It'd save me the embarrassment of having him look me directly in the eyes and tell me I was an old fart and uglier than Mother Teresa.

So, I pulled the red and black zip-down pullover sweater from the hanger and laid it on the bed next to my favorite pair of black jeans. This particular outfit made me look younger than I actually was, but still older than a college jock. It'd been lucky for me in the past, and I was counting on it again.

I undressed and walked to the shower. Was that Linkin Park I was whistling, I wondered, or MacArthur Park?

I was running a little late anyway, and had to stop at the store to buy a pack of breath strips. So by the time I got to Charlies it was already 8:15. Only a handful of people were milling about in both areas of the bar, and the show was running late, as usual. I took a quick peek around, but didn't see the hottie I'd been chatting with earlier, so I went to the bar to order a drink.

Just as I paid for my cocktail, my phone rang. It wasn't the regular ring of an incoming call, but the steady tone that let me know I had a voicemail message. I cursed for the millionth time that my phone didn't ring loud enough nor vibrate quite vigorously enough to be heard or felt over the drone of loud music and shouted conversations of the bar.

I pulled out my phone and listened to the message as I walked away from the bar and over to the more quiet ATM machine. So, his name was Kyle, and he was here. His voice sounded a little sad or disappointed, yet it also had an undertone of anger. I recognized that tone immediately. I'd used it often myself. We Geminis are not known for our mild manner or patience, and I smiled as I took note that this kid really was a true Gemini.

I saved the message because I loved the sound of his voice, and returned the phone to my pocket, then turned around to walk into the Party Bar, where the show was about to begin. It was then that I saw him walking toward me, and thought my heart would explode.

It was HIM. Not just him, but HIM. The kid I'd been noticing . . . on the verge of stalking, practically . . . for the past year. Why hadn't I noticed that *he* was HIM? His hair was a little different than in the picture online, and he was a little heavier. But still! As he walked toward me and smiled, I knew at once it was HIM. Why the hell hadn't I noticed it while I was chatting with him online? For the past year I'd noticed him almost every time I went out. His piercing eyes and full, pink lips drew me to him like some magical potion. I'd made a point of standing right next to him on the dance floor, or behind him in line for a drink every single time I'd seen him. I'd leaned in to get a whiff of his cologne. And I'd gone home alone and beat off to his face in my mind more times than I cared to count.

And now he was walking right toward me with the most seductive smile I'd ever seen, and I panicked at the thought that our first date would begin and end with him watching me being rolled out on a paramedic's gurney.

"Hi," he said, and thrust his hand toward me. "I'm Kyle. Please tell me you're Gemini_Angel."

I tried to smile and prayed my eyes were nowhere near as bugged or cross-eyed as they felt. "Hi, yes, I'm Gemini_Angel," I said as I stuck out my hand for him to shake. "But you can call me Preston."

His lips were moving, but I couldn't hear a word above the loud ringing that resonated through my head. When he motioned me toward the bar, I noticed the group of four or five guys watching us intently. I assumed they were his friends, and walked with him over to the bar.

Thankfully, the show started right away. About ten minutes later I felt myself relax a little, and my heart slowed to a normal pace. It might have been the show, but it was more likely the Malibu Rum with Red Bull that I'd milked less than delicately. Whatever the reason, I found myself emboldened and allowed my arm to slide behind Kyle and rest lightly on his shoulder. I reminded myself to breath, unsure how he would react to my sudden move. When he leaned back against me, and rested his hand on my knee, I relaxed and fell into a normal breathing pattern.

Normally I'm a little shy around cute guys, so I really have no explanation as to the events that came next. Okay, so I had another couple of drinks, and maybe that could be the answer. But I prefer to believe I'd found that renewed sense of self and confidence I'd been striving to achieve for the past couple of months. Whatever the reason, I found myself tickling the back of Kyle's neck, and when he moaned lightly and leaned against me a little harder, I kissed his neck softly.

He gripped my knee tighter. "You really should stop that," he whispered.

"I'm sorry. I didn't mean to . . ."

"Because I won't be able to stand up if you keep this up," he said, and smiled as he leaned back to kiss me on the mouth.

His kiss was soft and sweet, and instantly hardened my cock. Some guys—and especially those in their early twenties—are afraid of kissing. They go into it tentatively and cautiously, as if there might be something frightening inside the kiss. But not Kyle. His tongue licked my lips tenderly, then slipped inside. I sucked on it eagerly as he slid it in and out of my mouth.

I cheated, and peeked to see if his eyes were open or shut. Call it a quirk or a pet peeve, but I've never been able to tolerate guys who kiss with their eyes open. It always seemed like they were looking around for someone hotter while they were kissing me. Kyle's eyes were closed and when he gently pulled me closer to him, I knew he was into it one hundred percent.

That's all I needed, and when I relaxed and let my body rest against his, I felt I was in heaven. I reached down and let my hand rest at the front of his jeans. I immediately found out he wasn't kidding at all about not being able to stand up in public. We kissed for a few moments then sat back down and behaved ourselves. We were in public, after all, and I didn't feel we needed to make a spectacle of ourselves.

But that didn't stop us from being noticed.

"Wow," a shaved-headed twenty-something kid with multiple piercings said as he walked up to us and kissed Kyle's friend John on the cheek. "You guys are hot. I'd do you both. At the same time."

Kyle smiled and squeezed my hand, and I blushed.

"Well, I would," the guy repeated. "You make a very hot couple."

Kyle and I looked at one another and grinned. "We only just met about twenty minutes ago," Kyle said.

"Really?" the punk kid said. "Well, you should be a couple."

"Oh, please!" John said loudly, and turned to wave his hand at the bartender. "Don't encourage them. They're already out of control. We don't have time for any more. It's shot o'clock, for chrissake!"

Kyle and I laughed, and John passed out a round of Tuaca shots.

With the sexual tension broken, I relaxed and enjoyed the rest of the evening. But when the show ended, I felt sad. It was a Tuesday evening, and both Kyle and I had to work the next day, so I knew it was getting close to time to go. I didn't want the evening to end, and I didn't feel Kyle did either.

Sookie came over and excused herself as she grabbed Kyle and pulled him away from me and with her. Kyle laughed and shrugged as he was dragged away. "I'll be back in a few . . ." he whispered as he disappeared around the corner and out onto the patio.

I took the opportunity to get us another drink, wanting to postpone the inevitable as long as possible. When he returned, I handed Kyle another beer and kissed him softly on the lips.

"Okay, so I have a choice to make," he said as he broke the kiss and took a big swallow of beer.

"What's that?" I asked.

"Sookie wants to crash at my place tonight because his mom and dad are in town for a couple of days and staying at his apartment."

I raised my eyebrow and tried to smile.

"And he wants to leave now. So . . . I can leave now and go to my place with Sookie . . ."

"Or?"

"Or I can give her the keys to my place and go home with you."

My heart skipped a beat and I took a deep breath. "Well, I'm not one to pressure anyone," I said, "but you're more than welcome to spend the night with me."

Kyle looked at me and smiled, and my heart melted. "I'll be right back," he said, and he darted out the door. A few minutes later he returned, and grabbed my hand as he pulled me toward the door.

"Where are we going?" I asked.

"To your place."

Kyle

Preston's place was small, but I couldn't believe how neat and clean it was. The furniture was nice, there were no dirty dishes on the kitchen counter, no dirty clothes thrown around on the living room *or* the bedroom floor. He had a really nice wooden four-poster bed and matching dresser, and classy artistic prints of male nudes in expensive frames hanging on the walls.

I felt a little uncomfortable and out of place. The guys I dated were all my own age, and either lived at home with their parents, or in run-down ghetto apartments with roommates, like I did. We slept on mattresses on the floor and kept our clothes in large Glad bags. Our "artwork" consisted of cheap posters thumbtacked onto bare walls. And we had dirty dishes and dirty clothes lying around. That's just the way it was.

But Preston's place was different. When he lit a candle on the nightstand next to his bed and pulled me in to kiss him, I instantly felt comfortable and relaxed.

His kisses were like heaven in my mouth. I love a guy who knows how to kiss, and who likes doing it. It didn't usually happen with the guys I went out with. He undressed me and laid me on the bed, and then undressed himself. I watched him in the candlelight and couldn't believe what I saw. Yeah, sure, he was quite a bit older than me. I knew that going into the whole thing, and he looked older than me. He still looked hot, but definitely older. But his body was incredible. He was a couple of inches shorter than me, but his muscles were big and toned and bulging in all the right places. Even in the candlelight I saw thick veins running along his legs and arms. I couldn't take my eyes off of his naked body.

I broke out of my trance when he walked toward me, and I held my breath. Suddenly I wasn't comfortable being naked. I wasn't fat by any means, but I certainly wasn't anywhere near this guy's league when it came to having a nice body. The only time I ever spent in a gym was a year in high school when I took gymnastics class. But that had been a few years back. I never ate healthy . . . it was always the cheapest and fastest takeout available. So I felt a little self-conscious when he lay next to me in bed and leaned in to kiss me.

His kiss forced me to breathe, and when I did, I relaxed a little. Apparently Preston didn't mind my body. He scooted next to me, wrapped his arms around me and kissed me on the lips, and I in-stantly sprung a boner. He moved his kisses from my lips, to my ears, and then down my neck, and I moaned and wriggled beneath him. This guy was fucking driving me crazy just with his kisses.

He crawled on top of my chest and pinned my arms to the mattress on either side of my head, then licked down my neck and to my chest. He slid his body down so that his ass rubbed up against my hard cock, and licked and nibbled on my nipples. I moaned louder, and tried to squirm under him, but he was strong and kept me pinned beneath him.

"Oh God, that feels good," I whispered.

"You like it?"

"Yeah."

"Good," he said, then let go of my arms as he slipped between my legs and forced them apart.

I grabbed the sheets on either side of me and closed my eyes as he licked the lower part of my belly, around my bellybutton, and down to my cock. I hadn't had sex in over a week, and I thought I was gonna shoot right then and there, so I tried to think of anything sad or bad or ugly to keep from cumming.

He licked the head of my cock for a couple of minutes, then licked my shaft for a little bit, and I squirmed like a little kid being tickled. When his mouth wrapped around my cock and sucked me deep inside, I stopped moving and breathing all together. It took every ounce of strength and concentration I had not to cum. This guy sucked cock like no one I'd ever been with. There was no clumsiness or awkwardness to it at all. This was a mouth that had sucked some cock before and knew what it was doing. He swallowed me deep into his throat, and his throat muscles squeezed my cock. I lay there motionless, afraid to move in fear that I'd cum and it'd be over. Then, with my cock still buried in his throat, he licked around the head and the first couple of inches of my dick.

Well, that was it. I grabbed the sheets tighter in my fists, my body stiffened, and I let out some primal grunt that sounded like it came from one of the Jurassic Park creatures, and I shot my load down his throat. It wasn't my usual two- or three-shot loads, but six or seven bolts of lightning speared my body as I tightened every muscle and released myself into his throat. Preston didn't choke or gag or try to come up for air at all. He just kept sucking and kept swallowing until I'd drained myself into him, and then he sucked some more. It seemed like he didn't want to miss a drop.

"I'm soooo sorry," I said. "I didn't think . . ."

"It's okay," Preston said. "It was kinda sexy, actually. It's been a while since I've made someone cum that quickly and that easily."

"I'm not usually that easy," I said, and hoped he didn't see how red my face was. "But that was fucking incredible."

"Thanks," he said. "But I hope that doesn't mean we're done. Can you stay hard?"

"Umm, I'm twenty-three," I said in cocky voice that I'd practiced many hours and that normally pissed guys off. Something told me Preston wouldn't get pissed off, and might even like it. "What do you think?" I said, and looked down at my cock. It was not only still hard, but throbbing as if it hadn't cum in a week.

Preston grinned. "Good."

He leaned over and grabbed a condom and slid it down my cock in what seemed like one effortless move. I usually had to wrestle with a condom packet for what seemed like minutes, and usually ended up tearing it open with my teeth and slapping it on clumsily. But Preston never used his teeth and had it opened and rolled down my cock in less than a couple of seconds. Then he poured some lube onto the head of my cock, and slathered some on his ass. All of this happened in a nanosecond, and before I could really register what was happening.

"Just relax," Preston said as he positioned his ass at the head of my cock and leaned down to kiss me.

That sounded strange to me, since it was usually what the guy fucking would say to the guy who was getting fucked. But when he kissed me, I felt myself relax all over, and realized I'd been as tight and tense as a guitar string.

When my muscles relaxed and I returned his kiss, Preston slid down onto my cock until I was buried inside him all the way to my balls. I sucked in a breath as I kissed him, and pulled him closer to me. When he moaned and squeezed his ass muscles tight against my cock, I felt like I was being poked with thousands of acupuncture needles. My entire body felt more alive than it had in years. His ass was tight and warm and made me feel at home.

This was not something I was used to. Other than my first encounter with my roommate in college, I'd really only had a handful of real sexual experiences. Mostly I'd made out and fooled around a little with several guys. There were a few that I went all the way with, but they felt nothing like this. After getting fucked by Tony a few years earlier, I'd only been fucked a couple of times. I'd found early on that I much preferred being a top. But that wasn't always convenient, because, as I'd been told on more than one occasion, I come across as a little effeminate, and apparently I have a very nice, meaty, and fuckable booty that attracts mostly tops. But I like topping better, and usually end up debating the whole position thing, and when it finally comes down to either of us getting fucked, it's always awkward and clumsy and not really that great.

But with Preston, there was none of that. No debate, no discussion, no question. He wanted me inside him and he wasn't about to waste any time getting me there. And he definitely knew what to do with a cock up his ass. He continued to kiss me . . . gently and passionately, and then playfully biting my lower lip . . . as he slid his ass up and down my cock, and squeezed it tightly.

I wrapped him in my arms and returned his kisses, and licked his lips and kissed his neck. As he moaned and writhed on top of me, I began to fuck him. I wanted to go slow and make it last, but he'd already done enough of that, and now I had to fuck him—and fuck him hard. I rammed into him until our heads hit the headboard. I rolled him onto his back, and lifted his legs onto my shoulders and slid myself even deeper inside him. I smiled when he moaned louder and squeezed my cock with his ass to let me know he appreciated my effort.

I looked down into his eyes as I fucked him, and saw him smiling at me. *This is right*, I thought as I gazed into his eyes. He reached up and caressed my face in both hands, then brought my face down so he could kiss me. I fucked him some more, hard and fast at first, then slow and gentle, never breaking the kiss. When he finally did break the kiss, he smiled at me and winked. *This is home*, I thought with more clarity than I'd ever known.

Preston

Kyle's kisses alone filled a void in my heart and in my life that I'd almost given up hope of ever filling. The way he laughed and smiled and stared into my eyes made me feel complete again.

I'd had plenty of sex in the two years since my last relationship. Much more than any of my friends, as they never hesitated to point out. But it was always just recreational sex and nothing more. It was good sex, most of the time, at least. But it never left me wanting anything more with the guy. Which was a very good thing because, though I got lots of hookups online, and took home a few guys from the bars, and had at least a couple of booty calls a week . . . I never got a call from anyone asking if I wanted to go out for coffee or go to dinner or go see a movie.

That had been getting old for a couple of months at this point, and just when I was about to give up on finding something more meaningful, here was Kyle. I know it was our first night, it was our first sex, it was a bar pickup from an Internet connection, it was with someone half my age. But none of that mattered. None of it.

His kisses alone were good enough to write a book about. But it was more than that. Now, as he raised my legs and slung them over his shoulders and buried himself inside me, there was magic. I know it sounds corny, but to call it anything else would be doing it injustice—and it would be a lie. I'm not one of those people who believe there is one true love in your life and that's it. I'd already experienced real and true and complete love twice in my life, so I knew that wasn't true. I knew what it felt like, and I recognized it here.

As Kyle shoved his cock deep into my ass, he stared intently into my eyes, and his never left mine. Not for a second. Everyone has a gauge as to what makes something real and true and right for him, and that is mine. I've been told I have very expressive and intimidating eyes; they can't lie, and they are too intense. So I've grown accustomed to people looking at me for a few seconds and then looking away. Even in casual conversation this is the case, so you can imagine how little eye contact I have had while in the throes of sex. But Kyle gazed into my eyes, and I into his, and I could tell we were reading one another as he fucked my ass like it hadn't been fucked in a very long time.

I'm a good judge of people most of the time, and am very perceptive. It comes with the Gemini territory. I knew as he slid into my ass and stared into my eyes that he was thinking the same thing I was: *This is right. This is magical.* When I winked at him, he smiled, and then leaned down to kiss me again.

"Am I doing okay?" he asked between kisses.

"Oh, baby, you're doing much better than okay."

"Then why aren't you touching yourself?"

"Because if I do, I'll cum, and I don't wanna cum yet."

"Why not?" he asked.

"I want you to cum first," I said, and kissed him again.

"I did."

"No, I mean I want you to cum first while you're fucking me. I want you to cum inside me. I want to make you feel good,"

"Oh, you do make me feel good," Kyle said, and smiled. "Very good. I already came inside you while I was fucking you."

"What?" I asked, astounded.

"Just a minute ago was the second time."

"No fucking way." I just stared at him.

He nodded. "And if you don't cum soon, I'm afraid I'm gonna

go soft. I've never cum three times in one night. I'm not sure I can keep going much longer."

I rolled him onto his back and straddled his cock, squeezing with my ass as tightly as possible. "You came inside my ass twice?"

"Yeah. Sorry, I couldn't help it."

"Don't be sorry. It's fucking hot! I just didn't hear anything. I had no idea."

"Yeah, I don't make much noise."

"Well, I do," I said, and began riding his cock hard and fast. My moans grew in intensity as his cock grew harder and slid deeper inside me.

He grabbed my cock and pumped it as he fucked me from underneath. The bed was squeaking, and I was moaning like a cat in heat. I was sure the neighbors were calling 911.

I felt the buildup deep in my balls, and knew it would only be another couple of seconds. "I'm cumming, baby," I said loud enough for my elderly neighbor to hear.

"I want you all over me," Kyle said, and pumped my cock harder.

I didn't disappoint. My load sprayed all across his chest and face, and a couple of spurts even hit the headboard. Kyle gasped, and let go of my cock to wipe my cum from his eyes, but that didn't stop me from shooting even more onto him.

When I finished showering him with cum, I took a couple of seconds to catch my breath, and then I fell on top of him and began laughing. Because that's what I do when I am nervous. I laugh.

"What's so funny?" Kyle asked as he finished wiping his eyes and leaned in to kiss me.

I rolled off him and lay next to him on the bed. "Nothing's funny. I'm sorry. I just laugh when I'm nervous."

"And just why are you nervous?"

I stared into his eyes, and didn't answer.

"Preston?"

I felt the tears building in my eyes, but was determined not to let them fall.

Kyle kissed me passionately on the lips, and I tasted my own cum and felt my cock start to harden again. He squeezed my dick lovingly, and kissed me gently on the eyelids. He licked his lips, and I knew he had tasted my tears.

"You'd better not have any fucking plans for the rest of your life, mister," he said. "Or if you do, they'd better fucking include me. Because I'm not letting you go."

I laughed, because that's what I do when I'm nervous. And then I hugged him tight to my body and fell asleep in his arms.

PART III
Coupledom

"This is totally blowing my mind," Kyle said as he flipped through the book and stuck little yellow Post-Its on the pages he liked. "We're finally doing it. Five years together and we're finally getting married." He looked at Preston and smiled as he kissed him on the lips. "I mean, look at us. We're picking out wedding invitations, for crying out loud."

"Yeah, it is kinda weird, isn't it?" Preston said. He touched Kyle's knee and caressed it. "But good weird, right?"

"Absolutely, good weird. Never in my life did I think this would happen. Every time I thought about what it would be like to be gay, it was a depressing picture. Alone, going out every night and getting drunk almost every night, spending my life alone. Or worse, with a different nameless trick every week."

"That's what a lot of people want us to believe our lives as gay men are fated to be. But look what happens when we don't listen to them and we believe in ourselves and take control of our own lives," Preston said. "We get married."

They looked at each other for a long moment, and then kissed.

"I like this one," Kyle said, breaking the kiss and pointing to the invitation on the open page of the book. It was a simple design, a single red rose lying atop a grand piano. Inside the card was stylish but simple text that, of course, would be tailored for the couple.

Preston wrinkled his nose, and flipped the book back a few pages, and pointed to the one he liked. It was a picture of two guys, holding hands and dressed in nothing but long cotton pants rolled halfway up their shins and walking in ankle-deep water along a deserted beach. The sun was almost over the horizon, and splashed brilliant reds and oranges and purples across the sky and reflected off the water.

"That one is pretty," Kyle said, and sighed. "But it's a little girlish, don't you think?"

"Girlish? Those are two men holding hands. Where's a girl?"

"I didn't say there was a girl there. It's just kinda foo-foo. So colorful. You know all of the little queens are gonna love that one, but our butch friends are gonna laugh their asses off if we go with that one. And never mind what my parents will think."

"You're right. Never mind what they will think. Or anyone else, for that matter. This is our wedding. Yours and mine. You like the picture . . . the idea and the thought that comes to mind when you see it?"

"Yes."

"Then that's the one we're going with. Besides, we're going to Puerto Vallarta for our honeymoon. This card is perfect."

"But . . ."

"Wrap it," he waved the sales clerk over. "We'll take 250 of these."

"Are you sure it isn't bad luck to do this the night before the wedding?" Kyle asked.

Preston slid Kyle's underwear off and spread his legs apart so he could lie between them. Kyle's cock was fully hard and already leaking precum.

"No," Preston said, and licked the precum from Kyle's cock

head. "It's bad luck to see you in your wedding clothes before the wedding. Thank god no clothes are involved here."

He licked around the head and then up the shaft of Kyle's cock for a moment, and smiled as Kyle squirmed and moaned beneath him. Even after five years, Preston never failed to make his lover writhe in pleasure and struggle to keep from cumming too soon.

"Stop it," Kyle begged, with no conviction at all. He was lifting his hips up off the bed and moaning as he pretended to try to get away.

"You're not going anywhere," Preston said. He reached under the bed and pulled up a long, thin strand of leather. He tied Kyle's right hand to the right headboard post, and then did the same with his left hand.

"No, please," Kyle pleaded. It was a game they'd played every now and then for the past nine months or so. Both of them enjoyed being tied up, but usually Preston preferred it more. Tonight, however, Preston had taken control and hadn't really given Kyle much of a choice.

There was no sincerity at all in Kyle's voice as he asked for mercy. Preston knew his lover wanted it a little rough. "You talk too much," he said, and straddled Kyle's chest and slapped his hard cock against Kyle's cheeks and lips.

Kyle stuck his tongue out and licked at the hard cock as it hit his face, lapping at it and catching just the head of it in his mouth for a few seconds at a time.

There were few things Preston enjoyed more than having his cock sucked. And Kyle was an expert at sucking his cock. With most guys it would take hours for him to cum from being blown, and most guys, understandably, gave up after half an hour or so. But with Kyle it was different, and always had been. Even when they first got together and he wasn't as experienced at cocksucking, Kyle had shown an innate ability to learn quickly and master the art. His mouth was always hot and wet and strong, and he could usually get Preston to shoot his load in a matter of minutes.

Kyle smiled to himself as he swallowed Preston's cock and saw the look of pleasure in his lover's face. He watched as Preston closed his eyes, leaned his head back, and licked his lips as his cock disappeared down his throat. Then he tightened his throat muscles around the hard cock, and Preston moaned loudly before pulling his cock out of Kyle's mouth.

"Fuck, baby," he said huskily, "you're gonna make me cum too fast if you keep that up."

"What's wrong, honey?" Kyle teased. "Don't you wanna cum?"

"Not now. Not like this."

"Then how?" he asked in a much deeper and in-control voice.

"You know what I want."

"Then shut the fuck up and take it," Kyle said roughly, even as he struggled against the leather straps that bound him to the bed.

Preston moved between Kyle's legs and began sucking his cock. God, how he loved the taste and feel of his lover's hard dick in his mouth. Kyle moaned and wiggled around as his cock was being sucked, but Preston knew he was gearing up for something more. Something better. He made sure as he sucked Kyle's dick that there was plenty of spit left on the cock.

"Stop messing around and sit on my cock, baby," Kyle said, in a tone somewhere between early Marlon Brando and current Justin Timberlake.

That voice, that tone, those words, drove Preston crazy, and when he looked up into Kyle's eyes, his heart melted. Those long, black, curly eyelashes had always done Preston in. And right now Kyle's five o'clock shadow and soft, full, pink lips were making him quiver. He'd never been more in love with Kyle than he was at this moment.

Preston sat up and kissed Kyle passionately on the lips, then positioned the head of Kyle's cock right at his asshole. It was still slick with his saliva, and he slid down the length of the dick in one slow and deliberate move. When every inch of Kyle was inside him, he squeezed his ass, and smiled as Kyle moaned his approval.

"Untie me now," Kyle said. "I want to hold you as I fuck your ass."

"No," Preston said. "You just lie there and let me fuck your dick."

Kyle's eyes bulged, and he stared at his lover as if he'd never seen him. But he had to admit that his cock hardened even more as Preston kept him tied to the headboard and pinned to the mattress as he rode his cock mercilessly.

They usually switched positions and varied their styles a few times during a sex session, but tonight Preston was hot and wild and restless, and was having a hard time holding back his orgasm. So he gave in to the tingle that shot all the way through his body, and allowed himself to just go with the flow. He leaned down and kissed Kyle, causing his ass to tighten around Kyle's cock when he did. He slid up and down the hard shaft as he kissed his lover, and before long he felt the beginning tingles deep inside his balls. From Kyle's heavy breathing, he could tell he was getting close too.

"I'm close, baby," Kyle moaned, and slammed his cock harder and deeper into Preston's tight ass.

"Me too," Preston said. He slid off Kyle's cock and turned his body around and on top of Kyle's so that his cock hovered over Kyle's head and his own face was only inches from his lover's cock.

"FUUUUUCCCKKKK!" Kyle yelled between clenched teeth. A second later his cock shot three huge spurts of cum onto Preston's face, and then a couple more dribbled onto his own tummy.

Preston licked around his lips to get as much of his partner's cum as possible, and then licked the rest from Kyle's stomach. "Here I cum," he said.

Kyle opened his mouth and took five or six large squirts of Preston's load. More was coming, but Kyle started to gag, so he closed his mouth and let the rest of his lover's load land on his lips and chin and chest. He swallowed the load he'd taken in his mouth, then pulled Preston's cock into his mouth and sucked on it some more, milking every last drop of cum from his thick cock.

"Damn, that was hot," Preston said as he rolled onto his back next to Kyle. He put his arm around his partner, and kissed him.

"Yes, it was," Kyle said, still trying to catch his breath.

"Will you marry me? And fuck me like that at least three or four times a week for the rest of our lives?"

"You already asked me that."

"And what did you say?"

"I said yes." Kyle he smiled and kissed Preston. "But only if you untie me. These straps are starting to hurt."

"Oh fuck," Preston said, and began to untie the straps. "I forgot."

"It's okay. It was a lot of fun."

"And just when did we say we were getting married again?"

"Tomorrow, sweetie. Tomorrow."

"Oh yes, that's right," Preston said, and leaned down to kiss Kyle again. "Then we'd better get some sleep. We have a big day tomorrow."

Kyle laughed and rolled into Preston's arms and hugged him tightly. They fell asleep in one another's arms a couple of minutes later.

"That was one fucking amazing wedding," Kyle said, and kissed Preston lovingly on the lips. They were on the plane, about halfway to Puerto Vallarta, and Kyle was irritated by a few of the passengers who were giving them peculiar looks. "Our honeymoon is gonna be the best damned honeymoon Puerto Vallarta has ever seen," he said, intentionally loud enough for the annoying gawkers to hear. "It'll be one hell of a long time before that city forgets our honeymoon."

And that was a very true statement. They were there for ten days, and the first seven were nothing short of magical. Every day was the same routine for them. Magical, but exactly the same, with minor variations occasionally.

They stayed at a hotel/condo, where every unit was a one-or two-bedroom fully furnished apartment, and just a block and a half from the beach. They slept in until eleven o'clock every morning, and then went immediately down to the beach. The "Blue Chairs" section of Playa de los Muertos beach was the "gay beach" in PV. It was named for the blue lounge chairs used by the owners of the gay hotel and palapas along a section of the beach. The Blue Chairs and the adjoining Green Chairs were famous worldwide for being the gay mecca of Mexico. By noon, the place would be packed like a can of sardines, so Kyle and Preston woke a little earlier than most and got there just in time to get VIP seating under a shaded palapa at the front, closest to the shoreline.

They stayed at the beach, soaking up the sun, soaking up the alcohol, and soaking up the flirtatious attention many of the other men gave them. They even ate lunch right there on the beach. Local vendors swarmed the Blue Chairs area because it was a well-known fact that the gay tourists in PV were very generous. They easily supported a dozen or more of the more popular and gregarious vendors to the point that the vendors didn't need a second job, unlike most other people. Kyle and Preston got caught up in the energy of the beach culture, and bought much more than they should have. Kyle bought Preston a couple of ankle bracelets and a gorgeous handmade beaded mosaic painting of a sunset along the PV beach. Preston bought Kyle some handmade leather sandals, a couple of shirts, and a tiger's eye choker.

One afternoon they took a horseback tour into the foothills around town, and another afternoon they went on a snorkeling excursion that took them to a private island where all the gay boys had a barbecue and played volleyball in the nude and snuck off to private spots on the island.

But other than that, their afternoons were spent shopping and having at blast at the happy hour at Vallarta Cora, a gay condo/hotel just a few blocks from the beach. Happy hour was from four to eleven, and was always packed with a line out the door. The bar was situated around the pool, which sat in the middle of the court-yard surrounded by apartments. It was a clothing-optional resort, and most people at happy hour opted for no clothing. Guests who actually stayed at the hotel had a habit of being naked in their rooms with their doors left open as the night grew later, so the place became more of a bathhouse than a hotel. Everything was al-lowed here: drinks in the pool, balloons and balls in the pool, sex in the pool. And all of that was allowed, and taken advantage of, in every other corner of the resort as well. The newlyweds spent a lot of time there, and made many new friends.

They'd leave the Cora at about eight o'clock, run back to their condo, shower and change for dinner, and afterward head out to the clubs. One club or another would feature strippers or a drag show or both, or some other form of entertainment that kept the clubs packed to the rafters—and the clubs in PV stayed open until four in the morning.

Paradise Lost happened on day eight. Kyle sensed trouble the moment they walked into Paco Paco's, their favorite club. On that particular night, the club was hosting both a drag show and a strip-per show. One of the strippers, a beautiful, young Latino boy named Christian, took an immediate liking to Preston, and wasn't shy about letting Preston and everyone else know, including Kyle, who was less than happy about it. And if Preston had a type . . . which he did . . . it was exactly this kid. Clad in nothing but a leopard-print loincloth and a shitload of hardened and oiled muscles, Christian spent a lot of time rubbing up against Preston, even though Preston didn't put any money in his pouch. He had a huge uncut cock, and as strippers do in Mexico, pulled it out when it was fully hard. When Preston gasped, Christian grabbed Preston's hand and wrapped it around his big, thick cock, then kissed Preston fully on the lips.

"Oh, HELL no," Kyle said, and grabbed Preston's hand from

Christian's cock and pulled them apart. "He's mine," Kyle said as he stood between the two.

Christian shrugged and moved on to work the rest of the crowd for tips.

"What the fuck was that all about?" Kyle asked.

"What?" Preston said. "I didn't do anything. I didn't even give him any money. He was just all over me. There was nothing I could do about it."

"Bullshit," Kyle said angrily. "You could have moved away and said you have a boyfriend. A husband, now, in fact. That's what you could've done."

"I'm sorry, okay baby." Preston said. "I guess I just got caught up in the moment."

"Yeah? Well, if you wanna keep your nuts, you'd better learn to distance yourself from the moment."

"I'm sorry," Preston said again, and gave Kyle a kiss.

They left the back part of the bar, where the stripper show was, and headed back to the drag show in the main area of the bar. Kyle had a very bad temper, but could also let go of something when an apology was put on the table. They watched the drag show and danced a little. Then Kyle went to the bar to get a couple of drinks.

"Hey, I didn't mean to get you into trouble back there," a very sexy voice with a thick Mexican accent whispered into Preston's ear from behind.

He turned around and stared right into Christian's face. He was dressed in jeans and a tank top now, and looked just as good as he did naked. "Oh, you didn't get me into trouble," he said hurriedly, then looked at Kyle across the room. There was a huge line of people waiting for drinks. "He gets a little jealous every now and then, but it's all good. No problems. Besides, he's not my boss. I'm a big boy."

"Yes, I can see that," Christian said, and looked Preston up and down. He glanced over at the bar, too. "It looks like he'll be at least another fifteen minutes. Wanna come with me for a few minutes?"

He took Preston by the hand and led him through the crowd. Preston opened his mouth to say something, but then closed it quickly. He knew he was going through with this. Christian led him to a room upstairs in the back of the bar, and closed the door behind him.

"I'm not sure . . ." Preston pretended to protest.

Christian pushed him up against a wall and kissed him on the lips. It'd been a very long time since anyone other than Kyle had kissed Preston, and he drank it in like a fine wine. Christian's lips were full and soft, and tasted faintly of beer. When he slid his tongue into Preston's mouth, Preston sucked on it greedily, and his cock hardened instantly.

"I want you, *papi*," Christian said, as he slid his tank top over his head and kicked his jeans to the floor. His thick uncut cock was already fully hard and throbbing in front of him.

Preston dropped to his knees and licked at the head, savoring the taste of the large drops of precum that seeped from the tip. He took the entire head into his mouth and licked around it with his tongue. When Christian moaned his approval, Preston opened his throat and swallowed the entire cock deep into his throat.

Christian grabbed Preston by the head and fucked his mouth fast and hard. It was obvious he wasn't looking for tender loving that night. "That's it, baby, suck my fat cock," he said in his thick Mexican accent.

Preston held on to Christian's legs and sucked his cock as expertly as he'd ever done. He loved big cocks, and was adept at taking them deep down his throat and deep into his ass with equal talent. Christian's cock slid all the way inside his throat and pulled back out only after his pubic hair tickled Preston's nose.

"Fuck, *papi*," Christian grunted, and pulled his cock out of Preston's mouth quickly, "I'm gonna cum!"

Just then the door flew open, and Kyle stood in the middle of the doorway, staring at the two of them. Preston was fully clothed, and on his knees in front of Christian, who was naked and hard, and pumping his cock right at Preston's face.

"What the FUCK is going on here?" Kyle yelled into the room.

"Oh, fuck," Christian yelled. His whole body stiffened as he sprayed his load all over Preston's face and past it onto the floor behind him.

Preston just sat there, blinking as each spurt of cum splashed across his face, and watched as his lover watched, stunned, a few feet away.

When Christian finished emptying his load, he picked up his clothes and quickly pushed his way past Kyle without saying a word to either of the two American tourists.

Kyle just stood in the doorway, watched Christian hurry past him and down the stairs, then looked back at Preston. He was having a hard time catching his breath, and tears threatened to overwhelm him, but he bit down on his molars and forced them back. He would not cry over this.

"I'm so sorry," Preston said, as he began to wipe the huge load of cum from his face.

"You're sorry?" Kyle asked. "Some fucking stranger comes up to me and tells me that a trashy local hooker has just seduced my husband and I'd better go stop it, and all you can say to me is 'I'm sorry'?"

"I don't know what else to say."

"Well, at least you have that saving grace. Because if you think there is something you *could* actually say to explain this or make it better, then you'd be a complete fucking idiot. And so would I for ever having believed in you."

Kyle turned around and left the room. Preston saw him descend the stairs, and then he was out of sight.

Preston sat there for a moment, wiping his face, and trying to collect his thoughts. How could he have been so stupid? He was in love with Kyle. Madly in love with him. How could he have done this to the person he cared the most about?

"He left," Christian said from the doorway. "Stormed out the door. He's pretty mad."

"Gee, I wonder why?" Preston asked.

"You can spend the night with me if you want. I don't think it's gonna be very pleasant at your hotel room tonight."

"Thanks," Preston said as he stood up and brushed off his jeans. "But I think you've done enough for one night."

"I'm really sorry," Christian said as he grabbed Preston by the arm. "I really didn't mean to start any trouble. I just thought you were hot and I was a little out of control tonight. I didn't mean any harm."

"It's not your fault," Preston said, and kissed Christian one last time. "It's mine. I'm the one who should have had boundaries. You're amazing, by the way."

"Thanks."

Preston left the club and walked the ten blocks back to the hotel.

The moment he opened the door, he heard Kyle crying in the bedroom. His heart sunk to the pit of his stomach and he felt like vomiting. Watching his lover cry was the hardest thing he'd ever had to do, and in their five years together, he'd never once made Kyle cry. He walked to the bedroom door and knocked lightly.

"Don't even think about it," Kyle said.

"Baby, please. I just want to . . ."

"I can't deal with you right now. There are pillows and blankets on the sofa."

"Can't we just . . ."

"I swear to God, if you say another word, I'm gonna get up and leave. And I can't promise that this time you'll be able to find me."

Preston dropped his head and leaned against the closed bedroom door. "I love you," he said. When there was no response, he walked to the sofa and curled into a fetal position, fully clothed, and fell asleep.

* * *

The next morning Preston awakened to the smell of eggs and chorizo, and strong coffee. He was a bit confused. Where was he? What day was it? Then he looked around the room and remembered where he was. And why he was sleeping on the sofa and why Kyle was cooking breakfast and not sleeping beside him or getting ready to hit the beach.

"Coffee's ready, and the eggs will be in a couple of minutes," Kyle said from behind him in the kitchen.

"You didn't have to make breakfast." Preston stood and stretched to get the kinks out of his muscles.

"Yes, I did. I saw the frying pan there and thought I'd better start cooking some eggs or I'd find a better use for it while you were sleeping defenselessly."

"Kyle, I am so sorry . . ."

Kyle turned around and stared at Preston with that look that always stopped him in his tracks, and Preston shut up.

"Go shower and brush your teeth," Kyle said. "I'll pour you a cup of coffee and fix you a plate of eggs. We'll talk over breakfast. Make it a fast shower."

Preston did, and when they were sitting across the table from one another, he'd never felt like they'd been farther apart. From day one their relationship had been magic. They were that one "wonder couple" that every group of friends had and envied and wanted to be like. They were deeply in love and never fought over anything. So this was totally foreign territory for Preston.

"You hurt me last night," Kyle said, as he sipped his coffee and looked Preston directly in the eyes.

Preston felt like he'd been stabbed in the heart. "I know. And I truly am sorry."

"Do you love me?"

"Of course I love you," Preston almost choked on his eggs. "What kind of question is that?"

"A better question is, if you love me, why did you cheat on me? And especially on our honeymoon."

"Oh, God, I love you, Kyle," Preston said, and started to stand up.

"Sit down."

Preston sat down and poked his eggs around the plate for a moment. "Okay, so here's what I feel," he said, and pushed the plate away. "You and I are amazing. I've never known anything like this, and neither have you, and neither has anyone we know. We are *too* good together."

"What the hell does that mean?"

"It means that sometimes we're just too damned good and nice and sweet and . . . predictable."

Kyle gasped.

"Well, we are. Everything is so goddammed by the book and perfect with us. We don't smoke, we don't drink very much at all, we don't do drugs, we don't throw wild parties. We're clean and we're good and we're nice."

"And this is a bad thing?"

"Yes," Preston said a little too quickly. "I mean, no. It's not a bad thing. But sometimes I have the urge not to be quite so perfect. I grew up in a different era than you did, baby. Things were different for me."

"You never did drugs or smoked or partied before you met me. You're the cleanest guy I've ever met. That's one of the things that attracted me to you."

"You're right. I never did any of that stuff. But I did have a lot of sex with a lot of different guys. And that variety brought something special and unique to my life."

Kyle's eyes dropped, and Preston could see he'd hurt his boyfriend again.

"Don't get me wrong. I love you and sex with you is incredible. But after five years, it's beginning to get a little predictable and routine. I can't have predictable and routine in my life, and neither can you."

"You're right. I can't. But for me it hasn't gotten there yet. For me, every time we fuck it's a new experience, and an exciting one."

"God, you're incredible. Thank you for saying that. Especially for me, at my age."

"Well, it's true."

"The thing is, I didn't know I was feeling this way either, until last night. I mean, I guess I'd felt for the past few months that we were stuck in a little bit of a routine, but I didn't really think about it. But last night, when Christian showed me some attention . . .'"

"He did more than show you some attention."

"I know. But don't get pissy, please. Just hear me through. Then yell at me all you want if you still want. But at least hear me out."

Kyle took another drink of coffee and stared at Preston.

"When he came on to me and wanted me in that way, it made me feel alive. It made me feel hot and sexy and wanted."

"And I don't make you feel those things?"

"Yes, you do. But it's you. I expect it from you. I haven't expected it from anyone else in a very long time. So when it happened, I lost control. I couldn't help myself. He wanted me."

"And you wanted him," Kyle said.

"Yes. I'm not going to lie. I did want him. I didn't want to love him or be with him for the rest of my life. But I wanted him sexually. And when it happened, I have to tell you, a part of me came alive that I thought had died long ago. I know that's not what you want to hear, baby, and I'm sorry. But that's what I'm feeling."

"Do you love him?"

"Don't be ridiculous. I don't even like him. I just wanted to suck his cock."

"And if he'd wanted to fuck you?"

"Yeah, I'd have wanted that too."

Kyle's eyes never left Preston's. "Do you love me?" he asked softly.

"More than I've ever loved anyone in my life. You are my soul, baby."

Kyle stood up and walked over to Preston, and straddled his legs as he sat in his lover's lap. "Then what are we gonna do about this?"

"I don't know."

"I don't want to lose you, Preston. I want to work on this. I want to do whatever it takes to make you and me last forever."

Preston swallowed hard and fought back tears. "Me too."

"So how about this?" Kyle said. "New rules. Number one: We always be honest and communicate our feelings, especially if they're about us feeling like we're growing apart."

"Agreed."

"Rule number two: Let's start spicing things up a little in the bedroom. Let's get some toys and handcuffs and bondage stuff and have some fun. And let's start adding other guys to our sex life. I think that will add a positive element for us."

"Are you sure?" Preston asked. He'd never heard Kyle talk like this and had never even imagined hearing words like this come from his mouth.

"Yes. And rule number three: We never play with other people alone, without each other."

"I can do that."

"Good. Now kiss me and then take me to bed and make love to me. Just me this time."

Preston held Kyle close to him, and kissed him more passionately than he'd thought possible. Then he picked him up and carried him into the bedroom.

The Kit Kat Club was a hip and energetic restaurant/lounge in the heart of the Zona Romantica, the area in which ninety percent of the gay establishments in Puerto Vallarta, as well as the gay beach, were located. The décor was bright recessed neon lighting with modern chic avant-garde. They were known not only for the fine food they served, but for the creative martini list that "exceeds 100 delectable delights" and the festive staff and atmosphere that kept people waiting over an hour for a table.

"Wow, this place is incredible," Kyle said, as they were seated. He leaned over and kissed Preston on the mouth.

Preston returned the kiss and thought how lucky he was. He knew Kyle was trying really hard to put the night before behind him, and really work at making their relationship meaningful and successful. If the situation were reversed, he knew there was no way he'd have been able to forgive Kyle and move on. Though they were very similar in so many ways, they were different in a few, and this was one area in which they were very different. Preston held a grudge forever, and found it hard it forgive—and even harder to move on.

"Welcome to the Kit Kat Club," the waiter said as he opened their napkins and placed them in Kyle and Preston's laps. "My name's Chad, and I'll be serving you this evening. Can I get you a glass of wine or a cocktail while you browse the menu?"

Preston couldn't help but notice the way Kyle stared at Chad as he spoke. The waiter was standing right next to him, so Preston scooted back an inch or two so he could get a better look. He instantly knew why Kyle was looking at him so intently. Chad was beautiful, and exactly the type of man Kyle would consider the perfect specimen. He was in his late twenties, with dark blond hair and green eyes. His tall frame was lean, but muscular. He was obviously American, but tanned beautifully, as all locals and transplants there were. When he smiled, his eyes sparkled, and dimples popped out on either side of his thin pink lips.

He looked nothing like Preston, but everything like all the boys Kyle commented on when they talked about perfect boys, as they often did. Preston felt a little jealousy build up inside him, but forced it away. He, of all people, could not be jealous. Especially that night.

"I'll have a glass of Shiraz, please," Preston said.

"Me too," Kyle said.

"Excellent." Chad winked at Kyle and squeezed Preston's shoulder as he walked away.

"Did you see that?" Kyle asked.

"Yeah. He apparently thinks you're adorable. And I can't say I blame him. You are. And he certainly isn't bad on the eyes, either."

"Right?" Kyle said, barely able to conceal his excitement. "But then he flirted with you too. I saw that little squeeze on the shoulder."

"Ah, he was humoring me to keep me from being upset at winking at you. He can tell I'm the jealous bitchy type."

"Shhh, here he comes," Kyle said, and grabbed a menu and pretended to read.

"Here you are, gentlemen," Chad said as he set a glass in front of both them. "I'll give you a moment to check out the menu, and then come back for your order."

Kyle and Preston stared at him unabashedly.

"Let me help you with this, though," Chad said, and turned Kyle's menu right side up and handed it back to him. "It might make narrowing your choices down a little easier." He smiled and winked at both of them before walking away.

"Oh, my god," Kyle said, "I'm so embarrassed. How fucking stupid of me."

Preston laughed. "Don't worry about it. He's probably used to it. He is gorgeous. And he certainly knew how to handle the situation gracefully."

"Well, I could just die," Kyle said, and buried his face into his menu.

Dinner was amazing, and Preston noticed Chad was making extra trips to their table and paying them special attention. He made a point of touching them both quite a bit, and was very playful with them. When he insisted they try his two favorite desserts, compliments of him, of course, Preston knew something was brewing. He was about to bring it up himself, when once again, Kyle surprised him.

"What do you think about asking him to come back to our place when he gets off work?" Kyle asked as he bit into the bananas Foster.

"What?" Preston couldn't believe his ears. Kyle had always been the shy one, always a step behind Preston and the one to agree or disagree, but usually agree, to Preston's suggestions. Now he was taking charge and suggesting their first three-way only a few hours after they'd discussed opening their relationship up to that possibility.

"I think he's adorable, and I know you do too. And he's obviously flirting with us. We said we should add some spice to our relationship and bring others in to play every now and then. What better place to start than here? We'll never see him again after this weekend, so if it goes bad, it won't matter. I'm sure he'd be up for it. I just get that vibe. What do you say?"

"You like this guy?" Preston asked, even though he knew the answer.

"Yeah. He's very cute. I think it'd be hot."

"And I won't have to worry about you leaving me for him?"

Kyle stared at Preston with that one look that at the same time silenced him completely and made him feel like a three-year-old.

"I'm sorry. That was stupid of me. I think he's hot. Let's do it."

When Chad started toward them with the check, Kyle kicked Preston under the table.

"Was everything satisfactory, gentlemen?" Chad asked.

"It was great," Preston said, and took the check as he pulled out his wallet.

"Chad, we were wondering..." Kyle said quickly, and then stopped to work up enough saliva to swallow.

"Yes?"

"... if you'd like to come back to our hotel when you get off your shift tonight."

Preston held his breath as he handed the check and some money to Chad.

"Thank god," Chad said, as he took the bill. "I thought you guys were gonna be another one of those shy hot couples that never works up the nerve to ask. We are all encouraged to be very friendly and fun with our customers here at Kit Kat, but the house rule is that we can never be the one to come out and make the proposition. We can accept any and all invitations—we just can't be the one to make them."

Preston and Kyle both looked at him, neither blinking nor breathing.

"I'd love to join you two for some fun. Can you hang around for a couple of drinks and wait for me?"

"Absolutely," Preston said, and smiled, as he heard Kyle finally take a breath.

"Right on. Sit tight. Drinks are on me. I'm the first waiter to close out, so I should be done in about an hour. Then we can head out." He winked at them again, and walked back to finish closing out the rest of his station.

"Oh, my god. Are we really gonna do this?" Kyle said.

"Yeah, it looks like we really are."

"I've never done anything like this. I don't know if I'll be able to get it up."

Preston laughed. "Give me a break, baby. First of all, you're twenty-eight years old. Secondly, you got rock hard the very first night we met just by me kissing your neck."

"Yeah, but that was you. Of course I'm gonna get hard with *you* kissing any part of me."

"God, I love you," Preston said, and meant it. "But Chad is ten times hotter than I am. And he's exactly your type. Thanks for the compliment, but don't kid yourself. You'll be hard before we get back to the hotel."

Kyle blushed and smiled.

"Oh, fuck. You're hard right now, aren't you?" Preston asked.

Kyle started laughing and waved at the bartender for another round of drinks.

"It's a great night out," Chad said as the three of them walked into the apartment and through the living room. "Let's do it out on the balcony. I love fucking with the sound of the waves crashing against the beach."

Kyle and Preston followed Chad out onto the large balcony, being led like two little boys into a candy shop.

Out on the balcony, Chad stripped his shirt off and kicked his shorts to the floor. He'd obviously been in this position before. He pushed Kyle against the railing, and with one hand on the shoulder, gently pushed Preston to his knees in front of him.

Chad's cock was already hard, and throbbed in front of Preston's face. Preston licked at the head and sucked on it as he looked up and watched Chad kissing his lover. He wanted to be hurt or angry or jealous, but he didn't feel any of that. Instead, he was turned on more than he could have imagined.

Kyle returned Chad's kisses tentatively at first, but when he looked down and saw Preston sucking Chad's cock and winking at him, he kissed Chad more enthusiastically. He'd thought about what it would feel like to be in a three-way before, but hadn't really given it too much thought. Though few people ever believed him, he was pretty conservative when it came to sex, and always had been. He'd been told many times he was way too hot not to be into some kink and group action. He'd thought about arguing his point, but the truth was, the image people had of him was much sexier and more flattering, so he'd never denied it.

But now, as he stood naked out on the balcony, kissing a stranger and watching his lover of five years sucking the same guy's cock, he felt hot and sexy and slutty and nastier than he'd ever felt. He had to admit, it felt pretty damned good, too. His cock was hard and demanding attention, so Chad finished the kiss and dropped to his knees to suck his dick.

This waiter's mouth was hot and tight and had the suction power of a Dyson. He swallowed Kyle's cock and sucked on it greedily for a while, and then slid his lips up and down its length. As Chad sucked his cock, Preston stood and straddled Chad's back and kissed Kyle on the lips.

"Are you okay with this?" Preston whispered softly into his ear after kissing him for a moment.

Kyle moaned loudly, and his body stiffened. He grabbed Preston and pulled him tightly to his body as convulsions racked through him. He unloaded himself into Chad's throat and hugged Preston so tight he knew he had to be hurting his lover. It felt like he was shooting a gallon of cum down the guy's throat, and when Chad didn't even gag or come up for air, Kyle had to force himself not to laugh. Because that's what he did when he was nervous. He laughed.

"Fuck, dude, that was hot," Chad said, as he wiped his lips and stood up.

"You're not fucking kidding, it was hot," Preston said.

"Your boyfriend has a fantastic cock."

"Yeah, I kinda like it myself," Preston said, and kissed Kyle.

"Can you stay hard?" Chad asked Kyle.

"That definitely won't be a problem," Kyle said.

"Good. Because your boyfriend's ass looks really fucking amazing and I want to fuck it."

Kyle and Preston looked at each other, and Chad could see the tension and the hesitation. "I know some couples will only fuck each other, so if that's the game, that's cool too. But I'd love to fuck your ass," Chad said to Preston, "while your stud of a boyfriend fucks my brains out."

"Yes!" Kyle and Preston blurted at the same time.

"Good," Chad said. He leaned Preston forward against the rail of the balcony and bent him over, then leaned down and licked his ass.

Preston moaned and wriggled his ass against Chad's hot tongue, and watched as Chad beat off Kyle. He had always loved Kyle's cock and was amazed at how hard it got and how it could stay hard after coming once or even twice sometimes. And right then it looked like it was about to shoot off another load just from being fisted by Chad as the waiter rimmed his ass.

As he licked and sucked on Preston's ass, Chad reached into the pocket of his shorts and pulled out two condoms. He handed one to Kyle, and stood and slid the other one on his own cock.

Preston's ass was well-lubed with the masterful rimming he'd gotten from Chad, so when Chad positioned the head of his cock at Preston's hole and gently pushed forward, his cock slid right in. Preston moaned loudly and bit down on his bottom lip. Though not the biggest cock he'd ever taken, it was certainly impressive, and with only spit to serve as lube and it was not the easiest task to take it all in one stroke. But he did it. When Chad was all the way inside him, he tightened his ass muscles around the big dick and leaned back to kiss the waiter on the lips.

Chad rested his dick inside Preston's warm ass as Kyle moved behind him. He expected the kid to spit on his cock and slide it inside him, because that had been his experience with young guys and because Kyle seemed anxious and ready to explode. So he was surprised when Kyle knelt down and licked around his ass for a few minutes. It wasn't the most expert rim job he'd ever gotten, but it was good enough, and combined with the feeling of his throbbing cock buried inside Preston's ass, he was on fire. He moaned and wriggled his ass around Kyle's tongue, while he slid his cock in and out of Preston's ass, and all three men moaned loudly.

Kyle stood and pushed his dick against Chad's ass crack. Chad stopped humping Preston, and stood still as Kyle pressed the head of his cock against his hole and then slid it slowly inside. Kyle took his time sliding his cock into Chad's ass, and Chad closed his eyes and leaned his head back as he savored the feel of every inch sliding into him.

When Kyle was buried all the way inside Chad, and Chad was

buried inside Preston, all three men took a moment to breathe and relax and get used to the feel of their bodies working with one another.

And then they fucked. Chad started first, sliding his cock in and out of Preston's ass, which in turn caused his own ass to slide up and down the length of Kyle's cock. Then Kyle fell into the rhythm and the three men rammed into and onto each other as if they'd been doing it all their lives. Their moans couldn't be contained, and filled the quiet Puerto Vallarta night. Before long they noticed a few of their neighbors had come out onto their balconies and were watching the action, and a couple of them beat off as they watched the trio going at it.

"Fuck, dudes, I'm gonna cum," Chad said loudly. He tried to pull out of Preston's ass, but Kyle moaned louder and pressed Chad's shoulders into Preston's back, causing him to shove himself deeper inside Preston. The feel of his entire torso pressed up against Preston's hot back, and his cock being squeezed tightly by Preston's ass was too much. He felt several shots of cum shoot through his cock, and he grunted loudly with each spurt.

"I'm cumming too," Kyle tried hard not to yell. He pulled out of Chad's ass and ripped off the condom, throwing it to the ground.

Preston saw two giant wads of cum fall from above his head and drop to the ground. Then three large shots of warm cum hit his neck. Chad was still buried deep inside him, pressed tightly against his back, and hugging him from both sides. Preston felt Chad's head resting just below where the shots of Kyle's cum had hit his neck. A second later he heard Chad moan and felt him thrust his now softening cock deeper inside his ass. He knew that Chad was being turned on by feeling the remainder of Kyle's huge load land on his back.

Kyle's knees gave out and he dropped to the floor of the balcony. Chad pulled his soft cock out of Preston's ass and shakily sat next to Kyle. Preston turned around and faced the two young men. His cock was bigger and harder and redder than he could ever remember it being.

"It's my turn, boys," Preston said, as he pointed his cock at them. "Are you ready?"

"Fuck yeah," Chad said, and opened his mouth.

"Give it to me, baby," Kyle said, and leaned his head in so that he and Chad were cheek-to-cheek.

Preston was already so close, it only took a couple of strokes. "Here I cum," he said between gritted teeth. He always came a lot, but this load surprised even him. He showered both men until their faces were covered in his cum. Several drops landed in Chad's mouth, and he swallowed it and licked his lips for more. Most of the part that landed on Kyle's face hit his eyes and forehead, but he too got some on his lips and licked at it hungrily.

His legs gave out before he was finished shooting, and Preston fell to the floor and joined his lover and the waiter as the last couple of drops of his load hit the ground.

"Fuuuuuuuck," Chad whispered, as he tried to catch his breath.

"That was really hot," Kyle said, and pulled Preston to him. They hugged and kissed each other for a moment, and then pulled Chad down to join in on the kiss.

"You're welcome to stay the night," Preston said, as the quiet of the night and the several martinis they'd had earlier began to kick in. He was fading quickly, and he knew it was only a matter of minutes before Kyle would be snoring.

"Thanks," Chad said, "but I gotta get home. My boyfriend is gonna be wondering where I am. I'm not usually this late getting home."

"All right," Kyle said. "Well, thanks for tonight. It was fun."

"Fun?" Chad said. "It was hotter than hell. If you're in town for a few more days, come back by for dinner. We can definitely do this again."

He got up and dressed, and left a free meal coupon on the table as he left. Kyle and Preston didn't even bother to get up and move to the bedroom. They just hugged each other, naked in the warm Mexican night, and slept on the balcony.

"I can't believe it's over already," Kyle said, as he looked out the window and watched Puerto Vallarta grow smaller as the plane lifted off the runway and rose into the air.

"I know. It went way too fast." Preston was feeling so many emotions at once. He was elated. He'd married the man he loved more than anything, and they'd had an awesome honeymoon. But he'd also cheated and betrayed the man he loved, and hurt him. Yet he was forgiven, and Kyle let him know that he was loved more than ever. And now they'd discussed the next phase of their relationship. It would be exciting to add some spice and some new men to their relationship every once in awhile. But could that excitement possibly lead to him losing Kyle? Would Kyle discover that the twenty-year age difference really did matter and that he could have more fun with someone his own age?

"What are you thinking?" Kyle asked.

"Nothing," Preston said sadly.

"I love you. You do know that, right?" Preston had never been able to lie to Kyle. He knew exactly what his lover was thinking.

"Yes."

"And what happened with us here is a good thing. I know you need this new arrangement, because of all of your experiences. I don't need them, I don't need anyone else but you. But that does not make you a bad person. Please know I don't think that of you. You need excitement and fun and spice and variety. That's cool. And trust me, I liked it. I thought it was fun, and I will enjoy it when we do it again."

"I can't help feeling kinda bad about it," Preston said.

Kyle reached over and held his lover's hand. "Don't feel bad. We're all different people, and we all have different needs. I'm very lucky. I know a lot of guys like you who are so wrapped up in their need for excitement and variety that they can't ever settle down and love just one person. You can and you have with me, so if you want a little extra excitement every now and then, I can handle that."

"You're amazing," Preston said, and kissed Kyle on the lips.

"Just remember the rules of the game. Always communicate and be honest with each other. Spice things up in the bedroom, with or without bringing someone else into our bed, and only play with others together."

"I can definitely do that. And thank you for understanding me and for being such a damned amazing partner."

"It's not hard at all. Going through life with you by my side is the greatest journey and most exciting dream I could hope for."

They kissed and leaned in together to watch the last view of Puerto Vallarta disappear below the clouds.

PART IV

If I Could Turn Back Time
. . . I Wouldn't

I watched Kyle struggle with his tie from across the room. He hated very few things more than having to dress up, and never really got the hang of tying a necktie. It's not that he couldn't have gotten the hang of it; he just refused to do so. I could count the number of people I knew who were more stubborn than me on one hand, and Kyle was definitely one of them. Fucking Geminis. You can never reason with them because reasoning isn't a priority with them. Nor can you convince them of anything they aren't already convinced of, because they are never wrong. I know because I am also a Gemini, and I'm always right.

"Let me help you with that," I said, as I walked up behind him and wrapped my arms around his neck. His face was already beginning to redden as I took the two ends of the tie from him and looped them around his neck.

"I don't know why I have to do this," he grumbled. "I'm seventy-three fucking years old. You'd think I would have a say in my own goings-on at this point in my life."

"Oh, shut up. You're a spring chicken. You do have to do this, and you don't have a say in it. So shut up and finish getting dressed."

"This is really stupid, you know," he mumbled.

"*Cariño*, I am ninety-three years old, and you are seventy-three years old. We are a gay couple who has weathered every kind of storm known to man, and have still managed to spend fifty years loving and living together. That is an amazing accomplishment, and our community wishes to celebrate us and throw us an elaborate party."

"Which community is it, this time? I can't keep track."

"All of them," I said. "They're all coming together to make sure this is the social event of the decade. That's no small task, and we should be duly appreciative."

"It's just gonna be a room filled with C and D list celebrities wanting to touch you and hog all your attention and have their picture taken with you so they can brag to their friends that they were 'in your close circle of friends.' It's hideous, really. You write one or two international bestselling novels, and everyone suddenly has to be seen with you. Even as wrinkled and liver-spotted as you are. Truman Capote would not have let himself stoop to this level, I'm sure of that."

"I've written *twelve* international bestselling novels, thank you very much, and am considered one of our country's greatest literary minds. I'm a living legend. And trust me, Truman Capote would not *only* have stooped this low, but he would have organized the party himself."

"I don't like playing these games," Kyle whined.

"Who are you kidding? There are just as many of your fans down there as mine. You weren't the heartthrob of gay cinema for twenty years because you don't like playing games. You thrive on them, and trust me, as soon as you swoosh down that spiral marble staircase, your game face will be on and you'll be charming everyone until the saccharine drips from your oversized pores. You're just grumpy because you didn't have any part in planning any of this, and you aren't in control."

"Damn, you talk a lot."

"I have a lot to say, and I'm old and might not have much time. So I gotta get it all in now, while I still have breath in my lungs."

"It's a good thing you don't lean toward the melodramatic," Kyle said, and turned around and kissed me.

Even to this day, after spending fifty years together, his kisses sent chill bumps up and down my entire body. He didn't even have to tongue me. Just the feel of his lips on mine sent my heart racing. It was a good thing I'd been taking palpitation medication for the past twenty years.

"I love you, Preston."

"And I love you, Kyle."

"Shall we?" he said, and took me by the arm and led me toward the door.

The party was lavish beyond description. You'd have thought Kyle and I were Elizabeth Taylor and Richard Burton back in the day. There were a few successful and out gay couples around by this time. Society had crawled its way slowly toward acceptance, if not embracement, of the gay culture. Famous lesbian couples were everywhere, and had been for half a century. But there were only a handful of gay male couples whose relationships had survived their dual levels of success. And Kyle and I were the only such couple who'd endured the golden fifty years. So society and our friends and our various communities strongly believed we deserved such extravagent treatment.

And I agreed wholeheartedly. Kyle did too, I knew. He'd just never allow himself to admit it.

I was right, though. As soon as we descended the stairs and the applause started, Kyle's patented smile graced his face and he filled the room with his presence. I watched as he was touched and pulled and tugged and led around the room, and was amazed at how beautiful he still was. His Latino heritage had treated him well, and he didn't look a day over fifty. He still had a full head of shiny black hair. His thick (but carefully trimmed) eyebrows and long, thick eyelashes still made gay men of all ages melt. And his full, pink lips puckered and pouted even when he wasn't trying, which drove me wild. When he smiled and his dimples jumped out on his cheeks, I wanted to kiss them and dive into them and never leave.

I watched Kyle mingle and entertain *his* crowd. I could see that every man, and some women in the room fantasized about him. Even at his age. I was the envy of the room, and basked in that distinction as I strolled over to the quieter and slightly less gregarious group of *my* fans and friends.

Whereas Kyle's side of the room was mostly a younger (and by that, I mean the forty-to-sixty-year range) and gayer crowd, mine was a little more mixed. My books all had gay lead characters, but didn't necessarily revolve around gay-themed plots nor hold any gay agenda. I wrote a couple of romantic comedies that did very well, and one book of essays and a memoir that both hit number one on *The New York Times* bestseller list. But my real success was in the horror/psychological thriller genre. After the first, they were all at the top of the bestseller lists even before they were published. And so my "crowd" was quite a bit more eclectic than his. Young, old, in-between. Gay, straight, and in-between. Male, female and . . . in-between.

But both groups were equally pretentious, and try as we may to deny it, both Kyle and I basked in it all.

Silverware clinked against glasses, and I found myself being nudged toward the stage at the front of the room. I looked over and saw Kyle was also being ushered in that direction.

"Ladies and gentlemen," the mayor announced loudly, and the room quieted immediately. "We're here tonight to honor two great men, and undoubtedly the best role models this city, or any city for that matter, could ever hope to have."

The room erupted in applause. Kyle leaned in and hugged me.

"We gave them the key to the city years ago, we've made them honorary mayors, we've asked them to grand marshal more parades than anyone has a right to ask, and they've stepped up to the plate and made us proud every single time. So, tonight we aren't asking any favors or bestowing any honorary honors, or anything else. Tonight we just want to celebrate the lives of two truly great men, and one amazing couple."

Another thunderous round of applause, and this time Kyle cupped my face in his hands and kissed me tenderly on the lips. The crowd clapped louder and a few people wiped tears from their eyes.

I knew Kyle would get into it once he was on stage. Not that he didn't mean and feel every second of his affection and action toward me, because there was never a doubt in my mind that he did. But he thrived in front of an audience.

"How about a few words from our favorite sons?" the mayor asked, and handed the mic over to Kyle.

"Thank you all so much for coming out tonight to celebrate with Preston and me, and to share in the joy of this evening."

I watched in wonderment as my lover spoke to and enchanted the crowd. He made them laugh, made them cry, and left them wanting more. He truly was a gifted actor. But underneath all the polished training and careful diction, he meant every word he said, and that's what really endeared people to him.

". . . And so, thank you again for being part of such a special night for us. But I'm just a silly old actor. I'm gonna turn it over to the guy who is really good with words. Baby, it's all yours," Kyle said as he handed me the mic.

More applause and whistles and cat calls, which seemed ridiculous to me. At ninety-three, I felt like I should want the crowd to quietly clap their forefingers against the insides of their wrists to keep from startling me. But I was energetic and loud and boisterous, and had a reputation for being a ham, so the crowd knew exactly how to behave around me.

"Really good with words?" I asked, as I took a sip of my wine and winked at Kyle. "I was just gonna ask everyone to really drink up fast and get out so we can get to bed and fuck. I'm horny as hell tonight."

The audience cracked up, and a few people spat out their drinks as laughter erupted from their mouths. It's not like anything was unexpected. I'd always had a flair for shocking people, and though my fame came with legit mainstream books, I'd gotten my start writing porn, and most everyone knew it and expected me to go for the shock factor.

"Seriously, folks, thank you for being here tonight. Kyle and I have been blessed to have you in our lives." Looking over the crowd, I saw a few of the men we'd shared our bed with over the years. A few of them were guys we'd slept with only a few times, but a few more were men we'd regularly shared our bed and a good part of our lives with. We'd never even entertained the thought of having a committed three-way relationship, but there were four or five guys that we saw regularly for a couple of years each. They'd brought renewed energy and new perspectives to our relationship, and we remained good friends with all of them.

"At our ages and having been together for such an amazingly long time, we've obviously experienced some tough times. There were times when we didn't think we could go on. That life was too hard or that being in a committed relationship was too hard, or that achieving the level of fame we both did was too hard."

I looked over at Kyle and felt my eyes mist up. He'd always teased me about being so emotional, so I was determined to get through this speech without crying. I took another sip of wine and continued.

"But whenever we felt like that, we remembered the magic that brought us together in the first place. You've all heard the story a million times, so I won't bore you with it again. But it was truly magic. When we felt like we couldn't take one more minute of each other, we turned to you, our friends. You always kept us on track and reminded us that our being together was not a choice. It was fate. Thank you for that."

Kyle cleared his throat, and when I looked over at him, he smiled and raised his left eyebrow. That was my signal to wrap it up.

"So . . . thank you for coming. Eat all the food, drink all the booze, and have fun. But do it in a hurry, because I took my Viagra half an hour ago and that crap about lasting four hours is bullshit!"

Everyone laughed, and we all returned to the festivities. It wasn't long before the party began to die down, and an hour after I finished my speech, the place was cleared out, and Kyle and I retired to bed.

We crawled into our giant, king-sized bed and settled beneath the heavy, hand-embroidered comforter. Kyle leaned over and kissed me on the lips, told me he loved me, and rolled onto his right side, with his back to me.

I hadn't really taken any Viagra that night, and in fact, I hadn't taken Viagra in close to six months. I always kept a supply around, just in case. But they were more for my ego and pride than for my penis. But as I lay in bed, reflecting on the evening and reminiscing about the incredible life Kyle and I had shared, I found myself getting hard even without the aid of the little blue pill. It'd been so long since I'd had any erection, let alone one so hard and without the aid of pharmaceuticals, that I had to pull back the blanket and make sure I was feeling what I thought I was feeling.

Yesirree, I was. My cock was rock hard and throbbed against my belly. It hurt a little, but also felt wonderfully exciting.

I rolled over and pulled the top of the blankets back to expose Kyle's lower neck and upper back, and kissed him softly.

"Oh, my god," Kyle said sleepily. "I can't remember the last time you did that. You used to kiss me to sleep like that every single night. But it has to have been at least ten years since you kissed me there."

"Yes, it has been a long time," I said, and moved closer so that I pressed the front of my body against the back of his.

"Holy fuck!" Kyle yelped, and turned around onto his back. "Are you okay, Preston?"

I laughed. "Yes, I'm fine. Better than fine, actually. I have a boner."

"Yes, I can see that. How many of those damned pills did you take, anyway?"

"None."

"You're kidding me," Kyle said, shocked, and looked at me in the eyes.

I smiled.

"You got that fucking hard-on all by yourself? No Viagra?"

"Nope. Just me."

"What's gotten into you, baby?" he asked, and turned around to kiss me.

"You have," I said. "Well, you haven't actually gotten into me in quite some time now, and I'm afraid those days have come and gone long ago."

Kyle laughed and reached down to stroke my still throbbing cock.

"I was just lying here thinking about you and me and how great our life has been. We've both accomplished our dreams and have been very successful. We're richer than we have a right to be. We've both been healthy, for the most part, and have grown old together."

"Speak for yourself," Kyle said as he squeezed my dick and slid his hand up and down it's length.

I hadn't even beat myself off in so long, I'd forgotten how pleasurable it could be. As Kyle stroked and squeezed my cock, I rocked my hips back and forth, reveling in the friction and sensation of his hand bringing me closer to climax.

"God, we were hot back in our day, weren't we?" I said, and

pushed my head farther into the pillow as electric currents ran through my body.

"Back in our day?" Kyle said. "I think we're still pretty damned hot, even in our advanced age. You are a beautiful man, Preston Daugherty. And just look at this hard cock I have in my hand. My god, I know thirty-year-olds who would kill for a cock like this."

"You're sweet," I said lovingly as I closed my eyes and let his hand take me away. "But you're just saying that because you love me."

"You're right," he said. "I do love you. But I'm not saying this to make you feel good or to convince you that I love you. I'm saying this because it's true. You are one hot fucking man, Preston."

"Oh, stop it," I said, and felt myself blush.

"I'm serious. Feel." His hand left my cock and I felt him scoot from under the blankets and move around on the bed. A few seconds later he knelt next to my chest and his hard cock slid gently across my lips.

"Kyle!" I almost shrieked. "What in the world are you doing?"

"I'm showing you that I'm not just saying nice words to you. You fucking turn me on, baby."

I started to say something, but then he lay beside me, with his head at the foot of the bed. A second later I felt his tongue lick the head of my cock. I moaned and tightened my body as his mouth enveloped my cock and he sucked gently up and down.

"Oh my god, baby," I gasped for air.

I vaguely remembered how great a blowjob felt. But it had been so long since we'd been physically intimate that I'd forgotten just how life-altering it could be. Kyle and I had slipped into a comfortable life of lazy luxury. We wined and dined and entertained and traveled. But we fell out of the habit of making love a few years back. We never spoke about it, but just stopped without much hoopla. We hugged and we kissed and we held hands and we bought each other gifts. That's how we showed our love for one another. But I think somewhere down the road we decided we were just too old to fuck anymore, and so we stopped.

But we were wrong.

As Kyle sucked my dick, I pulled his cock closer to my face and sucked it into my mouth. It hadn't shrunk a bit over the years, and it filled my mouth. I could barely fit my lips around it, because *they* had shrunk and become less flexible. But I gave it the old college try and sucked on it as best I could.

Kyle didn't seem to mind, and moaned as he sucked my cock with more fervor as he tried to slip another inch of his dick into my mouth.

I was now bucking my hips fairly excitably, and Kyle could tell I was getting close.

"I want to make love to you," he said as he slid his mouth off my slick cock.

"You have got to be kidding me," I panted, and tried to push him back down to finish me off.

"No, I'm not."

"Baby, I'm ninety-three years old. I cannot get fucked. It's a physical impossibility. I'd break into a million pieces if you tried to shove that pole up my ass."

"Yeah, but I'm only seventy-three. A spring chicken, remember?" he said with that impish chuckle that ensured I'd do anything he asked. "You can fuck me. I won't break. I promise."

"Kyle, I don't think . . ."

"I want you to fuck me, Preston," he said, and leaned down to kiss me, and then got on all fours in the middle of the bed. "Go slow. I may be a spring chicken, but I haven't laid an egg in a very long time."

"Are you sure?" I asked, even as I got into position behind him.

"Think of the money we could get from selling the tape on Ebay."

I laughed for a moment, then held his hips in both hands. I looked down at his ass, and was astounded that even after fifty years, it still made me tremble with desire. Throughout our relationship I had been the bottom for the great majority of the time. But every once in awhile I got the urge to fuck Kyle, and every time I did, it was amazing. Now, as I looked down at his ass in front of me and my cock throbbing impatiently just an inch or so from his crack, I thought I must have died at the party earlier and this was my heaven.

I spat on my cock, and then spat some more on Kyle's ass, and rubbed my dick against his cheeks. Every nerve in my body tingled as I humped his ass cheeks, and I knew that once I entered him, it would only be a matter of minutes before I came. This would not be a marathon.

"Are you just gonna stare at it all night," Kyle asked sarcastically, and turned to smile at me, "or are you going to fuck it?"

I held his hips tightly, more to steady myself than to control him, and pushed my cock head just inside his asshole. I literally heard it pop when it slipped inside.

"Oh, fuck!" Kyle cried out, and squirmed beneath me.

"Should I stop?"

"Don't you fucking dare," he spat out, and took a deep breath as he slid back against my cock. He didn't stop until his ass was pushed against my pelvic bone. "God, you feel so great," he said. "You're filling me up with your big cock."

"Where did you learn to talk like that?" I asked, trying to distract myself from the pleasure that coursed through my cock and my entire body.

"I read your books," Kyle said. "I know you have a bad knee," he said as he slid his ass up and down my cock, "so you just sit there and let me do all the work."

"Like hell," I said, and pulled my dick all the way out of his ass.

"Noooo," he moaned. "Put it back in. Please."

I smiled, and slid my cock back inside his ass. I left it buried deep inside him for a couple of minutes, and then began ramming in and out of him. Okay, so ramming might be a slight exaggeration, but I slid in and out of his ass and fucked him like I remember we used to do. A little slower maybe, and more carefully, but every bit as hot and sensual.

"I can't believe we're doing this," Kyle said as we rediscovered our rhythm and began bumping and grinding against one another. "I wonder if we could be in the *Guinness Book of World Records* for the oldest fuck."

"You talk too fucking much," I said, and fucked him harder. "Shut up and take my cock."

Just hearing those words come from my mouth turned me on a little more than they should have. But when Kyle looked back and winked at me, and told me he loved me that was all I could take.

"I'm gonna cum, *Cariño*," I whispered as I pulled out of his ass. There was a time when I shot my loads all over the place . . . over the heads of the guys I fucked, all over the walls, all over the beds. But that was decades ago, and right then I was content with the couple of spurts that dribbled out of my cock and landed on Kyle's belly directly beneath my cock head. The orgasm felt as intense as any I'd ever had, and I was a very happy man.

"That was so hot, baby," Kyle said, and turned over to lie on his back. "Come here."

I laid my head on his stomach and watched him beat his cock. It only took a couple of tugs before he came. His load wasn't as grand as it had been years earlier, but a couple of shots hit me in the face. I licked them from my lips and wiped the one that hit me in the nose.

"That was incredible," Kyle said, and wrapped his arms around my shoulders.

"I can't believe we just did that," I said.

"Well, we did. And now that we know we can do it still, we're gonna have to make sure we keep in practice."

"I'm not sure I will be able to get hard like that again," I said as I rolled over onto my side of the bed.

"Well, if not naturally, you've got a year's worth of Viagra stockpiled over there. I don't think we'll have to worry about that."

I sighed deeply.

"What's wrong?" Kyle asked.

"I know I'm way too old to get fucked. You'd do some serious damage at this point."

"So?"

"So that means I'm gonna have to become a top. After all these years, I have to become a top. I mean, really. I have a reputation to think about."

We both laughed, and Kyle scooted over to my side of the bed and hugged me. It felt a little weird . . . we'd gotten so used to sleeping on opposite sides of the bed. But in no time at all we were both asleep, wrapped in each other's arms. The last thought I had before drifting off to sleep was that of all of the boys I'd fucked, or all the boyfriends I'd loved, and of the fifty years I'd shared my life and my dreams and my adventures with Kyle . . . none of them was more intimate or special as the feeling of him falling asleep in my arms.

FALL

According to *Dictionary.com* fall/autumn is:

> 1. *The season of the year between* summer *and winter, lasting from the autumnal equinox to the winter solstice and from September to December in the Northern Hemisphere; fall.*

> 2. *A period of maturity verging on decline.*

Already armed with the knowledge that I'm not a fan of the first definitions for the seasons given in the dictionary, I'll once again focus on definition number two. Let me say I'm not a fan of this definition, either. So I looked up the definition in a couple of other dictionaries . . . and they all said the same thing, almost verbatim. Then, I said, "Fuck the dictionaries." I'm thinking outside the box here anyway, remember?

I'm not thinking about natural progression of time across a calendar, but the natural progression of our maturation as human beings, and particularly as sexually and sensually and romantically and erotically positive gay men. As I wrote this book, the season of autumn was a natural progression of moving from the experimental and excitement and thrill-seeking days of summer into a calmer, more mature state of settling down. The men in these stories are in their thirties and forties.

All you gay versions of Jack Nicholson and George Clooney out there, please don't send me hate mail. I know not all gay men get involved to form a couple and that many live very happily as confirmed bachelors all of their lives. It doesn't make them any less significant because they are not partnered. BUT, very many of us gay men do meet the man of our dreams and settle down and become domesticated and grow into an old married couple, as my single and bitter gay friends like to refer to me and my partner.

Gay men in committed and long-term relationships are often over-looked or under-represented or sometimes even invisible. And that's a shame.

So, in keeping with the theme of the book, fall, or autumn, for our purposes is finding ourselves wanting something more out of life than anonymous sex in bathhouses, or one-night stands, or friends with benefits. It's about finding that special someone to share our lives with and to invest enough of ourselves to go through their life's journey with them as well. It's growing from two separate people into a single entity. And just how do we do that without losing ourselves in the process?

When you're part of a couple your perceptions of love and sex and romance and eroticism all change pretty drastically. After having "sexperimented" and having had fun with a variety of hot guys in your youth, you now wake up and go to sleep with the same person every day and night. How do you do that and still find excitement and romance in the relationship?

In these stories, the characters do that in a few different ways. They mix things up a little, add some spice to the marriage, surprise their partners.

Being part of a couple isn't all bouquets of roses and boxes of chocolates. It's hard work. It's disagreeing and fighting and wondering if it is all worth it. It's thinking maybe you'd given up too much, and wishing you were still twenty-one and beautiful and single . . . but realizing you're not and dealing with it. And ultimately, it's coming to the understanding that as you mature and life keeps rolling by . . . it's so much nicer to have someone you love along with you for the journey.

His Special Project

The ending credits rolled across the screen slowly, and I made sure to read every one of them. There wasn't a chance in hell I would recognize any of the names that appeared after the first five principal actors or so. Certainly I wouldn't know who the second assistant to the hair stylist for Ms. Streep was, or the "gaffer," whoever or whatever the hell that was. But I waited until the song ended and the television screen went completely blue before I turned off the DVD player.

Only then did I dare look at the clock on the wall above the bookshelf a few feet from the television.

11:30 p.m.

I sighed and wrapped my arms around my chest and tried with valiant effort not to cry. It was Thursday evening, which meant Robert would be walking in the door in about an hour and a half, with a shit-eating grin on his face. It had been exactly the same routine every Tuesday and Thursday for the past two months.

"Honey, I've got this really important project to work on and I'm under a lot of pressure to get it done. I could really use three days a week working late on it, but I would never do that to you.

I definitely need two, though. Please be patient with me. It's just for a couple more months, and then I'll be back to normal. Home at six and spending every minute of the evening with the man I love."

I know Robert was hard at work and trying for a promotion that would mean a lot to him. Hell, it'd mean a lot to both of us. It would almost double his salary. And I knew he loved me.

So I'd been putting up with being alone every Tuesday and Thursday evening for the last month. But earlier tonight, as I was cooking up a batch of spaghetti, I remembered Robert's mother had called that afternoon and asked me to have him call her. I'd completely forgotten until I was making dinner, so I called his office number, but got his voicemail, so then I dialed his secretary.

"I'm so sorry, Jason," she said. "But Robert leaves at 3:00 every Tuesday and Thursday. He has for the past month now."

"What?" I asked, stunned.

"I just assumed . . . I'm sorry, Jason."

I hung up the phone and stumbled to the sofa, where I fought to catch my breath. Never in the eight years we'd been together had I once suspected Robert of cheating on me. But thinking back on it now, it all made sense. Supposedly working late, coming home exhausted, too tired for sex half the time, secretive about what he was working on.

I'd sat there brooding for so long that I burned the spaghetti sauce and lost my appetite. That's when I curled up on the sofa and watched *Sophie's Choice* on DVD. I needed desperately to emote, and if anything could get me to cry, it was Meryl's stunning performance in the best movie ever made.

After a few moments of staring at the blue screen, I turned off the television and went to bed. I undressed and climbed into the king-sized bed, looking up at the ceiling through the dark of the room, and soon fell asleep.

* * *

The hot, wet tongue licked up and down the length of my ass crack, sending chills up my spine. Then a kiss on each cheek. I probably have more sexual dreams than anyone I know, and I fucking love them. I subconsciously concentrate on staying asleep so that I can carry the dream through to the end, and I'm almost always successful. I can't even count the times I've awakened to either the sheets or my stomach and chest covered in my own cum just from my dreams.

The tongue licked around my hole and then slid in slowly. I moaned loudly and wriggled my ass around the tongue, all the time willing myself to stay asleep. This was a good one and I definitely wanted to make it to the end before waking up. The hands on either side of my ass massaged the cheeks lovingly and spread my ass apart even farther so the tongue could work its way deeper inside.

I almost creamed right there. There are few things I love better than having my ass eaten out, and this dream was taking me beyond the limits within which most of my dreams reside. I didn't dare move a muscle lest I wake up and cause it to end.

"Come on, baby," I heard the voice from miles away. "Wake up. I wanna fuck you so bad, and I'm not really into necrophilia."

It took me a moment to realize this wasn't a dream, and that Robert was in bed with me. I rolled over and looked at him. He smiled sheepishly and rubbed his naked body against mine. His cock was hard and throbbing, warm against my leg.

"I burned the spaghetti sauce," I said defiantly and pouted, then scooted a couple of inches away from him.

"What?"

"Never mind. You wouldn't understand. It's a matter of the heart." I immediately regretted saying it. I've been accused, on more than one occasion and by more than one person, of leaning toward the melodramatic. Although I haven't completely embraced it, I have come to accept it as fact. But now, with my heart beating a million times a minute and my ass on fire, was not the time. My husband was naked and fully hard and smiling that fucking sexy smile of his that melts my heart every time.

"Come here, baby," he said, and I did. "Suck my dick." And I did.

The thing that struck me about Robert when I first met him was his commanding presence. Whenever he walked into a room, every eye was on him and he had control of the room. When we first started dating, I turned to Jello every time he told me to "get on your knees and suck my dick," or "bend over and don't even think about moaning as my cock slides up your ass." He was never cocky about it, but rather I think he sensed the excitement it elicited in me, and did it more to please me than himself.

The second thing that struck me about Robert was his cock, and even after eight years, it never ceased to take my breath away. It's not that it was so huge. I'd seen and had bigger. But it was a work of art, perfect in every detail. It was maybe between seven and eight inches, but so thick I could barely wrap my fist around it. Thick veins ran along the length and crisscrossed all around it. The skin, even when his cock was fully hard, was soft as silk.

So I didn't hesitate to wrap my lips around it and suck it at that moment. I licked the head first, then took it in my mouth and sucked gently on it. Robert loved having his cock head sucked, but I wanted his entire cock buried in my mouth, so I opened the back of my throat and swallowed him in one slow move.

"Oh, fuck, babe," he moaned. "You know I can't take too much of that. You'll make me cum too fast."

I teased him for a few more minutes by deepthroating him and sucking for all I was worth. When I knew he was close, I pulled my mouth off his cock.

"You're such a tease," Robert said as he caught his breath

I raised myself up and kissed him on the lips. He returned my kiss, licking lightly around my lips and then slipping his tongue inside my mouth. I sucked on it greedily, and savored the sweet taste of bourbon. But only for a second. And then it hit me. Why was he drinking bourbon if he was supposedly working?

"Where were you tonight?" I asked as I broke the kiss and leaned down to lick his nipples.

"Shhh," he said, and leaned forward to knead my ass cheeks as I licked his nipples and worked my way down to his belly button.

"You weren't at work."

"Turn around and get on your knees."

My heart skipped a beat, and I did as I was told. I knew what was coming, and as much as I wanted to know where Robert had been, I wanted, oh so much more, what was to come. I got on all fours and raised my ass in the air.

Robert got behind me and spread my ass with his hands and attacked my ass with his tongue as if digging for gold. I moaned and bucked myself back against his mouth.

"Do you want me inside you, baby?" he asked.

"You know I do," I answered. "Fuck me." I was already so hard and throbbing I thought I'd explode any second with anticipation.

Robert and I have made love hundreds of times over the past eight years, and every time it seems to get better. When he fucks me, it's almost always slow and gentle and lasts an hour or more. He enters me slowly and lets my ass adjust to the thickness of his cock before he slides in and out of me.

But not tonight. As soon as the words, "Fuck me," were out of my mouth, I felt Robert's cock head against my asshole, and a second later he slid his fat cock all the way inside me in one slow but steady and deliberate move. I yelped out in pain, and dropped to my stomach on the bed. Robert stayed inside me and lay on top of me.

"Robert, that hurts."

"It won't in a minute and you know it."

"But it hurts now," I said between gritted teeth. "Why did you do that?"

"Don't doubt me again, baby, and don't doubt my love for you. It hurts me and it upsets me."

He slid his cock out of my ass just an inch or so, and then went back deep inside, and that's all it took for me. The pain was gone. In its place every nerve in my ass tingled, and I wriggled my ass against his cock.

"Okay," I said. "Will you fuck me now?"

Robert leaned down and kissed my neck as he slid in and out of my ass. He started out slow, but quickly picked up his pace.

I reached up and held his chin in my hand and stared into his eyes as he fucked me. When he shoved his cock inside me with quick jabbing stabs, his eyes rolled back in his head and then closed. When he slowed down and slid into me slow and deep and tender, he stared into my eyes, and winked the sexiest wink I'd ever seen.

I kissed him on the lips, and then he moaned loudly. I knew he was close. I sucked on his tongue as I tightened my ass around his cock and moved up and down.

"I can't take any more, babe," he said. "I'm gonna cum."

"I already did," I said.

"What?"

I rolled over to my back without allowing his cock to slip from my ass. My stomach and the comforter were both covered in my cum.

"Oh, shit," he yelled, "here I cum!"

He pulled his cock from my ass just in time. I felt the first couple of shots splash against the outside of my ass. The next few flew across my torso and landed on my face. I lapped at it eagerly as the last couple of spurts of his cum landed on my belly and mixed with my own.

We lay there for a few minutes, catching our breaths.

Then Robert spoke. "Just exactly when did you cum?"

"When I looked into your eyes and saw the love behind your wink."

He pulled me close to him and cradled me in his arms. We fell asleep like that and woke up the next morning in the exact same position.

The next three weeks were a nightmare. Monday, Wednesday, Friday, Saturday, and Sunday were heaven for me. Robert and I seemed closer than ever. On the weekends we took trips to the beach and amusement parks. I was on a high during those days, and more in love with my husband than ever. But when Tuesday and Thursday rolled around, I found myself in deep depression. I'd called his office a couple more times after 4:00 and found, as I'd expected, that he'd left at 3:00.

Finally, I couldn't take it anymore. I called my best friend Carol.

"Honey, you've got to face the facts," she told me as she exhaled from her Pall Mall and took a swig of Bartles & Jaymes wine cooler. Even without seeing her, I knew what she was doing. It was her standard after-dinner routine. "He's having an affair."

"How can you say that?" I asked, even as I bit my nails because I knew it to be true.

"The signs are all there, sweetie."

"But he's so affectionate and loving when he's here. Sex is better than ever."

"That means the end is near. He's being affectionate and loving because he feels dirty and guilty and wrong for doing this to you, and is trying to atone for his sins." Another drag on the cigarette and big swig of wine cooler. "And the sex is so good now because he knows it's coming to an end, and as crazy as it sounds, he wants to remember you and the sex you had in the best possible way. Trust me, I know these things."

I didn't know how she knew these things. She'd never been married, and hadn't been able to even hold onto a boyfriend for more than six months at a time.

"I don't know, Carol. I love him so much, and I think he loves me too."

"He lied and said he's working late and you know that's not true, right?"

"Yes."

"And you always smell alcohol on his breath when he comes home, right?"

"Not always, but most of the time."

"And he's usually too 'tired' to have sex when he gets home at one in the morning, right?"

"Not always, but most of the time."

"He's cheating on you, Jason. Get the fuck out of there. If he wants someone else, let him have the bastard. You can come live with me."

The thought made me shudder. But her logic had worn me down, and I was determined to make a move.

"Thank you, Carol. You've helped a lot."

"That's what I'm here for, honey."

"I'll call you in a couple of days when I know what I'm doing and where I'm staying."

"You be careful, sweetie."

"I will."

I hung up and finished biting the rest of my nails to the quick. Then I got up and went to the bedroom, where I packed three suitcases. When Robert walked into the door a little after one a.m., I was sitting on the sofa with the suitcases next to me.

He stopped halfway through the door.

"Baby, what's going on? You've been crying. What's wrong?"

"I'm going to make this easy on you," I said, and wiped my eyes and then blew my nose into the same Kleenex. "You're in love with someone else, and I don't want to be one of those spouses who fall to the ground and wrap their arms around their husband's legs and begs him not to leave."

"What the hell are you talking about, baby?"

"Come on, Robert. I'm not stupid. Every Tuesday and Thursday you come home way past midnight. You told me you were working on a "special project," but I've called your office and you're not there. In fact you leave at three on those days. You come home smelling of booze and are too tired to have sex half the time."

"Jason, you're misreading this completely."

"Oh really? What else could it be? I thought you loved me. How could you do this to me?"

Robert came all the way inside the house and shut the door. "I love you more than anything in this world, Jason."

"Then who is this whore you're spending so much time with?"

He laughed.

"Don't you dare laugh at this, Robert. Don't demean our relationship like that."

He walked over to me and tried to put his arm around me, but I shook him off, and blew my nose into a new Kleenex.

"I was hoping we could wait another couple weeks to do this. It's all I really need to be done with it. But I can see how upset you are, so let's do it now."

I began crying in earnest and removed the ring from my finger and laid it on the coffee table.

"Baby, put your ring back on and don't ever take it off again."

"But . . ."

"Put your ring on and get your jacket. We're going for a little ride."

"Robert, I'm very vulnerable right now, and very confused."

"I know, but it'll all be clear in a few minutes. Just trust me and get your coat."

I did, and walked to the door where he stood.

He wrapped his arms around my waist and pulled me close to

him. Then he leaned in to kiss me. At first I pursed my lips and refused to accept his kiss. But it was impossible. I opened my mouth
and sucked eagerly on his tongue.

"I love you," he said. "Now let's go."

The ride was intolerable. Neither of us spoke, but the silence
was so deafening I thought my head would explode. We finally
pulled up to a large house in the middle of a cul de sac in one of the
nicer neighborhoods in the city.

"Where are we?" I asked.

"Come on," Robert said as he opened my door and took my
hand. He held it as we headed up the walk and even as he opened
the door with the key. Then he picked me up and carried me
through the door. The inside was even larger than it looked outside. Three stories with vaulted ceilings, elaborate lighting, and a
grand circular staircase to the second floor. It was right out of
Dallas or *Dynasty*.

"Robert, what's going on? Where are we?"

"We're home. Or at least it will be home in a couple of weeks."

"What?"

"This is what I've been working on the past couple of months.
I'm tired of living in our small apartment. I'm tired of you having to
live in our small apartment. I've never been more in love with you
than I am right now, and I want us to have a nice home. Our own
home. Big enough to have a couple of kids maybe in a couple years.
I've been renovating this place for the past couple of months.
Pulling up the old carpeting, installing hardwood floors, updating
the electrical system. You know . . . man stuff."

"Robert . . ."

"This is for you, Jason. Because I love you and I want to live
with you forever and I want to raise a family with you and I want
you to live in a home deserving of the amazing person and lover
you are."

Tears poured down my face. "I don't know what to say."

"How about telling me you love me."

"I love you so much," I cried as I threw my arms around him and hugged him.

He hugged me back, then lowered me to the floor, where he began undressing me.

"Robert, there's no furniture and the hardwood floor is cold."

"Shut up and suck my dick," he said, and winked as he finished undressing me while I sucked his cock to full hardness.

He threw his own clothes carelessly to the floor, then raised my legs into the air as I lay on my back. He licked my ass as only he had ever been able to do, and made me moan with animalistic lust.

"I want you inside me," I moaned.

Robert pulled his mouth away, and rested the head of his cock against my ass, then slowly pushed it inside. I took a deep breath and relaxed my ass as he slid slowly inside me. When he was all the way inside me, he leaned in and kissed me. My eyes had been closed, enjoying the ecstasy of feeling his cock fill me up. But as he kissed me I tasted something salty, and I looked up into his eyes. Big tears rolled down his cheeks and fell onto my lips as he kissed me.

"I love you so much, Jason," he said as he pulled his cock almost out of my ass and then slid back in, and another tear fell onto my lips. "I can't imagine my life without you."

Robert was big and strong and muscular, with a hairy, manly chest and strong jaw that immediately told you he was in charge and that everything would be okay as long as he was around. His strength and control were what made me fall in love with him. I'd never once in eight years seen him cry.

But now as he made love to me slowly and tenderly and passionately, he couldn't stop crying. And I'd never regarded him as stronger or loved him as intensely, as now.

I pulled his face down to mine and kissed him passionately, running my fingers across his strong back and cupping his muscular ass with my hands.

"I love you," I said awkwardly through the kiss, before breaking it. "And I'm yours forever."

His breathing grew deeper and heavier.

"Kiss me again," he said, and I did. He moaned loudly and shoved his cock deep inside me, and just left it there as he sucked on my tongue and kissed me with more emotion than I'd ever known in a kiss. And then he collapsed on top of me.

I took a moment to catch my breath, then rolled him over onto his side, and I rolled onto mine to look at him.

"Did you cum inside me?" I asked.

"I'm sorry," he said, and tensed up a little. "I didn't mean to. I just couldn't stop before it happened."

I looked at him for a moment, not knowing what to say. When we first got together we got tested, and were both negative. For the first four years we'd practiced safer sex, but after that we'd abandoned condoms. We were always sure we were both monogamous, and we still got tested every six months throughout our relationship. But we'd never once cum inside one another. I wasn't sure how I felt about it.

"I'm so sorry, babe," Robert said.

I kept looking at him, and knew without a doubt that he'd never cheated on me and that we were both clean and negative.

"I guess you were serious about starting a family, huh?"

Robert laughed and pulled me into his arms again. It took no time at all to fall asleep spooning one another. About an hour later we awoke because it was so cold. I felt Robert's cock hard and throbbing against my leg again.

"What do you say we go back to the apartment and go to bed?" he said.

"Good idea. I'm freezing and exhausted. I can't wait to fall asleep in our bed."

"Who said anything about sleeping?" Robert said, and slid his cock up and down the length of my ass crack before he slapped it and we got dressed.

over the past three months, and I couldn't help but think it meant something.

In the dream I was blindfolded and lying spread-eagle on my back on a sterile stainless-steel table. There were no ropes or leather straps or handcuffs, or any other restraints, but my arms were spread above my head and my legs were spread wide across the foot of the table, and try as I might, I couldn't move them. I struggled and wriggled against the table, but my feet and hands were held in place by some invisible force. And though nothing physical blocked my mouth and no tape stretched across it, I couldn't speak or make a noise of any kind.

Suddenly I felt a pair of soft, cold hands caress my chest and stomach. I took a deep breath and felt my cock twitch as adrenaline coursed through my body. The touch was light and the hands were soft, so at first I assumed it was a woman running her hands all over my body. But then I felt the unseen stranger's body shift so that it stood over my face at the head of the table, and a couple seconds later I felt the unmistakable weight of a semi-hard cock across my cheek and mouth. I gasped in surprise, and struggled against my invisible restraints as the cock grew thicker and harder against my mouth. Who was this unseen stranger and why was he touching me like this and sliding his hard cock across my lips? I halfheartedly wriggled across the table again, feeling like I should be mortified and feel abused. But my heart raced with excitement and my cock hardened to its full eight inches.

I tried to yell in protest, but instead a low animalistic moan escaped my throat as the unseen stranger tweaked my nipples and slid his hard cock into my mouth. It didn't take long for me to open my throat and swallow him completely, and my own cock began to ache with the force with which it throbbed.

"That's it, baby," I heard him whisper as his cock slipped past my tonsils and deep into my throat. "Take my big cock, Mr. Frye." His voice was familiar, and I began to panic as I wondered who he was, and how he knew me.

The Neighborly Thing to Do

"Ross, I'm not going to call you again," her voice yelled from downstairs in the kitchen. "Breakfast is getting cold. Get your ass down here now." I swear she sounded exactly like my mother, and for a moment I felt like I was back in my bedroom in my parents' house when I was in middle school.

I groaned as the sound of my wife's voice caused my cock to soften just slightly, and then I squeezed it harder and pumped my hand up and down the length of it faster to try to keep it hard.

"Shit," I cried, and tried desperately to stroke it back to life . . .

. . . "Ross, did you hear me?" her high-pitched nasal voice cried up the stairs.

. . . and it was useless. My cock shrank back to its fully soft size and my balls shriveled up against the base of my cock.

I sighed, and hit the sheets beside me with my fists, and gritted my teeth. "Yes, dear," I yelled as cheerfully as I could. I looked down and held my limp cock for a moment, hoping against hope. Nothing happened. "I'm coming."

My day at work was no better. I couldn't get the fucking dream I'd had earlier that morning out of my head. Where it original came from, I had no idea. But I'd had it no less than a dozen ti

But then it didn't matter, and I tightened my throat muscles around his hard cock and began to suck it. A moment later I felt his warm wet mouth wrap around my cock and swallow me in one move.

That's all it took for me, and I moaned loudly as I sprayed my load down his throat in wave after wave of ecstasy. He moaned as well, and quickly withdrew his cock from my mouth. A moment later he grabbed the blindfold and ripped it from my eyes. I looked up into the face of my neighbor's kid, Marc, and stared in amazement as he showered his load across my face.

And then, as unexpectedly as it began, it was over. *What the fuck was that all about?* I wondered the first few times it happened. And then I didn't care. In fact, I began to look forward to the dreams.

I don't know where they came from or why I was having them, but I remember the first time I had the dream. It was the day after Marc returned home from his junior year in college for the summer. I saw him out in the driveway washing his car when I got home from work, and couldn't help but notice his strong muscular legs or the washboard abs that tightened as he stretched to reach a spot on the roof. He smiled and waved at me as I walked to my front door, and I remember feeling my cock stir and a smile cross my lips. I didn't give it too much thought, though, until the next morning when I woke with a hard cock and sticky sheets.

But that was three months ago, and now, as I sat at my desk, trying to work, I realized I was hard as a rock again, for the umpteenth time that day.

"Dammit," I said, and hit the intercom. "Belinda, I'm going out for lunch. I'll be back in an hour or so."

I got up and walked out of my office and headed down the street. In the opposite direction from all the typical lunch spots I normally frequented.

Four blocks from my office was the Galaxy Theater. It was a gay porno theater that was infamous for the strip and j/o shows that ran every two hours, and for the sleazy anonymous sex its patrons engaged in. I'd never been there, but I knew where and what it was, and I knew without a doubt I was going there.

As I approached the door, I looked around to make sure no one saw me, and then I entered. The darkness in the foyer and the stench that immediately assaulted me was overwhelming. It smelled like sweat and sex and old, burnt popcorn. From behind the glass window I could hear the loud moans and the tacky music that accompanied them.

The smell inside the theater was even ranker, and the music pounded through my head. I looked up at the big screen, and gasped as I watched a giant cock slide in and out of a smooth white ass. I sat down in the closest seat, and tried to catch my breath as I watched for the first time a man getting fucked by another man.

Desire welled inside me as I stared at the screen, and I found it hard to breathe. My cock pounded so hard in my slacks that it hurt. I rubbed it for a moment, but realized very quickly that I would shoot all over my slacks if I continued, so I stopped. A couple minutes later I had to pee, so I stood up and made my way to the restroom.

The smell in the restroom was even worse than out in the theater. It contained the same odor of sex and sweat and old popcorn, but it also tried to cover all of that up with an overpowering scent of pine cleaner. I covered my mouth as I walked quickly to the urinal. But gray duct tape cordoned it off, and a sign said it was not in service. So I walked over and took one of the stalls at the opposite side of the room.

I unzipped my slacks, pulled out my still half-hard cock, and waited for it to soften so I could pee without spraying it all over the stall. Finally I was able to relieve myself. As I shook off the last few drops of piss, I heard a sound.

I looked behind me. To my side I noticed a round hole in the wall of the stall adjoining the one next to me. A second later two fingers appeared in the hole, and beckoned me closer. My heart raced as I looked at the fingers, and my cock hardened again.

"Come closer," the guy on the other side said. "Lemme suck it."

I hesitated only a moment, then leaned against the wall and slid my cock through the hole. Even before it was all the way through, the warm mouth wrapped around my cock head and sucked on it. When my dick was entirely inside the hole, he swallowed the rest of my cock in slow sucking movements until it was buried in his throat.

I thought I'd shoot right then. Nothing had ever felt so good. My wife had sucked my dick a few times since we'd married, but it never felt like this. It was only a couple of minutes before I felt I couldn't hold back any longer. "I'm gonna cum," I moaned loudly, and grasped the top of the metal stall divider.

His mouth was off my cock instantly, and I felt I'd had the breath knocked out of me. "No," he said. "Not yet."

"Please," I begged, and shoved my hips against the wall so that my cock was closer for him to take again.

"It's my turn," he said, and I felt his hot, hard cock push against mine through the hole.

I stepped back and looked at the cock. It was beautiful. I'd only seen a couple of other guys' dicks before, and never had they been hard . . . and begging to be sucked. This cock was at least as long as mine, but quite a bit thicker. Thick blue veins ran the length of the cock and pulsed visibly. A tiny bead of transparent precum peeked out of the hole at the head, then slid down the shaft slowly.

"Suck it, man," the guy said. "I gotta feel your lips wrapped around my cock."

I'd never sucked a cock before, and wasn't sure I could do it at all. Especially not one as big and thick as this one. But I wanted it more than anything, so I stuck out my tongue and licked the salty precum from the head of the cock. I moaned loudly as I wrapped my lips around the head and sucked it.

"Yeah, dude, that's it," they guy said. His voice sounded tinny and far away, as if in a tunnel. Probably because of the loud high-pitched ringing sound I couldn't get out of my head. "Suck my cock, dude. Swallow that big dick."

And I did. I took my time and swallowed a little bit at a time. But as I took more and more of his big dick in my mouth, I kept thinking that at any moment it would hit the back of my throat and I'd gag and have to stop. To my surprise, when his cock head pressed against the back of my throat, my throat opened wider and allowed his fat cock to slide all the way inside. When his pubic hairs tickled my nose, I thought I'd pass out any minute.

"Fuck, dude, you can really suck a cock," the guy moaned as he slid his cock in and out of my hungry mouth. "You're gonna make me cum," he moaned, and I prepared myself to swallow his load . . .

. . . "But not like this," he said, and pulled his cock from my ravenous mouth so fast that it hurt as his cock head slid past my tonsils and out of my throat.

"What?" I asked as I grabbed my own cock and began to beat it. "Come on, man. Lemme have it."

He pulled his cock back through the hole in the wall, and I felt my heart drop. He couldn't quit now. I was so fucking close.

A couple of seconds later the hole was covered. It took me a second or two to realize that I was staring at his exposed asshole. "Fuck me," he moaned loudly.

I stared at the marble-smooth ass in front of me. The pink hole puckered and beckoned me to enter it. My breathing quickened, and I could tell he felt my breath on his twitching hole.

"Come on, dude," he said desperately. "Fuck my ass."

Before I realized I was doing it, I stood up and pressed my hard cock against the crack of his ass as it peeked through the hole. A big wad of spit left my mouth, and it landed on my cock head, sliding down the shaft. I took a deep breath, placed the head of my cock at the entrance of his hole, and slowly slid forward.

I thought I'd faint as the heat of his ass enveloped my cock and sucked it deeper and deeper inside. It felt like an eternity before I felt my balls resting against the warm smooth skin of his ass.

I'd never experienced anything like this. Sure, sex with my wife was good. But it wasn't great, and more often than not it seemed like an obligation in which I was on automatic pilot. But it didn't even come close to this. Every inch of my skin and every nerve in my body tingled with electric bliss. I didn't want the feeling to ever end, and planned to take this fuck as slowly as possible and enjoy every minute of it.

But my friend on the other side of the wall had other plans. He grunted like an animal as the last of my cock slid inside his ass, and then he began thrusting back and forth on it faster and harder.

The room spun around me as he fucked my cock, and I held my breath and counted to ten to keep from cumming right away. But his ass was relentless, and refused to allow me any rest. It didn't take long before I felt the orgasm building in my balls, and a moment later my cock was on fire as the cum traveled up the length of my shaft.

"Fuck, man," I moaned as I buried my cock deep inside him. "I can't take it anymore. I'm gonna shoot."

"Hell, yeah," he said, and slid his ass off of my cock in a quick motion.

I pulled my dick back inside my side of the stall as I stroked it, and noticed his face was at the hole in the wall now. He stuck his tongue through the hole and then, I saw his eyes looking up at me.

"Mr. Frye?"

I recognized the voice immediately this time, and my heart stopped. But my orgasm didn't. In fact, the sound of his voice made the cum shoot from my shaft like a missile. My knees buckled and I slumped to the floor as the last of my spunk dripped from my cock. Now at eye level with the hole in the wall, I looked through it and into the face of my new buddy.

"Marc," I gasped, as I watched what seemed like a gallon of my spooge drip down his eyes and nose and cheeks, and onto his T-shirt below.

He licked a tongue full of it off of his lips and smiled at me. "That was fuckin' hot, dude."

"Marc," I stammered, as my cock twitched at the sight of his smooth white skin and pink lips as he licked my cum from his face. "This isn't right."

"When can we do it again?"

"I don't think . . ."

"My folks are gonna be away this weekend. You could come over."

My head was spinning.

"My wife . . ."

"Tell her you're helping me out with . . . a plumbing problem. You know, man stuff. Come on, Mr. Frye. It's the neighborly thing to do."

"Okay," I gushed, before I realized I was doing it.

"Right on," Marc said, and stood up to pull up his jeans. He left the stall and I heard the sink running out in the main part of the restroom.

I pulled up my slacks and stumbled out into the restroom. Marc was standing right outside my stall door, and as I exited, he grabbed me by the arms and pinned me against the wall. He leaned in and kissed me deep on the mouth. I could still taste my own cum in his mouth, and my cock swelled again as his tongue tickled my own.

"Saturday, three o'clock. Don't bother knocking. The door will be unlocked. Just come on up to my room. I'll be waiting for you naked on my bed."

I nodded stupidly and tried to catch my breath. He gave me a quick peck on the mouth, and left the restroom. I stood leaning against the wall, smiling like the fucking Cheshire cat, and waiting for my hard-on to soften.

Then I straightened my tie and left the restroom, and headed back to work.

The Honeymooners

"I just don't see the point," Lee said as he wrapped the fat end of his tie around the skinny end and pulled it through the loop. "I mean, we've been together for ten years, for crying out loud. Why bother?"

I glared at him through the mirror, and resisted the urge to smack him upside the head. "I want to be recognized. Officially."

"Honey, we have two kids in middle school. We drive a mini van. You're on my insurance and the sole beneficiary of my estate. We even share a hyphenated last name."

"It's not enough," I said stubbornly.

"Let's not get into this again," he said as he sighed deeply and turned around to kiss me. "We are more established and more normal than anyone I know. I just don't see the sense in all this. It'll cost a fortune and there's no real point."

I followed him out the bedroom door and into the kitchen. The girls had left for school twenty minutes ago, so we were alone.

"The point is, that barbaric cretin we jokingly called our leader for eight years is finally out of office, and he is now the laughing stock of the entire world."

"Oh, Jesus," Lee said as he swallowed his vitamins with a glass of orange juice. "Here we go again."

"Yes, here we go again, Lee," I said as I wiped up a couple of drops of OJ he'd spilled on the counter. "Our new President has been in office for just over a year, and already he's managed to turn things around. Not only did he single-handedly defeat the constitutional ban, but he convinced the nation . . . the entire nation, not just the two coasts . . . that we deserve to have all the rights just as opposite sex couples have. We're finally equal."

Lee kissed me on the lips and walked to the door. "No one is your equal, baby," he said, and picked up his keys as he opened the door.

"Don't patronize me, Lee," I said as I tried not to let him see me lick my lips to savor the taste of his own. Even after all these years, just a kiss from him melted my heart and made me shiver. "I want to get married. It's legal now, everywhere, and there's no reason we shouldn't."

"But there's no reason we should, either," Lee said through a deep sigh. "We already have all the rights as everyone else."

"We have the right to be married now, and I want to exercise that right. When women and Blacks were given the right to vote, they voted. Think about what might have happened if they'd been satisfied with just having the right and not exercising it. We have the right to marry, and we should get married. It's our civic responsibility."

"That's bullshit and you know it," Lee said. He looked at me sternly for a moment, then softened his expression. "I love you, Bronson. I've committed my life to you, and I couldn't be happier. But this conversation is over." He walked out the door and locked it behind him, leaving me staring at it from the inside.

The next few days were strenuous, to say the least. In front of the girls, Lee and I seemed perfectly natural. They never knew their daddies were arguing. We cooked dinner together, laughed at their jokes, and helped them with their homework. On Wednesday evening we watched a video of their choice after dinner, as was our routine. But once the girls were in bed and Lee and I were alone, it was like Winter had settled into our home. I didn't speak to him at all as we cleaned up and went to bed. I didn't respond to his attempts to get me to laugh. I didn't kiss him good night and I certainly didn't make love with him, as hard as it was to resist his gentle caresses and loving nibbles on my neck.

"You're being a fucking brat about this, you know?" Lee said as he turned around and pulled the blankets up under his chin. "It's very unbecoming."

"Whatever," I said, knowing that response pissed him off more than anything. I heard him sigh, and regretted saying it immediately. It wasn't an angry sigh, or a desperate one. It was a sad sigh.

Lee fell asleep fairly quickly, but I tossed and turned for another hour. Was I being a brat? Was I being unreasonable? For the first twenty years of my life I'd denied who I was and repressed the feelings that threatened to burst to the surface at any given moment. I felt bad about myself. I was ashamed. When I came out at twenty-one, I swore to live my life proudly and to fight for justice and equality. I met Lee at a Human Rights Campaign fundraiser, for crying out loud.

The fight grew increasingly more difficult and seemed like a losing battle with Asshole, Jr. in office for the past eight years. But we'd fought hard and persevered, and now we were being rewarded. Legal and nationally recognized gay marriage was a reality. Not domestic partnerships or civil unions, but Gay Marriage! I'd dreamt about it for twenty years, and now it was in my grasp. And I wanted it.

But Lee didn't, and that infuriated me. I knew he loved me, and was dedicated to our life together and with our kids. He'd always been very considerate of me, and supported me in my endeavors. He bought me great birthday and anniversary and Father's Day gifts. So I just didn't get why he was fighting the whole marriage idea. It pissed me off.

The energy it took to stay mad for this long and the exhausting day I'd had at work wore me down, and I eventually gave in to the sleep that had tried for the past hour to settle into my body and mind. And before I knew it, I was asleep.

As I awoke the next morning, I rolled over and threw my arms around where Lee should have been. But he wasn't lying next to me, and my arms flopped over his side of the bed. He wasn't in our bathroom or in the study or in the kitchen either. The girls were also gone. I looked at the clock: it was nine-thirty. He hadn't bothered to wake me, and I was now late for work.

"Shit," I yelled, and ran upstairs to shower and dress as quickly as I could.

"Nice of you to join us," Marcus, my partner in our architectural firm, said as I rushed past the receptionist and into my office.

"Don't start with me this morning, Marcus," I said as I slammed my briefcase onto my desk and reached for the cup of coffee Marie had set on my desk over two hours ago. "I'm not in the mood. Marie, please get me a fresh cup of coffee," I yelled to my secretary.

"Okay, well this is a side of you I haven't seen before," Marcus said.

"Sorry. I've just had a really shitty couple of weeks. My head is killing me, and I slept wrong so I have a crick in my neck."

"Hmm," he said, sounding like he didn't believe a word I was saying, and walked to the door. "Lee called about an hour ago. Sounded surprised you weren't here yet."

"Yeah, well maybe he should've thought about that before leaving this morning without waking me."

"You two having problems?"

I looked up from my paperwork and raised an eyebrow.

"Forget I asked," he said, and left my office.

The afternoon dragged on painfully slow, and I accomplished absolutely nothing. At two o'clock a dozen roses were delivered for me, and a note was attached: "I love you more than my Target luggage." It was a joke between Lee and me, and over the years had become our favorite term of endearment. He always said it to me as a means of apologizing. And even though I was still upset with him and wanted to stay angry, I found myself smiling, and looking forward to getting home to him later that afternoon.

At three o'clock my life changed. I'd noticed a certain energy in the office that I'd not felt before. Every time I looked out at Marie's desk, she was staring in at me, smiling. People were whispering and giggling, but when they walked by the open door to my office, they stopped, and pretended to be working on something very important and top secret.

Even Marcus was acting weird, not talking to me at all, but chatting it up with everyone else in the office, which was definitely not his style.

The grandfather clock in my office struck three, and I looked up at my door. The entire office was crowded around it, staring in at me.

"Am I missing something here?" I asked, with more bite than I'd intended. "Am I growing horns? If my pants were unzipped you wouldn't know it, because I'm sitting down. So what is it?"

Suddenly the group parted, and Lee walked into my office. He was holding another dozen roses in one hand, and held something else behind his back. The smile on his face stretched from one ear to the other.

"Babe?" I said stupidly as I stood. Of course it was him. "What are you doing here? I got your flowers earlier. They're beautiful. You didn't need to bring more."

"I know I didn't," he said, and leaned in to kiss me.

I backed away, out of instinct. We were in my office, and although everyone knew Lee, and were completely respectful of our relationship, I wasn't in the practice of public displays of affection.

"But I wanted to," he continued. "Now sit down," he said, and pushed me back down into my chair. He knelt between my legs. "I love you, Bronson."

"I love you, too," I said uncomfortably, and blushed as I looked beyond Lee and at my staff.

"I mean, I *really* love you, and I want to spend the rest of my life with you."

"Me too," I said, slower this time.

"Bronson, you are my entire life. I'm not a whole person without you."

"Lee, are you . . ."

He reached forward with the hand that was behind his back, and laid a small black box in my lap.

"Will you marry me, Bronson? Will you live with me and love me and raise our kids with me and share your dreams with me? Forever?"

Tears streamed down my face as my heart raced. I looked at the door, and everyone in the office was smiling and shaking their heads yes. Marie was crying.

"Yes," I said, and threw my arms around him.

To say the wedding was opulent would be an understatement. Charles and Diana would have envied ours. We rented out the ballroom on the 55th floor of the highest priced hotel in town, and I insisted we stay in the Presidential Suite. Asshole, Jr. had stayed in the same room with his Missus all six times he'd come to town during his tenure. The poetic justice was too tempting for me to pass up.

I'd insisted a honeymoon wasn't necessary, but Lee refused to listen. "You wanted a real wedding and a real marriage, so we're gonna do this right and have a real honeymoon," he said.

"But we've been together a decade. It's not like we're virgins who've waited for this special day to consummate our marriage."

"We could pretend." He smiled, and pinched my ass. "We're going on this honeymoon and we're going to have a very special time. We're newlyweds, afterall."

The six-course dinner was perfect, and the complimentary champagne worked its magic on me. When dinner was finished, Lee held my hand as we walked back to our room. And when we arrived at our door, he lifted me into his arms and carried me over the threshold.

I laughed. "I'm not a woman, you know. You don't need to do this."

"Oh, I know you're not a woman," he said, and kissed me. "But I want you to know I love you more than anything in this world. I'm yours forever, and I'm always going to be here for you. I'll carry you, like I'm doing now, when things are tough for you. I'll be your rock. And when I'm feeling down and need your help, I know you'll be there to carry me across the rough waters as well."

I looked into his eyes and swallowed hard as I fought back tears. "Yes I will."

Lee laid me on the bed and kissed me passionately. I wrapped my arms around him and held him tight as our tongues danced. Even after ten years together, his kiss made me tremble and caused the hairs on my neck to stand at attention. My cock filled with blood as he moved his tongue from my lips to my neck, and as he ground his hips into mine, I knew I wasn't the only one becoming aroused.

I moaned loudly as he kissed and licked and nibbled on my neck, then worked his way down my throat as he unbuttoned my shirt and tossed it to the floor. My entire body quivered as he bit my nipples and licked his way down my torso and to my bellybutton. I worked out a couple of hours a day, seven days a week, and my six-pack abs never failed to work Lee into a frenzy. Tonight was no exception, and he attacked my navel. He kicked off his shoes and struggled to kick his pants off.

In a matter of seconds, we were both naked and holding each other. Champagne always makes me a little horny, and I'd had three glasses. I rolled Lee over onto his back on the bed, and spread his legs wide as I lowered myself between them.

His cock had always amazed and excited me. Easily a full eight inches long and almost wrist-thick, it was the most magnificent dick I'd ever seen, and I thanked the universe every time I wrapped my lips around it. I pulled back the foreskin, and licked the head. Lee moaned his approval, and I put my lips around it and sucked a few inches into my mouth. Thick veins wrapped across his shaft in every direction, and throbbed as my tongue and lips slid across them.

"Oh, baby, that feels good," Lee whispered as he wriggled across the bed.

I swallowed his cock in one slow and deliberate move, and smiled inside as my husband moaned and arched his back off the bed. I sucked his dick for several minutes, relishing the heat and hardness of his head and shaft as they parted the back of my throat and slid in deeper. Before long, his cock pulsed harder and thick, sweet precum dripped from the slit. He'd always loved the way I sucked his cock, and was amazed at how easily I could make him cum just from sucking him. No one else had been able to do that.

But I wasn't ready for him to shoot yet. I was just getting started. I pulled my mouth from his cock and moved up to lie next to him.

"Please," he begged. "Please suck me some more. Finish me off, babe."

"No," I said, and licked his ear. "Not yet."

He smiled, and rolled on top of me. There was no need for further foreplay. My cock was already so hard it was turning red. He licked the head and rod for a moment, then slid his fingers between my cock and ass. I became defenseless every time he did that, and he knew it. When I moaned, he swallowed my cock all the way to the balls and slid one long, thick finger deep into my ass.

"Oh, fuck," I said through gritted teeth, and lifted my ass off the bed so he could get in even deeper.

Lee obliged and slid a second finger inside my ass, then wriggled them against the muscles inside me. All the time, he continued sucking my dick, and when my first drops of precum slid onto his tongue, he laughed.

"You're so easy," he said, as he removed himself from my dick and kissed me.

"Fuck me." I pushed him by the shoulders back down between my legs.

Lee spread them further apart and lifted them into the air, so that my ass was only inches from his face. He worked up a good amount of saliva and let the spit fall from his mouth onto my puckering hole. Then he leaned down and licked my ass, spreading my hole with his tongue and letting the spittle slide in so slowly that I thought it'd never get inside me.

"Do you want me to fuck you?" he said teasingly, then slid his tongue all the way inside my ass, and then out again.

My throat was hot and as dry as sandpaper. I couldn't speak, so I moaned my reply.

"Beg me, baby. Beg for my dick."

"Fuck me, Lee. Please."

"What? I can't hear you."

"I want your cock, baby. Please fuck me," I said as I somehow found my voice. "Shove your cock up my ass and fuck my brains out."

Lee looked down at me staring up at him between my spread legs, and smiled.

"I want you deep inside me."

He raised himself up and rested his cock against my upturned ass. It was hot as it throbbed against my cheeks, and I tightened my ass to squeeze it lovingly. I was resting on my shoulders, with my ass raised and my knees resting next to my ears. Now it was Lee who was crazed with lust, and he spat on his cock and placed the head at my hole. I winked at him, and he closed his eyes as he moaned loudly and slid his big dick deep inside me.

"Oh, my god," I whispered as my ass muscles spread and Lee's fat cock filled me up. I'd always laughed when people said they saw stars when they made love, but I wasn't laughing now. Bright lights—red and yellow and green and purple ones—exploded behind my eyes as my husband filled me completely.

He rested there, with his dick deep inside me. I knew he was waiting for me, but I wanted to feel that fullness as long as possible. I wasn't in complete control though, and before I knew it, my ass was twitching and squeezing Lee's cock, begging for more.

That was his sign, and he went to it. He slid his cock in and out of my ass as slow as possible. It took a full minute for him to slide out to the point that only his head remained inside me. Then he slid back inside all the way to the balls just as slowly.

"Fuck me!" I yelled and gripped his cock tighter inside as I slid my ass up and down his cock.

Lee wrapped his arms behind my back, and fucked me hard. He thrust in and out of my ass slow and tenderly, then fast and ferociously. Every time his cock rammed its way inside me, those damned lights burst alive inside my head again, and I whimpered like a lost puppy.

I felt myself getting close, and as much as I wanted this feeling to go on forever, I knew I had to cum. Before he had a chance to brace himself, I shifted my weight and rolled Lee over onto his back. Without allowing his cock to leave my ass, I was now sitting on top of him.

"What the . . ." Lee started to say.

"Shut up."

When he started to pump in and out of my ass, I planted my hands on his hips and held them still. My heart pounded as I struggled to catch my breath. But I wanted to be in charge of this. I leaned down and kissed Lee on the lips, giving us both a moment to catch our breath and allow our climaxes to retreat for a moment. It was useless, though. No matter how much I tried to calm down, I felt my orgasm right below the surface. There was no slowing down or turning back.

So instead of trying to hold back, I decided to finish us off. I licked Lee's lips and sucked on his tongue as I squeezed his cock inside my ass and slid up and down his dick. He moaned loudly, and I quickened the pace. Before long, my ass was devouring his cock, and the entire bed rocked.

"Oh, yeah, baby," Lee said between kisses. "Fuck my big cock!"

I sat up straight, impaling his dick all the way inside me. The cum was building up deep in my guts, and I knew it was now impossible to stop. "I'm gonna cum, baby," I tried to yell, but only managed to whisper hoarsely.

"Give it to me," Lee said, and thrust his cock deeper inside me one last time.

I grabbed my cock and held it tight as Lee wriggled beneath me. My entire body shuddered as the first wave shot from my cock and flew past Lee's head and onto the headboard. The next two shots splashed across his face, and he licked at my cum hungrily. Another few spurts landed on his chest and stomach before I collapsed on top of him.

His cock was still buried inside my ass, and as the last few drops of my orgasm leaked from my dick, my ass constricted around his shaft. That was enough for him.

"I'm gonna cum, baby," Lee said, and started to pull his cock from inside me.

"Don't," I said, and clutched his dick even tighter.

"I can't help it, it's too close," he croaked. "I can't stop it."

"I mean don't pull out."

"But . . ."

I wriggled my ass some more, and suddenly it was there. Lee raised us both off the bed, and gasped for breath. His cock thickened with each contraction as he spent himself deep inside me. A wet warmth spread from my ass into my intestines and what seemed as far as my heart. It went on for several moments, until both of us were exhausted and collapsed into each other's arms.

Our breathing patterns melded as we lay there as two people who were now one. I'd never felt more complete or alive.

"We've never done that," Lee said quietly as we untangled ourselves and slipped beneath the blankets. "You sure it's a good idea?"

"We've been together ten years. We've been tested several times."

"Yeah, I know, but . . ."

"You ever cheat on me?"

"Of course not," he said as he fluffed his pillow.

"Me neither. We're clean, we're healthy, and we're monogamous. So, there's nothing to worry about, right?"

"I'm not worried about that," Lee said and kissed me.

"Then what?"

"I'm just not ready to have another kid. The two we have are a handful. I think we should get your tubes tied."

We both laughed much harder than the joke warranted, and began hitting each other with our pillows. I finally gave up and we fell tiredly into one another's arms. I heard Lee snore softly, and knew it'd only be another minute or so before he was out completely.

"I love you, husband," I whispered into his ear.

"I love you, too," he said sleepily. "Husband."

Close Encounter

"Nothing's wrong, all right," I said as I pulled the blankets back and started to get out of bed. "I just have to get to work. God, it's not like I haven't had to do this for the past twelve years."

"Come on, honey," Brad said sleepily, and pulled my hand over to touch his hard cock. "I remember when you used to set the alarm a few minutes early so we could have a little fun before you left for work."

"Yeah, well, I didn't set it early last night," I said irritably as I looked over at him. A little shock of black curly hair fell across his forehead, and his eyes were still half closed from sleep. For a moment my heart skipped a beat. Then his eyes closed, and the smile on his lips disappeared as he looked away. "And don't read anything into that that isn't there."

"So go in a few minutes late," he said as he slid over and kissed my soft cock. "Tell them traffic was a bitch." He pulled the head of my dick into his mouth and sucked on it softly, and it soon began to respond.

"Bradley, get serious," I snapped as I stood up quickly, tossing him to the other side of the bed. "I've got a busy day ahead of me."

"You always have a busy day ahead of you lately," he mumbled, and pulled the covers over his head as he turned his back to me.

"And it's a good thing, too, since you haven't really been helping out much. Your last temp job was almost two months ago. Someone's gotta pay the mortgage and the car payments. Apparently that's me."

I heard a gasp from under the blankets, and immediately regretted what I'd said. Bradley was one of the most sensitive men I'd ever met. It was one of the first things that made me fall in love with him. But he was easily hurt, and I seemed to be hurting him a lot the past few months. I looked at the lump of blanket on the bed and saw it was shaking a little. I knew he was crying, and I wanted nothing more than to crawl back into bed with him under the covers, wrap him in my arms, and make slow and passionate love to him. To say how sorry I was. To make it all better.

Instead, I walked out of the bedroom and into the bathroom. I turned the water on so hot the mirror steamed up, and then stood under the stream of hot water for what seemed an eternity. If I stayed under the spray of scalding water long enough, maybe I could scourge myself from the filthy attitude I'd been having lately toward the man I loved. Maybe I could be clean and good and loving again. Maybe I could find my old self.

But none of that happened. Instead, my skin turned red and wrinkled. When I finished showering I quickly got dressed for work.

"I'm sorry, Brad," I said softly as I leaned down and kissed the top of his blanket-covered head. "I'll probably be home a little late, so I'll just grab some fast food for dinner."

I walked to the bedroom door, then stopped and turned around. The blanket was shaking even more visibly now, and I heard Brad sniffling. My heart ached, and again I wanted to wrap him in my arms and make it all okay. But instead, I turned around and walked out the door.

I don't know why I bothered going into work at all. Who was I kidding? There was no way I'd be getting any work done. Not in the mood I was in.

And what the fuck was that mood all about, anyway? Why had I been treating Brad so badly the past couple of weeks? I wasn't mad at him. I didn't resent that he wasn't working. We had more than enough money to take care of our bills and still enjoy what most would consider a better-than-middle-class lifestyle. In fact, it was I who'd encouraged him to quit the job he hated and do a little temp work on the side while he tried to finish the novel he'd been working on for more than a year.

I looked to make sure the blinds were drawn on my office window that looked out into the lobby, then cleared my desk of the cluttered papers on which I should have been working. Then I typed in what I knew would be my only means of stress release and allow me to actually get some work done in the afternoon.

www.getmesomenow.com

I quickly signed in and entered the Denver chat room. It was filled with profiles and pictures I was very familiar with. Denver might be a big city, and even have a large gay community, but the fags who stalked these rooms were pretty much a core group. We all knew one another, or at least were familiar with the names and pictures.

I immediately received three or four Instant Messages (IM's) from some guys I'd flirted with a few times.

<< I need to suck your dick >> one said.

<< And it needs sucking >> I responded automatically.

<< So when are we finally gonna hookup? >> asked another.

<< I'm free this afternoon >> I typed as I scrolled down the list and checked out the other guys in the room.

I recognized all of them, and had chatted with ninety percent of them in the last six months. But then I came across a name I hadn't seen before: *Desperate4It*.

<< So am I >> the last guy wrote back. << Let's meet at 4 and I will fuck your brains out >>

<< No. Let's meet at 4 and I will fuck *your* brains out >> I typed back as I opened the profile of the new guy.

<< That works too. Where? >>

<< Meet me in the restroom at the Safeway on 6th and Corona. Have your pants down, your cock hard and, your ass lubed. >> I was such a tease. It came so naturally. I led guys on like this all the time, but never followed through with any of the flirtations. Sometimes I wondered if any of them actually went where I told them to.

<< I'll be there and ready >> he typed.

<< See ya then >>

I read the profile for *Desperate4It*. "30 y/o. Very cute, hot, and in great shape. I'm mostly a bottom, but inhibition is not in my vocabulary. Tight bubble butt and nice thick cock. Must be discreet. But let's have some fun."

The profile sounded hot. A little generic, but most profiles were on this site. He had a couple of pictures linked to the profile, but they were locked. Users could only get access to the locked pics if the profile owner unlocked them. What the fuck, I thought. He was the only guy in the room I hadn't seen or chatted with before.

<< Hi >> I wrote. << Nice profile. What's goin on? >>

<< Not too much >> *Desperate* wrote back. <<Just getting out of bed and trying to get going for the day >>

<< Kinda late for just getting up, isn't it? >>

<< I'm spoiled. I get to sleep in a lot >>

<< Nice. So what are you looking for? >>

There was a long pause, almost five minutes, and I thought I'd either offended the dude or scared him off. But then his response came.

<< I don't know, really. Well, I do, but I'm a little confused and torn >>

Normally I wouldn't continue with this guy. I'm not one to beat around the bush, and I have little patience with those fags online who pretend to be shy and reserved and yet spend the entire day on hookup sites. But something about this guy seemed a little different. So I played along. << Awww, come on >> I typed. << Don't be shy. We're all here for the same reason >>

<< Yeah, I know. I'm not playing games. I do know what I want. But I shouldn't want it, and I'm having a little trouble dealing with that >>

<< And just what is it you want? >>

<< I want to get fucked >>

My cock instantly hardened, which was weird. I'd read those words from other guys a thousand times with no reaction whatsoever.

<< And I want to fuck you >> I wrote.

Again, several minutes passed with no response, but I noticed he was still logged on.

<< Hello? >>

<< I want it. I really do. But I shouldn't. I'm not a tease. Please believe me >>

<< I do >> I typed back, and was surprised to realize that I really did. << Why shouldn't you want me to fuck you? Are you a good little Catholic or something? >>

<< No >>

<< Then just listen to what you want and not what you feel you shouldn't do. It's usually a lot funner that way >>

<< More fun >> *Desperate* corrected me, and I smiled.

<< I really do want to fuck you, and I can come over right now. Can I see your pics first >>

<< I dunno if I should be doing this >>

<< Of course you should >>

Another few moments of awkward silence.

<< Please >> I typed, and then stared at the words on the screen. I'd never pleaded with anyone on these sites. They all wanted *me*. My profile made it clear that I was hot and masculine and built like Adonis. The fact that I had an eight-inch, wrist-thick

cock didn't hurt either. And I had pictures to back up my claims, when I chose to unlock them and tease the players a little more than usual. *They* always begged me.

<< OK >> *Desperate* typed back. << But please don't share them with anyone. I really shouldn't be doing this >>

<< I won't >>

A moment later I received a message that his pictures had been unlocked. I clicked on the first one and stared at the most beautiful ass I'd ever seen. It was as white as snow and silky smooth. The back and legs that were also visible were deeply tanned, and as smooth as the tightly muscled bubble butt that was exposed on top of . . .

. . . Wait. That was my bedspread in the picture. I leaned in closer to the screen and looked at his ass. There it was. The tiny mole at the bottom of his back where his spine met his ass. I quickly clicked on the second picture, and Brad's smiling face stared back at me.

A sharp, stabbing pain shot through my heart, and I fought to catch my breath. Tears welled in my eyes, and I wiped them away before they could fall down my cheeks.

<< Hello? >> Brad typed. << I hope your silence doesn't mean you've changed your mind >>

I stared at the pictures and tried to type something. But my hands wouldn't move.

<< It's OK if you're not interested. I understand >>

<< No, it's not that >> I typed quickly.

<< Then? >>

<< I want you >> I typed as I wiped a tear from my eyes. << Can I fuck you now? >>

Another moment of pause, and then . . . << Yes >>

<< Good. What's your address? >> I couldn't stop the tears now, and my heart felt like I'd swallowed it.

<< Can't do it here >>

<< Why not? I'm at work now. We can't do it here >>

<< OK, look. I have a boyfriend, and I can't bring someone into our home. Sorry if that offends you, but that's the way it is >>

I sniffled and wiped snot from my nose. Brad was getting a little feisty now, like he did when his mind was made up. I wanted to smile, but couldn't.

<< If you have a bf, why are you having sex with someone else? >>

<< Are you judging me? >>

I did smile at that one. He could be so pissy at times. I loved him for that.

<< No. Just wondering >>

<< He's been a little . . . preoccupied the past few months. Not real responsive, and I'm horny as shit, OK? >>

<< OK >>

<< Look, I'm not looking for anything serious here at all. I'm in love. But I just need to get fucked. It's been awhile >>

<<I understand >> I typed and swallowed hard.

<< I'm beginning to think this isn't such a great idea. Maybe we should just forget it >

<< NO!! Let's do it. Just say when and where >>

<< I don't know >>

<< Meet me at the Safeway at 6th and Corona in half an hour >> We lived only two blocks from there, and I knew he wouldn't argue. << I drive a white Honda Element. I'll be at the front door waiting for you >> It was a lie. I drove a black Lexus, and I had no intention of meeting him at Safeway.

<< OK >>

<< I'll see you in a few minutes >>

<< Bye >>

I signed off the site and wiped the tears from my eyes. My god, how could I have let it go this far? How could I have neglected the man I love so much that he actually was looking for sex elsewhere? Sure, I played around online a lot, but I only teased. I never met or intended to meet anyone. I was pretty sure Brad had every intention of meeting me at Safeway.

I turned off my computer and walked out of my office.

"Rhonda, I'm gonna be gone for the rest of the afternoon. Cancel my appointments. Tell them I'm sick. I'll be back tomorrow."

"Yes, Mr. Peterson."

It took me about fifteen minutes to get home. I parked a block away, and sat in my car for a couple of minutes, gathering my courage and trying to catch my breath and slow down my heartbeat. Then I walked up to our house. I stood on the front porch, just to the side of the door so Brad wouldn't be able to see me if he were to look toward the door or window.

After about five minutes, Brad opened the door and took a step out onto the porch. Before he could put both feet outside the door, I stepped forward and pushed him backward into the house.

"What the . . ." he started to yell.

I saw the fear and surprise in his eyes and heard it in his voice, and wished more than anything that I could take it all away and make him feel safe. Then the look in his eyes softened as he realized it was me.

"Steven, what's going on? What are you doing home?"

"I came for you."

"What?"

"Where were you going, Brad?" I asked, trying very hard to keep my voice from shaking.

He hesitated for a moment. "I was . . . we're out of . . ."

"Shhhh," I said, and kissed him softly on the lips. I sucked on his tongue as he darted it in and out of my mouth, and hugged him tightly as he allowed his body to relax against mine. "We're not out of anything, do you hear me? Nothing you can get at Safeway or anywhere else. We're not out of anything. We have all we need right here."

Brad pulled away my body and looked at the floor. "How did you know?"

"Because I'm the guy you were chatting with. I'm the man you were going to meet at Safeway."

"I'm so sorry, Steven," Brad whimpered, and raised his hands to his face. "I didn't mean to . . . I don't know what . . ."

"It's okay. Don't cry. And don't apologize."

"I didn't want to . . ."

"I've been such an ass, babe. I should never have treated you like that. If you'd have left me for the way I've been treating you lately, I would have deserved it."

Brad grabbed me by the back of the neck and pulled me into him. He licked my lips, and then slid his tongue slowly into my mouth. I tasted the toothpaste and mouthwash and knew they were meant for someone else. Some anonymous trick that he'd have given himself to completely for an hour and then never see again. Hopefully. But I didn't care. It was me tasting it now, and I sucked on his tongue and kissed him passionately.

He began undressing me as he kissed me and pushed me backward toward the bedroom. When we reached the bed, he threw me down onto it, and ripped my slacks from my legs. And he didn't bother pulling off my underwear, but instead ripped them in half and threw them to the floor. I'd never seen him like this.

"I love you, Steven," he said huskily as he straddled my naked body and leaned in to kiss me as he undressed himself.

"I love you, too," I said, helping him with his jeans.

"But I need more than what you've been giving me lately," he whispered in my ear.

"I know . . ."

"Shut up. I need you to hold me tight and tell me you love me. I need you to laugh with me and make me laugh with you. I need you to bring me flowers and tell me every day that you can't live without me."

"I will," I panted as he rubbed his naked ass across my hard cock. "I promise. I can't stand the thought of losing you. I don't know what I was thinking. I don't know what came over me."

"And I need you to fuck me. I need you to fuck me right now and every day for the rest of our lives." He reached behind him and positioned my cock head at the entrance to his hole.

He took a deep breath then slid his ass down onto my cock until just the head slid inside. He moaned loudly as his ass tightened around the head of my cock. "Every day that I tell you I want it," he whispered into my ear as he licked it and then slid all the way down my thick shaft.

I closed my eyes and moaned as he squeezed my dick. The heat of his ass muscles warmed my cock like a wet electric blanket. It was so tight it felt like he had my cock wrapped in one of those blood-pressure cuffs. He's been that way from day one, and even though we'd had sex hundreds of times, it never ceased to amaze me how tight and in control his ass was.

"God, I love you, babe," I moaned as I slid my cock in and out of him.

"Then start acting like it," he said as he bit my lower lip roughly, then kissed me softly. He'd never been aggressive like this before, and it made my cock harder inside him. "And don't ever disrespect me again." He pulled his ass all the way off my cock to prove his point.

"I won't," I panted, and pulled him by the waist back onto my throbbing cock. "I promise."

"Good. Now shut up and fuck my ass."

As if I needed prodding. I lay on my back for several minutes, sliding my big dick deep into his ass, and then out again. I hadn't realized how long it'd been since I'd fucked Brad until I felt the cum churning in my balls after only a couple of minutes.

"I'm gonna cum," I moaned.

"Like hell," Brad said, and slid off me in one move. He lay on his back and lifted and spread his legs.

I took a few seconds to catch my breath, and allow the cum to retreat. Then I went back in. I put the head of my cock against his already wet and hot hole and let it rest there for a moment.

"Don't tease me, Steven," Brad said huskily. "Shove your cock up my ass and fuck me."

I was in no position to argue, so I slammed my dick into him in one move. He cried out in initial pain, and bit his arm. Then he began to moan as he lifted his ass off of the bed and up and down the length of my cock. I tried to pretend I was in control, shoving inside him slowly at first and then more forcefully. But I was kidding myself. Brad's ass was so strong and commanding that I was completely at his mercy. He squeezed my dick as he slid himself up and down my cock. I finally stopped moving altogether and just let him milk my cock.

He moaned and thrashed his head back and forth as he impaled my dick, and that was all it took. I couldn't take any more. I slammed into him several times until my balls slapped against his ass.

"I'm cumming, baby," I said loudly.

"Me too," he said, and slid his ass off my cock.

I pointed my dick toward his torso just in time. Cum flew everywhere—the headboard, the wall behind us, the pillows on either side of Brad's head, his chest and stomach. But the majority of it landed on his face. He was covered in it, and it turned me on more than I'd expected. I leaned down and kissed him, licking my own still-warm cum from his soft, sex warmed lips.

"Oh, FUCK!" Brad yelled, and a moment later I felt the wet heat of his load spray across my back and ass. When it finally stopped I found myself wishing it hadn't.

I collapsed onto him, relishing the feel of his cum drying on my back and ass as our chests and stomachs slid against one another with the slickness of the part of my load that had landed on his torso. We lay like that, chest to chest and feeling one another's heartbeats, for several minutes before either of us spoke.

"I need more than just your money and your security, Steven,"

Brad whispered into my ear as we caught our breath. "I need more than what you've been giving me lately."

"I know, baby."

"I need you to kiss me."

"I know."

"I need you to love me."

"I do."

"And I need you to fuck me like you'll never get the chance to do it again."

"I will."

"A lot."

I laughed and kissed him tenderly, then looked into his eyes. Tears were streaming down them. "I know, baby. Really I do," I said as I wiped his tears and kissed him again. "I realize that now. I've been a jerk. But I can't lose you. I can't bear the thought of not having you by my side for the rest of my life."

"I love you, Steven."

"And I love you. I'll never let you doubt that again, or feel like you need to go elsewhere."

"Thank you. And now, just one more thing," he said as he rolled me off of him and leaned on one elbow as he looked into my eyes.

"What?"

"Get rid of that website account and don't ever get another one."

"I've never done anything with anyone I've talked with on there . . ." I started to explain. But his single raised eyebrow silenced me. "Done."

"Good," Brad said, and wrapped himself around my naked body. "This isn't some fluke, you know? This is you and me together for the rest of our lives."

I heard the sleepiness in his voice and knew he'd be asleep in less than two minutes. "For the rest of our lives and then some," I whispered in his ear.

"I like that," he said, barely audible, and then I felt him snoring lightly.

I hugged him to my body and allowed the tears to flow freely. I'd come way too close to losing the one meaningful thing in my life, and I knew without a doubt I'd never let it happen again. I kissed his ear and snuggled closer to him as sleep washed over me and I thought about how I was the luckiest man in the world.

A Call Boy's Tear

Mykel leaned against the bay window and drew his knees up to his chest. White moonlight mixed with the amber glow from the streetlamp halfway down the block and created an eerie, yet comforting radiance that seeped through the window and pierced the darkness from the room behind him.

He took a long drag from his cigarette and inhaled deeply, wincing from the sting as the smoke penetrated and staked claim to his throat and lungs. When he exhaled, very little of the smoke he'd sucked in came back out, and he thought that could not mean anything good.

The big wooden window creaked and moaned as he forced it open a few inches. It was a little after three in the morning in San Francisco, and the cold air and fog caused the wood to expand and protest as he manhandled it up the metal track. He hadn't been able to bring himself to replace the old windows when he'd bought the house three years ago. He could update much of the interior of the old place, but not the windows. They had too much character.

Mykel stretched his body out across the wooden seating area in the bay window and looked down at his naked body. It was long and lean, with smooth, well-defined muscles that flexed impressively with the smallest effort. He'd just gotten out of the shower a few minutes before, and tiny pellets of water still clung to his skin. As the brisk bay air whispered across his body, his wet skin tightened and chill bumps covered every inch of his body. His tiny nipples hardened, and he felt his cock constrict in protest.

He looked down at it as he drew in another mouthful of smoke and swallowed it. Even cold and wet and shrinking, it was fucking impressive. At its very smallest and softest, as it was right now, it was still just under six inches long and thicker than most cocks at full hardness. The veins that snaked across the shaft pulsed with his heartbeat and promised to double the size of his cock at a moment's notice, which it often did with no effort at all.

The curl at the ends of Mykel's lips could be interpreted as a sneer or a smile, and depending on his mood, either would be correct. It was virtually impossible to distinguish between the two anyway.

He reached down with his free hand and cupped his balls, squeezing and rolling them for a moment. They were freshly shaven and filled his big hands. When his cock began to respond to the touch and harden, he let go of the balls and stared emotionless at his dick. He loved his cock. When he was much younger it had actually brought him quite a bit of pleasure. And now it was responsible for the lavish lifestyle to which he had become accustomed. To this day, at his own slightest touch, and often without a touch at all, it hardened and sent shockwaves of pleasure through his body.

Yet sometimes, at times like this, he loathed his cock. As much pleasure as it had brought him over the years, it had brought him twice as much pain. Why couldn't he have been less blessed? More like a normal kid? Why did men have to desire him to the extent they did? Why did he have to love sex as much as he did and still be hurt and betrayed by it?

He continued to glare at his dick. The snarl/smile stayed the same as it always did, and an onlooker would not be able to decide which it was. But the increasingly squinting eyes and tightening of the muscles around his jaw were unmistakable.

Mykel stood and paced around the room for a few moments. He walked over to the wall-sized, mahogany-framed mirror and looked at all of the leather furniture, granite and marble statues and crystal chandeliers behind him, and forced himself to contain a snorted chuckle. The reflection staring back at him showed no emotion at all as he glared at it. He ran long fingers through his thick black hair and watched as the reflection did the same. Who was the hot guy with the piercing blue eyes, silky white skin and dimpled smile looking back at him through the mirror? Was this guy with the smooth, chiseled body really the Greek god he appeared to be, or was he a complete fake? A masterful painting that was beautiful and mysterious on the surface, but nothing but messy oil and a jumble of color when one dug deeper into the canvas?

And then he realized it didn't matter. He didn't like that guy anyway. He never had, and he probably never would.

The phone rang, and he smiled when he looked down at the caller ID display. He recognized the name and the New York City number immediately.

"What the fuck do you want?" he barked into the phone, as he walked into his room and pulled the carry-on suitcase from his closet and began to pack for a couple of nights in the Big Apple.

"Good evening, Mr. Christian," the doorman said as he opened the heavy glass door and stepped aside to allow Mykel entrance.

Mykel nodded at the doorman without saying a word. He glided through the large, sparsely decorated lobby and to the elevator, where he pressed the Penthouse button, and then entered the private code when instructed to do so. The ride was fifty-eight floors, and the elevator was relatively slow. Still, there wasn't much time to fuck around, and so he stripped quickly in the elevator. He reached into the suitcase and pulled out the leather harness and jockstrap, and pulled and strapped them on quickly. Then he reached deeper into the suitcase and pulled out a thin black leather mask that covered the upper half of his face, but that allowed his piercing blue eyes, his nose and mouth to be seen, and slipped it snugly over his head.

When the elevator reached the top floor and the doors slid open, Mykel was already fully hard. He walked inside and set his suitcase against the wall just outside the elevator, and looked around him.

There were a few candles lit throughout the living and dining areas, and from behind the kitchen he could see the flickering light from the television coming from the bedroom.

Right on. He liked this particular scene very much. It was his favorite, in fact. The other scene, where the homeowner comes home to find his apartment being robbed, was cool, too. But this one was even better. Because in this one, there was a third party who never knew what was about to happen. The sincere fear in the stranger's eyes and voice fucking got his blood flowing and his cock even harder than usual, and he really got off on all of it.

He walked quietly over to the closet between the living room and the dining room, and reached carefully onto the upper shelf. There, he found a very realistic looking toy pistol and several long strands of leather rope. He draped the rope around his neck and shoulders, and closed the closet door halfway shut. And then he walked slowly and quietly toward the bedroom at the end of the hall.

"What the fuck do we have here?" Mykel said loudly as he walked into the bedroom. "A couple of faggots?"

The two middle-aged men had been in the middle of a sixty-nine session. His client shrieked, and acted surprised. The other guy lay frozen on the bed, his eyes wide and glued to the plastic pistol in Mykel's hand. He opened his mouth to say something, but was frozen with fear.

"Both of you, lie down on your backs," Mykel said roughly, and waved the gun around, as if he could really shoot them at any given moment. "And don't even think about screaming for help. Unless you want it to be the last word you ever gasp."

The two men lay side by side on their backs. The frightened guest was beginning to form tears in his eyes, and his cock went completely soft in a matter of seconds. He was shivering, and trying hard not to cry or make any noise. The client had a gleam in his eyes, and was as hard as a rock, but he stayed motionless on the bed, and played along.

Mykel walked around the bed and tied both men's hands to the head of the four-poster bed, and their feet to the shorter poles at the foot of the bed. He walked over to the client's side of the bed and stood next to him.

"Suck my cock, bitch," he sneered, and shoved his huge dick into the client's mouth. The guy had never been a great cocksucker, and had never been able to take more than a couple of inches of Mykel's giant dick. So Mykel just slid enough in to make him choke a little and make it sound like he was taking much more than he really was. Hey, he was paying Mykel five thousand dollars for a couple hours of work, and if he wanted it to look like he was swallowing this intruder's huge cock, then Mykel was more than willing to oblige. He always aimed to please.

He noticed the other guy was looking over at them from the corner of his eyes, and despite his obvious fear, his cock was starting to twitch.

"What the fuck are you looking at, punk?" Mykel said, and pulled his cock from the client's mouth and walked over to the other side of the bed.

"Nothing," the man whimpered, and tried to look away.

Mykel pointed the toy gun at the man's head. "Look at me."

The man looked him right in the eyes, and Mykel noticed his cock begin to harden even more. He was used to this reaction. Even at their most frightened and vulnerable, he'd never encountered a man yet who didn't get rock hard just staring into his eyes.

"Open your mouth," he said, and moved closer as he pointed the gun right at the older guy's now fully hard cock. "And you'd better hope to god you're a better cocksucker than your friend here."

He slapped his cock against the man's cheeks and lips for a couple of seconds, and smiled when the old guy began to whimper and wriggle beneath the ropes. He slid his cock into the man's mouth, and shoved several inches down his throat. He could tell the dude was trying his best to take all of him, but with three or four inches of hard cock still to go, the old guy choked and giant tears rolled down his face.

"Fuckin' amateurs," Mykel said as he pulled out, and then slammed back into the old man's mouth. He face fucked him for several minutes, and had to give it to the old guy. He gave it the good old college try.

"Oh, shit," the stranger said quickly as he pulled his mouth from Mykel's cock and turned his head to one side. "I'm gonna cum."

"You cum, and it will be the last time you do," Mykel said angrily, and aimed the gun only an inch from the man's face.

"Oh, god," the man cried, and bit his lip hard.

Mykel watched as the guy's cock throbbed for a moment, and then began to soften. When he looked into the guy's face, he noticed huge tears dropping down the dude's cheeks. He wanted to feel bad for the guy. To feel guilty for scaring him and making him cry. But he didn't. He didn't feel anything.

"You'll cum when I tell you to cum, and not before. You got that?"

The guy kept biting his lip as his cock softened, and nodded his head.

"You!" Mykel said forcefully, and waved the gun toward his client. "I'm gonna fuck your ass now, and I don't want to hear a word out of you. Is that clear?"

"Yes . . ."

"I said not a fuckin' word. What part of that don't you understand?"

His client remained silent.

"Good boy. Now, I'm going to untie your legs so you can get on your knees with your ass toward me. Your hands will stay tied. You got that?"

The client nodded, and Mykel untied his feet and pushed him into the doggie position. Then he walked over to the foot of the bed and stared at the stranger.

"I'm going to untie you and you're going to crawl under this fucker and suck his cock while I fuck him," Mykel said to the other guy, knowing that this was his client's favorite position to get fucked when there was a third person. "I know you're not stupid enough to try anything silly. Right?"

"I won't, I promise," the old man said.

"Good," Mykel said, and untied the man's hands and feet, and pointed the gun for him to crawl underneath the client. When the man was in place, Mykel said, "Now get into a sixty-nine position, like you were when I walked in, and suck his cock."

The guy positioned his head right under the client's cock and so that his cock was directly beneath the client's head. He reached out with his tongue, and licked the head of the client's cock, and then took the whole thing into his mouth.

Mykel stood behind the client, and spit a huge wad of saliva onto the client's ass. He knew from experience that the guy's ass would already be well lubed. He'd hooked up with this particular client at least twenty times, and knew him inside and out. The spit was purely to make it look more legit to the stranger.

"Please don't . . ." the client began.

"Shut up and suck your girlfriend's dick," Mykel spat out. He rubbed the head of his cock against the client's ass a couple of times, and then slid it just inside the red hole.

"Oh god," the client cried out in mock pain. "It hurts. Please don't . . ."

"You're a fucking glutton for punishment, aren't you?" Mykel said, and shoved his gigantic cock deep into the bowels of his client. "Suck his cock, and if I hear a word or even a grunt out of you, I'm gonna kill you both. Is that clear?"

The client didn't verbally respond, but sucked on his friend's dick as his friend did the same to him.

Mykel fucked his client relentlessly. The old dude was a freak when it came to getting fucked. He couldn't get enough, even of Mykel's big cock. His ass wasn't tight at all, which Mykel didn't experience very often. Given his length and girth, even the biggest sized queen was usually fairly tight. But this client was actually rather loose, and so Mykel was able to fuck him for several minutes before working up a load.

With the sixty-nine action going on with his buddy, the client worked himself to a climax fairly quickly. He moaned and wiggled his ass, which was Mykel's clue that he was about to shoot.

"Your buddy's gonna cum now," Mykel said to the stranger, grabbing him by the hair underneath his client's ass and cock. "Don't even think about moving your mouth. You're gonna swallow every last drop of his load. Got that?"

The guy grunted a reply, and Mykel quickened his pace and shoved his cock deeper and faster into his client's ass. The client moaned loudly, and his body stiffened. Mykel knew he was spraying his load down his buddy's throat, even though he couldn't feel his client's ass tightening around his cock, like he usually felt when he was fucking someone as they came. The stranger beat his own cock as he swallowed his friend's load, and soon shot his own all over his belly.

Mykel smiled genuinely for the first time since he'd arrived in New York City. He was almost done here, and the entire scene had taken less than an hour. Sometimes sex with this particular client took only a couple of hours, but he wanted Mykel for the whole weekend. Just the company. But he'd let Mykel know when he called that it was just a one-niter. As it turned out now, it was only a one-hour gig. Better yet for Mykel. He got the same five thousand dollar fee, regardless.

He pushed the client roughly onto his stomach next to his friend, with his hands still tied to the headboard, and pulled the stranger by the hair, closer to his cock at the foot of the bed. He closed his eyes so he wouldn't have to stare at the two older men, and concentrated. It didn't take long. His cock was pretty much at his command within a couple of seconds.

"Open your mouth and eat my cum," Mykel said to the stranger, and grabbed the post of the bed with his free hand that wasn't holding the gun, which he pretended to point at the client.

He felt the geyser build deep in his balls, and then shoot up the length of his shaft. It shot out of his cock with its usual gale-force and sprayed in every direction. It not only covered the stranger almost completely, but landed on the headboard, the wall behind them, the client and all over the bedspread on either side of the stranger. It was a pretty normal load for Mykel, but he could tell by the moans of admiration from his two "victims" that they were quite impressed. It was something he'd become very accustomed to over the years.

When the last of his cum had been drained of his cock, he looked at the two men covered in cum on the bed. It appeared as if he were contemplating their fate.

"I'm going to assume that you two aren't completely stupid, and that if I allow you to live, you will not get out of this bed or try to phone the police for at least fifteen minutes. Is that a safe assumption?"

Both older men nodded eagerly.

"You," he pointed the gun at the stranger, "lie right where you are for fifteen minutes. Then you can untie your buddy here. My suggestion is that at that time, you both do the smart thing, and decide not to call the police at all. But that's your call, and I'll be long gone by then, so I won't be able to stop you."

The poor guy just nodded.

"Good boy," Mykel said. He walked out of the bedroom, and into the kitchen. He could hear whispered conversation coming from the bedroom, and knew his client was convincing his friend to wait the full fifteen minutes, and not to say a word to anyone. They both had reputations to protect, after all.

He put the ropes and the toy gun back in the closet and changed clothes in the dark in front of the elevator doors. Then he reached into the top drawer of the desk next to the closet and pulled out the check written out to his name. He double checked the amount, touched up his hair in the mirror hanging next to the doors, and then walked into the elevator and pressed the lobby button.

"You look like shit, you know." Mykel's best friend, Laura, sat across from him at the small table at Café Flor. It was just a few blocks from his house, and his favorite hangout.

"Thanks for the boost of confidence. I'm tired, that's all. I just got back from a quick trip to New York."

"Mmm hmm," she said, as she blew into her cup of chai. "It's always a quick trip somewhere. New York, LA, Chicago, Rio, London. The list just goes on and on and on. It never stops with you. You're running yourself into the ground."

"I'm staying busy," Mykel said, and swallowed half a chocolate croissant in one bite. "That's a good thing. A very good thing. I'm still in high demand. In fact, I'm having to turn some gigs down. I only have a few more years before I won't be able to say that anymore, so I am taking advantage of it now."

"Whatever. You're twenty-seven years old and fucking gorgeous. You don't look a day over 20, and you have the body of a fucking god. You're going to look hot forever, and I hate you for it. Besides all that, you have more money than God. You could stop hustling right now and live like a king forever."

"Okay, you're hitting all my buttons today, bitch. I won't look hot forever. I have three good years left in me. Four at the most.

But I love you for saying that. And I don't have more money than God. He's still a few million ahead of me, and I won't be happy until I at least catch up."

"You're by far the richest guy I know," Laura said, and picked at the chocolate from the last half of Mykel's croissant. "And I know quite a few rich fuckers."

"And I do *not* hustle. I'm an escort and I provide a very expensive service that is worth every penny. Hustlers walk the streets, baby, and I definitely do not walk the streets."

"Semantics," Laura said, and waved the waiter over for another cup of chai. "My point is, that as gorgeous as you naturally are, you look like shit today. You're not taking care of yourself."

"I am too. I'm spending the entire afternoon at the spa. Facial, mani and pedi, massage . . . the works."

"That's not what I'm talking about, and you know it. You're not taking care of your heart, honey."

"Oh Christ, not that shit again."

"I'm serious. You never need to work again. You can retire and travel the world if you want."

"It's not about the money, sweetie, and you know it. Daddy dearest left me quite comfortable when he croaked. But even before I inherited all his millions, I'd already made and saved a couple of mil myself."

"Seriously?" she asked, looking in shock over the top of her cup. "A couple of million just from fucking?"

Mykel smiled, and tossed the last bite of his breakfast into his mouth. "I'm very good," he mumbled through a mouthful of pastry.

"Wow! But, see, that just proves my point. You don't need the money. Why do you keep doing it? Why not relax and take care of yourself and enjoy life?"

"I'm a philanthropist."

"You're full of shit, that's what you are."

"I'm serious. I love sex, and I'm good at it, and guys pay me crazy amounts of money to fuck them. I don't keep any of it. Not a cent. Everything I make, I donate to charities."

"Shut up!"

Mykel laughed. "I'm not lying. I have four charities that I am very generous with. I live off my inheritance and my investments. Everything I make from my escorting services goes to the charities."

"But why not just donate it outright? Why bother with the hust . . . the escorting services at all?"

"I get bored easily," Mykel said flippantly. "It's a nice distraction. I love sex anyway, and if I can get guys to pay me good money that I then turn around and donate, then why not? It keeps me off the streets and I get to travel and see the all the most exotic places on earth. It's the best of all worlds, really."

Laura just stared at her friend for a moment, and then raised her eyebrows. "But how are you going to find a boyfriend if you're off slutting around the globe?"

Mykel rolled his eyes. "Are we really gonna revisit that page? You know I'm not looking for a boyfriend. I don't want one."

"Who doesn't want a boyfriend?"

"Me!"

"Everyone wants a boyfriend, darling. Even you, underneath that tough exterior. You're just afraid of committing yourself to someone and letting yourself love them. And it's no wonder, with the fucked-up role model your parents gave you. But you know that not all relationships are like that."

"You're forgetting about Alex."

"No, I'm not. I'm intentionally ignoring him. He was after only one thing. Okay, well two. Your huge cock and your huge bank account. He was definitely bad news. But no one gets it right the first time around. You just gotta keep putting yourself out there, and make yourself available for love."

"No, I don't. I can keep fucking as many men as I want, whether it's for pay or not. And then I can send them home."

"Like you sent Victor home?"

Mykel looked up at her with searing eyes. "That's not fair. We agreed not to bring him up."

"Yeah, well, I changed the rules. He's a really good man, and all he wants is to settle down with you. Build a life together. Have a healthy relationship with you."

"I don't need the mess of a relationship, and I don't want it, either."

"Mykel Orlando Christian, you know that is not true. You have way too much love in that big heart of yours not to want to share it with someone. You're just giving up on yourself, and I won't allow that to happen."

"Apparently," Mykel said, as he signed the charge tab and stood up to leave. "And I love you for it." He kissed Laura on the forehead, and opened the door for her, allowing her continued rants to be lost in the fresh breeze as they walked outside and headed for the spa.

When he got home after the spa treatment, he had six voicemails. One was from Laura, thanking him for the full day of pampering. Four were from clients, requesting dates with him. He knew immediately that he would turn down three of them. But the guy from Rio was special. He'd worked with the guy and his boyfriend four or five times, and each occasion was better than the previous. They flew him out to Rio first class for a full week, put him up in a luxury hotel right on the beach, took care of all his expenses, and only asked that he fuck around with them two or three times while he was there. All of that, and a check for ten thousand dollars made it pretty hard for Mykel to say no to them. He made a mental note to call them the next morning to make the travel arrangements.

But the last call was from Victor, and that was the call that kept him awake right now, lying naked in bed and staring at the ceiling. Their last conversation had been almost a month ago, and as much as Mykel tried to convince himself that he was okay with that, and that he didn't miss Victor, he knew it was a lie. His cock began to harden at the thought of Victor's face, and his voice, and his laughter. He rolled over onto his stomach, to smother the impending erection, and quickly found himself falling asleep.

"That was amazing, you know," Victor said through a smile as he spooned himself against Mykel's frontside. They'd just made love and were lying in Mykel's king-sized bed.

"Thank you," Mykel said, and kissed Victor on the neck. "I do aim to please."

"Hey, I'm not one of your clients."

"No, you're not. And you'd better be glad, or you'd be bankrupt by now."

Victor laughed, and snuggled closer against Mykel's body. This was their seventh or eighth time together, and he was already more comfortable with Mykel than he'd been with his last two lovers, each of whom he'd lived with for a couple of years. There was something special about Mykel, and he'd felt it from the very beginning.

They met at a party that Victor's best friend was hosting. Victor had noticed Mykel the moment he walked in the door, as had everyone else. Mykel had a way of commanding a room like that. But Victor was shy, and certainly not in this guy's league, and so he kept his distance. But Mykel did not. No more than fifteen minutes after he'd arrived, he walked up to Victor and staked his claim. His eyes never left Victor's. He never allowed the conversation to drift away from the subject of Victor. He made sure Victor's glass was never empty. And at the end of the night, he invited Victor to go home with him.

"What was it about me that night that made you come and talk

with me?" Victor asked, as he tried to hold back a yawn. "You obviously weren't looking for a new client. You never asked me for money, and didn't even tell me you were a call boy until our next date. So what was it?"

"It was this ass," Mykel said, as he reached down and grabbed one cheek in his hand. "It was the hottest ass in the room, and I wanted it." It was right on the tip of his tongue to tell Victor the truth: that the second he looked into Victor's eyes, his heart quivered in his chest; that when Victor smiled and his dimples popped up on his cheeks, he, Mykel wanted to dive in and get lost in them; and that when Victor walked past him and Mykel smelled his sweet scent, he thought he'd die if he didn't have that man. It was right there on the tip of his tongue, but he didn't say it.

"That's it?" Victor asked, and turned around to look into Mykel's eyes. "I had a nice ass and you just wanted to fuck me?"

Mykel looked into Victor's face, and noticed how the moonlight from the window made his blond hair shine. He could see those big blue eyes, and those long, thick eyelashes, and those beautiful pink lips that were trying to part into a smile, but weren't quite successful. He thought he was going to say the right thing, was right on the verge of it. But when he opened his mouth, all that came out was, "Yes."

Big tears welled up in Victor's eyes, and when he pushed himself away from Mykel and up from the bed, Mykel knew he'd fucked up. Once again he'd screwed everything up. He should go back and retract everything he just said. Start all over and this time say what he was really feeling. But he knew he wouldn't. He couldn't.

"Where are you going, Vic?" he asked as he watched Victor get dressed in the dark. "You know me, I always say all the wrong things. I'm sorry. Come back to bed."

"Then say the right thing, Mykel," Victor said as he sat on the edge of the bed and tied his sneakers.

"I can't. You know I can't."

Victor sat motionless on the bed, with his back to Mykel, and then took a deep breath. "I love you, Mykel," he said as he turned around *to look at the guy who'd just made love to him. "I kinda thought you felt the same way. Or were at least moving in that direction."*

"Victor, I told you upfront that I was not looking for anything serious," Mykel said, as he sat up in bed. "I can't have any strings in my life right now."

"It's not that you can't," Victor replied, and stood up and began putting on his jacket. "It's that you won't."

"Okay, so it's that I won't. What difference does that make?"

"It makes a big difference, Mykel. What we just did, what we have, is more than just being fuck buddies. It's special. Or at least it could be, if you just let it."

Mykel closed his eyes so that he would not have to look at Victor, and to give him the strength to say what he knew was going to come out of his mouth, even though it is not what was coming out of his heart. "I don't want something special, Vic. I just wanna have a good fuck every now and then."

He heard Victor gasp in the dark, and then he heard Victor walk out of the room and down the stairs. A moment later the front door downstairs shut quietly.

Over the next week, Victor called Mykel at least once every day. Mykel looked at the caller ID display, and let the calls go into voicemail. He just wasn't ready for the kind of relationship Victor was looking for. Victor finally caught on, and to his credit, stopped calling after that first week.

Mykel woke up the next morning and knew at once he'd had another of his nightmares. His heart felt heavy and pained. What was it he'd dreamed about? He couldn't remember, and after very little thought, decided it didn't matter.

He showered and returned the call to Rio, getting the travel arrangements. There was a flight leaving later that afternoon, and he planned on being on it. He called Laura and arranged for her to housesit while he was gone, and then walked into his room to begin packing.

* * *

"Are you sure that thing will hold both of you?" Mykel asked as he looked at the leather sling attached to the ceiling in the basement.

"Yes," Rafael said as he climbed into it and lay on his back. "It's securely screwed into a cement beam. It's not going anywhere we don't want it to."

Mykel took a moment to gaze at Rafael's body. His client was perfectly built: a little over six feet of solid and defined muscles, completely smooth body from head to toe, dark copper skin, and a thick uncut cock that was almost, but not quite, as big as Mykel's. He was a very successful model in South America, and his face was sculpted perfection. He was one of only a handful of the thirty-years-and-younger crowd that Mykel knew who was anywhere near as rich as he was.

Paolo walked up behind Mykel and kissed him tenderly on the neck, and then walked over and joined his lover at the sling. He wasn't in the same league as his Rafael, but was certainly no slouch. He was about five feet eight inches tall, with creamy beige skin and sandy blond hair and green eyes. His smile broke many hearts of both sexes, and there wasn't a soul who knew him who wasn't madly in love with him. He was tender and caring and emotional, and always cared for others way above himself. Everyone thought they were the perfect couple, and Mykel had to agree.

Paolo took Rafael's big uncut cock in his hand and sucked on it for a moment, as Mykel watched from a few feet away. Then he carefully climbed onto the sling and straddled his lover's body. Rafael's thick cock stood straight in the air directly below Paolo's ass, and Mykel found himself breathing heavily as he walked toward the couple.

"Sit on his cock," Mykel said, and reached up to kiss Paolo as he pushed him by the shoulders down toward Rafael's cock. He heard Paolo gasp and felt his body tense up a little for a second or two, and then relax as he slid all the way down to the base of the big dick. "I want to see him fuck you until you cry out in ecstasy and shoot your load all over me," Mykel said, and kissed Paolo passionately on the lips as the two lovers fucked.

The sling began to rock back and forth rapidly, the chains clanging with the fury of the sex. Paolo pushed Mykel back about a foot, and then leaned forward with his ass still impaled on Rafael's cock, and began to suck Mykel's big dick. The three had played around several times before, and Mykel had always considered the couple among his favorite clients. But there was something different about this time. The sling, the clanging of the chains, the heated grunts from the lovers, the dark room and candle light . . . it was all turning Mykel on more than he'd been turned on in quite a while. And Paolo was an expert cocksucker, as well, and so it wasn't long before Mykel felt himself getting very close.

"I'm sorry, guys," Mykel said, because he prided himself on always lasting until he'd made his clients cum. "But I'm gonna shoot. I can't help it."

"NO!" Paolo yelled, as he pulled his mouth from Mykel's cock, and grabbed it forcefully at the base of the cock, cutting off the circulation.

"Oh shit," Mykel moaned, and ground his teeth to prevent from cumming. Two large drops of cum dripped from his cock head, but he was able to hold back from actually shooting. "I'm sorry," he repeated, and shook his head to clear the cobwebs. "What's wrong?"

"Nothing's wrong," Paolo said, and pulled Mykel in for a kiss. "But I want you both inside me at once. I want to feel both of your huge cocks fucking me."

Both lovers were breathing heavily, and speaking in Portuguese, telling each other how hot the other was, and how much they loved one another. Paolo moaned and slid his smooth ass up and down the length of Rafael's giant cock, and Rafael pounded his cock deep into Paolo's ass, squeezing and hugging him as they fucked.

"Are you sure, Paolo?" Mykel asked in Portuguese. He had

many clients who were into fisting and taking things such as traffic cones and baseball bats up their asses. But Paolo wasn't one of them. Paolo was nice and sweet and playful. Almost innocent, if not for the huge cock up his ass and the fury with which he fucked his lover's big cock.

"Yes, I'm sure," he panted, and licked his lips at Mykel in a way that made it impossible for Mykel to deny him. "I want you both inside my ass. Now."

He leaned way back, so that he was almost lying on top of Rafael's torso. From this angle, Mykel could see Paolo's smooth ass stretch to what seemed its limit to take the massive cock that was buried deep inside him. Rafael's cock throbbed, and the giant vein that ran the length under this shaft looked like it was about to explode.

Mykel's own cock was as hard as it had ever been, and he took a step forward and pressed his cock head against Paolo's ass.

"Fuck me!" Paolo said loudly.

And so Mykel did. He slid his cock inside Paolo's ass slowly, until only the head popped in. Rafael and Paolo both gasped, and when he slid his fat cock all the way inside Paolo's hot ass, both lovers held their breaths.

In all his years of fucking, Mykel had never felt anything like this. Paolo's ass was hot and tight as it squeezed his cock from the top and both sides. And Rafael's huge cock was as hard as a rock, and when it slid against the underside of his own cock, it sent shock waves of pleasure throughout his body.

He couldn't believe that Paolo was taking both gigantic cocks up his ass. But there he was, moaning loudly as both men fucked him fast and hard. The two lovers kissed and hugged one another as Mykel held onto the chains at the foot of the sling and pounded his cock relentlessly into Paolo's ass.

"Oh fuck, I'm cumming," Rafael said as he gasped for air. He left his cock buried deep in his lover's ass.

Mykel felt Rafael's cock throb and expand inside the hot ass, pressed against his own as Rafael shot his load deep into Paolo's ass.

"Me too," Paolo said.

A second later Mykel felt the stud's hot ass grab his cock and squeeze it several times as he shot his load in every direction. It seemed to never stop, and with every spurt, the tight ass gripped Mykel's cock it a little tighter and swallowed it a little deeper.

"Shiiiiiiit!" Mykel yelled, and quickly pulled his cock from Paolo's reluctant hole. He barely pulled it all the way out before he began shooting. His load landed all over both men, and when he finished, they were both covered in his cum.

The three men took a couple of minutes to catch their breath, and then Rafael and Paolo stood up and wrapped Mykel in a hug.

"Come to our bed tonight," Paolo said. "Sleep with us."

"I shouldn't really. It's your bed. The hotel is just a couple of blocks away."

"No," Rafael said. "We insist. Sleep with us tonight."

Mykel didn't really feel comfortable with the idea, but they were paying him ten thousand dollars, and so he didn't feel he could refuse, either. "All right," he said, and followed them upstairs to their bedroom.

The two lovers lay on either side of Mykel, and wrapped their arms around him and touching one another. Each of the couple kissed Mykel tenderly, but separately, and fell asleep almost immediately.

But Mykel did not fall asleep immediately. He lay awake for a couple of hours, fighting back tears that he did not know where they came from, and shivering, even though it was quite warm in the room. He listened to the two lovers sleep, and felt them reach for one another in the middle of the night as they wrapped their arms around him, and sensed the love they shared.

And he knew his life would never be the same.

* * *

The plane ride back to San Francisco was a long one, and so Mykel had plenty of time to think and reflect on his life. So much had gone on in the past few months, and it seemed to be spinning out of control. He was not a person who was comfortable or accustomed to being out of control.

Why had he agreed to take the trip to Rio? Of course, it was the money. Who in their right mind would turn down ten thousand dollars, plus all of their expenses for a weekend in Rio? But if he'd just not taken the proposition, then everything would be fine right now. He wouldn't be second guessing himself. He wouldn't be tearing himself up inside.

Seeing Rafael and Paolo together, and interacting with them the way he had, was really fucking with him and his sense of self. And he didn't like it one bit. He'd worked very hard over the past several weeks to convince himself that he needed no one . . . and indeed, wanted no one . . . in his life. He was good alone. He wanted to be alone. He needed to be alone.

And then he spent one weekend with a couple of clients that he'd spent multiple times with . . . and everything suddenly changed. What went wrong? What was different? And then he realized, as if the stereotypical lightbulb blinked on inside his head: He'd slept with them. Not just fucked them and then left, as he'd done on numerous occasions, but actually slept in their bed, wrapped in their arms. As funny, or more accurately, stupid, as it sounded, he'd felt the love between them as he lay in the middle of the two lovers.

And as much as he hated to believe it, let alone admit it . . . he wanted that. Undeniably, he wanted that love. With Victor.

"Fuck!" he said a little too loudly, as he ran his fingers through his hair. The elderly lady across the aisle from him gave him a stern look, and he smiled charmingly and whispered, "Sorry."

He'd known for quite a while that he wanted Victor. Wanted to make a life with him and to love him. He wanted to stop working and settle down and live a normal, happy life. But he'd always felt like that was not an option for him. Everyone that he'd ever loved, ever trusted, had let him down. They'd hurt him.

His parents had hated one another and fought incessantly. They never spoke of it, of course, but he was certain they'd never loved each other. They'd married because it was expected of them. They were the children of two of the wealthiest families in the state, and they'd attended the same school and they'd both become very successful lawyers. Both sets of Mykel's grandparents had pushed them into the marriage, to create some super powerful dynasty, and he couldn't help but think of the prearranged marriages in some of the more traditional societies of the East. His parents had fought vigorously over the smallest thing, and never tried to hide any of it from Mykel.

When his mother was killed in a car accident, there was some talk of his father having arranged the accident. There was a short investigation, but his father was never implicated, of course. He inherited all of his wife's millions, and added to his own, became one of the elite super wealthy.

Mykel and his father seldom spoke, and when they did the conversation was strained and usually one-sided: his father's. Mykel left home when he was sixteen, and hit the streets of San Francisco. It didn't take long to move from common hustler to call boy to extremely high-priced call boy. His father, eager to be relieved of his son's presence, made sure his rent and all of his bills were paid on time, and a hefty "allowance" was deposited into Mykel's bank account every month. His father never asked about his life, and Mykel never offered up any details.

A couple of months after his twenty-fourth birthday, Mykel's father died, and left every cent of his fortune to Mykel. By then Mykel had already made and saved a couple of million of his own, and was just getting comfortable with the term "rich." But when he was instantly in possession of high triple-digit millions, he became numb to it all. He found that he wanted a family . . . a mother and father who loved one another . . . more than he wanted the fortune. And for a while he resented and hated the money. It couldn't buy him what he wanted the most, and so what good was it?

His parents had disappointed and hurt him.

It was about six months into his inheritance that he met Alex. They met by accident at a movie theater. The mysterious bad boy with the boyish looks and the sex-god body and the attitude of a gang of testosterone-ridden body builders. He was standing just outside the door of the theater, smoking, and glaring so hard at Mykel as he stood in line for popcorn that it made Mykel a little uncomfortable. And Mykel was not one to feel uncomfortable very easily or very often. But the look in Alex's eyes said, "I can have you in a heartbeat without even trying. I could turn you around and fuck you right there on the popcorn counter, and have you begging for more."

Mykel had never met anyone who'd made him feel like that before, and so he was intrigued. He walked outside, and began chatting with Alex. Less than half an hour later they were back at Mykel's place, and in his bed. Turned out that it was Alex who was all about getting fucked. Underneath all the tough exterior, he was an insatiable bottom, which was perfectly fine with Mykel.

The guy turned out to be a sweetheart. He bought Mykel flowers and sent him cards and cooked him dinner. He was attentive and affectionate in bed, and it didn't take very long at all before Mykel was besotted with Alex. He bought him a new sports car and expensive jewelry and high-end electronics.

Mykel didn't see it at the time, but the more he bought Alex, the more Alex clung to him and the sweeter and more intimate he became. Mykel fell hard for him, and after three months was ready to ask Alex to move in officially and to share his life. It was then that he overheard a phone conversation he was obviously not meant to overhear.

"He's such a fucking sap," Alex said to an unknown person on the other end of the phone. "You should see the way he looks at me with those puppy dog eyes of his when he's fucking me. Sometimes I honest to god think he's gonna start crying. Yeah, he is richer than the fuckin' Sultan of wherever the fuck he's from. Which is the only reason I'm still around. I mean, he's got this fucking cock from hell, don't get me wrong. He fucks my brains out, and I love it. But shit, I can get that from any two-bit hustler on Market Street anytime I want it. And without all the fucking baggage, you know what I mean?"

Mykel braced himself against the wall, and grit his teeth as he listened.

"I just need to hold out a couple more weeks. I've already got him wrapped around my little finger. He'll give me the money, I know he will. I just have to make sure he really believes I love him first. He does, I know. But just gimme some time to cement it in his head. It won't be long 'til I'm added onto his bank account, and we'll be cool. And then I'll be in his will and we'll be set for good. Just be patient. These things take time."

Mykel walked into the room quietly, and stood behind the sofa on which Alex sat. When Alex finished with his call, and turned around, Mykel landed a right hook directly to his nose. He heard and felt at the same time, the bones breaking as Alex fell backward and hit the ground.

Alex started to get to his feet, and Mykel kicked him back to the ground. "I dare you to try and get up again," he said angrily, and looking directly into Alex's eyes.

Alex glared back, but didn't move.

"Get out of my house right now. I'll pack up your shit and have it out on the front lawn in an hour."

"The car's mine," Alex said aggressively. "You put the title in my name."

Mykel laughed. "Take the fucking car. Like I'd ever want to sit in that thing again? It's yours. But you have about three minutes to get your ass out of my house before I begin ripping your limbs from your body. Come back in an hour and pick your shit up off my lawn."

Alex literally ran out the door, and it was the last Mykel ever saw or heard from him.

Mykel leaned his head against the airplane window. His heart felt like someone had reached inside his chest and grabbed it and squeezed it until it might explode. He became short of breath, and felt a pressure building behind his eyes.

This must be what it's like to cry, he thought to himself. He wasn't quite sure, because he'd never actually cried in his life. Well, he supposed he must have cried, when he was a baby, but certainly not even once that he could remember. He took a couple of deep breaths, and forced his emotions back. He'd come this far in his life without shedding a tear. He wasn't about to start now.

"Ladies and gentlemen, we're about to begin our descent into San Francisco International Airport. In preparation for landing, please make sure your trays are locked in front of you, that your carry-ons are stowed safely under the seat in front of you or in the overhead bins, and that your seat is in its full upright position."

Mykel was successful in holding back the tears, but not in curbing his feelings and emotions for Victor. He'd known for several months that he wanted to make a life with Victor. But he'd been burnt before, and hurt beyond belief, and he hadn't wanted to go through that again. And so he'd pushed Victor away.

Laura was right, though. He had to put himself out there for the possibility of love. For the real thing. Seeing Rafael and Paolo had made him see that perfectly clear. He wanted what they had, and he wanted it with Victor.

The landing and deboarding seemed to take an eternity. And the taxi ride home seemed even longer. He couldn't wait to get home and call Victor and ask him to come over. They needed to talk.

It was just before six in the afternoon when the cab pulled up to Mykel's house. He saw Victor sitting on the front steps from a block away, and felt his heart pound uncontrollably in his chest.

"What are you doing here?" he asked as he stepped out of the cab. It came out of his mouth sounding much more accusatory than happy, and he mentally punched himself in the stomach.

"I'm sorry," Victor said. "I know I shouldn't have come. But Laura told me when you were gonna be back. And . . . well . . . I just couldn't stay away another day. Not without telling you one last time that I love you, and asking you to look me in the eyes and tell me that you don't love me. I know you did it before, and I walked away. But I don't believe you, Mykel. I need to hear you say it again to believe it."

"I can't," Mykel said. "I can't say that to you. Because I love you with every fiber of my being."

"What . . ." Victor started to ask, having been taken by surprise. But Mykel rushed over to him, held his face in his hands and kissed him passionately on the lips as he pushed him backward through the front door and into the house.

Mykel took his time undressing Victor. This was not one of his jobs, and Victor was not one of his clients. He kissed every inch of his lover's naked body as he undressed himself, and then lay next to Victor on the bed.

"I do love you, Vic," he said as he wrapped his arms around him and kissed him.

"I can't take another false alarm," Victor said, "so please make sure you mean it before you say that to me."

Mykel looked Victor in the eyes, and then leaned in to kiss his eyelids. "I love you, Victor."

Victor leaned up and kissed Mykel passionately on the lips. He felt Mykel's cock harden against his leg, and smiled. "I love you, too."

Mykel reached down between Victor's legs and squeezed his cock into full hardness. Then he slid down and licked on the cock head and sucked it gently into his mouth. He loved sucking cock, but didn't do it all that often. He never did it with his clients . . . they paid him to be the hot stud, always in control and always the butch top who wouldn't think of sucking a dick, let alone enjoy it. But there had been a few guys he'd actually cared for over the years, and he'd sucked their cocks and he'd enjoyed it very much.

But this was so much different, he thought as he felt Victor's cock head slide past his tonsils and deep into his throat. This was so much better. He tightened his lips around the shaft, and closed his throat around Victor's big dick. When Victor moaned and grabbed the sheets as he arched his back, Mykel felt himself try to smile with his mouth filled with cock.

"Oh my God," Victor gasped as Mykel deepthroated him. "I didn't know you . . . you never . . . oh fuck!"

Mykel sucked on his lover's dick, slow and easy at first, letting almost the entire length slip from his lips before slowly going back down on it until the whole thing was buried deep in his throat. Then he sucked harder and faster, tightening his lips around the veiny cock as he slid up and down the thick pole.

"Jesus, Mykel," Victor moaned as he wriggled underneath him. "I'm so close."

Mykel sucked even harder, and squeezed Victor's balls lightly with one hand as he entwined his fingers of the other hand with Victor's.

"I'm cumming," Victor warned, as he tried to pull his cock from Mykel's mouth.

But Mykel squeezed both Victor's hand and his balls harder and swallowed the entirety of his cock. He meant for Victor to know that he loved him. He knew in his heart that sex was not the way to show it, but he wished it could be a start, and that Victor would recognize the difference in him. As Victor emptied himself into his throat, Mykel swallowed every drop, and hoped that he'd be successful in swallowing his pride along with the sweet taste of his lover's load.

"What was that all about?" Victor asked, as Mykel sucked the last few drops of cum from his cock, and then slid up to lie next to him.

"I know I always say absolutely the worst thing . . . the wrong thing. And I don't want to do that again. I know sucking your cock doesn't prove that I love you. But I wanted to show you that I'm serious. I do love you, and if you let me, then I will show you that with my heart."

Victor stared into Mykel's eyes. "That was absolutely the right thing to say."

"Can you stay hard?"

"Ummm, yeah," Victor said, and took Mykel's hand and moved it to his still throbbing cock. "I don't think he's going anywhere anytime soon."

"Good," Mykel said. "Because I want you to fuck me."

"What?" Victor asked, and turned to face his boyfriend. "You don't get fucked. Everyone knows that. And you made it perfectly clear to me the night we met."

"Correction. I have never been fucked. Because I was hiding something, protecting myself from something that I feared. But I don't fear it anymore."

"Are you sure?" Victor asked. "I mean, don't get me wrong, I'd love to fuck you. But I want you to be sure that that's what you want."

"I've never been more sure of anything in my life," Mykel said, as he leaned in and kissed Victor on the lips. "I want to feel you inside me. I want to feel you make love to me."

"Done," Victor said, and moved down to suck on Mykel's cock. He was always amazed at the big dick . . . how fat and long and hard it was, and how the thick veins coursed through it. The way the foreskin slid back and rested behind the bulbous head. If ever there was a perfect cock, Mykel had been blessed with it. And Victor was fascinated with it.

He sucked on it for several minutes, knowing when Mykel was getting close, and forcing himself to stop just short of bringing him to the point of no return. When Mykel was all worked up, and grinding harder against him, Victor pushed his lover's legs up against his chest, so that his ass was completely exposed.

When his tongue flickered against the tight, puckered hole, he heard Mykel gasp, and felt him grab the sheets on either side of him. He made sure there was plenty of saliva on his tongue, and then slowly slid it inside Mykel's tight hole. It took a couple of minutes, but he finally was all the way inside, and slid his tongue around the inside.

"Oh fuck, that feels incredible," Mykel moaned, and wriggled his ass against Victor's tongue.

Seeing and hearing Mykel respond to his touch and his tongue like that turned Victor on even more than he was, and he didn't just *want* to fuck his lover, he *needed* to. He raised himself onto his knees and slid into position between Mykel's slick, spread cheeks. He rested his cock head against the hot, wet hole, and bit down lightly on his tongue to keep from shooting right there. He hoped silently that Mykel was not expecting a really long fuck, because even though he'd just cum, he could tell that he would not be able to last too long inside that hot virgin ass.

"Fuck me," Mykel begged. "I want to feel you inside me."

Victor leaned down to kiss his lover, and as he slid his tongue into Mykel's mouth, he slowly slid his cock into his ass.

Mykel groaned loudly, and every muscle of his body tensed up as Victor's cock head slid inside. His mouth tightened around Victor's tongue, and sucked desperately on it.

"Relax, baby," Victor said as he broke the kiss. He licked Mykel's neck and nibbled on it, eliciting another deep moan. He smiled as he felt the sphincter muscles relax just a little, and another inch of his cock slid deeper into Mykel's ass. "Fuck, Mykel, your ass is so hot and tight. I've never felt anything like this." He knew Mykel well enough to know that he'd get off on this kind of talk. "It feels so good wrapped around my big cock."

Mykel stroked Victor's back, and his hands moved down to Victor's ass. He took a cheek in each hand, took a deep breath, and pulled Victor deeper inside him until he was buried deep inside Mykel's ass. A deep, animalistic groan erupted from Mykel's throat as he felt Victor's big dick slide against his prostate. His own cock throbbed uncontrollably across his stomach, and a big drop of pre-cum slid out of the head.

"Fuck me," he whispered.

Victor tried hard to keep himself from becoming manic. He counted prime numbers in his head to keep from shooting too soon. His brain flipped to auto pilot as his cock slid in and out of Mykel's ass.

"Harder," Mykel said, and began tightening his ass and slamming it deeper onto Victor's cock.

Victor pulled his dick all the way out of Mykel's ass. He was so close, he needed just a few seconds to calm down. He leaned down and kissed Mykel again, and as he broke the kiss he turned his lover around, and then raised his hips from beneath, so that Mykel was on all fours in front of him.

"Get back inside me and fuck me," Mykel instructed.

Victor slid his cock deep to the base in one stroke, causing both men to moan loudly in ecstasy. In this position, Mykel's ass was even tighter and hotter, and Victor was able to slide in just a little deeper. There was no holding back now, and he fucked Mykel like a wild man, slamming into him in long, deep thrusts.

"I'm so close," Victor gasped as he fucked Mykel's ass fast and hard.

"Slow down," Mykel said.

"It's too late."

Mykel dropped to his stomach, causing Victor's cock to slide out of his ass.

"Here I cum," Victor moaned, and a second later his load began to spew from his cock. It flew everywhere . . . across Mykel's back, onto his ass and upper legs, onto the bed beside them. It seemed to go on forever. When it finally stopped, he dropped limply on top of Mykel's body. "Are you gonna cum?" he asked between labored breaths.

"Are you kidding me?" Mykel asked. "I blew my load the second you put me on all fours. Your cock slid into my ass in one long, sweet move, and I shot all over the bed."

"You did?"

Mykel laughed, and pointed at the puddle beneath him and all around them.

"I can't tell which is yours and which is mine," Victor grinned as he looked at the cum-soaked bedspread.

"Doesn't really matter," Mykel said. "It's all *ours*, and that's the way I want it to be from now on."

"Seriously?"

"Seriously. I want us to be 'us' from now on. I want you here with me . . . or me with you. I don't care which, as long as we're together."

"What about your work?"

"I'm done. I was only doing it as an escape mechanism anyway. To hide from the truth."

"The truth?"

"That I love you. That I want you. That I need you."

"I love you, too, Mykel. Are you sure you can give it all up just like that?"

"In a heartbeat. It's all in the past, starting right now. My present and my future are with you. If you'll have me, that is."

"I'll definitely have you. You know that was never a question."

"I know, and I'm sorry I was so stupid. So afraid."

"Don't worry about it. We're all entitled to a little stupidity."

Mykel laughed and hugged Victor close to him. "Wanna take a trip somewhere?'

"Where?"

"I don't care. Anywhere. I just wanna get out of this town for a little bit. Go somewhere where no one knows me, and where no one can get ahold of me. I just want to spend some time with you alone."

"It's gonna be hard to find somewhere that no one knows you."

"Shut up!" Mykel laughed and hit Victor with his pillow.

"But I hear Japan is nice."

Mykel had a couple of clients in Tokyo, but thought it better not to mention them to Victor. Besides, he hadn't heard from either of them in over a year.

"Done!" he said. "First class to Tokyo this weekend."

"What about my job?"

"Quit your job. You won't be needing it anymore. When we get back from our trip, you can go back to school and finish your degree. Then you can get the job you really want. You don't have to settle anymore. Not for love or a job or anything else."

The grin on Victor's face was priceless, and Mykel kissed his head as he pulled him to rest his face on Mykel's chest. A couple of minutes later, Victor was snoring softly, and only then did Mykel allow the couple of tears that had been welled up inside him to fall down his cheeks.

Crying wasn't as horrible as he'd thought it would be, he decided, and drifted off to sleep entangled with Victor's body.

WINTER

Okay, now don't hate the messenger. I have to be consistent and give the definition of this word from *Dictionary.com* just as I have with all the other seasons. So here it is:

> 1. *The usually coldest season of the year, occurring between autumn and spring, extending in the Northern Hemisphere from the winter solstice to the vernal equinox, and popularly considered to be constituted by December, January, and February.*
>
> 2. *A year as expressed through the recurrence of the winter season.*
>
> 3. *A period of time characterized by coldness, misery, barrenness, or death.*

Personally I hate Winter. It's cold and I miss the heat of summer. It snows, and I miss strolling along the beach. The days are shorter, and I get depressed when it's dark at five o'clock. So I just don't like the winter months.

Thankfully, we're not looking at winter as a period of the coldest three months of the year. In this book we're viewing winter as the time in our lives when we've lived a long time and had many experiences that, for good or bad, have influenced us and molded us into who we are. The men in these stories are in the age range of fifty to ninety-three years old.

With that much experience and that many years behind us, we can't help having a unique perspective on life. Love doesn't necessarily mean the same thing it did when we were twenty or thirty and green under the collar. Romance looks a whole lot different now. Sex is often a memory or a dream at this point . . . but not always. And intimacy is much more important than any of the other things I've just touched on. Or so younger gay men, tend to—or have been taught to—believe.

But we can be so wrong. In talking with some gay men of this age group, I found some very interesting things. The last definition given above of winter was "A period of time characterized by coldness, misery, barrenness, or death." I was a little shocked when I spoke with some men of that older generation and they didn't totally disagree with the definition. I thought they'd be furious. But they told me they often have found themselves being cold, and miserable and lonely. And the older the men were, the more they thought about and focused on death. It's natural.

But I also found out they believe they feel this way because they've been taught all of their life that they are supposed to feel this at this age. Many cultures teach their young to respect their elders. In some, older people are revered and celebrated and honored. But in American culture, we have a long ways to go before we can come anywhere near that kind of attitude and honor for our senior citizens. Especially in the gay male culture or community, older men are very often forgotten completely, or even worse, pitied. Again, I'm not lumping the entire gay male community into a pot and saying we all feel that way or treat people that way. But we'd be lying if we denied it was a prominent sentiment and way of life for a majority of our community.

What I learned is that life doesn't stop at age fifty, or sixty, or even eighty. Men of this age still feel very much alive. They laugh, they cry, they dance . . . and they have sex. To them, their sex is every bit as hot as that of twenty-year-olds. The difference, I am told proudly, is that everything means so much more to them than to the younger generation. Physical beauty is relative. Beauty to these men is often found in their partner's laughter or his experience or his kindness. Gray hair and a few wrinkles here and there can be a turn-on. Intimacy and companionship are much more important than getting fucked every night of the week.

As I said, life doesn't stop at this season, and neither does sex. Often the sex is even better, because the men have to be a little more creative, and a lot more tender with one another. Views on sex and beauty and intimacy change as we get older, as does our perspective on nearly everything.

We can learn a lot from men in their winter season, and I hope the men I've created in this section of the book are real and alive and able to teach us a thing or two about love—and about life.

Walter's Phoenix

"It's all bullshit, every last word and picture of it," Walter spat out at no one in particular. He wiped the trail of spittle from his chin. "Bullshit!"

"Walter," Jeremy scolded, "we've had this discussion before. You simply cannot throw these tantrums and tirades at every session. It makes it uncomfortable for everyone else in the group."

Jeremy was fifty years Walter's junior, and Walter hated nothing more than to be reprimanded by him or told what to do or how to act. At seventy-five years old, Walter had lived a full life, and understood it. What did this punk know about real life? And what the hell was he doing facilitating a group called "The Excitement of a Fulfilled Gay Life"? How could he know anything at all about a fulfilled life of any kind? He was barely out of diapers.

"I'm sorry," Walter said, not meaning a word of it. "But that movie is pure nonsense."

"I loved it," Christopher said. He was a freshman in college. "I think it's a wonderful representation of gay life in the twenty-first century. This is how it works today."

"It's that easy?" Walter asked. "You walk down the street and see a cute boy, you stop and talk with him for less than five minutes, and then you go home and have sex with him?"

"Yes," several members of the group chimed in at once.

"I've never seen it happen," Walter said defiantly.

"How often do you walk Santa Monica Boulevard in the middle of the day?" Christopher asked.

"I don't. I live more than a mile from that area."

"So do I," another member said, "but I make a point of cruising the Boulevard almost every day, and I get laid almost every day."

Walter wrinkled his nose, waved his arm dismissingly at the young man, and crossed his arms as he looked away.

"I sense you're a little anxious about this movie and the discussion, Walter," Jeremy said. "What exactly bothers you about it?"

Walter thought about the question for a moment before answering. "It's too easy. You kids, all of you here in this group, take it all for granted. You just walk up to some guy, whip out your dick, get off, and then move on. There's no thought of consequences or the possibility of something more. And there's no appreciation of the fight that us older gay men fought to get you to this place. Had I known the fight would have led to something like this, I wouldn't have bothered."

"Oh great, here we go again," Christopher said. "*In my day we had to walk a mile to school in the snow with no shoes.*"

This drew laughter from the crowd, and that was enough to get Walter on his feet and reaching for his coat.

"Please, Walter, don't leave," Jeremy said. "No one here means to be disrespectful. We just have some different dynamics and perspectives here that lead to some meaningful conversation."

"I'm tired. I want to go home."

"Will you be back next week?"

"I don't know." Walter slipped his coat on.

"Can I ask you one more question?"

"What?" He said tiredly as he exhaled loudly.

"Have you ever been in love, Walter?"

Walter looked at the younger man leading the group, and then around the room at the other dozen or so young men watching him with varied expressions of boredom. Then he buttoned his coat and walked out the door.

"I'm not sure we should be doing this," Robert said. "What if the captain comes in?

"Relax," Walter said. "He's taking a nap. It's like clockwork. He'll be by in an hour and fifteen minutes. That gives us plenty of time."

He leaned in and kissed Robert as he unbuttoned the younger man's shirt. Robert had just turned twenty-one two weeks ago, a month after the ship had set out for the South Pacific. Walter had been infatuated with him from the moment he laid eyes on the boy. Not that Walter was that much older than the kid. He was only twenty-five himself. But Robert was fresh off the farm in a small Nebraska town and as naïve as anyone Walter had met. Walter was from Seattle, and was a little wiser in the ways of the world. Young enough to be adventurous and seek out a little private fun every now and then, but wise enough not to get caught.

It turned out Robert was much more hungry for sex than Walter had imagined. He ripped his clothes off in seconds and dropped to his knees in front of Walter's crotch. He unbuttoned Walter's pants and pulled them to his knees. Then he reached inside Walter's shorts and pulled out his cock.

Up to this point, Walter was sure the kid had never sucked a cock in his life. Maybe never even seen one other than his own. But now he was convinced otherwise. Robert lapped at the heavy cock for about a minute, and had it fully hard and throbbing. When it stood at full attention, Robert sucked the head into his mouth then slowly swallowed Walter's dick until it was buried deep in his throat.

"Holy shit, man," Walter whispered as he gasped. "Where the hell did you learn that?"

"Neighbor kid back home and I used to fool around a little. You like?"

"Fuck yeah, I like," Walter said. "Suck it some more."

Robert sucked Walter's cock for several minutes, and much to his

surprise, Walter found himself getting close. He'd never been able to
cum from a blowjob.

"You better stop, kid. I'm getting close."

Instead of stopping, Robert wrapped his hand around Walter's
balls and squeezed them gently as he sucked harder on the fat cock.

"Robert?" Walter asked, quickly running out of breath.

Robert looked up and winked at Walter as he swallowed more of
the cock and squeezed it with his throat muscles.

Walter grabbed Robert by the shoulders and moaned loudly as he
poured his jizz down Robert's throat. It seemed to go on forever, and
by the time he finished, his knees buckled and he slumped to the
floor, pulling his cock from Robert's throat.

Robert lay down next to Walter, and leaned up to kiss him on the
mouth. Walter could still taste his own cum on Robert's tongue, and
that made his cock stir again, even though it had just been spent.

Robert and Walter fell in love immediately and spent every mo-
ment they could together for the next two years. It would have lasted
forever, had Robert not been killed in action right in front of Walter's
eyes.

Walter woke up with tears on his cheeks and a lump in his throat.
He hadn't dreamed about Robert in several years. Goddamn Jeremy
for asking if he'd ever been in love. What fucking business was it of
his anyway?

But Walter noticed a strange tingling in his cock. It almost felt
hard, and he anxiously pulled at the elastic waistband of his sweats
to check it out. No such luck. It just lay there against his leg, as flaccid as it had been for the past five years. It seemed a little plumper
than usual, but Walter figured that was more wishful thinking than
anything else. He couldn't remember the last time he'd had an
erection, and even less what it felt like to have one.

He lay on the sofa for a few more moments, then took a deep
breath and forced himself up and into the kitchen. He was hungry,

but had ordered pizza the night before and it hadn't agreed with him. Chinese food agreed with him even less, so he found himself in a dilemma. He hadn't cooked in over ten years. There wasn't much of a chance there was anything in the pantry, but he opened it and looked anyway. An expired box of cereal, half a box of stale crackers and two scoops of Skippy peanut butter. Not much promise there.

So he could either go out for dinner or starve to death. If he were completely honest with himself, he'd admit the latter sounded more appealing. But he was stubborn and never took the easy way out with anything.

He slowly went about his routine of getting dressed. First he put on his socks, and walked around the room twice to make sure they didn't slide down his skinny calves. Then he slipped on a pair of boxers and headed to the closet. He decided on a pair of brown slacks and plaid shirt. Then he put on his favorite blue bow tie and fedora.

His favorite restaurant was only three blocks away, so he walked to the Patriot Buffet and sat at his regular table. He was right in the middle of enjoying his roast beef with mashed potatoes and steamed carrots when someone came up to him and addressed him by name. Walter was not pleased with interruptions, and at first didn't look up from his plate.

"Walter," the guy repeated, louder this time.

Walter looked up and saw Jeremy, the leader of the group at the Gay and Lesbian Center he'd been to earlier that evening.

"What is it?"

"Hey, I just wanted to come over and say hi."

"Hi."

"I'm here with my granddad. This is his favorite restaurant."

"Mine too, but only when the food is actually hot. Which it tends not to be when one allows himself the habit of conversation during dinner."

"Walter, don't be such a grouch. You can go back and get as much hot food as you want. I wanna bring my grandfather over here and introduce you."

"Nope."

"Why not."

"I'm not interested. I wanna finish my dinner, have a little desert, and a cup of decaf and then go home and go to bed."

"It'll only take a minute, Walter, and I'm not taking no for an answer," Jeremy said, then walked back to his table. He spoke with the old man sitting across the booth from him for a moment, and then called the waitress over and spoke to her and pointed toward Walter.

"God damn it," Walter mumbled as he saw Jeremy and his grandfather leave their plates behind and walk toward him.

"Hey, Walter," Jeremy said jovially as he sat next to Walter and the older man sat on the other side of the booth. "This is my grandpa, Micky."

"Mmmph," Walter said as he nodded toward Jeremy's grandfather.

"Nice to meet you, Walter," Micky said, and extended his hand.

Walter sighed and shook the hand in front of him, just as the waitress brought over two plates filled with fresh, hot food and set them in front of Jeremy and his grandfather. He wanted to be annoyed at Jeremy for this invasion of his privacy. But the truth was, it felt kind of nice not to be sitting alone. And to tell a bigger truth, Walter found himself somewhat attracted to Micky. Or at least he thought that was what was happening. It'd been so long, he wasn't quite sure anymore.

"So Jeremy tells me you attend the gay men's social group he heads up over at the Center," Micky said.

"Yes, that's right," Walter said as he made a concerted effort to eat slower.

"You've got a hell of a lot more balls than I do," Micky said, and took a spoonful of soup. "All those young kids just get on my nerves."

"Oh, they get on my nerves, too," Walter said, "especially this punk you call a grandson." Jeremy and Micky both laughed, and Walter surprised himself at his successful attempt at humor. "But that just means I have to go all the more."

"But we don't have anything in common with them," Micky said.

"We have more in common with them than you think," Walter said. "At least I do. I guess I shouldn't just assume that you're . . ."

No one said anything for almost a full minute, and Walter was just about to excuse himself and walk home.

"Yes, I am a confirmed bachelor, I'm afraid. Not so much afraid of being a homosexual, but of being a confirmed bachelor. It's more than just a phrase at our age, I suppose."

"I know what you mean. It does get lonely sometimes." Walter noticed the glint in Micky's eyes. "Although being alone does at times have its advantages."

"True."

"So, Walter," Jeremy butted in. "Grampa was just saying he might be willing to try the group out next week if he weren't the only elderly gentleman there."

"Now, Jeremy, I didn't quite say that," Micky said.

Jeremy looked at his grandfather and raised an eyebrow. "I've been trying to get him to come to the group for a while now, but he won't ever come," Jeremy said to Walter "Grampa, if Walter were there, would you come?"

Micky and Walter both kicked Jeremy under the table.

"Come on, Walter. You're always complaining that no one in the group understands what it was like being gay when you were young, and that none of the representations we have in the group are real. This will be your chance to have someone collaborate with and understand you. And grampa, you're always saying it's depressing to leave the house because there are only young kids outside anymore and you get tired of being the dinosaur. This is the perfect solution for both of you."

Walter looked across the booth at the man facing him. He had a full head of gray hair that one could tell was once dark black and wavy. His gray eyes were once sparkling blue, and had probably broken more than one heart in their day. When he looked at you, it was obvious you had his full attention, and it made you want to keep it. He was thin, but appeared toned and in shape. Walter was undoubtedly attracted to this man, and as uncomfortable as that felt after so long, he also felt alive for the first time in many years.

"I'd be honored if you'd accompany me to the group next week," Walter said. "We can show those punks what being gay really is, and that it's more than just a quickie in a park or behind the Pizza Hut."

"It is?" Micky said. Everyone laughed. "I'd be happy to join you."

That night, after dinner with Micky and Jeremy, Walter found it difficult to fall asleep. He couldn't get Micky out of his mind. Though he'd long ago stopped thinking of men as attractive or fantasizing about them, he couldn't stop thinking about how handsome Micky was, and how attracted he was to him. As he drifted off to sleep, he pictured Micky as a young man.

"You're not really gonna make me work this hard for it, are you?" Micky asked.

"I don't know what you mean," Walter said.

They were at a seedy hotel, far away from everything and everyone they might know. They were naked, and Micky stood behind Walter with his arms wrapped around Walter's arms and chest. Both men had recently finished their tours of duty in the Army, and were in excellent shape. Walter was an inch or so shorter than Micky, but was smooth and muscular. He'd worked out every day of his tour, and every inch of skin and muscle was taut and defined. His blond hair and piercing brown eyes with inch-long eyelashes made women and men alike stare.

Micky rubbed his hands across Walter's smooth and muscular chest and tweaked his nipples until Walter moaned and leaned backward against Micky's naked body. He felt the hard, hot meat of Micky's cock rub against his ass and leg. Walter looked in the mirror and admired Micky's reflection. A couple of inches taller than himself, Micky was the most beautiful man Walter had seen. Thick black wavy hair and sharp blue eyes that pulled you in and refused to let you go. His skin was olive and smooth everywhere except for the short curly hair on his chest. But what made Walter's heart drop were the dimples that graced either side of the most beautiful smile he'd ever seen.

"Come on, Walter. You know what I want."

"I know. But I've never done that. I don't think I can. Can't I just suck your dick?"

"All right," Micky said as he walked Walter over to the bed and sat him down so that his face was level with Micky's already throbbing cock. "We can start there, anyway, and then see what happens."

Walter reached out with his tongue and licked Micky's cock head and then the entire length of his dick. When Micky moaned, Walter sucked half of the long cock into his mouth.

"My god, that's good," Micky said, and slid his cock in and out of Walter's mouth.

Walter had sucked a few cocks in his time, but never had it felt like this. His own cock throbbed so hard it hurt, and was so hot it felt like it was on fire.

"Okay, you can do it," Walter said as he stopped sucking Micky's cock, not sure where the statement came from.

"You sure?" Micky asked.

"Yes, I want you to fuck me."

Micky wasted no time getting Walter in position, before he changed his mind. He laid Walter on his back and pulled his legs into the air. He spat a couple of large drops of saliva onto Walter's ass, then slid his head inside.

"Oh, FUCK, that hurts," Walter said as he bit his lower lip. *"Take it out."*

"Come on, man. It won't hurt for long. Trust me, you'll be begging for more. Just relax and let me keep going, okay?"

Walter nodded, and bit his lip harder as Micky slid his cock in and out of his ass, first slowly and then a little faster. Micky was right, it didn't take long before the pain turned to ecstasy, and Walter was bucking up to meet Micky's thrusts.

"Fuck me harder, Micky," Walter said. *"Gimme more."*

Micky laughed. "That's my boy," he said as he slammed in and out of Walter's ass.

Both men found their rhythm and were soon fucking like they'd been doing it for years. Walter shook his head back and forth against the pillows and begged for more, and Micky pulled his cock all the way out then slammed it back inside in one swift thrust.

"I'm gonna cum!" Walter screamed.

"Me too," Micky said, out of breath.

Micky pulled out and sprayed his cum all over Walter's face and torso. The ripples on his abs filled with cum and dripped over his sides. That was enough to send Walter over the edge. His cock was pointed straight up, and he shot several jets of cum a foot or so into the air.

The two young men collapsed onto each other and fell asleep drenched in cum.

"Everyone, this is my grandpa, Micky," Jeremy announced. Several audible moans could be heard throughout the group.

Walter and Micky were seated next to one another, and looked as if they might get up and leave.

"Look," Jeremy said, a little more aggressively than he'd ever spoken to the group. "This group is about empowering gay men to live to their full potential. It's not the local meat market or pick-up club exclusive to twenty-somethings whose biggest care in the world is whether to wear their Armani Exchange T-shirt or their

Abercrombie and Fitch. We're here to support one another, listen to one another, exchange ideas, and learn from one another. This is a loving and supportive group, goddammit, and if any self-involved punk isn't welcoming of other members, then the door is right over there," he said as he pointed behind him.

The other younger men just stared, open jawed, at Jeremy and said nothing. Micky smiled and blew a kiss at his grandson, and Walter allowed one corner of his lip to curl upward into something resembling a smile.

"All right then," Jeremy said as he smoothed his own A & F T-shirt. "Last week we watched *Trick*, and I for one, loved it. And though for many years I've been one of Tori Spelling's harshest critics, I must admit she's made a convert of me."

Everyone laughed and clapped.

"But tonite we're gonna watch a different kind of movie. It's a little older, but it's a gay classic and absolutely one of the best gay films ever made. It's called *Torch Song Trilogy*.

"Puleeze don't tell me it stars Walter Matthau and Jack Lemmon," one of the younger guys in the group snipped.

"No," Jeremy said. "In fact, it stars Matthew Broderick when he was in his early twenties."

"Oh, God, he's still yummy even though he's a little old. I bet he was drop-dead gorgeous when he was young."

Walter and Micky looked at each other. They were both familiar with Matthew Broderick because of his outstanding performance in *The Producers*, and they were stunned these kids could think someone in their late thirties or early forties could be considered old.

The lights went down and the movie started. For the first few minutes, there were some scattered mutterings among the younger group members, but they soon settled down and got quiet. Walter and Micky both took notice that the youngsters were actually getting into the movie, and when they looked at each other again, it was very natural to reach over and hold the other's hand.

When the movie was over, there wasn't a single dry eye in the room. A few of the younger members even had to leave at one point or another to retreat to the restroom to cry properly and not be seen by their peers. When the lights first came up, no one said a word. Everyone was looking at their laps and fidgeting with their hands.

"I just don't get it," Reggie said, as he dried his eyes for the fifth time.

"Don't get what?" Jeremy asked.

"Well, a lot of it, actually. It was very emotional, don't get me wrong. I can't stop crying, as you can see. But, okay, first of all, why would Alan fall for Arnold to begin with? Alan was cute, he was young, he was successful. What would he see in an old, unattractive drag queen who lived in a basement apartment and who had more emotional baggage than Courtney Love?"

"He saw Arnold's heart," Walter said quietly. "When you looked at Arnold, is that all you saw? An old, wrinkled drag queen?"

"No," Reggie said, and looked back down at his hands. "But I don't think I could fall in love with him."

"He was hilarious, man," Chandler said. "And he loved Alan with every ounce of his being. It might have taken me a little bit longer to fall in love with Arnold than it did for Alan, but I would have done it. Shit, at this point in my life, I'd *love* to find someone who felt his world revolved around me."

"Get serious," Josh said. "You're one of the biggest sluts in West Hollywood. You sleep with a different guy every night."

"Yeah," Chandler said, looking straight at Josh. "And when those online hookups or guys I pick up from the clubs get dressed and leave at four in the morning with promises to call me 'sometime soon,' then I cry myself to sleep. Almost every night. I'd give anything to have what Alan and Arnold had."

No one said anything for awhile, and then Jeremy asked, "What did you think of Arnold's relationship with Ed?"

"I think it was stupid," someone yelled out. "Who would waste their time even thinking about someone who didn't show any interest? For crying out loud, Arnold was obsessed with him. Even after he was with Alan."

"Your first love is a very powerful force," Micky said. "You never forget it. And though you might move on and fall in love with someone else, you never stop loving your first one."

"Okay, so if that's true, then after Alan died and Ed wanted to be with Arnold, why didn't he get with him if he never stopped loving him? It's stupid."

"You don't love someone like Arnold loved Alan, and then settle for anything less after that," Micky said. "It's true, Arnold still loved Ed, but not in the same way he loved Alan. Sometimes people can lose the love of their life and eventually find someone else who will never replace that love, but who can bring love and joy back into their life. Arnold and Ed had too much history and too many issues to ever have their love become *that* love. They could never be more than friends. And that's not a love to sneeze at, lemme tell you."

The conversation went on for over an hour, and many more tears were shared. As the group dispersed, Micky and Walter were both shocked that several members of the group came up to them and hugged them and thanked them for teaching them something about love and life.

Micky followed Walter home without either of them speaking of it. They made small talk in the kitchen for a few moments, and then Micky scooted closer to Walter.

"I want to make love to you, Walter," he said as he reached over to hold Walter's hand.

"What?" Walter almost yelled, and jerked his hand away from Micky's. "Are you out of your mind?"

"No, I'm not," Micky said, and took Walter's hand back into his own. "I haven't felt like this toward another man, hell, for another human being, in over twenty years."

"And neither have I. That's because we're old."

"Exactly. Which is why we shouldn't waste any time playing games. We might not have enough time to fall in love like Arnold and Alan did. But then again we might. The only way we'll ever know is if we give it a try."

"I like you a lot, too, Micky . . ."

"Then stop being such an old fart and come to bed with me."

"I haven't had sex in more years than I care to count. I don't think I can do it anymore. I'm sure my ass has cemented over by now. Nothing's getting up there, I'm pretty sure of that."

"No one said anything had to get up there."

"Well, I haven't had an erection in at least five years. I'm quite certain I couldn't get it up your ass either."

Micky laughed.

"Besides, we're so damned old, Micky. We could die of a heart attack just from the exertion. Heaven forbid my niece Heather walk in someday and find us locked in rigor mortis with my dick inside you. I don't think I could live with that."

"You wouldn't have to. You'd be dead."

"This isn't funny, Micky."

Micky stood and lifted Walter to his feet and led him to the bedroom. "There are more ways of being intimate and making love than fucking, Walter. Take off your clothes and lay down with me."

The two men undressed and lay down next to each other in bed. Walter shivered uncontrollably as Micky leaned into him and wrapped his arms around him. He couldn't stop thinking about the wrinkles and folds of skin and age spots that defined his body. But Micky's body was so warm and soft and comfortable that Walter soon stopped shivering.

"You okay, now?" Walter asked.

"I think so."

"Good."

Micky scooted up and kissed Walter. At first Walter took a deep breath and refused to open his mouth. But Micky's tongue was persistent, and soon Walter opened his mouth and allowed the warm, wet tongue inside. He let it lay there for a moment, and then he began to suck on it lightly. It tasted slightly of peppermint, and felt better than anything he could remember feeling or tasting in years.

Micky slid his tongue in and out of Walter's mouth then sucked on Walter's tongue too. As he did this, he held Walter's face in his hands for a while, and then let them travel down his neck and chest.

"Don't," Walter said, as he broke the kiss. "This can't be exciting for you. I'm as wrinkled and dried up as a prune."

"This is the most exciting thing I've experienced in I don't know how long. Your mouth, your skin, your body all feel so incredible."

"Please," Walter said.

"You don't believe me?" Micky asked, and moved Walter's hand down to his fully hard cock.

"Micky!" Walter gasped. "How the hell did you do that? Are you taking that Viagra?"

Micky laughed. "No. It's all you. You do things to me and make me feel things I thought I'd never experience again."

"I'm not sure what to say," Walter said. "I love what we've been doing, but I'm not hard at all."

"Leave that to me," Micky said, and lowered himself down the bed.

"Micky! Don't be ridiculous. We're seventy-five years old. Men our age don't . . ."

Suddenly Walter's cock was surrounded by a wet warmth he only vaguely remembered. Micky was patient, and licked and sucked on it slowly for several minutes. Walter was embarrassed that he wasn't responding, and was about to tell Micky to give up, when he suddenly felt a little lightheaded. His cock tingled, and when he looked down at it, it was fully hard and sliding in and out of Micky's talented mouth.

"Oh, my god, Micky," Walter gasped. "I'm hard."

"Yes, you are. And I never would have guessed you were quite that well endowed," he said as he came up for air and wiped his mouth.

"Me neither. I forgot."

Micky laughed.

"So now what?" Walter asked. "I really don't think I can get fucked."

"And I'm certainly not letting that thing up my ass, either. They really would have to carry me out of here in a sheet-covered gurney."

"So . . . ?"

"So who needs anal intercourse? I've had it already in my life. Have you?"

"Yes."

"Completely overrated. Let's take it to the next level."

"There's a next level?"

"Lie on your side facing me."

Walter did, and Micky did the same. Micky leaned in to kiss Walter again, and this time he pulled his body so that both naked bodies were pressed against each other. At this point, Walter did not need to be told what to do, and both men rubbed their cocks against each other as they kissed and caressed the other's face.

"You are the most amazing man I've met in years, Walter," Micky said as they broke from a kiss. "You feel incredible."

"You too," Walter said, a little breathless.

Micky could tell Walter was getting close, and so was he. He reached down with one hand and tugged on Walter's balls as his other hand pulled Walter's face closer for another kiss. His own cock was throbbing and he knew it would only be a few more seconds before he shot.

He thrust his tongue deeper into Walter's throat and squeezed harder on his balls. When Walter moaned, Micky's body tensed and he felt himself release years of pent-up cum all over Walter's legs and stomach.

Walter bit down lightly on Micky's tongue and his body tensed as well. A second later, he sprayed his load all over Micky's hand and crotch. It wasn't that much, but it felt like the latest NASA launch had just occurred between his legs.

"Oh, my god, I had no idea I could still do that," Walter said.

"You just needed a reason to."

Walter gazed into Micky's eyes.

"What?" Micky asked.

"Will I have a reason to again?"

Micky smiled. "As much as you'd like."

"I don't know how often I'll be able to do that . . ."

"We don't have to do *that* every time. There's so much more to intimacy than having sex. We can just cuddle. We can spoon each other and fall asleep in one another's arms. We can take bubble baths with champagne and candlelight. We can kiss until we fall asleep with our tongues still inside the other's mouth and then wake up kissing again."

"All of that sounds great," Walter said, and hugged Micky tightly so that he couldn't see the tears.

"And we can make love like we did tonight too. As much as you'd like."

"So it really is that easy? As easy as the kids say it is?"

"What is?'

"Finding this. Finding love. And intimacy"

"Don't be ridiculous. Those kids are sweet, but they don't know the first thing about love or intimacy. It's that easy for them to find the biggest dick or the tightest ass. Because that's all they know to look for."

"I suppose you're right."

"Do you think it was easy to find this? What we just had? Love and intimacy?"

"No."

"You're damned right it wasn't. Took over twenty years for both of us. It'll take at least that long for many of those kids. And some of them will never find it. Some of them don't even want it."

"That doesn't seem right or fair. What can we do to help?"

"Remember that kid Chandler tonight?"

"Yeah."

"He wants it. And so do a few of the others. So we talk with them. Nothing too overbearing, just casual. Coffee or something. And we show them that it is possible to get what you want out of life, as long as you don't compromise along the way."

"Those kids won't listen to us."

"Not all of them, but some will. I think Chandler will. And if we get him to listen and get it, then he can pass it on to the others. We older gays have been educating and passing on empowerment to younger generations for centuries. It's what we do. That and making sure we still make enough time for loving ourselves. You and me."

Walter looked at Micky for a couple of minutes without saying anything. Then his eyes filled with tears.

"I know," Micky said. "Me too."

Hot Hands on the High Seas

"Elizabeth," I almost yelled into the intercom, "who the hell authorized a $3,000 expenditure with the Robinson Travel Agency?" I stared at the statement in disbelief, and leafed through the rest of the mail to try to find an explanation.

Instead of responding through the intercom, Elizabeth walked into my office and closed the door behind her. "I did."

"What do you mean you did? You don't have the . . ."

"Of course I do. I make your travel arrangements all the time. Cindy at Robinson is one of my closest friends. We do lunch at least once a week. She's arranged all your travel plans for the past three years, and I've ordered the trips and authorized the company's credit card payment for all of them."

"But I'm not going anywhere. My next trip isn't until next month when I have that meeting with Harrison in London. This statement is for a cruise to the Mexican Riviera next week."

"Yes, it is."

"I'm not going to the Mexican Riviera next week, Elizabeth. What the hell is going on?"

"Yes, you are," she said, and folded her arms across her ample breasts. "Next week is your fiftieth birthday, and you haven't been on a vacation in more than two years. You need to get away."

"That's ridiculous. I travel someplace new at least once a month. It seems all I do is travel."

"Yeah, for business meetings. Jim, it's your fiftieth birthday. That's a big deal. You need to take some time off work and take a real vacation and celebrate the magnificent life you've worked so damned hard to build for yourself."

"Impossible," I said. "I've got meetings all next week. Important meetings."

"Not anymore you don't," Elizabeth said, and walked around my desk and pulled up my Outlook calendar. It was blank, except for a very large "Bon Voyage" typed across the entire week. "I cleared all your meetings. Every single one. Rescheduled them for the following week, so you'll be busy as hell when you get back. You'll be giddy. But you're going on this trip and you're going to have a great time."

"Elizabeth, you had no right to do this. I simply can't pack up and take a vacation right now. Those are important meetings you tampered with."

She leaned in close to me and looked me right in the eyes. "How long have I worked for you, Jim?"

She was the only person in my company who had enough balls to call me by my first name. To everyone else I was Mr. Thomas. "Nineteen years," I said softly.

"That's right. And I've taken good care of you for those nineteen years, haven't I?"

"Yes, Elizabeth, you are the best personal assistant anyone could hope for, but . . ."

"No buts about it. You *will* be taking that trip next week, and you *will* have a wonderful time. Because if you don't, you'll be finding someone else to put up with all your bullshit for the *next* nineteen years. Do I make myself clear?"

"Yes, ma'am," I said, and smiled. I knew she meant every word. Elizabeth wasn't one to say anything she didn't mean one hundred percent. I loved her like a sister, and couldn't imagine my business or my life without her.

"Good," she said, and leaned in to kiss me on the cheek. "I ordered you a bunch of new beach and cruise-type clothes from the Internet. They'll arrive tomorrow. I suggest you get busy."

"Busy doing what? You've cleared my calendar for the rest of this week as well."

"Planning your vacation. I planned the dates and the venue, but you and I both know there's no way in hell you're taking a vacation without having every minute scheduled. Your itinerary is there with the statement from the travel agency. Look it over, get on the Internet and get busy planning your vacation."

I laughed and watched her close the door quietly behind her, and thanked the Universe for sending Elizabeth my way so many years ago.

The ship was huge and elaborate and gaudy and everything I hated about overpriced vacation packages. Not that I knew that much about them, since I hadn't really ever taken one. But the *idea* of them made me sick. The floors were obviously fake or very cheap marble; the wood was obviously fake or very cheap mahogany; and the uniformed staff was obviously fake *and* very cheap people. But there was nothing I could do about it now. I'd promised Elizabeth I'd go on this trip, and now that I'd checked in and boarded, I was stuck. Five whole days on this tacky *Love Boat* reject.

My cabin was a decent size, and clean, if not tastefully furnished. I unpacked my luggage and stared out the port hole as we pulled away from the loading dock. No turning back now, I thought. I turned on the TV and flipped through the channels. There was nothing of interest on. There rarely is for me. So I pulled out my laptop case, and opened it up, anxious to log into my workspace remotely and get some work done.

I wanted to scream. I wanted to throw something. I wanted to fire Elizabeth. But of course, I didn't do any of those. Instead, I laughed out loud. My laptop wasn't inside its case; in its place were several travel books and magazines about Mexico. There was the *Damron North American Gay Travel Guide*. The *Ferrari Guide to Gay Mexico*. The *Fodor's Gay Guide to the USA and Mexico*. And a handful of magazines of a more erotic nature, all of which prominently featured hunky Latino men. I'd always been careful not to mix my private life with my professional life, and I am as discreet as they come. Still, it didn't surprise me to know that Elizabeth knew I was gay. But that she knew my preference for Latino men did throw me for a loop.

I flipped through a couple of the magazines, and then fell asleep as I adjusted to the floating sensation of the big boat as we drifted away from the San Diego shores.

In my dream, I was younger. At my age, I'm almost always younger in my dreams. At least in my dreams that involve sex with other hot and younger men, as this one did.

His name was José, and he was the centerfold in one of the mags Elizabeth had put in my laptop case. But in this dream he was a concierge on the ship. He was nineteen, and built like a Greek god with the face of a Latin angel. I was twenty, and horny as hell for José. I made up any excuse to talk with him, and feigned ignorance of the city and the Spanish language when we pulled into port in Acapulco. He was a very dedicated concierge, and offered to give me a personal tour of all the hot spots.

The hottest spot in Acapulco, apparently, was at the end of a long alley. At dusk no one could see us from the street. José pushed me up against a fence post, and stripped me in no time at all. He dropped to his knees and sucked my dick deep into his throat. I tried to hold back, to make it last a little longer, but I was helpless against his talented tongue and throat. I blasted my load deep into his gullet and collapsed against the fence, exhausted.

But José wasn't finished with me yet. He stood up and lowered his slacks to his ankles. His massive, thick, uncut cock sprung up and slapped against his belly. Precum was already dripping from the head.

"Suck me, papi," he said, and gently put his hand behind my head and guided me to my knees in front of his hard cock.

I was only twenty, remember, and wasn't that skilled at cocksucking, so I stuck my tongue out and tentatively licked at his cock head. José moaned and slid another couple of inches of his fat dick into my mouth. I tightened my lips around his hard member, and sucked as if my life depended on it. José begged me not to stop and fucked my face deeper and harder.

"I'm gonna shoot, baby," he said in his thick Mexican accent. And then he did. His cock thickened to unbelievable proportions, and squirted a dozen or more thick streams of warm cum into my mouth and deep down my throat.

I'd never tasted cum before, and was surprised how warm and sweet it was. When he'd finished pouring his load into me, I licked my lips to make sure none of his cum was wasted. He lifted me up and kissed me on the lips.

"I love you, papi," José said.

"I love you, too, José."

A knock on the door woke me up. My cock was fully hard, and showed a long line down the legs of my jeans. I pulled my T-shirt out to cover the bulge, and answered the door.

"Mr. Thomas, I'm Robert Clark. I'm the Assistant Steward on board. I just wanted to make sure everything is satisfactory so far."

He was cute. Tall, blond hair and blue eyes, nicely muscled body and a movie-star smile. I thought for a moment about pulling him inside and having my way with him. But he was no José and I didn't feel like settling.

"Yes, everything is fine. Just fine. Thanks for asking."

"If there's anything I can do to make your stay with us more comfortable, please don't hesitate to ask."

"I won't. Thank you again."

I watched his ass as he walked down the hall, and then shut my door and took a long, hot shower to get ready for dinner.

I spent the rest of that evening pretty much brooding. I couldn't get my mind off all the work I had ahead of me that had been pushed back to allow me this extravagant vacation. At dinner I was seated at a table with a bunch of strangers. And not just any strangers, but all straight and married strangers. It was all I could do to swallow my prime rib without vomiting it back up after listening to the excited chatter of their mundane lives.

I retired to my cabin right after dinner. I just didn't feel like being social. I lay in bed and read through some of the travel material Elizabeth had packed for me. Now that there was no turning back, I was actually kind of looking forward to visiting Mexico again. It'd been more than ten years since my last trip, and I'd never been to Acapulco. I made note of a few bars that sounded interesting, as well as a local bathhouse. Then I pulled out the magazine with José's centerfold, beat off, and fell asleep.

I woke up the next morning feeling like a new man. The sun was bright and the air warm, but not stifling hot. The sea was calm and brought in a nice, cool breeze. Even I couldn't stay in a bad mood on a day like this. I signed up for a little tennis, and in less than ten minutes, I had a partner. His name was Brian, he was thirty-two years old and on vacation with his wife and two kids. They were watching a movie, so Brian snuck off for a little tennis. He was "more of an outdoors kinda guy." He was definitely hot, and just the kind of guy I'd normally go for, when I felt the need to deviate from my Latino fixation. Tall, thick wavy blond hair and beautiful blue eyes, muscles sculpted from a couple of days a week at the gym. But I'm not one of those gay men who chase after married straight men. So I concentrated on playing tennis, and was having a great time . . . until I reached for a shot and pulled my hamstring.

"FUCK!" I yelled as I scrambled to the ground, and then looked around quickly to make sure there were no kids within earshot. Damned family-friendly cruises, anyway.

"Are you all right, buddy?" Brian asked as he jumped the net effortlessly and ran to my side.

"Yeah," I said as I tried desperately not to wince, or worse yet, cry. "I think I pulled a muscle, though. I'm afraid I'm done for the day."

"That's too bad, buddy," he said, and helped me to my feet. "You were giving me a run for my money there for a while."

If he called me buddy once more, I was gonna smack him with my racket. "Thanks."

"Lemme help you get to the infirmary."

I started to say no, but when he put his shoulder under my armpit and pulled me close to him, I decided I could do much worse. Every muscle on his body flexed as he helped me wobble to the infirmary. The sweat he'd worked up playing tennis mixed with his natural scent and made my cock swell. When we reached the doctor's office, I thanked Brian for the game and for the help, then watched his ass as he walked away. It's a habit I had not yet been able to break. I love a nice ass.

The doc confirmed the pulled hamstring, gave me a pain pill, and made an appointment for me with the massage therapist for later that afternoon. There wasn't much else I could do, so I grabbed a book and sat on one of the lounge chairs next to the pool. The book was good, the guys playing around the pool were for the most part hot—or at least worth a glance—and the Vicodin was wonderful. I was enjoying myself, and before I knew it, it was time for my massage.

I hobbled to the spa, and had to wait only a couple of minutes before I was seen. The receptionist was very sweet and said she was sorry I hurt my leg, but that she was sure Antonio would be able to get me better in no time, and then pointed to the last door down the hall on the right.

The moment I laid eyes on Antonio, I knew I was in trouble. He was tall and tanned and toned and quite possibly the most beautiful man I'd ever laid eyes on. He wore white shorts and a white muscle shirt with the ship's logo, and his dark skin contrasted with them wonderfully. His black hair, soul patch, and dark brown eyes mesmerized me. He had a wide smile with thin, pink lips, and his eyes sparkled when he spoke.

"So, I hear you have a boo-boo," he said in a deep voice and sexy accent that made my knees shake.

"Yes," I managed to squeak out. "I pulled my hamstring."

"Well, let's get you undressed and on the table. I'll have you feeling better in no time at all."

I'd like to say that my eyes didn't bulge or that my breathing was not noticeably labored as I listened to Antonio speak those words. But neither is true.

"Don't worry," Antonio said, and smiled. "I'm a professional. You can leave your underwear on if you like, although the massage will be more helpful without the hindrance of clothes. You can crawl under the blanket if you want. To start out, anyway."

I'm sure I looked like I'd just swallowed a bucket of barbed wire.

"I'll be in the next room getting some oils and candles ready. Just lemme know when you're ready." He walked out and closed the door behind him.

I stood there for a moment, paralyzed. I was fifty years old, for chrissake. I'd been naked in front of dozens of men. I worked out three times a week and walked around the locker room completely naked with no care whatsoever. I played racquetball on the courts at work and changed in front of my co-workers on a regular basis. I went for a physical checkup with my doctor every six months. So why should I have this reaction to stripping down for Antonio?

Because when I looked at all those other men, I didn't envision them naked and oiled up and hard, picking me up and carrying me to a king-sized waterbed and fucking my brains out. That's why.

I undressed, shaking like a third grader at his first public spelling bee, down to my underwear, and crawled under the sheets, lying on my stomach. "Umm, I'm ready," I stammered quietly, "anytime you are."

Antonio walked into the room, and placed candles around the room. He dimmed the lights and turned on some soft, relaxing music that emanated from unseen speakers. He was shirtless now. "Sometimes the shirts just get in the way of a good massage," he said, and smiled. "And they tend to get oily, too. You don't mind, do you?"

"No, I suppose not," I said. I couldn't take my eyes off of him, even though it was hard to look up and around at him while lying on my stomach. His chest was powerfully built, with tiny brown nipples in the center of each pec. It was covered in very short (probably impeccably clipped), thick black hair that dropped down to leave a thin trail right between his two rows of hardened six-pack abs. The hair got thicker and a little longer as it disappeared into the waistband of his uniform shorts.

"We'll start on your stomach, then pay special attention to your injured hamstring. But it's important to work over your entire body, so that the muscles around the hamstring are relaxed as well. They're all connected, you know, and all work together to make you work properly."

He started massaging my feet, and I felt every muscle in my body tense up. My breathing became shallow, and my heart raced.

"You know the old song, 'The ankle bone's connected to the shin bone'," he said as he massaged around my ankle and my shin. "Well, the same thing goes for your muscles. They all connect and work together as a machine."

"Mmm hmm," I moaned as he rubbed oil into his hands and began working his way up my calves and shins. His hands were really working magic on my legs, and I fought the urge to fall asleep. He worked delicately but deep as he massaged my hamstrings and stretched and pulled them in positions I didn't know were possible.

As his strong hands squeezed the backside of my upper legs, they brushed against my ass cheeks and perineum, and I hardened instantly, vanquishing any thoughts of sleep.

"This is where the underwear becomes a problem," he said, and skillfully removed them with one hand as he caressed my ass cheeks with the other. He kneaded them as if they were bread dough being prepared for the king of the world.

"Relax," he said softly as my reflexes kicked in and I tightened my ass as hard as possible. "There's no need to impress me here— which I am, by the way. The point here is to relax as much as possible."

I took a deep breath and relaxed as he continued working my ass muscles. My cock grew harder the more he worked me over and pressed my hips deeper into the cushioned table. He eventually moved to my lower back, which I was grateful for, and then up to my shoulders and neck.

"Okay, my friend," he said as he massaged my scalp. "Time to turn over so we can work the frontside."

"Is that really necessary?" I said a little too panicky. "I mean, it's my hamstring that's injured."

"Yes, it really is necessary," Antonio said, and gave my scalp an extra little squeeze. "Hamstring muscle connected to the chest muscle and all that, remember?"

"I seriously don't think I can . . ."

"Turn over," he commanded, and I did.

Most men's cocks will lie right across their belly when fully hard. It's natural. But mine does not. It points straight up in the air, reaching for the ceiling, and that's exactly what it did as I turned onto my back on Antonio's massage table. My cock was hard as a rock, and red in some places and purple in others, and I could've died of embarrassment.

"Looks like your hamstring isn't the only muscle that needs

some working," Antonio said, and moved closer and spread his legs so that he was straddling my face. He reached down and massaged my neck and chest, tweaking my nipples a little as he did, but avoided touching my cock.

The ship had a strong reputation for complete and absolute customer satisfaction. In most circumstances the staff was to anticipate the guests every whim and desire. But when it came to sexual services, it was a different ballgame. No one wanted a sexual harassment suit, so when sexual favors were in play, the staff was well trained to wait for the customers to request something. Never assume you know their wishes or desires. So Antonio stared admiringly at my hard cock, but continued massaging my chest and abdomen. At this point his crotch was only inches from my face, and his cock was hard. The tip of his dark, uncut cock peeked out from the underwear and I caught a glimpse of his foreskin as he spread his legs further.

I was so lightheaded that I reached up and squeezed his cock from inside his shorts leg.

"Do you want it, my friend?"

"Yes," I managed to squeak out.

Antonio pulled his shorts and underwear off in one move, and his long, thick cock bounced in front of him and thumped me in the face a couple of times. His balls were huge and shaved and smelled lightly of baby oil. I took a deep whiff and then licked them lightly and sucked them into my mouth. He moaned to let me know he enjoyed it, so I took them both in my mouth and sucked on them for a couple of minutes.

He leaned over and licked my balls and cock. His own cock found its way to my mouth, and as he sucked my cock into his mouth, I did the same with his. We worked in perfect harmony. He deepthroated me, and as he slid up my cock to catch his breath, I swallowed his cock deep into my throat. We went at it like that for several minutes, and I had to really concentrate on not cumming too quickly.

He stopped and looked at me with the most adorable, puppy-dog eyes I'd ever seen. I saw the desire in them as clearly as if it had been written in ink across his forehead. But he was well-trained and couldn't assume anything or make the first move.

"Fuck me, Antonio," I said.

"Oh, thank god." He moved to the foot of the table and he spread my legs wide, forgetting about the pulled hamstring. He knelt between my legs and licked and kissed my asshole as if it were a chocolate-filled sopapilla and he were a chocoholic.

I moaned and wriggled and pushed my ass closer to his probing tongue. It was long and strong and filled me up.

But he was just getting started, and had grander plans in mind. When my ass was quivering and puckering, begging for more and dripping with his saliva, he stood and placed the head of his cock at my asshole. I couldn't believe how hard and hot and big it felt as it pressed against my hole.

"Shove it inside me, Antonio," I said, and pressed myself tighter against his cock.

He was well-trained to listen to his customers, and slid his huge cock deep inside my ass in one deliciously slow stroke. It felt like a baseball bat going up my ass, and deep in my consciousness, I made a note that I should have felt some hesitation and a little pain from the experience. But I felt neither. As each inch of his fat cock slid deeper inside, I became more alive. My body tingled and grew hot and squirmed to get even more of this hot man inside me.

Antonio was a very skilled fucker, and he pushed and pulled and twisted and maneuvered me into positions I'd never have thought possible—especially with an injured leg muscle. But I felt no pain at all, only ecstasy. He pounded me hard and rough for a few moments, pulling his cock all the way out and then slamming it back in a few times . . . and then slid in slowly and gently and left his big cock buried in my ass as he wiggled it around inside me. The contrast of styles drove me wild, and brought me to the brink several times.

But when he fucked me slow and deep, and then sucked my dick at the same time, I lost it all together.

"Fuck, man, I'm cumming," I cried out, and grabbed the sides of the table. When he didn't let go of my cock, but intensified both the sucking and the fucking, I warned him once more. "Dude, I'm seriously gonna blow . . ."

He swallowed my cock deep in his throat and slammed his dick deep to his balls inside my ass as I exploded inside his mouth. My body convulsed as I blasted my jizz down his throat. I fought to catch my breath as seven or eight shots spewed from my cock. Antonio didn't remove his mouth from my dick until he'd sucked every last drop of cum from it.

He quickly pulled his cock from my ass and moved to stand next to my face. From this angle, I couldn't believe how huge it was, and that it'd been so deep inside me. He pumped it a couple of times, then grabbed my head. A second later the first jet of hot, thick cum splashed across my face, and several more quickly followed. About a minute later, my face was completely covered in Antonio's load. I licked as much as I could into my mouth, and then Antonio leaned down and licked up the rest. He leaned in to kiss me, and I sucked on his hot tongue to taste as much of him as I could.

"Fuck, that was hot, my friend," he said as he broke our kiss and rested against the table.

"That might possibly be the understatement of the century," I said, taking in deep breaths.

"I want to see you again."

"Absolutely. I'm here for the duration of the trip."

"And after that?"

I looked at him as if I'd taken the short bus to school when I was young. "After that I live in San Diego and you work on a cruise ship."

"But I have a place in San Diego."

"Look, Antonio, you're very hot. Quite possibly the hottest man

I've ever been with. But I'm fifty years old. You're what? Twenty-three, twenty-four?"

"I'm thirty-five. And you don't look or act a day over forty. You're very hot, Mr. Thomas. I find you extremely attractive."

"Thank you. And please call me Jim. Antonio, I'd love for you to fuck my brains out like you just did every day for the rest of this trip if you want to. But I'm just not looking for a relationship. I work a lot and really like living alone."

"Me too. I'm not looking for a husband. I like my independence very much. But I am in San Diego a couple of times a month for two or three days at a time. It'd be really great to be able to hook up with you when I'm in town, go to dinner, hang out a little, and fuck our brains out, as you say."

I laughed. "I'm fifty."

"Yes, I heard you."

"That doesn't bother you?"

"I find it very sexy. I find you very sexy. And if you find me very sexy too, then I don't see any reason why we shouldn't become regular fuck buddies and good friends. I'd love to come home knowing that I get to fuck that incredible ass of yours."

"But . . ."

"Don't make me stalk you."

I laughed again, and leaned up to kiss him. I still tasted his sweet cum on his tongue, and knew right then that I'd go along with the plan.

"I want gifts from every trip," I told him.

"Done." He leaned down to return my kiss. "Now, get out of here before people start talking about how long we've taken. Wrap the leg and use alternate heat and cold compresses every four hours or so."

"Yes, Doctor."

"And I think we need to make an appointment for every afternoon for the rest of the trip. You know . . . to make sure we stretch those muscles and get you healthy. Work it out with Karen at the front desk."

I laughed and left the massage room, and made my daily appointments with Antonio.

And then I resisted the urge to skip back to my cabin.

Like Riding a Bike

Harry watched from his window as the cab pulled up to the half-circle drive. Earlier that day he'd overheard one of the orderlies say that a new resident was arriving later that afternoon, and he'd sat at the window ever since, waiting. The building was a U-shaped brick single-floor design. Harry had one of the choice rooms, in the center wing. Not only was he closer to the nurses' station than most, but he also had the best view in the entire home. From his window he could see everyone that was arriving, and also the windows of most of the rooms on the other wings. At least the rooms that faced the front of the building, as his did.

He looked at the wings on either side, and saw no fewer than a dozen curtains pulled ever so slightly to one side. Mrs. Goldsmith, Mrs. Rubio, Mrs. Felter, Mrs. Callahan, and Mrs. Schooler. Those were the ones he recognized right away, and it didn't surprise him at all that they were gawking out their windows. Goddamn piranha, they were. They were always in everyone's business, and anytime a new resident was admitted, they were all over them. Didn't matter if they were male or female, those catty old biddies pounced on them even before they'd signed the paperwork. If the new res was a man, the piranha cuddled and coddled and pinched him like he was a tomato at the market. The unsuspecting gentleman would later that evening find several slips of paper with the women's names and room numbers in his various pockets. Harry knew, because they'd attacked him before he'd even made it inside the building when he first arrived. If the new res was a woman, they'd still be right there on top of her, clutching her arms and walking with her, immediately filling her in on the gossip of the house, and warning her which of the "taken" or "unavailable" gentlemen to steer clear of.

"Goddamn snakes," Harry mumbled under his breath.

The cab door opened, and the passenger stepped onto the sidewalk. Harry gasped as he took in the beauty of the man. He was tall and slim, but seemed to be well put together, according to the way his shirt and slacks clung to his frame. His hair was a shiny silver, and he had a mustache of the same magnificent color, but speckled with several black hairs. Even from this distance, Harry saw the guy's eyes were blue-gray, and they scanned the premises like a practiced hunter. Those eyes seemed to rest right at Harry's window, and Harry closed the curtains quickly, and took a couple of deep breaths before he opened them again and looked back outside.

The man was walking toward the main entrance now, and swatting away the attempts of staff to help him get from the cab to the door. *He's still strong, and still proud*, Harry thought. He could now see the man more clearly. He was right, the eyes were a steel blue, and filled with life. At this range, Harry saw they were framed with long black eyelashes. The nose was long and distinguished, and his jaw was square and set strong.

The man took Harry's breath away. Literally. He had to take a couple of deep breaths before he allowed himself to head toward the door. It was vital that he get to this handsome stranger before the Ya-Ya Sisterhood did. He was seventy-three years old, for crying out loud. This might be his last chance. And even if it weren't, it would probably be the last time he had a chance at someone this handsome and self-possessed.

But Harry was too late. He heard them cackling from way down the hall even before he turned from the window. When he reached his bed, the entire gaggle of them were zipping past his door, cackling and whinnying like an escaped stampede from the local zoo. They were pressed against one another, standing on their tiptoes and pushing others aside to get a better look.

Goddamned piranhas, Harry spat out not so quietly, and looked around to make sure no one heard him.

"Okay, ladies, make some room." It was Sandra, the head nurse. She was the one person on staff that Harry had befriended, and had held in confidence. He'd often told her that if the Universe had been kinder and made him normal, that he'd have asked her hand in marriage. And she would happily accept, she'd told him dozens of times, and then kissed him on his very balding head. She looked over at him now and winked, as she muscled her way through the mob at the door. "I said, make some room. Let the gentleman through. You don't want to look desperate!"

Desperate would be an upgrade to first class for this coven, Harry thought. Gasps spread through the group of women at the tone of Sandra's words, and they disassembled from around the door. As they scattered around the desk and entry area, Harry smiled, and tipped his hat to them. "Gloria," he said to Mrs. Rubio, and blew her a kiss. She grunted and gave him the finger.

He laughed and watched with all of the interest and hopefully none of the desperation of the widows as the new res walked through the door. The cooing and girlish giggles were immediate and deafening. The new guy stopped halfway through the door and scanned the place. Harry thought he looked like he was assessing an enemy attack.

"Ladies, I am not kidding, here," Sandra said as she cleared a path and motioned for the new guy to follow her. "There will be no cheesecake tonight for any of you if you don't head back to your rooms."

It was as if someone had dropped a tear-gas bomb right in the middle of the room. The ladies stiffened and began to move quickly out of the reception area and back to their rooms. Apparently they'd forgotten that when a new resident was admitted, the kitchen staff prepared cheesecake to welcome him. It was a treat, and one the ladies couldn't get enough of. They were really booking it now, as Harry's grandson often said, and moved away from the new guy as if he'd been pronounced a leper.

But to Harry, the prospect of companionship and real friendship and maybe a little affection was much more appetizing than cheesecake. Truth be known, cheesecake gave him gas. It wasn't pretty for anyone involved. He'd much rather stroll through the gardens with this new guy and snuggle with him afterward. And at this point, he'd rather daydream about that than have cheesecake. Not that he was kidding anyone. He knew he wouldn't get anywhere with this man, and he knew he'd have his cheesecake tonight, too. Sandra would never deny him.

"Harry, would you be a gem and escort Mr. Michaels to his room?" Sandra said as she looked at Harry and winked. "I have to go check on Mrs. Winters. She has a bad cough this afternoon."

Harry just stood in his doorway, stunned and unable to move or speak.

"Harry?" Sandra said again, louder this time.

"Huh," Harry said, sounding about as stupid as a *Three Stooges* movie. "Yes, of course," he said, and grabbed his cane and moved one foot in front of the other.

"Mr. Michaels will be in Room 110. Mr. Roberts' old room."

"Okay," Harry said, and tried not to look in Mr. Michaels' eyes. "Sure, no problem."

"You're a gem," Sandra said, and kissed him softly on the cheek. "They don't come any better than Harry, here, Mr. Michaels. He'll be a good friend for you, and I'm sure he'll be happy to show you the ropes. Right, Harry?" She made sure Mr. Michaels wasn't looking before she winked at him.

* * *

"You know, Harry, I've been here a month now," James leaned in and whispered just inches from Harry's face. He'd stopped being Mr. Michaels to Harry after the first couple of days at the home. "You'd think they'd figure out I'm not interested."

Both men turned and looked at the group of ladies sitting at the table a few feet away. The women made a production of giggling and fixing their hair and sipping their virgin cocktails. They all waved over at James, and a couple of them winked at him.

"Nah," Harry said, and swatted at them as if they were mosquitoes coming to suck the blood from both of them. "They aren't the sharpest tools in the shed, I'm afraid. They're old and blind and senile. Look at poor Mrs. Callahan. She has her wig on backwards, and none of them has noticed. Not a one."

James laughed, and Harry thought he could fall inside the depths of that laugh and never return.

"Still, I haven't beaten around the bush or been sly about my disinterest. You'd think they would catch on."

"Hmph," Harry said, and moved his bishop within striking distance of James' king. "Check."

James looked down at the board and smiled, then moved his king out of danger without thinking much about the move. "And you'd think that you would catch on as well."

Harry scratched his head and pondered his next move. "Oh, I get it. You're not interested."

"That's right. In the women, Harry. I'm not interested in the women."

"Oh, I see," Harry said, and slapped James playfully on the shoulder. "Then it's Mrs. Felter you have your eye on, huh?" Harry laughed so hard at his own joke that he began coughing and choking.

James stood and moved behind Harry, patting him on the back. When Harry stopped coughing, James leaned in and whispered into his ear, "No, Harry. I'm interested in you."

Harry gasped so hard that he almost started coughing again. He looked up at James. Those steel-blue eyes were boring into Harry's soul, and he couldn't tear himself away from them. Those eyes were saying things to him that Harry had not heard in over thirty years, since his lover Paul had died in a car accident. For so long he'd wanted to hear those things more than anything else. But now that they were being said through James' eyes, he wasn't sure he was ready for them. Or even if he was actually hearing what he thought he was.

"James . . ."

"I know how that sounds, Harry," James said as he took his chair next to his friend. "I know it sounds ridiculous and stupid and impossible."

"No, it doesn't," Harry said, and struggled to keep control of his voice that wanted to jump and shout and sing at the top of his lungs.

"I'm a very upfront kind of man, Harry. I don't believe in pussyfooting around the issues. Besides, I'm as old and as senile as the coven over there. Hopefully not as ugly or desperate, but every bit as old and as senile. I don't have time to waste. So, I speak my mind."

Harry smiled, and wanted to cry, but knew he shouldn't. He forced himself to count to ten as he stared deeply into James' eyes. They were no longer hard or calculating or darting around him to assess any unforeseen calamity. Instead they were bright and alive and filling with tears as they looked into Harry's soul.

"I love you, Harry Johnson," James said, and reached out to place his hands on top of Harry's. "And if you spit in my face for saying that, I will stake claim to that aforementioned senility and hold onto it for dear life. I'll suggest they triple my medication because I'm *that* senile and had no idea what I was saying."

Harry laughed, and squeezed James' hand.

"But I do know what I'm saying, just between the two of us. And I do love you."

"I love you, too, James," Harry whispered. He looked over at the old ladies and resisted the urge to lift his hand entwined with James' and to shout at the top of his lungs, *"He loves me. James Michaels loves me and I love him. So take your dried-up, pruny old venom somewhere else, old biddies. He's all mine."* But he didn't say that. Instead, he smiled at James and repeated, "I love you too."

"Oh, thank God," James said through a burst of breath he'd been holding. "Because I seriously don't know what I'd have done if you'd have laughed at me or shaken my hand from yours."

"I would never do either."

"Thank you for that. Harry, I've been struggling with my feelings for you from the moment I walked into this place. When you led me to my room I wanted so badly to pull you inside the room, shut the door and kiss you until we both collapsed."

"It took you that long, huh?" Harry said through a smile, and caressed James' long fingers. "I wanted to push you back into the taxi and let you have your way with me as soon as I saw you step out of the cab."

James looked at his watch. "We've got about an hour and a half before dinner. Would you care to accompany me to my quarters?"

"I'd love to," Harry said as they stood up. "But an hour and a half might be a little overly ambitious."

"You don't know me very well," James said, and winked at Harry as they walked hand-in-hand toward the door.

"Should we close the curtains, do you think?" Harry asked as he stepped aside to allow James room to enter. It was only four in the afternoon, and the sun was shining brightly into his room.

"A little bit," James said, and leaned in to kiss Harry. "We don't want the coven peeking in from outside and seeing all the action. But don't close them all the way. I want to make sure I can still see you."

"Not all that much to see, really," Harry muttered as he pulled the chain on the vertical blinds so they were a little more than halfway closed.

"That's not the way I see it," James said from only a couple of inches behind him, and pulled Harry into his strong embrace. He locked his lips onto Harry's, and kissed him.

As James' tongue licked around his lips and then slowly slid inside his mouth, Harry felt the wind knocked out of him, and thought he might fall. How long had it been, exactly, since he'd been kissed like this? Thirty-two years? Thirty-five? A hundred? He wasn't sure anymore. He sucked gently on James' tongue for a long moment, then tentatively returned the kiss. James' response was not as gentle as his own, and he sucked Harry's tongue into his mouth and moaned.

It was Harry who broke the kiss. He pulled back and stared into James' eyes, and felt himself blush. "It's been a very long time," he whispered.

"Too long, I'm sure," James said, and leaned in to kiss Harry's neck.

"Over thirty years."

"What?" James said, and stood back to see if Harry was kidding with him. He could see he was not. "Well, that's absurd. A hot number like you shouldn't have been left alone for thirty years."

"Thank you," Harry said, and smiled as he felt his blush deepen another shade.

"That is going to change right now," James said, and pulled Harry's hand over to rest on his crotch. "You will never again have to experience the absence of a man's touch. A lover's touch."

"Good Lord," Harry gasped, and withdrew his hand quickly, as if he'd been burned. He looked up at James' smiling face, and smiled back. "Have any more?"

"Any more what?"

"Viagra."

"Oh, I don't need that stuff," James said. He noticed the embarrassment on Harry's face, and smiled. "And neither will you."

"It's been . . ."

"Yes, I know. A very long time. All the more reason you won't need it. Now come over here and let me undress you."

Harry stood as still as a statue as James disrobed him. His knees shook and his teeth rattled as if it were twenty below inside the room. When he was completely naked, James took a couple of steps back and stared at him. Harry looked down at his own body, and wanted to die. His skin was pasty white and clung to his bones in some places, while it sagged against muscle in others. Dark freckles dotted his torso, and wiry white hairs stuck out sporadically across his scrawny chest. His knobby knees were still knocking, and looked like they might collapse at any moment.

"James, I . . ." He started to say that he didn't think this was such a great idea.

"You are an amazingly beautiful man," James said in a very soft voice that let Harry know immediately that he meant every word.

"Thank you," Harry said.

He looked at James, who now stood naked in front of him. James was only a couple of years younger than Harry, but it was obvious he'd been in much better shape all his life than had been Harry. Even at seventy-one, he was muscular and toned. Sure, there was a little extra skin that hung loose in a couple of places, but not an ounce of fat to be seen anywhere. And when James flexed, the extra skin smoothed out and clung sexily to his muscles. His penis was fully hard, and throbbed anxiously. Harry was shocked at how beautiful it was. The perfect length, the perfect thickness. Big, hairy balls swung low beneath the shaft, and Harry couldn't remember wanting anything so badly in all his life. "You're beautiful too."

James wrapped Harry in his arms and kissed him gently on the lips again, as he pressed their bodies together. When he broke the kiss, he laid Harry gently on the bed. Harry inched up to the head of the bed, and scooted over to make room for James next to him, but James didn't follow. Before Harry knew what was happening, he felt James' warm, wet mouth envelop him from below, and his world threatened to go black.

Harry looked down the length of his body, and was amazed to see his fully hard penis disappearing inside James' mouth. He pulled almost all the way out, so that he could make sure he was actually seeing what he thought he was seeing. Satisfied he slid back inside James' mouth and moaned as pleasure coursed through his body.

It took a couple of minutes for the bright spots behind his eyes to fade away, but when they did, he was more alive than he could ever remember being. "I want you," he said as he continued pumping in and out of James' mouth.

Not one to disappoint, James arranged their bodies into a sixty-nine position, all without letting go of his grip on Harry's cock. He moaned loudly as his cock was enveloped in warm, wet ecstasy. At first Harry's mouth and tongue were a little hesitant, so James reminded him how it was done. He licked around the head of Harry's cock, then sucked it into his mouth. He smiled around Harry's cock head as he felt his new friend copy his every move, and moaned his appreciation. He took a couple more inches into his mouth as he wrapped his thumb and forefinger around the base of Harry's cock, where it met his balls.

From here James could see Harry's ass cheeks perfectly, and between them the dark hair that barely concealed the hole beyond. He spread Harry's ass cheeks and there it was in all its splendor. He couldn't remember ever seeing a more beautiful ass. He was sure that at some point many years ago, he could not have said that, and wouldn't have thought this old man's wrinkly ass was at all sexy. But he was much older now, and had a wealth of experience behind him, and at this particular point in his life, the ass was glorious. Every inch of Harry's skin, every word out of his mouth, every essence of his being, was intoxicating to James. He might not wear his loneliness as visibly as Harry did but he had been every bit as lonely for the past eight years. He'd continued having sex after Burton passed away, but it never meant anything. It was emotionless and joyless, and he'd even paid for it on more than one occasion. But now, with Harry, he was experiencing the real thing all over again, and he knew he couldn't live without it again.

"I want to make love to you," he whispered, as he let Harry's cock slip from his lips.

"You are making love to me," Harry said, from somewhere deep inside what had to be a dream.

"No. I mean, I want to be inside you."

"You have got to be kidding me." Harry looked down between their naked bodies and into James' eyes. "You're not kidding me."

"No, I'm not."

"James, really! The last time I was penetrated, Mrs. Schooler still wore stockings and didn't drink a gallon of Scotch a day."

"It's like riding a bike," James said, and maneuvered himself between Harry's legs.

"Yeah?"

"Yeah."

"A couple of years ago I tried riding a bike again after many years," Harry said. "I fell and almost broke my hip. I'm too old for that. And if I'm too old for riding a bike, well then . . ."

James laughed, and spread Harry's legs a little farther apart.

"Seriously, James, I don't think this is such a good idea," Harry stammered, and realized that even as he spoke the words, he wanted James inside him more than he'd wanted anything in a long, long time. "I'll never be able to get my ankles behind my ears, and if I do, they'll never come back down. Not in one piece, at least. They'll have to bury me like that, and with a big smile on my lips. People will talk."

"So, we'll try another position," James said as he kissed the inside of Harry's legs.

Harry had already decided he was going to try it, despite the butterflies in his stomach and all common sense. "Be gentle with me. I'm sure after all this time, I can be considered a virgin again."

James just smiled, and turned Harry over onto his stomach. Harry spread his legs as wide as they'd comfortably go, and then thought, *James is right . . . it's just like riding a bike!*

There wasn't a whole lot of foreplay and Harry didn't expect much. At their age, one didn't waste valuable time. He felt a drop of saliva slide between his ass cheeks, and when it reached his hole, he quivered. This afternoon had been filled with wonderful surprises, and continued to be. First, he'd discovered that his best friend and probably last true love of his life was playing on the same team as him. Second, he was now lying naked in bed with that man. Third, his cock was fully hard for the first time in almost ten years, and looked mighty impressive, if he did so say himself. And finally, he was about to be fucked. At seventy-three years of age, that was amazing. Worthy of an award.

James rested the head of his cock at Harry's hole for a moment, letting him get used to the idea of the penetration. He leaned down and kissed Harry on the ear, nibbling at it a little, and then slowly slid inside. As each inch worked its way inside with little resistance, James realized he was in heaven. He'd fucked many an ass in his seventy-one years. And with Burton it had even been the real thing. But even then, it didn't feel like this. When he was fully inside Harry, he was home. He was alive.

"Are you okay, my friend?" he asked.

"Yes," Harry answered. "I think so."

James slid almost all the way out of Harry's ass, and then slowly back inside. "Let me know if you want to stop. I don't want to hurt you."

"Not a chance," Harry said, and leaned back to kiss his lover on the lips. He vaguely remembered the sensation of being filled with another man. He'd had a few men in his time, and in his prime he was quite chased and considered a very good catch. He even vaguely remembered what it felt like to be filled with the man he loved. It was that feeling he was now experiencing. Again, miraculously, after so many, many years. "Please don't stop," he said.

He moaned loudly as James moved in and out of him. When he was much younger and in this position, he would tighten the muscles down there and make his men moan and whimper in ecstasy. But he knew better than to try that now. At this juncture, he'd be thankful if all of his internal organs remained in their original positions. But from the sounds James made behind him, and the way he expertly moved in and out of him, Harry figured it didn't matter that much that he couldn't create a vice grip with his ass.

James felt them sneaking up on him before he could prepare for them. He'd experienced them precious few times in his life, but knew what tears were, and he knew enough about them to know they wouldn't be a welcome addition to this lovemaking session. He gritted his teeth and pounded into Harry with more force, hoping to prove he was strong and powerful. To drive the tears away. But the harder he thrust into Harry, the more his lover moaned and moved back into his dick. And the more James was convinced he was in love again, after the seemingly endless loneliness that had become his spouse. The tears were not to be deterred, and they soon broke surface.

He laid his chest flat against Harry's naked back, and hugged him tightly as he wriggled his dick in and out of his lover's ass. Tears trickled down his cheeks, and he couldn't stop them from landing on Harry's face and shoulders.

"James, are you all right?" Harry asked, suddenly frozen beneath James.

"Yes," James said, trying hard not to sniffle or cry. "I'm very fine. Just a little . . . overwhelmed."

"Overwhelmed?" Harry asked, surprised. "With me?"

"Yes, with you," he continued sliding in and out of Harry, and felt the familiar stirrings of orgasm deep inside his guts. "With all of this."

"Overwhelmed is a good thing, right?" Harry asked as he lifted his left leg enough to reach below it and grasp his dick. He was still rock hard and felt like he would explode at any moment.

"Oh, yes," James moaned loudly, and thrust in and out of him faster. He was short of breath as he said, "It's a very good thing."

"I can't take much more of this, James," Harry said hoarsely.

"Does it hurt?"

"No. It feels great. But I think I'm about to cum."

"Me too."

"I want to see you cum, James."

James pulled out of Harry, and rolled over next to him. Harry turned around onto his back, and lay next to his lover. James put his arm under Harry's head and around his shoulders as they stroked their cocks.

"Here it comes," Harry said.

A couple of seconds later it did. His semen shot out of his dick and past his navel. He moaned loudly and took in a couple of deep breaths as a couple more shots landed on his lower belly and in his pubic hair.

"Oh, my God," James whispered, "here comes mine." His body grew rigid as he stretched from toe to head. The first couple of shots flew past his navel and landed on his neck and nipples.

Harry gasped in amazement as he watched the final three or four spurts land on James' ribs and tummy and across his pubes.

"That was incredible," Harry said as he leaned over and kissed James on the lips.

"Yes, it was," James said between kisses. "And it can only get better. I want to spend the rest of my days with you, Harry Johnson."

"And I with you."

"You're not sleeping with Mrs. Rubio or any of the others, are you?" James asked as he hugged his lover to his chest. "There isn't going to be a big dramatic breakup scene to deal with, is there?"

Harry laughed, and tickled James in the ribs. "No dramatic

breakup scene. I promise. I might not have too many days left on this earth, but what I have left are yours. If you want them."

"I want them," James said. "I want you. And there will be plenty of days left for both of us, and they will be filled with love and joy."

"Promise?"

"I do."

Rock, Paper, Scissors

Neither of us saw it coming. We'd gone to the county fair every year for the past ten, and not once did the psychic or fortune-teller inform us of this new development. We certainly didn't run an ad in the local rag, and neither of us had profiles in, or frequented, the Internet sites that inundated every nook and cranny of society. So as I say, neither of us saw it coming, and it was honestly the last thing either of us expected. But it happened, almost two years ago to the day, and when it did, it changed our lives forever.

I'm sixty-one years old, and a tenured professor of Philosophy at the local State University. From the time I was in high school I've never wanted for dates or affection or sex or love. I guess I've been blessed. The thick, jet black hair I'd always had is now trendily salt-and-peppered and fashionably styled. I have, by some miracle, been spared most of the wrinkles and loose skin that afflict most of my contemporaries. I work out three times a week and am as healthy as anyone I know half my age. My eyes are an unusual mix of green/blue/hazel and I've been told they sparkle with life. I'm not at all unaccustomed to being the object of crushes from both my male and female students, and even a few teachers. I'm not trying to be pompous or conceited here, just stating the facts for better clarification of this story.

Rodney and I have been together for eighteen years, and for the very vast majority of that time, we've been faithful and even monogamous to one another. There were a few times when we slipped; we're human, and gay men, after all. At fifty-three years old, Rodney is still a beautiful man, very much in demand for modeling and some small-time acting parts. He doesn't look or act a day over thirty-five. So, truth be told, there are very few men who tempt us to stray.

But Jeromy was an exception. He was one of my students-and not just any student, but one of my best. He was twenty-four, and as ambitious as they come. He was only a year away from getting his Master's degree in Psychology, with a minor in Philosophy. His mind and his pensive demeanor were definitely his most attractive qualities. But he wasn't bad on the eyes, either. Somehow, with all of his classes and extra study sessions, he still found time to work-out several times a week, and his muscles were quite impressive. He was shorter than most guys I find attractive, about five feet eight or so. But with his copper-brown skin, dark brown with blond-tipped hair, and blue-as-ocean eyes, his physical beauty could not be ignored.

That day two years ago started out exactly like every other. I woke up, had a poached egg, dry toast, and a glass of orange juice for breakfast, and kissed Rodney goodbye as I left for work. I was very set in my ways, as Rodney frequently reminded me, and to tell you the truth, that never bothered me. It gave me comfort. My first class wasn't until ten o'clock, so I always showed up a couple of hours early to workout in the school gym before class. There weren't many people there at that time of the morning. That particular morning there were maybe ten or twelve ambitious persons working out with me. Jeromy was one of them, and I admired his bulging muscles as I went through my routine. I thought I'd noticed him watching me, too, but chalked it up to wishful thinking.

But when I was finished with my workout, and began showering, I knew I'd been right all along. Jeromy showed up only a couple minutes after I did. The showers in the gym were communal, with no stalls or walls to divide the naked men lathering up. I'd often lingered there longer than I needed to, watching and admiring the student athletes as they washed their sleek, muscular bodies. But I'd never messed around with anyone, or even stroked myself in front of anyone there. It was too risky.

But this day was different. From the moment Jeromy walked naked into the showers, I knew I was in trouble. His thick, uncut cock swung heavily in front of him and refused to be ignored, even when flaccid. I swallowed hard and tried to turn around and not look at him. But it was useless. I couldn't keep my eyes off him, and couldn't help but notice his eyes didn't leave my body either. When he lathered his cock, it hardened instantly, and stood out almost a foot in front of him. I felt my own cock begin to harden as I watched in amazement as Jeromy stroked himself boldly in front of me.

"Wanna help me out a little, Mr. Henry?" Jeromy asked as he pulled back his foreskin and pointed the hard red head of his cock right at me, and smiled mischievously.

I found myself taking a step toward him before I realized I was doing it. Then I stopped halfway, my own hard-on seemingly trying to stretch the last few feet to get to him. "I can't, Jeromy," I said, finding it difficult to work up enough saliva to swallow. "I mean . . . it'd be wrong. I could get . . . ."

"Only if we're caught." He stroked his giant cock again. "But we won't. The door to the locker room is noisy as hell, and I put a chair in front of it so it'd make even more noise if someone opens it." He leaned his back against the wall and used both hands to stroke himself, and moaned loudly. "So, come on. Come over here and help me out."

I looked at the door and made sure the chair was there. Then I walked over to where Jeromy was leaning against the wall. I dropped to my knees and cupped his shaved balls in my hands as I opened my mouth and sucked the entirety of his big dick deep into my throat.

It'd been a couple of years since I'd had anyone's cock in my mouth other than Rodney's. And never had I had one this big or this thick. I sucked and lapped at it with everything I had, then massaged his balls as I took him as far as I could into my mouth. His big cock leaked a healthy amount of precum, and I swallowed it greedily.

"That's it, Mr. Henry," Jeromy whispered in a deep and hoarse voice. "Swallow my cock." He grabbed the back of my head and held it in front of his crotch as he pumped his dick in and out of my mouth.

As I sucked on his cock, I looked up into his face and fought to remain in control of my vital signs. My heart was beating at triple its normal rate, and I could barely breathe . . . and it had nothing to do with the fact my mouth was filled with Jeromy's cock. This kid was beautiful beyond description. He hadn't shaved that day, and his dark stubble only added to his masculine beauty. His bright blue eyes had always commanded my attention before, but now I couldn't take my eyes off of his full, pink lips as he licked them and then winked at me as he slid another inch of his fat cock deeper into my throat.

I shouldn't have been attracted to him at all. He was almost young enough to be my grandson, for fuck's sake. And I'm not usually attracted to boys. I like *men*. Men who are strong and intelligent and have been around the block a couple of times and have a sense of adventure and a sense of their own sensuality. I don't normally look twice at someone under the age of forty. They just don't interest me.

But Jeromy was different, and I was defenseless in my attraction to him. Even in my classes he'd stood out. He asked smart questions and demanded smart and complex answers that required even more thought to comprehend. That alone made me notice and respect and admire . . . and desire him. Around campus he was always the center of attention. People milled around him, and he was always laughing and smiling and making those around him do the same. He had a charisma like no other I'd ever seen. Yet he was very unassuming and undemanding. All of that with his clothes on.

Now, with him completely naked and wet under the shower spray and fully hard with his monstrous cock fucking my mouth, I was out of my mind with desire for him. There was no way I could get enough of him. I sucked on his cock and tried to swallow it all into my throat, until I gagged and came up choking.

"I'm so sorry, Mr. Henry," Jeromy said, as he put his strong hands under my arms and lifted me up to standing position. His face was red, and I wasn't sure if it was from the hot water or from the intensity of the blowjob I was giving him. He blinked his long, thick eyelashes a couple of times, then looked away from me as his face reddened a little more. Suddenly I realized he wasn't hot from the shower or the blowjob, he was nervous with me. "I didn't mean to hurt you," he said softly.

"You didn't hurt me, Jeromy," I said, and leaned in to kiss those delectably soft lips. "I'm just not as talented as I once was. And I'm not used to working with such a fantastic tool."

"Thank you," he said, and shook the water from his hair. He looked me directly in the eyes, and his blush deepened another shade. "I really want to suck your dick," he whispered as he wrapped his fist around it. "That's the reason I followed you in here. Can I?"

I nodded, and switched places with him, leaning against the shower wall as he knelt between my spread legs. He stuck out his tongue and licked very softly around the head of my cock, and that alone nearly sent me over the edge. The tip of his tongue tickled the sensitive skin that was tight around the head; it sent shivers up my body, even though warm steam swirled around me. Then his mouth closed around my cock head, and black dots floated in front of my eyes. His mouth was so warm and wet and tight; it felt as if one of those heated gel packs athletes use for sore muscles had been wrapped around my cock head. Jeromy barely gave me time to register that feeling before he swallowed my cock deep into his throat. Every inch of my cock was hot and wet and being massaged by his throat muscles, and I gasped as I clutched the wall behind me. I'm nowhere near as huge as Jeromy is, but in all the years my cock had been sucked, not a single guy had ever been able to swallow me completely like that without a considerable amount of work and patience.

But Jeromy swallowed my cock all the way to the base, until my pubic hairs pressed against his nose. Then he tightened his throat around my cock and playfully massaged it for a few moments. I wish I could say it was more than a few moments, but I can't. Before I could prepare myself for it, I felt my orgasm build in my balls and quickly work its way up my shaft.

"Oh, god," I moaned loudly, and tried to pull my cock from Jeromy's mouth. "I'm gonna cum!"

Jeromy refused to let me pull him away, and instead squeezed my cock harder inside his throat.

Every muscle in my body tightened and my knees shook violently as I unloaded myself into his throat. My orgasm shook me to the core, and seemed to last several minutes. Spurt after spurt of jizz shot from my cock, and when I thought it was all over, another series of spasms rocked my body, and I felt more of my seed spill into his still warm and sucking mouth.

He finally stood up quickly. He was beating his own cock, and leaned in to kiss me. His lips were so full and soft that it made me to never want to stop kissing them. I tasted my own load on his lips and tongue, and sucked greedily as he kissed me. He moaned, and I felt his muscles tighten as his load sprayed across my stomach and legs.

When he finished, he let his body lean against mine. We moved under the showerhead and allowed the hot water to rinse his cum from our bodies. Neither of us said a word as we showered and dried off. My mind was racing with a million thoughts: *I have to have him again. I love Rodney. I can't live without sucking Jeromy's cock again and making love to him. I love Rodney. I'll never be able to get through a class with Jeromy again without stuttering and looking like a complete and utter fool. I love Rodney.*

"I want to meet him," Jeromy said as I was tying my shoes.

"What?"

"Your boyfriend. I want to meet him."

"That's not a good idea, Jeromy," I said, suddenly panicked. I'd seen *Fatal Attraction* and was not at all fond of the ending.

"Sure, it is," Jeromy said, and kissed me on the mouth. "I've seen you two out on the town, at dinner several times, at the movies."

"Yes. We've been together eighteen years. We're very established. We're boring and conventional. We cook lasagna at home and read in bed, for crying out loud. He'd not at all be pleased in anyway about this little rendezvous."

"Once at the bathhouse," Jeromy said quietly, looking me directly in the eyes. "He was in a sling with your cock up his ass."

I just stood there with a very dumb look on my face, my eyes wide and my mouth dropped completely open. Rodney and I sometimes played at the bathhouse to spice up our sex life. More often than not we played together alone, but sometimes we'd have some fun with another guy there. We didn't frequent the bathhouse that often, and I knew exactly the visit of which Jeromy spoke. It had happened three weeks before. We'd gone out dancing, and Rodney had had a little more to drink than usual, and was particularly horny. At the bathhouse he demanded to be restrained in the sling and fucked mercilessly. I'd been a little hesitant, because the sling area was open and we were drawing quite a crowd. But that only heightened Rodney's excitement, and we fucked like a pair of wild rabbits.

"He didn't seem boring or conventional at all," Jeromy said slyly, and smiled. "Neither of you did. It fuckin' turned me on like crazy."

"Jeromy . . ."

"Invite me to dinner. This week sometime."

"That's not a good . . ."

"Please," he begged, and kissed me again, very softly and gently on the lips. "I don't want to cause any problems, I promise. I'm not that kind of guy. I just wanna have some fun with the two of you. You're both very hot separately, and together you're smokin'."

"Rodney would never go for it," I said, picking up my gym bag.

"Just ask him. Please. That's all I'm asking."

"Okay," I said as I kissed him quickly, and turned for the door. "But don't get your hopes up. I'm not promising anything."

"Cool," Jeromy said, as he pinched my ass and winked at me. "I love lasagna."

Dinner was delicious, and elaborately laid out. I could tell Rodney had had a more boring day than usual. The house was immaculate, there were fresh flowers on the table and around the house, and he served the chicken cordon bleu on our good china. All of this could only mean one thing. He was having writer's block and was frustrated. His constant fidgeting confirmed it. My suggestion could go either way. He'd either be all for it and look at it as an opportunity to add more spice to our sex life . . . again . . . or he'd be pissed and throw a tantrum. Possibly even cry. But if ever there would be a time to bring it up, it was now.

"Honey, this cordon bleu is delicious," I said as I looked over the rim of the glass at him and took a sip of wine.

"Thanks," he said, a little listlessly, and pushed his food around on his plate.

Here goes, I thought as I took a deep breath. "So, the funniest thing happened to me at school today."

"Oh, yeah? What's that?"

"One of my students actually flirted with me." I took a large bite of chicken.

"That's not unusual. They're always flirting with you. You just don't always pick up on it."

"Well, I picked up on it this time," I said, and took another sip of wine. "He actually did a little more than flirt with me."

Rodney looked up from his plate. "Really? What happened?"

"I was showering after working out, and he came in and joined me in the shower."

"What's his name?"

"Jeromy."

"And?" he asked, and suddenly found enough appetite to eat a bite of veggies.

"Well, as I was showering, I noticed he was playing with himself. It was obvious he wanted me to see him."

"Did he get hard?"

"Oh, yes."

Rodney stared at me for several seconds before saying anything. I knew him well enough to know he was deciding whether to be turned on by the story or to get really pissed. It was always a fine line with Rod.

He took another bite of his dinner, then wiped his mouth. "So, what happened?"

"I couldn't help it, Rod," I blurted out. "His dick was so big and hard, and he kept waving it at me and daring me to suck it."

"How big was it?"

"Huge. I could barely get a few inches of it into my mouth."

"Really?" he said, and I could tell he was turned on.

"Yes. It had to be close to a foot long and so thick I couldn't put my fist around it. I sucked on it for a few minutes, but then he wanted to suck me instead."

He flinched a little and looked at me again. "Did you let him?"

"Yes."

Rodney took a big drink of his wine, and pushed his food around on his plate again. "And how was it?"

"It was hot, what do you think? We were in the shower and someone could've walked in at any time. I have to admit, it was kind of exciting."

"Did he make you cum?"

For the first time in our life together, I thought of lying to him. But I couldn't. "Yes, he did. He swallowed it."

Rodney's face was turning red now, and I was sure I'd gone too far and pissed him off.

"Fuck, that's hot!" he said, and stood up from the table and grabbed me in his arms. He kissed me hard and rough-housed me into the bedroom, where he turned the tables on me, and fucked me harder and rougher than he'd ever done before.

Jeromy was ecstatic when I told him Rodney had agreed to a get-together. By the time all our schedules allowed us to hookup, we'd decided to forego dinner and get right down to the sex. We'd suggested Jeromy come to our place, but he had another plan in mind, and Rodney couldn't have been more willing once he heard the idea. I had to admit, I was excited about the prospects myself.

"Let's meet at my place instead," Jeromy said, leaving little room for discussion. None, actually. "I've got a huge house, and the basement is specially furnished."

"What do you mean?" I asked over the phone.

"Show up at eight and leave your inhibitions at home. You'll find out."

I couldn't believe this was the same Jeromy I knew from school. He certainly wasn't quiet, by any means. He often broke the ice and started conversation when no one else was talking. But he was always soft-spoken and thoughtful and respectful. This new Jeromy was forceful and strong-willed and in charge. I had to admit, it really turned me on.

Rodney and I showed up at Jeromy's house ten minutes early, and waited in the car until eight o'clock. Rodney spent the time asking if I was sure I could trust this kid, and plucking stray hairs from his nose and ears. I spent the time convincing him Jeromy was no one to be afraid of, that he wouldn't be chopping us into unidentifiable pieces and storing us in his freezer—and also plucked stray hairs from my nose and ears.

Then we walked up to his door.

We knocked twice, and when Jeromy opened the door, he pulled Rodney in by one hand, leaned him against the wall next to the door, and kissed him hard on the lips. With his other hand he pulled me inside, kicked the door shut, and pulled me in to join them in the kiss. His tongue was warm and soft and wet and sweet. He moved in to kiss me, and I tasted my lover's saliva on Jeromy's tongue.

I hardened instantly, and when I reached down to feel Rodney's crotch, he was rock hard as well, and moaning like an animal in heat as Jeromy alternated kissing one of us and then the other, and allowing us to taste one another on his tongue and lips.

"Let's go downstairs," Jeromy said, as he began unbuttoning his shirt, then pushed Rodney and me toward the basement stairs. "It's dark down there, but don't worry, nothing down there will hurt you. Just hold the wall as you walk down the stairs."

I went first, with Rodney holding my waist with both hands. I felt movement around his body, and from his moans, I knew Jeromy was undressing and fondling him as we descended.

"Stop there," Jeromy said as I slowly advanced into the dark room. He pushed us both against the cold wall, and undressed us. As he did, he kissed and licked and bit us lightly. My cock was harder than it'd been in quite some time, and from the sounds coming from Rodney, he was having the same reaction.

"Do you trust me?" he asked Rodney.

"Yes," I heard my lover say in a voice I barely recognized.

"Mr. Henry?"

"Yes," I said, and meant it.

"Good."

Jeromy moved me a few feet from Rodney, and kissed my lips and neck softly and tenderly. I was aware I was being moved farther from Rod, but wasn't worried about it. I felt strangely safe. Then Jeromy moved over to Rod, and I heard him whisper something into Rodney's ear. Rod responded with a moan. A moment later I heard chains rattling.

"Hey," Rod said with a slight tone of panic. "I'm not so sure about this."

"Shhhh," Jeromy said. "You trust me, remember."

More chains rattling, and some scuffing, and then deeper moans of lust from Rodney. "Oh, yeah. Suck my cock, man," Rodney said from a few feet away in the dark. I was beginning to feel a little left out, and then I heard my partner sound a little more panicked this time. "Hey, what the . . ."

There was the low sound of a motor, and then:

"Let me down from here. This isn't funny."

I started to move toward Rodney's voice when a very soft purple light illuminated the middle of the room. I saw Rod several feet directly in front of me. His wrists were shackled with leather restraints and suspended with chains a few feet from the ceiling. His feet were bound with the same leather restraints and connected to more chains that fell from the ceiling about a foot and a half lower than his hands. He was swinging slowly back and forth in the air, as if he were supported by some invisible sling.

My cock twitched at the sight of him bound and exposed like that.

"Do you like seeing your boy like that?" It was Jeromy, whispering in my ear only an inch or two behind me.

"Yes," I said hoarsely.

"I want you to stay right here. Do you understand me?"

"Yes."

"No matter how badly you might want to come over and make

love to your boyfriend, I want you to stay right here until I call for you."

"All right."

Jeromy brushed past me, and I felt his naked skin against mine; a drop of precum slipped from my cock head. A second later he was in the middle of the purple lighted area of the room, and standing between Rodney's legs. He stroked Rod's hard cock, and caressed his skin from head to toe. Then he knelt between Rodney's spread legs.

Rodney looked over at me. His eyes were a mixture of fear and lust and confusion and desire. But when Jeromy began licking his ass and shoved his tongue inside his hole, Rodney's eyes rolled back into his head and he moaned with animalistic lust. Jeromy attacked Rodney's ass with his tongue, and Rodney rocked himself back and forth onto Jeromy's tongue for several minutes. I stroked my cock as I watched, wanting to join them, but knowing I couldn't.

Jeromy stood up, and Rodney's body seemed to go limp. They were both drenched in sweat. Jeromy slid a condom onto his massive cock and dripped some lube onto it.

"No," I said, and started to take a step forward.

"Stay there," Jeromy said. "You said you trust me and that you'd do as I say."

"Yes, but he hasn't . . . he can't . . ."

"Yes, he can," Jeromy said.

"But we don't . . ."

"Let him fuck me," Rodney whispered as he looked over at me and winked. His eyes were dazed and filled with lust. I could see at once that he wanted Jeromy's big dick inside him.

I just stood there, a few feet away, and watched with a stupid look on my face. I knew without a doubt that Rodney loved me. He'd never want to leave me. But he wanted Jeromy's cock inside him in a bad way, and that was something completely foreign to me.

Jeromy positioned the head of his dick at the entrance to Rod's asshole, then slid it inside slowly. Rod gasped, and clutched the shackles at his wrists as he gritted his teeth. Jeromy slid a couple more inches inside and rested there. Rodney's grasp on the chains relaxed a little, and he began writhing around on Jeromy's cock, sliding his ass farther and farther onto it until the entire fat cock was buried deep inside his ass.

I looked up into Rodney's face. It was red as a beet. But it was also smiling and his eyes had a glow to them. When Jeromy began to slide in and out of his ass, Rod moaned and matched his strokes one for one. His cock throbbed with life on top of his belly as he was being fucked.

"Come here, Mr. Henry," Jeromy said.

I walked over and he leaned in to kiss me on the lips. "Stroke his dick while I fuck him." He kissed me deeper as I wrapped my fist around Rod's cock and slid it up and down the thick length of him.

"I can't take much more of that," Rodney said as he panted. "I'll cum if you keep that up."

"Do you like the feel of my cock in your ass, Rodney?" Jeromy asked coyly.

"Yes."

"Good, because I'm gonna keep fucking you until you spray your load all over yourself. Do you want that?"

"Yes."

I felt my heart drop into my stomach.

"I want your boyfriend to fuck me while I fuck you."

Suddenly, my heart was back where it should be. And my cock throbbed to full hardness again.

"Is that okay with you?" Jeromy asked.

"Yes," Rodney said without hesitation.

Rodney and I had fucked other guys on such rare occasion that I was taken aback by how easily he was swayed. But I remembered Jeromy's cock, and imagined how great it must feel up Rodney's ass . . . he *did* love to get fucked by a big dick . . . and realized this was an opportunity. I wasn't afraid of losing my lover. He'd be mine forever. And I had to admit, Jeromy's tight, round ass did look inviting.

"So, you just gonna stand there, Mr. Henry, or are you going to fuck my ass while I pound your boyfriend?"

I stood behind Jeromy, and rubbed my hard cock against his tight ass. Just the feel of his hard ass as he slid inside Rodney almost made me explode before I entered him. I grabbed a condom and slipped it on in a hurry, then spat on my cock. I tried to be calm and cool and collected and take my time, but I failed miserably. I positioned the head of my dick at his asshole, and before I knew it I was buried deep inside his ass.

"Oh, FUCK!" Jeromy yelled as he stopped thrusting in mid stroke and stood still to allow his ass to get used to my thick cock.

"Don't stop," Rodney begged.

"I mean, it looked nice and big and all when I was sucking it, but I didn't think it'd feel *this* big," Jeromy panted. "It fuckin' hurts."

"Come on, pussy," Rodney taunted. "If I can take your huge cock, you can certainly take my husband's."

"Fine," Jeromy said, and suddenly thrust himself deep and hard into Rodney's ass.

I slammed myself just as deep and just as hard into Jeromy's ass, and before I knew it we were all fucking like a well-oiled machine. When Jeromy slid into Rodney's ass, he pulled his ass off my cock, and then when he slid out of Rod's ass, he impaled himself onto my dick. It took only a couple of strides before we were all moaning and thrusting ourselves into and onto and out of each other.

Rodney was a great lover, and I knew Jeromy was getting the fuck of his life. But so was I. It'd been so long since I'd fucked anyone but Rod that I'd forgotten how wonderful and exciting and different sex with someone else could be. Jeromy's ass was hot as molten lava and as tight as a vice grip. It took all I had not to explode the second I shoved my cock into his hot ass. But after a few moments, I couldn't take it anymore.

"Fuck, man . . . I'm gonna shoot," I said loudly, and grabbed Jeromy's waist and pulled him deeper onto my cock.

"Me too," he said, and thrust his cock all the way inside Rodney's ass. I leaned forward to keep my cock inside him as he unloaded himself into my lover. I felt his ass cheeks tighten with every spurt of his cum, and could tell he was filling that condom.

I grunted like a pig being roasted alive, and shot my load deep inside Jeromy's ass. It seemed to go on forever, and my knees were just about to go out on me when Rodney said,

"I'm coming, baby. Come drink my load."

He loved for me to swallow his load, and it was one of my favorite activities as well, so I pulled out of Jeromy's ass with no tact or delicateness or fanfare. I rushed over to Rod's side and took his cock all the way into my mouth and throat. I'd barely wrapped my lips around it before he exploded into my throat. Rodney always has amazing loads, but this one gagged me. I swallowed three mouthfuls in quick succession before I choked and had to pull back. The last few drops leaked from his cock, and Jeromy lifted Rod's still hard dick and sucked the remaining cum from him.

"Kiss me," Jeromy said. "I want to taste him on your mouth."

I kissed him long and hard as he sucked on my tongue and licked every last drop of Rodney's cum from my mouth and lips. Then we moved up to Rodney's head and the three of us kissed for what seemed an hour.

"Honeys, I'm home," Jeromy said as he walked into the foyer and kicked off his sneakers. "It's been an exhausting day at school, and I'm famished. What's for dinner?"

"You have your nerve asking what's for dinner, Mister," Rodney said, and leaned in to kiss Jeromy softly and longingly on the lips. "It's your turn to cook and you know it. It's been two years. You know the routine."

"But . . ."

"No buts about it. It's your turn. And I don't want any of that instant-salad crap either. I want meat tonight."

"Oh, you'll get meat tonight," I said as I walked into the room. "Both of you will get all the meat you can handle."

"Don't be crude. Jeromy's trying to get out of making dinner again."

"I am not," Jeromy pouted. "I was just kinda hoping we could do dessert before the main course. I've had a hard day at work." He smiled slyly. "And I need a little stress relief."

We all three looked at each other, then ran to the bedroom and jumped onto our king-sized bed and wrestled around for awhile.

"I wanna be top tonight," Rodney said suddenly.

"Me too," Jeromy said.

"That's not fair," I whined. "Rock, paper, scissors?"

"Okay," my two lovers said in unison.

We hit our palms with one fist three times and then showed our strategies.

"Damn it," I said, and smiled widely as I got on all fours and watched Rod move to my mouth as Jeromy spread my ass.